Looking for Dawn

James Calvin Schaap, 1948 –

Looking for Dawn

A Floyd River Press book

Looking for Dawn

James Calvin Schaap

For Mary.
This is a book, but
it's also a symbol of what
retirement opens up for you.

Floyd River Press
103 Andrews Court
Alton, Iowa 51003

Be blessed,*
Jim & Barb

*as you have been for so many, a blessing!!

"There's more room in a broken heart."
Carly Simon

"Such instances of parental affection, and such love of home and native land may be heathen in origin, but it seems to me that they are not unlike Christian in principle."
Judge Elmer Dundy,
Standing Bear vs. Crook,
U.S. District Court, Omaha,
May 12, 1879

"We all are the work of thy hand."
Isaiah 64:8

Spend every bit of grace you got

Once the bedlam subsided and the halls emptied, Woody Dekkers sat at the keyboard in his classroom, looking for the right words, then decided against an e-mail because it would be way too easy, too chancy, and finally too thin a medium for what needed to be said, even though what he had to tell Karin wouldn't need to be lengthy. Besides, the Fabers were neighbors, for pity's sake.

He spoke to no one, pulled on his coat, slung his scarf around his neck, wiggled his fingers into the fleece gloves his granddaughter gave him for Christmas, and walked out of school the back way, down wooden hallways that creaked and screeched beneath his feet, reminding him of his own joints and the dang thoughtless people in the school district who wouldn't fork over bucks for a new school.

The Fabers would want to know. Karin would, at least. No, both of them, he thought—they'd both want to know because somewhere inside he knew there was something real and alive connecting them, even though Dawn Burnett had been a part of the story they tried so dang hard to put behind them and couldn't. He pulled out of the parking lot into unlikely traffic, but then, it was Friday, thank goodness. School's out.

Dawn Burnett. Some things could never be simply forgotten, even if most if not all could be forgiven, he told himself. Isn't that the run of the proverb?

The young guy, Trent Sterrett, had handled the whole mess well. A hurriedly-called meeting before school. The staff was supposed to be in the building by eight anyway, so right on the money he'd let it be known that he'd like to see all of them in the band room, where there were enough chairs and where they'd be out of the way once kids barreled in off the buses.

It had to be bad news. Hasty, early morning, spur-of-the moment meetings were never pep rallies. Never. But the moment he'd heard the name of the girl, he'd thought of Karin Faber, who would most certainly want to know.

And he wasn't surprised—no one could have been. It was Dawn Burnett.

"We have to ask ourselves what we can do better," Sterrett told them, one hand up against that thin presence of a beard of his, as if he might have been only mistakenly unshaven. Sterrett didn't use the word *suicide*, but no one missed the suggestion. Booze? —some, at least, or so the cop had insinuated. An accident, and the girl was in the hospital. She was going to make it, thank God, Sterrett said. He'd started with that good news—that she was going to make it. Much of the story he claimed he didn't know, but what he did, he said, came from the police and other credible sources. Woody just simply assumed he was likely not the only one in the room who guessed that Sterrett was talking about this new teacher, Coby whatever, who was likely more to the new guy than just another credible source.

"I'm not blaming us," Sterrett said. "I mean, there are things here far beyond your and my control." He looked down at whatever sheet music was on the podium in front of him, then straightened it without thinking. "No one knows, I guess, just what exactly happened, but when things like this get out, you know, we have to ask ourselves how we can do more."

Woody knew Trent Sterrett didn't know the long back story here, and neither did most of the others. So he did a head count--Fred Stanley, Arch Mentink were the only other ones who might have remembered what went on way back when Dawn Burnett was born, and even they didn't know everything. He was the only one there who knew the whole story, as much as anyone could. Principal Sterrett's impassioned pleas notwithstanding, Woody wasn't sure if anyone could have done any more for the girl. She wasn't in his classes, not this year, and besides, she didn't take to him the way her mother had. Back then, he was so much younger, so much more a part of life. Back then kids sought him out.

Sterrett stopped, looked around as if something inside told him he had to look at every one of them. "I mean, me too," he'd said and shrugged his shoulders. "*All* of us—we *all* have to do more." Then he raised both hands in front of his face, brought them together, finger to finger. "That's the news this morning—a grim way to start the week. I'm sorry." He took the pen from behind his ear and stuck it in an inside pocket of his sport coat.

It wasn't Wal-Mart, Woody knew. Meetings like this morning's didn't happen every blessed week. It was, for all intents and purposes, Sterrett's first real scare. Sometimes he and his wife used to think there was more horror out on the limitless plains than other places, other worlds, even when there were so many fewer people. Maybe everything just got exaggerated out in the middle of nowhere, she used to say, Thomas Hart Benton-ed.

Anyway, Karin Faber would want to know about the girl, he told himself as he passed Pioneer Acres at the edge of town; and Karin would be the one to tell Scotty, her husband, even though there was nothing either of them could do but die a little more inside when they heard what happened. And it could have been worse—someday it just might be, in fact. They'd know that too. They'd known that for a long, long time.

Sometime after his sophomore history class the idea had just come into his head that Dawn Burnett herself wouldn't let either of them forget. Just wouldn't. She was living, breathing testimony even if she never said a word or even knew who the hell she was herself. She was history, his history, their history.

The ex-coach in Trent Sterrett wouldn't let them out of the room in the shape he'd left them. He ginned up the encouragement. "I trust you," he told his teachers, most of whom were older than he was. "I've got confidence—you're professionals, you care." He tightened his lips, never once taking his eyes off any of them. "These things get out of hand—I don't have to tell you that. You know better than I do. In some perverse way, it's catching—this kind of thing, especially here." He meant, "this close to the reservation," of course, where suicide was epidemic. "And we're not going to let it happen." He raised a finger, as if he were an older man than he was. "We're going to beat this thing before it gets a chance to get any larger."

Honestly, for a moment, Woody had thought that Trent Sterrett, just a kid himself, might actually pray, which wouldn't have been out of line at Cottonwood. Worse things happened. And it was in Sterrett to do it—you could see it in his face just then, as if he was leading them all in a confession that required some ritual commitment to be ended with some incantation.

"Give yourself away," he told them, this young guy right in the middle of his first administrative tour of duty out here in the middle of nowhere. "If kids need some time or something extra, I've got people coming in. Otherwise, just give yourself away. Be flexible. Spend every bit of grace you got." And then he nodded, solidly, several times, as if what he really meant was amen.

He'd accounted himself well, Woody thought.

Trent Sterrett was stocky, barrel-chested. He wore his hair down around his shoulders, which isn't to say he looked Sioux. The bright red cheeks seemed almost scarlet-fevered, although he was far too young to have gone through a bout when he was a boy. And the truth is, Woody liked him. He liked to say that a school like Cottonwood ran through principals and supers as if they were paper figures in one of those little books you could fan into a video. Woody had been around himself forever. In the last thirty years, if he'd put notches in his desk for every hot shot principal Cottonwood had hired and dumped, the desk would look as if it'd come out of a butcher shop instead of an army barracks.

Trent Sterrett was a catch, he'd already told Tieneke, his wife. The guy was running from something. In Cottonwood, lots of people seemed to be, maybe even he was. About that, Woody wondered sometimes.

What Sterrett couldn't have understood was how marginalized a girl like Dawn was, even though her parents were who they were. Rough and rebellious, Dawn Burnett was not about to be prom queen. Most kids found her and her friends—however few of them were in school—almost contemptible. She was everything they were told never to become, made flesh before them, as if some wicked suicidal virus was going to spread though the school—and such things happened, especially here. People called them "suicide clusters." But it would have to start with a kid most others held in greater esteem than disdain. For Dawn Burnett's faux-suicide attempt to catch on, what she may have attempted would require a more precipitous fall, something almost theme park-ish. She would have had to be a popular kid—that's when there'd be copy cats. Or she'd have had to have been successful, death being the real grim reaper. If Dawn Burnett wouldn't make it, if she'd die, other students would grab for breath. But still, privately most of them would say that she who sups with the Devil had best use a long spoon, an ancient proverb none of them knew but most of them understood when he'd bring it up in class.

He'd not been close to Dawn, not ever—and maybe he should have been because he probably knew even more than she did about her own history. He'd been there at the beginning—not literally, of course, but he was there when she was no more than a couple centimeters long, a little, kidney-shaped fetus. He was there when she shouldn't have been.

Woody had spent his prep hour thinking maybe he'd stayed away from Dawn Burnett when she was in his classes *because* he was there back then, because he knew so much, because there was so much that needed to be forgotten, or at least concealed, so much he couldn't tell her, shouldn't—and wouldn't even if he'd wanted to. Dawn Burnett had so many faces, so many parents, that it had been hard for him to know how to talk to her, a kid with too much history. When first she came into his class, he didn't even know how to look at her. When her tests—when she took them—were awful, he didn't call her out because even when she sat before him he didn't know who to see behind her, over her shoulder, which parent, which step-parent. When he looked into her face, which he rarely did, too many faces looked back, too much grief and anger, even though the Lakota part of her rarely looked back at all.

What happens when you get old, Woody told himself, is that nothing seems all that long ago, even when it is, almost seventeen years having passed since he and Tieneke had sat in two different churches for two different christenings within just a few months. One of those babies had been born to two kids whose marriage vows had so piteously unraveled they were barely capable of sitting in the same sanctuary, much less the same pew. The other was a child born to a single mom whose chances back then looked as inevitable as they did bleak. Together, he and Tieneke had listened as all three pledged themselves, sort of, to do all in their power to raise these kids—same-old, same-old, he'd thought back then. Fat chance.

Sometimes he wondered if he should have stayed at Cottonwood for all these years, or whether a teacher should look around for another job once he gets to know too much. His father, the preacher, always said six years was it, time to hightail it because you both knew each other too well, the guy on one side of the pulpit and the natives on the other.

They might have left after their own Teresa died, the foster daughter, a sweet Native kid they'd adopted—that would have been the best time to get the heck out since everything stopped then anyway. Cottonwood could have just as well been Cincinnati back then, everything shot. They might have left, might have moved to Ohio or Idaho, and it wouldn't make a lick of a difference anyway with the empty spaces all around.

Anyway, a teacher gets to know more than he or she needs to, probably more than he should, no matter where you read your hundred-thousandth student paper, he told himself. Sometimes these days his students would flat out astound him with their naiveté, far more innocent than they once were, an innocence that made him only more cynical, more give-a-shit-ish, a state of mind he'd seen in a lot of old teachers, a sour old whiney-ness he'd once wished deeply to avoid.

The truck whined angrily in the cold, didn't want to start, then finally whinnied and coughed and got up on its feet.

On bad days when he'd leave school, the ride home through the country might just relieve him, the gentle slope of the plains in a landscape for the most part barren—wasn't it Black Elk who called these hills the soft lines of woman reclining? That endless rolling motion suggested something more somewhere beyond, something that mattered, bigger and unknowable, something the Lakota people called the big mystery.

To get home took him no more than ten or twelve minutes, depending on whether he trailed the school bus, and whether or not he just poked along, left the blacktop at any place at all and took gravel east and north. He'd never lost that enchantment he'd learned to feel when he was out in all that blessed openness. If he wanted to, he could take his good-natured time. Tieneke wouldn't miss him. They had been married way too long for that.

But this Friday he was going to have to tell Karin. That he knew. He was going to have to tell her because she would want to know because Dawn was part of her story too, part of their story, even though so many people didn't know. And didn't have to.

There was lots he didn't know

The two of them had worked together, held down jobs at Swifty's, the grocery store in Cottonwood, where at closing time once in a while, Marcus would sell LeRoy a twelve-pack if Cletus, the owner, was in back cleaning up the pizza kitchen. If he was somewhere out of the way anyway--you know, if things were all clear up front. He and Leroy were both underage, but buying was no sweat at Swifty's because the doors would be locked, and nobody would see a thing. Sometimes LeRoy would grab wine too because women love wine, he used to say, and wine coolers. LeRoy was tough and smart, and people respected him, or so Marcus thought. Marcus didn't know really if he'd call it respect or if they were just damn scared of him. It could have been that too, he thought, respect that sometimes looked a whole lot like white-in-the-face fear.

Leroy himself used to say that if he hadn't been so good with customers, Cletus would have fired him in a week. But LeRoy had this way with people—he knew how to talk to them, the only one who ever got tips for carrying out groceries, the only one, He wore his charm like that gold necklace, and people loved him, even older people, even if they didn't know him. They loved him because he took time with them when they came into the store, asked them questions, acted as if he really cared. It was something LeRoy was good at, Marcus used to say of the guy he lived with. LeRoy was older, of course. And this business of talking to old people--it was something all white kids just had, it seemed to him—not all of them either, really, but most of them anyway. Like they were trained in it, trained in talking. There were lots of misfits like himself, he thought, just different--most of them--and lots of Indians.

It wasn't that Marcus didn't respect old people either—like his own grandma. It's just that he didn't talk to them the way LeRoy did, playing up to them almost, as if they were the ticket to some place he'd never been to, but wanted to go.

Most teachers eventually grew to hate LeRoy because none of them knew how to deal with him. He used to say he could read a chump right off, so he dropped out of school because there was nothing anybody there could teach him that he'd need to know or didn't already, he said. Some teachers thought he was the kind of kid who was worthless in school, a real pain in the ass; but some told him they thought he'd take some weird idea someday and make a million dollars by the time he was forty. Thirty, maybe.

One day, LeRoy asked Marcus if he needed a place to live. Marcus's mother had some issues and his dad had been gone for years already so Marcus jumped at the chance, not only because he needed a place, but also because it seemed to him that hanging out with LeRoy was like being around a party just about to happen. That and the fact that LeRoy was, in so many ways, just so right, better than his grandma at least. Marcus loved his grandma, just wasn't so hot on living with her in that trailer on the reservation for the rest of his born days. She could talk, too, almost like a white guy. At least she had things to say.

Marcus was 17 and still in high school on those days he bothered to show up. The night Dawn Burnett came by to pick up her things was not the first time he was ever with a girl in bed either, but that night was unlike any other in his life. And then it was Dawn Burnett, LeRoy's girl, sort of. . .well, no more, at least to hear LeRoy talk about it, which he did, often enough. LeRoy loved women, loved talking about them. He talked all the time.

Dawn was LeRoy's girl, until she thought she was pregnant and all sorts of other things happened that Marcus didn't really know about or didn't need to since they weren't his business to start with and he wouldn't ever have thought of asking about if she hadn't wanted so badly to talk that night, hadn't needed him the way she said she did, hadn't told him all about what had gone on between LeRoy and her, or at least all she wanted to tell him about all of that, which probably wasn't the whole story either and he knew it, but true enough at least to make him feel sorry for her. She was the girl LeRoy stuck it to, in more ways than one. But all of that ended, and when it did, it ended slowly and not without some pain—at least for Dawn.

Marcus wasn't stupid. The old farm house where the two of them lived wasn't soundproof, after all. Wasn't even that big. Dawn came in that night and found LeRoy there, even though he wasn't supposed to be home. She'd told Marcus later that she'd thought LeRoy was gone or she wouldn't have even stopped by because she hated his guts so much. When she found him there and didn't expect it, what happened between the two of them got broadcast all over the house, yelling and screaming that sounded like something of the devil got let loose that shouldn't have. Marcus had tried to shut his bedroom door, but the volume was up so loud that all he could have done to cover it was pull on headphones, which he didn't want to do either because, truth be told—and it wouldn't be something he'd tell anybody either—when things get that hot just outside your room, you start thinking something's going to burn, and he was worried about the girl, about Dawn.

LeRoy was the way he was, and he didn't take crap from anybody. He'd whaled on people before, didn't matter who. All of that was going on right down a floor beneath him, and Marcus thought it best to give the battle a kind of listen.

He'd seen LeRoy hand it out—Marcus did. Never got beat on himself, but LeRoy wasn't someone to mouth off to. Certainly, no girls that Marcus could remember, but with all that yelling going on downstairs, he'd told himself that night that LeRoy was what he was—a nice guy, but a short fuse if he had some bug up his ass and didn't like whoever he was dealing with.

So Marcus didn't pull on his earphones. Instead he listened in to what he could hear from downstairs—words sometimes, but mostly just anger, which sure wasn't music. There were moments he honestly thought he was going to have to be the one to make some kind of peace between the two of them, or else get Dawn out of there before she said something she shouldn't have, something that pulled a trigger somewhere on LeRoy, in which case nobody would come out for the better, the way he had it figured. Dawn would get herself messed with and LeRoy get in major trouble with the law for beating on a girl. The truth was, the cops were more than anxious to hang LeRoy's ass for something most of the time anyway.

But the Lord Almighty or someone got in the way because all of a sudden, the whole battle was over. The door slammed. It was LeRoy who left, not Dawn. When Marcus turned down whatever music it was he had on right then, he heard her, crying. Muffled, sort of. Not loud. You had to listen in hard to hear it.

Anyway, that's when it started. That's where the whole long night began: Dawn was downstairs, wiping away tears--and she didn't cry much or hadn't, as far as he knew. Tough as a saddle horn, even LeRoy said so. And he couldn't help hearing her there—not sobbing either, but crying for sure. That's what got him out of his headphones and his room. Not like she fell apart or anything because she didn't. That wouldn't be like Dawn Burnett either, he'd told himself. She was just sad, he figured, because the whole thing between her and LeRoy, whatever it was, was over and done with. Marcus knew that because LeRoy had told him it was going to be over and ended. Dawn Burnett, as beautiful a chick as anybody could imagine, was really broke up, which she had a right to be.

There was some anger in there too, shaking out the tears, red hot anger--a kind of mixture of the two, really, mad and sad. You could hear it.

He pulled the door open a bit, not to see her—he couldn't see her from his room—but to be sure that what he was hearing was real. And it was. He crept slowly downstairs because it wasn't his business really, and it was too, you know? LeRoy was long gone, and Dawn was sitting there, her fist beating a little on the arm of the couch. She looked up at him with eyes like you see on some animal in a trap, not just angry. Anger, he figured he could deal with, one way or another. He knew anger, knew it very well ever since he was old enough to have a good look at the world he'd been brought into. This wasn't just anger. It was something more.

"What you looking at?" she said. She was a snapping turtle a mile from the river.

He wondered if she knew he'd been home from the moment she'd walked in the door, or if he'd surprised her. Could have.

He didn't know what to say exactly except what was on his mind before she arrived. All during the big fight, he'd thought about it, so that's where he started. It was his big speech, his only one. "We had this dog," he told her, "—you remember? Mangy thing in winter, big shoulders, big chunks of fur."

"Roland," she said.

"You remember? —used to chase cars."

"Every time I left," she said.

"Sure, sure," he told her. "You remember him."

That Dawn Burnett was sniffing didn't change a thing on her perfect face. There she sat, wiping her nose with the sleeve of that old blue sweatshirt she always wore, gorgeous as some early summer morning.

He honestly didn't know if she'd talk to him, but she did. She shifted her shoulders as if to make it clear that he was mistaken about the tears she'd been wiping out of the corner of her eyes. "Where is he anyway? —he hibernate or what?"

"Somebody opened a car door on him," Marcus told her, then mimicked the motion, pushing open an imaginary door as if slapping some imaginary dog.

"Killed him?" she said. "I haven't seen him around."

"I killed him," he told her.

"Hurt that bad?" she said.

He hunched his shoulders. "I couldn't let him suffer."

She sat up as straight as she could on the old couch, grabbed the pouch of that hoodie in both hands and touched up her face as if what she was holding was a hand towel. She took this big gulp of air, blew it out slowly, head back, then just lay there, half sitting up, on the couch, her head back against the towels laid there over the open stuffing. Took a breath as if she'd just finished running. "At least he's out of here," she said.

He didn't know whether she was talking about LeRoy or Roland or whatever, maybe somebody else.

"I miss him," he told her. "First movie I ever saw when I was a kid—I don't remember the name. Big dog got rabies and the farmer shot that dog between the slats of a cage or something he'd built when that dog couldn't be around the kids anymore, just growling and snapping."

"*Old Yeller*," she said.

"Don't remember the dog's name," Marcus told her, "but I think I cried, not in front of anybody. I was just a little kid, little Tonto."

Just like that, she said, "You didn't cry about Roland? I mean, that you had to put him down?"

He didn't know what to say, whether or not he wanted to confess. He didn't know what she'd think of him if he said he did cry, which he didn't. "Got to have heart of stone looking into the eyes of a dog that's hurt like he was," he told her, "who needs your help, you know, and you just know what's got to be done."

"Ugly dog anyway," she told him, not meaning it.

He let that sit for a minute as if to get her to reconsider. "Nothing in those eyes that was a bit ugly."

She sniffed a couple of times, as if she was pulling herself onto shore to get her bearings. "I didn't even know Roland was gone," she said.

"People can miss things," he said. "Sometimes not, too."

She put her head back on the couch. Her eyes were closed, and what she said then wasn't necessarily addressed to him. "Better part of me is gone," she said, not so much to him, maybe; just to the world in this little wreck of a house.

He assumed she was talking about LeRoy, but as much as Marcus liked him—and he did, in certain moods, at certain times—he knew LeRoy wasn't of the same mind about her exactly, because LeRoy wasn't going to miss her, knew it first hand, heard him say it, which isn't to say that every last word LeRoy said was gospel truth either, almost never was. But there was no sense in her truly thinking that LeRoy was some great man or something.

"I got news," he told her. He was sitting on the arm of the couch, and he reached for whatever he could touch easily, and it ended up being her arm, right at the muscle. "LeRoy i'n't going to miss you, my sister," he told her. "I don't want to upset you more than you are, but the plain and simple fact is he told me as much." And then he took his hand away because he thought touching her like that was maybe a little too pushy, even though he wanted to make the point. "I think the quicker you get over that dipshit white boy, the better," he told her, "and I know—I live with the dude."

"He's your friend?" she said as if scolding him.

"Yeah," he said. "What's that got to do with it?"

"I didn't think you'd side with me," she said.

"Not a matter of sides," he said.

LeRoy used to say that Dawn was sometimes hot, sometimes not, sometimes so ratty that a guy didn't even want to be seen with her—and then sometimes drop-dead gorgeous. Strange that way—in and out—almost like two people, or three, or four. He knew what LeRoy meant, knew that even though right now wasn't one of her good times, he himself hadn't really ever talked much to a girl so blasted beautiful.

"What you going to do now?" he said.

She looked up at him in a way she hadn't before, as if something written on her face wasn't supposed to be there. "What'd he tell you?" she said. "What'd he say about me anyway, the son of a bitch?"

He just spit it out because there was no sense hiding it. "He said you were going to have a baby," Marcus told her. "He told me some time ago—I don't remember when exactly."

And then she told him in a way that he thought was the whole truth and nothing but the truth, so help him God. She said how she'd found out about the kid already before Thanksgiving when she figured it was what was happening, and she'd bought one of those kits from the store where you check and find out and she did and she was, she said, dead-on pregnant. So she knew. And she'd been sure some time ago, before they had that big fight. "You remember that?" she asked him.

He told her he didn't remember a big fight but that there was lots he didn't know or remember and mostly that was because it was his thing to just let LeRoy have his life and he had his, or something like that. He said to go on with her story, which she did, which he thought she was happy to do.

She patted the couch, got him down beside her, where she could snuggle her shoulder into his, and then she took his hand—they were friends in a way, so it wasn't as if she was trying to come on to him or whatever—at least not right then.

And then came the thing about ditching the baby, which he'd heard about from LeRoy too, although he didn't tell her how LeRoy had told him what he wanted her to do, about how she should just take care of the whole mess because there were places where that job could get done and he could find out how and where and everything and how it wasn't anything at all because lots of women do it, lots of women just take care of things when things have to be taken care of. And he said he'd pay for what had to be done because he was the one who got her that way.

That's when she looked at him just about the way Roland had, that same kind of pain. "It's gone," she told him.

"You mean the baby?" he asked her.

She nodded and pulled herself into him, closer and closer, like a sister, he thought, and he threw his arm around her. Marcus's own sister was 19, but he hadn't seen her for a while, didn't know where she was exactly except that she'd left to go look for their father somewhere in New Mexico. She was older than he was, and he missed her, would have loved to have someone around other than LeRoy. Well, and his grandma too.

"You come here tonight to tell LeRoy that—that the baby was gone?" he asked her.

She told him that he'd already known, that she'd told him a week ago already at least, that it wasn't news, and that even then, when she'd told him, she picked up all these little things in the way he acted to make her feel he was going to dump her now that there would be no baby, which is not to say he wanted the baby—*he* didn't want the baby. That much, at least, LeRoy had made very clear: *he did not want the baby.* He was the one who'd told her to get rid of it, she said. LeRoy said he was going to be one piss-poor father and the world was already too full of bad-ass dads, is what he told her, which was nothing at all like he'd told Marcus, but then again probably true, Marcus thought, because it wouldn't have been the first time that people he knew said one thing and did another like that.

"So, it's just over now?" he said. "The thing between you and him—it just ended?"

She nodded.

And then he said something he thought he might regret: "You're better off without the bastard."

And she said, "I know it."

They were sitting there on the couch together, and she didn't let any grass grow under that line, not a bit, came right out with it. “Losing him is not why I’m crying, Marcus. That’s not the shits here,” she told him, shaking her head. “You don’t have to tell me that him being gone is a blessing. I already know it better.”

“Then what we ought to do is celebrate,” he said. He thought there was just too much beauty in that face to let it fall into all that sadness. He knew this much too—what they did, it was the right thing to do. She needed to celebrate. Tonight, she needed her own little party. Of that he was sure.

I just went in the ditch, all right?

It took just four and half minutes to get that Healthy Balance dinner hot in the microwave, just time enough for Coby St. James to get out of her school clothes and into her sweats. There were no plans for the evening, no plans at all. And the truth is, to her, that didn't sound bad at all.

The house was cold, very cold, and her cat followed her to the bedroom as if staying close promised a couple degrees of extra warmth. She looked at the thermostat, but the light from the sun—desperately low in the western sky—was shining directly on its face, which meant the rest of the house was impossibly frigid. She picked up the cat and hugged it—poor Lexi.

By the time she got back to the kitchen, the buzzer had already sounded, but the idea was to keep the dinner in for a while, cooking or cooling or whatever; so she ran water from the kitchen sink and filled up the plastic watering can, even though her plants—she wasn't blessed with a green thumb—weren't doing much at all in the scanty December sunshine. It would be like her, she thought, to find that water can—still there, still full—tomorrow, totally forgotten. There was a reason she wasn't good with plants. And for a nurse, too--at least a used-to-be nurse. Shit's sake, she said to herself, she ought to be ashamed.

Lexi followed her back into the kitchen, batting at her ankles with clawless paws, hungry for attention in addition to being cold, starved in a way that made the two of them soul-mates, her only companion, she told herself, smiling. Pets were great therapy for old people, she being one of them these days.

She pulled on her slippers, form-fitted after all these years, then stood at the sink for a moment and waited, thinking about this beautiful young girl who'd seemed so strung out but who'd not been in any immediate danger when she'd been brought to emergency—at least that was the report. Almost had to be drinking. Some frostbite, but fortunately she'd walked away from the car she somehow put in a ditch somewhere way west of town. Had she decided to try to walk away, she would have died and been written up like so many out here, or so the nurses said, white nurses. All too many of the dead ones were kids, but not all of them either. Nella had been the one who told her, reminded by Alice, both of them having remembered some beautiful Indian kid two years ago found frozen stiff along some snowy road out towards the river, body rigid and distorted, snow-swept, with thick cobwebs of ice through the edges of her clothing and across her face.

"You don't forget those," Nella told her. "Here's hoping it doesn't start a trend." She slipped her pearl ring up and down her finger habitually. "That happens, Coby," she said, as if she needed to be reminded. "Like dominoes."

"They're just kids," Coby told her, trying out a smile.

And that was it for conversation until break. Coby was the newbie, and she was Native, although she liked to say to people—some at least—not "*native* Native." That her presence created some difference in how the story was discussed was evident, even though the reservation wasn't all that far west, less than an hour and, people liked to say, maybe less on gravel.

But this beautiful young lady *wasn't* dead. Her ears may have been nipped—she wore her hair in braids, very traditionally, even though people said she lived not all that far outside of town, not way out on the rez, and that she came from caring parents. Just the same, there was enough mystery about her and what really might have gone on—she wasn't even an adult, just sixteen--to draw everyone in. Who had called it in was a mystery too. Someone had called 911 in the middle of the night.

Dawn Burnett was her name, and she didn't look as if she'd been through a chamber of horrors. There was some question about drinking, although no bottles or cans were found in the car or anywhere around so some kind of road-loading wasn't going on. She may have been smoking something. She was fully clothed, Nella said, no buttons left undone, everything in place, no sign of struggle. But still.

What the EMTs had suggested was that there was no clear reason for her to go four-wheeling the way she did. Wasn't really a blizzard, after all, and it certainly didn't look as if she has met some other car or truck. They didn't need to tell the others how far out all of this really was, where it happened—miles and miles from the beaten path in all that ice-house cold.

"Where?" she'd said.

"Sort of no-man's land between here and the rez," Nella explained. "Like, nobody lives out there."

No bruising, but there were suspicions, in part because this dark beauty of a girl had come through the ER before—more than once, and thereby left a well-documented trail. One didn't have to be given to idle speculation to imagine what might have happened. The police claimed there was no sign she'd lost control, the tracks from her Chevy swerving slowly into a ditch snow-filled to the brim. Where she came to rest was far enough off the road to make you wonder who could have found her there in the middle of the night, and how. The whole thing just felt suspicious, as if she'd deliberately plowed her way into that field a mile away because she didn't want to be found.

The hospital had waited to call Coby until morning because this young thing wasn't in great danger, and they didn't really suspect rape anyway, there being no signs of struggle. So when Coby had walked in to the girl's room that morning, what struck her the moment she saw her was her magazine-cover beauty. What had happened that early Friday morning would have been a huge story in the city simply because once a camera got an eye on a face that perfect, it wouldn't have let go quickly. Some reporter would dig up all the facts, determining exactly what had happened. But out here in the middle of the Plains, what went on last night, whatever it was that led to her aiming her car into a ditch in the killing fields of blowing snow, would be known only to a few and likely be held close to the chest or vest or whatever.

The girl was okay, basically. There was some question about frostbite, but was nothing broken, not even any bumps and bruises, nothing requiring major repair. But they'd called

Coby in anyway because of circumstances; the kid needed an advocate and the rape counselor idea was the closest thing. Hitting that bank of snow, plowing into it, was probably akin to slamming into a pillow; and that's what made the rumors fly—that there almost had to be some intent, some will on her part, not to end things exactly but to make it look for sure as if that's what was in the plans. It happened way too often, Coby knew, even though this one was her first since coming to Cottonwood and seemingly so very unlikely, Dawn Burnett being knock-out gorgeous.

The police claimed the girl's record spoke for itself—or so they'd told her on the phone. Miss Burnett still needed to rest, needed to be watched, needed to be cared for; she'd stay the day in the hospital—that was the report—even though she probably didn't need to. By the time Coby had come in, the girl's parents were already gone, their daughter sleeping soundly.

Coby pulled her dinner tray out of the microwave without a mitt and slid it on a plate, burning her fingers in the process, then grabbed the dishrag to cool them. Cottonwood school system wasn't some dream job, but she'd lost a heckuva lot of dreams anyway and there was this rich blessing here because it was nowhere close to where she'd been. It was "the lure of the West," some remnant of her own white parentage, she'd told people, the pioneer's resolve to cut out a new life in the middle of a land so wide people seemed ridiculously small. That's what she'd said, smilingly, to her friends.

Besides, she really didn't mind frozen dinners. They were nothing to write home about, but sitting there alone in a little old house in a tiny town in South Dakota on a snowy night? —there were worse fates. Worse fates she'd already lived through, in fact.

What had been amazing about the girl was how openly she had told her the story, or what she chose of the story to tell. Young women who find themselves in unforeseen hospital beds could be notorious liars, just about always for completely understandable reasons. In a half hour conversation—sometimes even less--just exactly what happened could change shape and form the way thunderclouds flexed and waned in a June sky. All through the telling, Coby had never been sure how much of what the girl had told her was the self-defense we all create. No one tells a story without spinning, she thought. But Dawn Burnett had given up something at least, a good deal more than an outline.

She had been angry at the kid who dumped her, this Ms. Burnett told her, so she went out to his place to fetch some things of her own—that was the plan. She was an artist, or fancied herself so, she said, like her mother; and she'd given him some things she'd done, some drawings, and now that he was an ex-, she told him she wanted that stuff back. It was over between them, Dawn had said, and she wasn't about to leave those drawings with a guy who didn't want her or them. Just to get this stuff because she thought he'd be gone, that was her reason for going back to this guy's place, a rental acreage, she said, a house that's falling apart—the Brethower place. Coby had taken care to write it down. Dawn Burnett hadn't wanted to see this guy, to end the deal or whatever. That was already a done thing. That wasn't it. Just to pick this stuff of hers up is why she was there. All of this she told to Cody slowly, deliberately, but with enough earnestness to make Coby believe the story she spun was something approximate to truth.

"I wasn't raped, if that's what you're after," Dawn had told her, straight up, anticipating the question. "I mean, if that's all you really give a damn about, forget it. Be a handy thing to say, but I can't. It didn't happen."

What Coby had wanted, at least for a while—maybe it was just pure suspicion on her part—was for the girl to take a rape test. She wanted to edge that request into the conversation because it wasn't easy with a girl like Dawn, young and seemingly guarded, no matter how thick her file. It was like kids in small towns like Cottonwood *not* to want to give up the whole story, instead to swallow horror because it was prudent of them—or so they thought—to keep their mouths shut and their reputations unsullied, no matter what kind of suffering they'd gone through. Coby had lived in cities for all her life long, but small towns weren't so far back in her DNA that she didn't understand the role guilt could play in a place like Cottonwood. Experts said that not giving up the truth only compounded problems down the road, but then most experts weren't sixteen and scared to death, and didn't live in a place so small that coming and going didn't take much longer than a good sneeze.

She determined that this Dawn was neither silly nor foolish. "You understand that lots of kids like you say exactly that when it's really a bald-faced lie," she'd told the girl with a smile. "There's a lot to be guarded about."

"Didn't happen," she said.

"Then what did?" Coby'd asked her.

Street-wise Native kids like Dawn know very well that if you're going to die, the cold may well be the killer most blest, she thought. Dawn Burnett, who Coby assumed simply had to be Native, some flavor of Sioux most likely, understood long before she'd turned sixteen that death came slowly, even obligingly, in any icy silence. She wouldn't have been the first, after all. About that, the other nurses weren't wrong.

Slowly, Coby lifted the clear plastic from the black packaging and the smell of the dinner—beef and carrots—swept up in a wave of steamy heat. Lexi was at her feet, nudging her ankles to remind her of what wasn't there in her dish. She let the dinner lay and turned to the cupboard to get cat food.

When she filled the dish, some of the cat food spilled out over the floor because Lexi couldn't keep her wet nose out of the Tupperware, so incredibly anxious to eat she was, as if she were starving. It was a game Lexi played, inflicting guilt. In thirty seconds, she'd be right there at her side on the couch, trying to find a way to get at the beef on her microwaveable plate.

She picked up the dinner and headed for the TV when she saw the phone light flashing. She had a cell but put in a landline because she knew she had to be in the book, someplace people could find her. There were emergencies in her life, of course—she'd been a nurse herself and a rape counselor—so she packed the cell but didn't give out the number to anyone other than the hospital. And maybe a couple of others.

She told herself she was falling into the old darkness again by reminding herself of the silence all around her in this old house. Like the stupid Christmas tree in the corner—how many people had such an ugly tree? She simply had to get one, or something anyway—so she did. There was still a week before

Christmas, but just a couple days before school vacation, when she'd head back up north to her folks anyway, right? So, who needs a tree if there is no Christmas? She looked out the window just for a second, then remembered how unearthly cold it was.

She hit "voice mail" even though she knew it would be Trent. Had to be. And that was good. Sort of.

"Coby," he said. "Here's the deal. Got something every night this week—basketball, Honors Club, what not. Got to be 'the man,' you know. Comes with the territory."

Pause. Long pause. She held her fingers over the keypad.

"Just thought I'd tell you that because I'd rather be doing other things," he said. And then he hummed a couple of bars from "How Am I Supposed to Live Without You?" Not well either. That wasn't the point. Music wasn't his thing.

The cat jumped on the counter beside her and pushed her face into her hand.

"I'll call you," he said. And then, "Yeah, well, sounds like a lie, even to me," he said. "But it's not." And then another long pause—terribly long, long enough for Lexi to push her nose into Coby's hand again. "I don't know how to do this exactly," he said, "so I hope you'll forgive me when I fumble the stupid ball."

What he meant was that he didn't know how to negotiate the territory between them, or what she figured he thought was happening—the two of them just plain coming closer. She could see him sitting at his desk at school, door closed, hallways empty, the place finally quieting down after another big day. Even so, he'd be cupping the phone like a narco.

And then, "Phone tag is better than no tag at all, right? Later."

He couldn't hang up. She knew what that felt like. She remembered, because there was too much of that in her life for her to forget so easily.

"The girl's been released, right? —Dawn Burnett? She must be gone by now, I take it. If you got any news, I'd like to hear, hear?" he said. "What on earth happened anyway? —there's tons of stories goin' round." Yet another long pause. "Yeah, well, like I said, 'later,' I swear."

Click.

The phone announced he had called just before five. She could probably still reach him at school and would have loved to, but she didn't want to lie and she couldn't tell him what she knew about Dawn Burnett. There was the law after all.

"I just want to make sure," she had told this pretty girl. "I'm a nurse, and I'm concerned that you're well. It's not all that intrusive, but it's a good idea because things happen, you know?"

To describe Dawn Burnett's eyes as wary wouldn't have been accurate, because deeper than their shiftiness, beneath that quick movement that felt like a hasty retreat from Coby's questions, there was something even darker, some pain and more than a little hostility. She could read it clearly because there were moments when those eyes wouldn't dart away, when she would study Coby's face, her own eyes, as if to measure something, find some trust. All of that somehow beneath what seemed pure disdain.

"I fell asleep is all," she had told Coby. "That's what this is about. I don't get all the damned fuss. People fall asleep all the time. I'm not hurt, right? What's the big deal? My car isn't even wrecked."

"We just want to cover all the bases," Coby told her.

"What damned bases? —and what business is it of yours? You're not the cops," she said. "And I didn't break a law. I went in the ditch," she said. "I just went in the ditch, all right? Now will you just leave me the hell alone?"

Sins of the fathers

The truth is, what Woody Dekkers had thought about between classes that day was Trent Sterrett, just a kid but a terrific catch, scarred by a failed marriage Woody knew nothing about, a boss who was prize for a district as pitifully small and out-of-the-way as Cottonwood. He was a young warrior who thought no problems insurmountable if we'd only hug kids a bit tighter, but he was no sappy fool either.

For a while after that 8:00 meeting, Woody had toyed with the idea of going down the hall and telling Sterrett the entire Dawn Burnett story; but sometime after lunch he'd decided not to—and besides it's not just something you plop down on the desk like homework, he thought. Just let him think what he does, Woody told himself, because just one of the lessons he'd learned himself, the older he got, was that innocence, no matter how blind, can be a Godsend. If Sterrett knew the whole blamed story, whatever had happened to Dawn might just seem worse—more unyielding. The shadow cast by whatever the heck the girl had done to herself might seem significantly bigger and darker, even paralyzing. Years ago, a young Woody Dekkers would have ridden into the band room on a white horse, worked up a posse, and hit the streets to make the world a better place. In fact, he'd even tried—with Dawn Burnett's parents, seventeen years ago, to be exact.

He came out of the parking lot slowly because school was out and cars were everywhere, the one moment in town when people could actually get stuck in traffic.

The thing was, he told himself, whatever happened had roots. When he and Tieneke had lived in town, an ash tree blew over on a night that wasn't even all that windy. He got a guy to saw it up for firewood, then rented a huge saw-like thing that plunged into the dirt where that tree had stood, churning the roots into mulch, two feet deep. But so much stayed in the ground, he remembered thinking, that whole mammoth root system. You couldn't burn it out, you couldn't dig it out, you couldn't dissolve it out because the truth is that everything down there just has to rot into oblivion, and that takes time, a lot of time, he thought.

He decided against telling Sterrett the whole Dawn Burnett story because there are things even the new guy didn't have to know, things not even Dawn had to know. In fact, he wondered exactly what the child knew—whether all those tangled roots were part of what made her veer off the road when death in the frozen cold was all she had out there in the middle of nowhere's open spaces.

The snow was snake dancing across the open fields just like it must have been when Dawn had gone into the ditch the night before. For anybody who grew up out here or knew the territory, *not* to speculate that what had happened was willful was nigh unto impossible. Visit some rez cemetery and any of a dozen graves marked dead men and women who breathed their last in some deadly blizzard, a way of death that was a way of life. Roll your beater on some country road when the temps were in the deep freeze, and you're baiting death, and everyone knew it, he thought.

Dawn Burnett was little more than a kid—16 or 17--but she knew tradition. She had to know. Men and women and kids too, far too often, just threw in the towel on life. Happened so often out here it was hard to know what was willful and what was just plain stupid. And everybody knew Dawn Burnett was street-wise, a good half-lifetime beyond innocence. She had to want to die in a perfectly Indian way—falling asleep in the freezer.

Another deer dead along the highway, when the road turned west. Must have come up out of the river bottoms like always, or so it seemed. Once a week at least, they'd get killed on the road, lie there half in the ditch, heads thrown back.

He and Tieneke had moved out into the country because he wanted to live in a place where he could take a leak out the back door, he'd told her. They'd never guessed they'd get a place so close to the river, but when this place came open—the Mattels left for the Twin Cities when the packing plant folded—they put in a low bid and somehow got it: a grand place, not huge, a place they'd quickly learned to love. The Fabers were right down the road, former students. But then who wasn't a former student after thirty years at Cottonwood? If he wanted to run from grads, he'd have to light out for Denver, and even there he couldn't hide.

An old friend of his used to say that living forever in one spot—a small town like Cottonwood—fills the heart with stories, every generation playing cause/effect with the next, the sins of the fathers tagging along like unwanted friends. And of the mothers too. The kind of pain Dawn had already created was equal-opportunity, he thought. Cities spill over with great momentary images, an old friend used to say, bright and engaging snapshots; but towns are overstuffed family albums, full-length feature films; every kid, every generation, gets its own chapter—but it's just one story.

Sins of the fathers, his father the preacher would have said.

He turned off the highway and up the gravel towards home, towards the neighbors. Scotty and Karin would want to know what happened to Dawn Burnett; and even if they wouldn't want to hear, they wouldn't want to *not* know.

He didn't think much about Tieneke spotting him driving right on past their place because not even in the first week of their marriage had she ever window-sat, waiting for her man. Had to laugh to think about it—that she might be looking out the window right now, wondering when he'd be home from school, so she could serve up coffee in a clean apron or meet him at the door wearing nothing but cellophane. Somehow, he'd chosen right, way back when, and so had she. Things like that had to be in the stars.

Likely as not she was reading or cooking, probably cooking, something she'd taken up with a passion since Teresa's death, a place to hide sometimes, he thought. He wished she were in her studio spitting paint at some massive canvas he'd need her to interpret; but she hadn't been in the studio they'd both spotted when they toured the house for the first time, a place she could work. She hadn't been putting anything on canvas for a long time, in part because the whole room—it overlooked the river--was hung with Teresa's work, a kind of museum, probably too much a shrine. She told him once, years before, that the longer she painted, the more abstract she got. That was before she'd stopped on a dime, too full of grief and guilt—who cared about the difference anyway? He told her he did too, got more and more abstract as years went by, even though he never touched a brush. It just happened—the more you know, the less you believe. That kind of thing.

Ceramic deer on the lawn. A windmill. The Fabers were too young for that old plywood woman in the flower garden bending over her petunias, her polka-dot bloomers jumping out, but Scotty and Karin would be just the type to add some silly lawn ornament someday, maybe just outside the playhouse Scotty had built when KayLee was nine or ten. Everything was neat; Scotty, an unmercifully hard-worker. Good night, could the guy work. Took out his loader and ripped out an entire hedge on a Saturday morning last fall, had it all but gone—jerked out and dragged away, the new ones in the ground—in the time it took Woody to go to town to pick up donuts for his grandkids. Buildings neatly kept, painted. Whatever wasn't needed on the place was gone, burned.

The gravel beneath his tires quieted when he slowed up a bit because he wasn't all that interested in delivering news sure to be heard in helpless pain. Why was he was doing this? —he asked himself. The two of them would certainly find out themselves soon enough, if they hadn't already. KayLee was in high school after all, and the Dawn story would have been front page stuff all day around town. Probably texted all over the Great Plains 24 hours ago already. Maybe they already knew.

He pulled into the driveway in front of the new garage they'd had built in the same old farmstead design as their Sears home, vintage 1922 or so—a house from the catalogue years ago and from *Better Homes and Gardens* today, thanks to Karin. Tieneke would say Karin had left no corners untenanted. Perennial flower beds filled every last open space on the yard, an old oaken bucket hanging from the pump out back, plump with daisies come June. All girls, too—four of them, all Faber beauties, pretty as pictures.

They were converts, really, even though both of them had grown up in church, born Methodist, born-again Independent Baptist—that kind of thing. They were sweet and wonderful people who'd come to see the errors of their ways, the sins of their youth, as people used to say. They'd come to see the light, and the light of the world had changed everything.

Well, not everything, he told himself. Almost everything.

He'd hadn't planned exactly what he'd say, although it wasn't the first time he'd rolled up with a grocery bag stuffed full of bad tidings. Karin had told him--not long after they'd moved in and Dawn had some kind of run-in with the law—he couldn't remember what anymore, or which time—that she wanted to know those things, always wanted to know, needed to.

She wasn't angry, and he was confident she didn't use Dawn Burnett like a weapon because the early years of their marriage had been the Wild West in every which way. He knew that too. He'd raised hell, but Karin hadn't been sitting home knitting afghans. Back then, they'd separated no more than a year after they'd married, bottomed-out, then later had come back together, and found the Lord—that kind of redemption story could have been on Christian TV, he thought. If they were given to making money, they could have started doing retreats with the testimony they could spin. They weren't. Thank the Lord.

But there were residuals, after all, and one of them was Dawn Burnett.

Four times he rang the doorbell before anyone came, but he knew Karin was home and so were the kids. It was a three-car garage—everybody needed a three-car garage these days. Two cars out front. Scotty's pickup was gone, out on a job somewhere.

"Woody! How long were you out here anyway?" Karin said finally, scold in her voice. The sounds of the piano came from behind her; they had been practicing, she and KayLee, their oldest.

"Not quite long enough to die," he told her, "but pretty near. It's wicked cold."

"Get inside here," she told him, holding open the door and grabbing his sleeve with her left hand. "We were going over some things because KayLee's got to sing at Medford this week—I think it's Medford. God knows where."

"I'm sure he does," Woody told her, unpeeling his scarf.

"Let me take your coat," she said, but he didn't mean to stay. When he didn't oblige her, her face fell because in that flash, just that quickly, she knew why he was there and it wasn't good tidings. But then, he figured, she probably knew the moment she saw him because it wasn't his thing to just drop in as if she had the only fresh coffee on the river. She looked behind her, swung the kitchen door closed, then folded her arms across her chest because the old hallway didn't do much to keep out the cold. "What happened?" she asked.

"KayLee didn't say anything?"

"I'm not sure my daughter even knows who Dawn is," Karin told him.

He couldn't just drop it down in front of her, couldn't just run through it quick as if to ask if she could feed the dog while he and Tieneke were in Omaha or something.

"What happened?" she said again.

He'd long ago thought Karin was prettier today than she was when she was 17 and in his history class. Money pays, after all, and so does Jesus, he thought.

"She's in the hospital," Woody told her. "There was this accident."

"She's okay?" Karin said. That she didn't pause made it clear to him that somehow it wasn't a surprise, and of course it shouldn't have been, not with Dawn's criminal record.

He nodded.

That's when the silence began.

Later, he thought about Karin being frozen the way she was right then as perfectly understandable. There was something so conspiratorial about the two of them standing there with the inside door closed, paralyzing cold rolled into a fist just outside because no mention of Dawn Burnett could be coaxed into that pretty and righteous place without soiling something. Dawn's graduation picture—if ever she would graduate--would never stand alongside KayLee's on the baby grand where Dawn's beautiful and talented half-sister right now sat plunking out notes for some ministry in music in a church somewhere down the road, one of a string of performances she'd been doing since 7th grade. "What a talent," people would say come Sunday morning. "What a testimony."

"Is there more?" Karin asked finally. And then it broke. "We shouldn't do this," she said. "I mean, it's so cold out here. Why don't you come in?"

"There's not much to say," he told her. "I thought you'd want to know—you said—"

"I do—I do. You're right about that—I always want to know. *We* do." She leaned down from the step and took his elbow. "I won't have this," she said. "Come in—even just for a moment."

There was this tinkling from the music room. KayLee was still there, singing a melody. No lyrics. KayLee had to know. The story got headlines all day in school. She had to have heard, had to know, but there was so much she didn't know.

He put a hand up as if to keep it all out of the house by himself. "I really don't know a lot," he told her again.

"I won't have it," she said and backed up the hallway, opened the door to the kitchen, and ushered him in. "This isn't right—come in, come in and sit down."

He hiked up the stairs behind her, deliberately kept his coat around his shoulders, then stood there in the warmth, slipping off his shoes beside a refrigerator jammed with pictures and assignments, notes and recipes, groceries to be picked up--all of it full of life, full of joy.

Karin took him into the sun room they'd added in the last few years, windows for walls, a room Scotty told him actually lowered their heating bill by catching everything the sun could offer all winter long. She pointed him at a wicker chair and remembered wishing he and Tieneke had a space like that when they'd been younger. An enormous Christmas tree, flocked in a pastel pink, nearly took over the entire western wall.

He kept his voice hushed. "There was an accident," he said. "She was alone. Some drinking maybe, I guess, somehow, the cops said. It was last night, and somebody must have come along and spotted the car in the ditch—you know how it was blowing."

She asked where.

He told her what Trent Sterrett had reported—a long way out, somewhere far away.

She asked what on earth Dawn was doing way out there, but it was a rhetorical question. She sat there across the room in a small arm chair, her hands tightly wound, shoulders slumped so that the cottony sweatshirt she wore bowed a bit and showed some soft lines of flesh across her chest. It was hard for him to remember that Karin—like Scotty, for that matter, and so many others—wasn't a kid anymore.

"No drugs, I guess," he told her, "but the way I hear it—we got it from the honcho himself, Trent Sterrett—he's a fine kid, really. The way people talk about it, there may well have been something willful about it."

"How can they say that?" she said.

He let that one go because she knew the answer: it wouldn't have been the first time.

"Sterrett said it wasn't life-threatening," Woody told her. "There's some exposure stuff, I imagine. It's lucky somebody called it in, you know? —a blessing, really, almost a miracle, out there where she was."

Dawn Burnett had been a long way from town.

"I don't know much more than that," he said, taking a deep breath. "I tried to keep my ear to the ground all day, but I didn't hear much from kids. They don't talk to me much anymore."

The moment he said it, he sweat a little, hoping she wouldn't think of what he'd said as some kind of memory. She didn't.

He pulled at the fingers of his gloves as if to take them off, then remembered he was going to leave—KayLee was home, after all, and the little girls. "You told me once—I remember you told me you wanted to know, and I respect that, Karin." She was looking at her hands. "I wouldn't have stopped by if I didn't think it was right—that you *should* know. And I didn't want it to surprise you, you know—somebody mention it at school or something." He deliberately cast a glance into the piano room.

"She didn't mention it," Karin told him. There was something totally unpracticed about the smile she gave him. "Ever since Dawn came back here, I think about her a lot—I do." She meant the smile, but it left as quickly as it had arrived. "It's a load, Woody," she told him. "And it's not an *it*—it's a human being, a girl, a young woman." Her hands were balled up, but she rubbed at her eyes. "And there's really nothing we can do—there's really nothing."

"She'll be okay," he told her. "She's a tough kid."

"This time."

"She'll grow up. We all do."

She nodded and drew a Kleenex from the box on the glass table beside her. "I don't know what's worse," she told him, "carrying her like a cross or not carrying her at all."

"Or carrying her cross," Woody said, but he wasn't sure that he'd been heard.

Once, maybe a year ago, he'd thought the whole story through to this point at least—he had simply determined that it was a blessing Karin herself had been less than faithful way back in those first years of their marriage, because if she had been virgin-pure she could have put her husband on the rack any day or night of the week. Max Backus had cheated on his wife seven years into their marriage—Woody remembered because it sounded almost biblical. When he wanted back in, Cheryl made his life miserable for three decades, maybe more—after all, they hadn't seen the Backuses in a long, long time. Cheryl Backus figured she had a right. Karin didn't, and she knew it.

When Karin would be telling Scotty what had happened to Dawn, to his own daughter—wherever that midnight hour would occur, whenever it would—the news, maybe no more than a sentence, would drudge up their mutual sin, not just Scotty's. If that wasn't true, Woody told himself, he likely wouldn't have told them when Dawn went astray because telling Karin would have made him feel like an arms dealer. The Fabers had a good marriage; tested and tried, but a good marriage. About that, he had no doubts. Both of them had just needed some growing up a couple decades ago like so many did, like Woody did, as he reminded himself. The church he'd grown up in would have crucified the both of them, but that church was long gone.

Karin looked around as if someone was standing just beyond her shoulder. "I've got to practice," she said awkwardly. "You know—with KayLee." She pointed back behind her.

"I didn't intend to stay," he told her, getting to his feet, drawing a deep breath as he did. "It's such a gorgeous room,

Karin," he told her, but she looked at him as if he'd lapsed into another language.

"Woody, you can sing," she said, her arms clasped across her chest as if this sweet room wasn't almost tropical. "Why don't you sit there with her for a while?" She both didn't mean it and did—he knew that. She balled up the Kleenex she'd used and jammed them into the pouch of her sweatshirt. "That girl has my husband's own blood, part of his heart too, you know—and soul. She's as much his daughter," she stopped herself, bit her lip, looked away, then back again toward him—"as much *his* as our own," she told him, pointing somewhere toward the music room. "It's a blessing, I guess, that they aren't in the same class."

"They'd never suspect—either of them," Woody said. "They don't look at all alike, don't hang with the same crowd, couldn't be more different."

"Pray with me," she told him. She got up from her chair, reached for his hands. "Woody, you pray, okay?" she said. "It's all we can do."

He did, quietly, even though he was cautious about closing his eyes.

That he'd cared

When Dawn Burnett told Marcus what she had about her ex, LeRoy, she was shedding tears but then catching them as if they weren't there. But when she had told him that what just about killed her didn't have much to do with LeRoy, all Marcus could guess was that the anger and sadness and whatever else was brewing was all about how she just got rid of the kid. It had to be about that, he thought, if he could believe her; and he did believe her, because Dawn was no liar. Straight-up honest she was about most everything. She was no white girl, worried that somebody, some place, was thinking something ugly. She didn't need to lie about things because kids thought the worst of her anyway, he told himself.

All that heat and smoke and anger, if it wasn't about LeRoy then it almost had to come from her knowing she was going to have a baby, that for a time in her life she was really "with child," as Grandma would say, and then in an afternoon or whatever it takes to snip it out, she wasn't. She'd done what LeRoy told her to do, gotten rid of the kid. That's what killed her, getting rid of that baby—that's what Marcus had figured. It happened to girls. He knew that much.

He reached around her and took her in his arms and held her, just held her, because, honest-to-God, right then his own heart just about broke for that girl. He knew she didn't have it easy, even though her folks were all right now and had money and stuff. But money wasn't everything. Just because you had it better than most kids didn't mean you couldn't crack up, he thought.

And besides, Dawn Burnett wasn't her father's daughter, and she knew it. And sometimes it made a person just say to himself or herself that there was so much trash and shit in the world that sometimes you can't help feeling as though the ground you're walking on is spread with shards of glass everywhere you look, every direction, even under your own bare feet that are already bleeding when you take the time to look. Nothing but stuff beneath you that'll cut you up in pieces like some rag doll. You feel that way sometimes, he thought, but he didn't say it just then, not to Dawn, who didn't need to hear it.

She had pulled away from him slowly. "I came to get my things," she told him. "Even though they're sketches of him, he doesn't deserve them. I'm the one that drew them," she said, "and I'm the one's going to toss them—not him, that's for sure."

"You going to take them home?" he asked her.

"I'm not going home," she told him, just like that, flat-out.

He knew better than to think she might be planning on staying here, not with LeRoy sure to come back. The truth was, he didn't know what she might have meant; nor could he even begin to think where she might go that night if she didn't stay here, which she wouldn't do, or go home, where she didn't want to go. And that scared him.

"Maybe I can help," he said. "Want to go look for that stuff?"

And so the two of them had gone into LeRoy's room and taken a couple of those drawings off the walls, found another one on the floor, not yet hung. Five in all—one of them maybe a foot wide or so in a frame, not expensive, all of them drawings, sketches she did in one of those big sketch books kids had for art class, then ripped out and stuck into frames. Three of them were of his face, and two of them were like his whole body, no clothes at all, although they weren't what you might think of because the pictures weren't like photographs or anything. They were different than that, although somehow it was clear—maybe only because he put two and two together—that the figures in the drawings were LeRoy.

He liked them too—LeRoy did. Marcus knew he was sort of proud of the big one, where he was sitting on the floor in a way that made him look beefier than he was, that tattoo running up over his shoulder, nothing of his package showing, just undressed.

It's not like she'd spent hours and hours on those drawings either. You could see that. They were charcoal or something, just a few strokes with some shading and a little bit of close work. They weren't art and they weren't on canvas, just paper.

"You want 'em?" he asked.

"I just don't want him to have them," she told him. "They were for him and from me, and I just didn't like it at all that they'd still be here when I wasn't, you know?" She pointed at the drawings, shrugged her shoulders. "About him I couldn't care less."

So Marcus had been the one who suggested they burn the whole bunch. Marcus said to pull them out of the frames and just take them out back and burn them all, have a bonfire in the frozen cold just off the back step. That'd be easy enough.

"Frames too," she told him. "I bought the whole bunch from Wal-Mart." She pointed at the big one. "Less than five bucks, I think."

"Good," he said. "They'll make a better fire."

There was no end to the trash lying around the place, so Marcus found a couple of shopping bags and filled them with stuff, then pulled on his jacket and gloves when she did, and the two of them pulled everything tight up around them because the night was freezing; horrible wind, ugly weather. He pulled a scarf off the shelf in the back hall and wound it around her neck, and when he pulled it up tight, he pulled her to him, and gave her a kiss on the cheek he meant like someone who loved her and not in the sex way, not at all. And she knew it.

"Honestly, we're going out there?" she asked him.

"Hey, the old ones lived in teepees, right?" he said. "You got something against heritage?"

"You got something to drink?" she said.

It just so happened he did, or LeRoy did, in the basement to keep it cold and not so obvious to the cops, if they showed up. He brought it to her and the two of them took a swig—maybe three or four, then grabbed a flashlight before heading out back.

He had thought of making the fire on the back step, then thought it should be the burning barrel; but the wind blew so hard that he knew he'd never pop a flame with a match or a lighter. He knew she needed to see those things burn, so he took her out to the machine shed, where they could sit inside and out of the wind, where they could light a fire and not worry about burning the place down. He didn't have much but old cereal boxes, but then those sketches wouldn't take long to burn up anyway. Wasn't going to be trouble, not really.

He'd never given a thought to LeRoy coming back because it wouldn't be like him to show up again so quickly, as if he were just running into town for gas or something. And besides, LeRoy just now had that new job, at night. Sometimes he'd simply be gone—two, three days at a time.

So there he and Dawn sat in the middle of the machine shed, wind singing through the cracks in the walls. He dumped the trash on the floor, raked it into a pile with his gloves, and grabbed wooden matches from the back-door ledge. He wadded up some Kleenex and jammed it in a Cheerios box, hoping to get things going, cupping the match after he lit it.

"You wonder how people lived out here with sticks and flints and everything," he told her. "I mean in winter, you know? You wonder sometimes, don't you?"

"Can you do that string thing?" she asked him, twirling some imaginary sticks in her fingers.

"Shit, no," he said. "I don't have patience to be an Indian."

"They were in the trees, you know--in the Hills, in *Paha Sapa*," she told him. "That made a difference, I think—you know, not being out in the open in all this wind. Maybe winter wouldn't be all that bad in the Hills, you think?"

"Still cold out there," he said, striking another match on his jacket zipper. "Even in the trees. Too much snow. Way too cold for me."

If he'd been smarter, he'd have hauled a blanket off his bed because the cement floor was a hundred and fifty degrees below zero, and she couldn't sit there or at least he wouldn't let her. Once there was at least the hint of a fire, he wandered off because he knew there was some hay in the far corner. "Don't let this go out," he told her.

"What am I supposed to do?" she asked.

"Blow on it," he told her. "Shoot, woman—you forget everything?" He grabbed the flashlight. "I'm going to get us something to sit on."

"I'm not dancing," she said, giggling.

"How do you know?" he told her. "Pow-wow hasn't even started."

It wasn't until he turned around and shone that light on the east wall that he wondered how blasted many four-leggeds he might disturb in here, how many possums and skunks and coons or whatever else might be holed up in some random corner of the shed to stay out of the wind. And right away he had this horrible feeling that they'd both get nailed by skunk piss and have to sit together in some hot bath to try to get the dang smell off, which, when he thought about it, wouldn't have been the worst thing either.

"Skunks in here," he said when he was far enough away from her to scare her.

"Marcus!" she yelled, like some pissed sister.

"Don't worry—I'm a warrior."

He could hear her laugh all the way over in the corner, even though the wind kept up the kind of siege you never get used to. He grabbed a single bale of hay by both strings, then spotted a whole stack of old barn wood just behind it. He hoisted the bale up on his knee and carried it back before putting it down, still wishing he'd have taken a blanket off his bed or from somewhere anyway—there were some old sleeping bags in a closet, even though going back in the house to get one didn't sound good. Still, he thought, it was going to be much sweeter sitting on that bale with a sleeping bag. "You want me to get you a blanket or something?" he said.

"I'm not camping out here when it's this cold," she said. "I got way too much white blood in me."

"So do I," he said.

That's when he remembered the sleeping bag he'd left in the back of the seat in the pickup, two of them in fact, still there from the summer, left there purposely because it was just smart to pack something along mid-winter, Grandma said, when you lived so far out. "Be right back—I swear it," he told her, pulling that stocking cap back over his ears.

"I just want to burn these things," she said. "It's all I want to do is just burn them, Marcus. Doesn't have to be some big ritual shit," she said. "Doesn't have to be a Sun Dance."

"Wait," he said, and he chased out to his truck, opened the door, then felt around behind the seats. Old wreck never had interior lights that he could remember, so he had to reach around until he found the sleeping bags. He pulled them out and wound them both around his shoulders before heading to the machine shed, then gave her one when he got inside.

"I'm not camping out here," she told him again.

"Neither am I," he told her. "That doesn't mean this has got to be over in a minute," he said. "We're going to do this right," he told her. "We're Injuns." He pointed at the sketches. "This is going to be something," he said. "We're going to take our blessed time. Has to be done with reverence, like the old ways." He smiled broad enough to make sure she saw it.

"What you think you know about the old ways?" she asked him. "You're just a kid."

"Grandma's way then—"

"Your grandma skin buffalo?"

He slapped his head like some comedian. "You born a fool or just grow into it?" he said. "She ain't Sacajawea." What he liked was the way she was smiling.

When the fire got started, more than enough light opened up the room and more than enough heat shook off the chill. The hay bale was better than a church pew, and the sleeping bags did things up right. So did the wine coolers.

Together, wrapped in bundles, they watched the fire in a silence that seemed right to him because sometimes, when you didn't talk, you could say more than you could when you did. It was almost a trance, middle of December, gusts of punishing wind outside the shed in another world altogether, just the two of them and a roaring blaze inside. Even beautiful, he thought. He couldn't help thinking that he'd done things right for once in his life.

"Now it's time," he said, and she pulled herself up from the bale, holding the blanket around her with her left hand, then reached for the first of the sketches. By that time, he'd grabbed some old wood from the east wall and fed it to flames that were already better than knee-high.

She used one hand to keep the blanket around her, the other to hold one of the charcoal sketches. Then she stood over the fire in its own radiant gold, and looked at him as if she needed his permission. He nodded. She placed the frame directly on top. Just a minute, no more, and the whole thing began to darken then burst out in flame.

He motioned toward the others, and she took the larger one. It would have been a good thing to sing, he thought. Somehow, it would have been right just then to sing, if he knew the song for sorrow about a baby gone, and if there was a drum, of course. He'd need some warrior with a drum to sing.

What he remembered later about that time sitting over the fire in the machine shed was that it was good, the two of them watching those drawings curl up into flame, a blessing on a night so dark and cold.

And he couldn't get out of his mind how beautiful Dawn was—that too. There she sat in a crouch, that sleeping bag pulled all around her, up to her face, her eyes shiny with flames. She was a painting, he thought. She ought to try something like it or he should because she could sell it, if he'd let her.

"You ought to draw what I see," he told her.

She looked at him as if she was suddenly surprised to see him there.

"That fire in your face," he said. "Some time you should paint that. It's like gold." He pointed at his own face, chin to crown. "It's like a painting—what I'm seeing here."

"Myself?" she said. "I should draw myself?"

"Paint," he said. "Not draw. I could tell you exactly the right color if I stood beside you. I could get it right. I could show you."

For just a moment when she stared at him, he couldn't help feeling she'd found a place for him in her soul. Those dark eyes full of fire were thanking him, maybe even asking him in.

She held the last drawing over the fire, watched it curl into flame, then sat back and drew the sleeping bag around her again, all the while staring into the flames.

When they were all black sheets, he nodded to her that it was time to go. He unwrapped himself from the blanket, then draped it around her as well, pulled on his gloves, and stepped outside the shed. He picked up an old pail that stood at the doorway and filled it up with snow, dumped it over the unsuspecting fire four times to douse the flames, then kicked the ash around to scatter what was left before dousing all of it again.

He reached for her hand, and she pulled hers from the blanket and took it, told him his hand was very cold from the snow. He nodded, and the two of them left the barn, wrapped in sleeping bags, headed back for the house. "You and me," he said, "—we're blanket Indians."

"I want to be warm," she told him, still holding his hand when they got back to the house. "Let's get warm, okay?"

So they climbed into his bed, fully clothed, then slowly undressed each other as the warmth rose preciously, the two of them together beneath the covers, all of it done in perfect silence. Once naked, they held each other to find their way back, just cuddled; like kittens, maybe, was the way he thought of it for a while. Not long, though.

Then she said what he told himself he'd never forget. "Love me, Marcus," she told him. "Love me nice, okay?"

With both hands on her lower back, he pulled her into him, wrapped his legs around her, her face at his shoulder, her hair against his cheek. When he kissed her, her lips were wet with her tears.

We're one flesh and all of that

It had been a good move to move his office right on the yard. Mostly Scotty Faber wasn't much more than a glorified secretary, just another dispatcher, except he owned the trucks. He didn't drive all that much anymore, and he missed it sometimes. He ran some cattle too—did it himself, more of a hobby than anything; but he's got it in his blood so that's what he does. But he was often pleased that he'd moved his whole business home a couple of years ago after they bought the house in the country. He liked being home and safe.

Karin doesn't come out to the office often, doesn't bother him much or hound him at all, never has. Some of his drivers--they say, like, "The old lady bug you much, does she, Scotty?" as if Karin's an old lady, which she's not, and besides neither is he an old man. That's what he likes to tell them. And the fact is, the old lady doesn't bug him at all.

But the afternoon Woody Dekkers came on the yard, she left the house all right and trekked out to her husband's office in the barn. Scotty hadn't seen Woody drive up or leave. He was busy—he is almost all the time. Sometimes he sees people drive up when they come to the shop, but mostly he doesn't see what goes on across the yard at the house.

Mitchell was in the office that afternoon, but he was accustomed to Karin dropping by, even though she didn't come out often. This time, when he saw her face he didn't stick around. "I got some things to check in the shop," he said. If he hadn't left, Karin would have wrestled Scotty outside or to the shop.

"You ought to come out here more often," Mitch said to Karin. "I think you're prettier every time I see you."

She gave him a smile that cost her a lot just to make it appear. Mitch saw that just as clearly as Scotty. Neither of them knew what was coming, but Mitch knew to clear out.

"Things are pretty much done on that Hutchinson contract," he told Scotty, pointing to his desk. "Twenty minutes max."

Karin Faber doesn't cry easily. She's been through enough that she doesn't get hijacked emotionally. It's one of the reasons Scotty says he liked her way back when, one of the reasons he fell in love, and probably one of the reasons those first couple of years were so shaky--hard as steel, tough as nails she was, nobody's fool. He knows it and she knows it. They're two of a kind, in stubbornness at least, or so people say, even if people who say that don't know a thing about those early years.

People in Cottonwood these days, most of them at least, think that Karin Faber is the kind of woman who gets out of bed looking like a million bucks. But she's not just a pretty face. What brought Scotty back to her finally, what pulled the two of them again together when the odds were against it, was her surly toughness, not her looking like something he didn't want to leave.

Seventeen years ago, she had stood at the door of their little house on the prairie that Super Bowl Sunday, stood there and told him what had to be said, not a tear in her eyes. "I'm not taking any more of this," she said, and he knew she meant it, a day he'd wished he didn't have to remember but didn't know how to forget.

"Woody was here," she announced to him once Mitch walked out of the office.

She looked straight at him as if she were praying, he thought. But this visit wasn't about Woody.

"She's okay?" he said. He knew.

"There was an accident," she told him, looking straight into his soul.

When she didn't say more right away, he simply assumed that Dawn Burnett was dead. In a moment, in a flash of a second, his mind filled with terror, not by way of her death, but by the thought that he'd have to go to a funeral and stand there buck naked, doling out best wishes to her parents, being a presence at least. He hated himself to the core for dreaming up that nightmare because he knew he was obsessing about himself, not even thinking of her, the girl. No matter what anyone said, no matter what he felt himself, no matter what was acknowledged and what was secret, he would always know Dawn Burnett was his own.

"She's okay, I guess," Karin said, shrugging her shoulders, "but there was some guess work about whether she wanted it that way."

"She's alive?" he said.

Karin looked at him as if he was feeble-minded. "Not even hurt that bad, I guess—not even bumps and bruises. She was out in the cold for a while—all alone, a one-car accident. That kind of thing."

Karin stood there at the door, not as if that was all she needed to say, but as if she wanted him to fill in some lines because she didn't know herself. Dawn wasn't a child anymore, he told himself, hard as that was to believe. Neither was KayLee.

"You're thinking maybe we ought to do something?" he said, and she turned her eyes away for a moment, then walked up to the high desk he was sitting behind, crossed her arms and leaned over, brought a hand up her face and ran her fingers through her hair, but said nothing, hunched her shoulders again, shook her head. She picked up a pen and clicked it over and over.

"We're coming to a place in the road where we're going to run stuck, Scotty. We're going to have to make some choices," she said, "and none of them are going to be easy."

He had no idea what Mitch was doing in the garage, but there was nothing but silence between the two of them. He squared the tablet on his desk, lined the pen up parallel with the wire at the top, and with his knee shut the drawers that were open.

"I don't know what to think," she told him. "She's yours, after all—and mine too. We're one flesh and all of that."

He motioned toward the chair to his left, but she refused, wanted to stay there standing at the desk. "The minute you came in almost, I was thinking *funeral*, honey," he told her. "And all I could think of was how stupid uncomfortable I'd be—how I could make myself invisible or whatever."

She put her head down on the desk in front of her. It stands up high—that desk does, for customers. It stands up chest high.

"What are we going to do?" Scotty said. And then, "It's *my* problem, isn't it?"

"You know better," she said. "Wouldn't life be simple if it was?"

Once she'd apologized for how loud the clock ticked—it had been a gift from her. "I never hear it," he'd told her when she complained. Now it sounded like someone's heartbeat.

"Woody said she's going to be all right?" he asked.

"He didn't seem worried." Karin leaned back, took a breath he honestly could feel in his own lungs, something cleansing, as if now it was time to go on, once more, keep going. "Won't be long and I'll have supper," she said.

"And then what?" he said.

She pulled up the back of her hand and rubbed at her right eye as if she had something there. "'And then what?'" She shook her head. "Maybe we dodged a bullet," she said, grimly, lips tightened. "We got to go on, honey," she said. She reached a hand to him because he knew very well she wanted to be touched. He took it, held it a minute, turned the ring she was wearing—her right hand—in his fingers. "But there's no more road, you know?"

He said he knew what she was saying.

"Maybe we're not there yet, but I see the yellow warning sign, and it's not much more than a quarter mile off." She kept her hand in his. "This suicide thing, you know?" she said.

"They know that?" he asked.

"You can't know anything for sure, but it wasn't like she was about to hit a steer or something," she told him. "Woody says the tracks just veered right into the field."

"Cold as it was?" he said. He hadn't seen Dawn for a long time, knew only—and would never forget—that she was the same age as KayLee. Same age. If he had no memories of those years, he told himself it would be damned hard to imagine him doing what he did.   The way Karin looked away at the wall over his head made it clear it was some thought she wasn't interested in thinking about. "You got Bible study tonight--remember?" she asked.

"I got to go," he told her. "I'm leading the dumb thing."

"Maybe that's a good thing," she told him. "I don't know."

"Or what?"

"Or else there's simply some things that got to be said here—don't you think? It's just time for something to happen, something we start."

He got to his feet behind the desk, still holding her hand.

"Maybe we should have someone around, someone like the preacher. Maybe Woody and Tieneke. Maybe Glen or Mitchell. I don't know, and she's my daughter, too," Karin said. "I could make the case in a lot of ways."

"Not flesh and blood," he told her.

"Not flesh maybe," she said, pulling her hands into the pockets of her jacket. "But blood—that's another story."

"Maybe we ought to give it a night to think through," he said. "Nothing's going to change, right? The girl is going to be fine."

"Her name is Dawn," Karin told him, "and she's your daughter." She meant that one to float in the wind like something frozen, a reminder and not a scolding. "It was a gift—I mean, for Celine to leave town back then—out of sight, out of mind," she said. "I remember thinking what a blessing it was I never had to look at that child."

Why was it so dang hard for him to imagine that? He knew it was true, knew it for a fact. The girl was something he figured was simply easier not to have to remember. "Let me ask a question," he said. "Why do we really have to say anything?"

"Don't be stupid, sweetheart," she told him. "Your daughter isn't."

"KayLee?"

"Yes, of course—KayLee."

"How on earth could she know?"

"I'm not thinking about her, Scotty, about Dawn. It's our daughter I'm thinking about. Maybe it's even me—I don't care to live a lie anymore."

"A lie?"

"It's not a lie," she said, and she came from around the front of the desk to sit at the chair beside him. "It's just not the truth, the whole truth, so help me God. Don't you ever think that KayLee's not knowing about her parents, about us, about this kid she sees in school, is some lie, some falsehood or something?"

He pulled her hand back to his. "I don't have a clue how to tell her—"

"Maybe we ought to talk to someone, some counselor or something. What happened. . ." And then she stopped, looking for words, and reached for his hand in both of hers. "What happened to us back then—what we did. We're not the only ones who know, for shit's sake." She reached out for him and took him in her arms, or he took her, and they held each other. "I don't think I want to live on the edge of KayLee figuring something out without our telling her. I'm sick of it. If nothing else, Dawn Burnett is going to bring down the whole thing sometime soon. She must be a wreck. Did you ever see her?"

Scotty shook his head—he hadn't. Neither had he wanted to.

"She's as gorgeous as her mother ever was," Karin told him, eyes edging up just slightly. "She's got every last bit of her mother's looks."

"How can she be such a wreck?" he asked.

She pulled her hands away and wiped them over her eyes. "Because she knows—she has to. And what's to prevent her from telling KayLee? —that's what I'm thinking. Meanwhile, the two of us sit here waiting for the sky to fall—I can't do that anymore."

"Maybe this is the time--" he told her, "this accident or whatever. Maybe we ought to go see her ourselves first."

Karin reached for his hands again but shook her head. "She's not so much our problem right now as our own daughter is," she told him. "I hate to say it that way, but it's true."

"Now?" he asked.

"Yes, now--soon," she told him. "I don't want to wait."

"Maybe we ought to talk to the preacher—tonight yet," he said. "I'll call him and tell him we're coming in after Bible study."

"Bernie doesn't know anything about any of this, honey—nothing," she said.

"You don't want him to know?"

"That's not it," she said, "but I don't want to go through the whole story—you know. How about Woody and Tieneke—they're neighbors."

"Not much they *don't* know," he said. "I remember him chewing my ass."

She shrugged her shoulders as if that wasn't a problem. "I'll call them," she said. "Look at it this way, honey--we been through far worse."

"Ain't that the truth," he said. "Tonight yet?"

She pulled her hands up to her face as if she were beat. She looked down at her watch. Supper would be late. "Not tonight," she said. "I'm not sure I've got it in me—but tomorrow for sure."

He'd walked away as if there were no pain

It wasn't that Coby St. James wasn't hungry—she was. Healthy Balance wasn't just leftovers either. But she couldn't help thinking about this little hot-headed, drop-dead gorgeous girl in the hospital. Dawn Burnett's thin, sculpted face might well have suggested royalty if she hadn't been or seemed to be so profoundly angry. Her dark eyes were so sharp, so defined that they could have, if called upon, pierce or drill almost anything, eyes to die for, eyes that could kill. Her hair had suggested that somewhere along the line she'd chosen a heritage, something Coby had never done. She was light-skinned, although her prominent cheekbones created shades of darkness that drifted down. Then there was the nip of frost, her skin hard to the touch. That would all pass. In a day or two, Coby knew, she'd be just fine. Maybe even more quickly. She had seemed so determined, a tough kid.

"You throw out a lot of heat for someone who's spent the night in the cold," Coby told her, and she reached for the girl's forehead, laid a hand there as if it was the professional thing to do, check for fever. She swept back Dawn's hair from her forehead. "Perfect," she said. "You're still chilly?"

She knew the answer. The chill would have disappeared once they got her wrapped up. By the time she got to the hospital last night, she was already warming—you could see in her face that the cold was somewhere behind. She was going to be just fine.

"You know," Coby told her, "we still don't have any idea who called it in." She sat beside her on the bed, something she rarely did. "You think maybe the spirits these days use cell phones?"

The very first half-smile appeared right then, after a searching stare, and a turn of her face that suggested something more than tacit attention.

"My mother was Ojibwa," Coby told her. "From Red Lake, in Minnesota."

"I've been there," Dawn said. "Your dad?"

"Paleface," she told the girl. "A doctor. I grew up in Rochester—that's Minnesota."

"I'm not an idiot," she said. "They make it?"

She didn't know what the girl meant.

"I mean, did they stay together?"

"Made in heaven," Coby told her. "Doctor marries his nurse—hot time in the old ER, I guess—like TV. What about you? —Sisseton, Rosebud, Wahpeton?"

"Mutt," she said, but there was a smile.

"A breed?" Coby said. "Like me?"

"Like Obama," she told her.

And then they talked—or maybe she should say, then Dawn talked, told her the story, at least those parts she chose to. It was all about a guy, somebody with whom she'd been close.

"How close?"

Dawn shrugged her shoulders.

"I mean, really close or just, you know, 'friends with benefits' or something?"

Really close. But not *really, really* close.

Something happened to end it—what, she didn't say and Coby didn't push her. She'd called over there to the junky place where this kid lived as if to make sure that this guy—she never named him, not in the whole recitation of events—to make sure the old boyfriend wasn't home. She didn't want to find him there, didn't want to see him again—ever. That kind of thing. It was a place out in the country somewhere, some run-down, abandoned farm place. She'd called before she left home because she honestly didn't want to see him again. A whole ream of expletives. She made it very clear that she didn't want to see his blankety-blank face.

By the time she got there he'd somehow showed up, and there was some screaming and yelling and all of that. No violence, she said. "He never hit me once if that's what you're thinking," she'd said. "What he did to me—sometimes I think I'd rather have been hit."

"Don't say that," Coby had said. "Don't ever say that."

"What do you know?" the girl shot back. "You sure don't have no scars."

"Are you kidding? —I'm a nurse," she'd said. "Besides, we all got scars."

Coby asked about a name, but she had the distinct feeling that if she had tried to figure out exactly who this guy was, all talk would have ended, even though Dawn snarled whenever the story spun out close to him.

Some ruckus, some ugliness, some shouting and cussing and the guy left. It was his home, but he shrugged his shoulders and walked out of his own house.

"Angry?" Coby had asked.

The girl didn't know exactly how to answer that. "Maybe if he'd have been angry," she told her, and then she waited, "—maybe if he'd have been super pissed, I wouldn't have done what I did."

That was it. What happened to her wasn't an accident. That much she knew at least. The guy wasn't mad. He'd simply walked out as if he didn't care. That's what pulled her heart right out of her chest.

So there was this other guy there—roommate or whatever. He lives there too anyway, or hangs out there, Coby didn't ask. There was this other guy around and he's privy to all the stuff that had gone on, and of course he knows the story—or at least the outline, the relationship, the history, the two of them—she and this guy she was seeing—having been close— "not really, really close," she said. Whatever that meant. But then it would have been easier to characterize the whole relationship that way now that he'd walked out on her, walked away as if there were no pain. This guy—whatever his name is, Coby thought.

Coby liked to think she could read a lie, even though she knew better. She'd been a nurse. Dozens of time she'd been lied to and missed it completely, a mile wide of the truth. Dawn the mutt, as she'd called herself, wasn't raped, she told her. There were no shadows anywhere on her face when she made it clear that this guy, whoever, hadn't touched her. Coby'd believed her but kept her options open.

Somehow the real pain had focused later, when her going off the road miles from anywhere wasn't just some species of inattentive driving. "That's what caused all of this," the girl had said at one point—*that* meaning whatever went on in that old farmhouse with a guy who walked out of her life without giving her a look.

There had to be more. Always was. Coby knew she would never know it all, not even if the girl would pull the blinds on the whole night, not even then. No one ever told the whole truth. No one.

Lexi was eyeing her Healthy Balance. Coby had forgotten to eat. The carrots were still a little cold in the middle, but she'd had worse and there were supposedly few calories. Still, she couldn't help wonder about the girl. Darn sweet cat wasn't thinking about anything but what, by this time, her mistress should have downed.

"There was some drinking?" she had asked Dawn after a while.

The girl measured an inch or two between thumb and forefinger.

"I'm supposed to believe that?" she'd said.

"I can't tell you what to believe." Dawn pulled in her lips, wetting them as if they were drying out. "Makes no difference to me anyway what you think," she said, "whether or not you believe me."

Coby wondered if she had it right, that there might have been two guys in one night. Beautiful girl, really gorgeous. No way did this young lady have to give herself away. Years ago already, Coby's father had told her that after half a lifetime in general practice nothing surprised him. He was beyond surprise when it came to human beings. Nothing surprised her anymore either, she told herself.

Anyway, this second guy was a roommate. He was there for her, she said—when the other guy walked out cold as ice. Then, there'd been a tone change, real tone change in how she told the story. This other kid was nothing like his roommate or whatever.

There'd been a fire. She'd taken the things she'd come to get off the walls, she said, held them under her arm. How many? *Five maybe*. Big paintings? *Little ones*—she held up both hands, five-by-seven-ish or so. Of what? Her eyes ran up toward the television. Of him? *Yeah.* You painted him? *Sketches, sort of.* There was more to it somehow—things she wasn't saying. Naked? The girl shrugged her shoulders. *Wasn't porn if that's what you're thinking.*

And you burned them?

Burning them wasn't her idea because she hadn't really thought of that when she'd come, but then she didn't think the ex-sweetheart was going to be there either, out at the place, the Brethower place, she said, let it slip. *And when he left the way he did--*

Explain, Coby said.

Those lips tightened, and the shiver in her face, in her chin, was unmistakable. She was choking, trying to hold back tears. *I can't tell you. I won't.* So you burned the stuff? *Marcus said to.*

First time she'd referred to anyone else, either of the guys by name. A load of trash was piled up in the place anyway, and this kid Marcus was going to take it out to the barrel beside the barn out back to just burn the stuff up.

"Shit begonia, kid, it was cold outside!" Coby told her.

The kid had a little Jack Daniels or something a lot cheaper—maybe wine or something, she didn't say—that came along with them out there, and there was so much garbage in the bag he brought out that soon enough there was a fire, a big one. It was all the same night—after the fight. All of that was Thursday night.

"Outside?" Coby said. "You had a bonfire outside last night?"

"Machine shed," Dawn told her. "Think we're crazy?"

"Nothing shocks me anymore," Coby said.

So I tossed them. This guy Marcus told her it was like ritual, like a cleansing or something to see them burn. *We even danced, you know? —sort of traditional. Sorta' making fun. Sorta' not.*

And then she looked up, straight into Coby's eyes as if to say that no matter what else she believed or didn't believe, what she was about to admit was the real bottom-line. "I'm lying about the dancing," she said. "Maybe I had too much to drink. I think I did. I can't hold the stuff."

For the first time, Coby knew for certain that what she was getting wasn't the whole truth. Happens with kids all the time. They start to talk, and you believe everything they're saying because what you're hearing is close to the truth and besides, the telling isn't easy and you want to love them, too. But then, there's this cold fence or wall, some kind of protection that goes up, and falsehoods roar.

"Why did you tell me that?" Coby had snapped at her then, and she knew it herself.

Just like that, the girl's face turned cold as steel.

The conversation had ended.

Her dark eyes rose to the TV, which was on, even though there was no audio. Dawn Burnett pulled her hands under the blankets and stared, tightening her lips once again, then quickly turned away, turned on her side, as if she wanted to sleep and wanted Coby not to be mistaken about it.

Who was this Marcus? —some guy looking to take advantage, Coby thought, looking to pick the goods out of someone else's trash. But there would be no more answers right then. That was it for a while, but at least it was a start.

"Marcus called 911?" she asked the girl.

"I don't give a shit," she said. "I don't care."

"Is that what he said?" Coby asked, and she knew she was pushing. "This guy—the one you painted or drew or whatever, this guy you had this thing for—is that what he told you when he left— 'I don't care'? I bet that's it, isn't it?"

"It's none of your damn business anyway," she said. "Who asked you to care?"

When she'd laid a hand on the girl's side, she recoiled as if she'd been shot, like a child might have, like the child she was. "Sometimes I think it's the worst thing someone can say, you know—'I don't care.' It's like the worst cussing out you could ever have."

She lay there cold and still as death.

"You can put all the f-words in you want, but what it comes down to is 'I don't care' is worse than any of it," Coby told her.

Dawn Burnett was hiding her face.

Coby let the silence work, but she didn't want to leave.

"So what brought you up to Red Lake?" she'd asked the girl. "I hope it was summer. Incredibly cold there now."

No response. Nothing.

"Look," she had said, "I don't want anybody to get away with stuff they shouldn't because Lord only knows there's too much of that in the world," she said. "Too many people carrying too much on their shoulders—way too many, and you're too young, Dawn. Trust me—you are way, way too young. I'm not trying to get back at anybody."

"What do you want?" the girl said.

"I'm just wanting you to get better," she said. "I don't want you to get hurt anymore, and if somebody's still hurting you, I want to know because the whole world would agree that that's got to stop."

"I didn't get raped," she said. "How many times do I have to say it—'it didn't happen,' alright?" She looked around and stared, her body still turned away from the side of the bed where Coby was standing. "I swear it."

Then a battle of eyes, and it was Coby who backed down. "Okay, I believe you," she said. "I do."

And she did. Sort of.

For a while, that was all that was said. Dawn Burnett wasn't just a good kid who got caught in something bigger than she was. No, Dawn Burnett was a tough kid who wasn't about to let herself down again after whatever it was that had happened.

She made it perfectly clear she didn't want to say another thing. Coby had heard some of the story anyway, enough for her to say that all of it—whatever it was—was enough to drive anybody in the ditch, maybe especially on a cold night. Was it suicide or just some kind of public bawling?

Honestly, she told herself, it had to be just some really tough public bawling.

But she'd been wrong before. Too often.

He needed them tonight maybe more than ever

That night—at supper—neither Scotty nor Karin had the strength or desire to play through what they were facing, so they were quiet, more quiet than usual. The little girls were chattering as they always did, but neither of them said a whole lot—and neither did KayLee.

The way Scotty saw it, they really had no choice but to go on, even if this wasn't the time to try to say what they'd never yet thought to tell her, to tell stories that—Karin was right, he thought—needed to be told. Someday. But with the little girls there and all, it just wasn't right, so he'd announced that it was Bible study night. When Karin wondered whether there'd be any Bible study at all in the horrible cold, he told them all, joking around, that nothing stood in the way of Bible study.

KayLee never looked up. Which was not like her.

The other guys would be there, he said, and besides, that night it was his job to lead, Larry having a sore throat or whatever it was that kept him home. Passage from Ephesians, second chapter.

KayLee acted as if she hadn't heard a word he said.

Scotty wouldn't have missed Bible study for anything in the world that night, not only because it fell to him to lead—leading really wasn't a huge problem because they all liked to talk—but because Bible study got him out of the house and away from what had to be faced and feared.

Not that long before he'd picked up a book his daughter left on the table beneath that lamp Karin had grabbed from her grandmother's sale, a wooden prairie schooner with a team of plastic oxen beneath an aging shade. A month ago maybe, not more. He never was a reader, but he liked to tell his Bible study buddies that since he got old and far less ADD, he'd take a shot at a book now-and-then and page through magazines more than he ever had because, for better or worse, he had got more sit in him these days, with the kids growing up.

The book was a paperback about dating, not thick, a Christian book with a cover featuring a pair of dream kids, a book he knew Karin would want their daughters to read. Karin was gone that night—PTA or something; the little girls were upstairs and out of the way. So was KayLee. He was alone in the sun room, and he picked up that book because the TV wasn't that good a friend anymore anyway. He started paging through, flipped that book open, you might say, didn't start with the first chapter or anything, just skipped pages. He guessed it belonged to KayLee, seemed that way anyway, and he wondered—how could he not? —what kind of stuff his daughter—she was becoming a woman all right—was reading. Besides, he was alone.

The book was about why Christian kids shouldn't date, shouldn't see the opposite sex at all or something like that. *Dating for Life* or something was the title. He didn't remember, but what was in it wasn't something he'd forget.

Karin bought it--that he was sure of because she bought all the books, kept the girls knee-deep in reading stuff, maybe deeper. Probably some friend of hers recommended it somewhere along the line, he thought, and she'd picked it up for KayLee, and for the little girls too because soon enough the house was going to be full of women, young ladies. Who would have ever believed it? Scotty Faber and his own harem.

He was paging through that book, not really paying much attention, when he stumbled on a bookmark with one of those pictures of Christ with lambs and a couple of verses from Psalm 23, all of which meant that KayLee was actually reading it. That made him pay attention. He started following, not as if he needed to hear what was being said, but because he was reading with his oldest daughter's eyes and heart, with KayLee's mind, at least what he could know of her anyway. Reading that way made the book interesting and way more strange.

"What seems remarkable to us," the book said—he looked at the back cover and saw the husband and wife team who wrote it," is that some of the kids we know, most of them in fact, simply don't assume that every person they date, every boy or girl with whom they seek a relationship, should be someone, someday, they might think of as marriageable. BUT THEY SHOULD."

All caps. He didn't know that was acceptable, hadn't had that much schooling himself, and what he'd had went pretty much in one ear and out the other. He'd flipped through more pages.

"You're seventeen, in your last year of high school," the book said. "Would you even think of choosing a college without seeking the advice of your parents? Of course not. You're about to choose some kind of profession. Can you imagine making a choice like that without your parents' advice? And yet, most kids we know never once ask their parents about their own dating partners. . ."

"'Dating partners,'" he thought to himself. Like square dancing.

"Since the only way in which a husband or wife becomes part of his or her spouse's family is by first of all being a dating partner, we believe parents should be far more involved in decisions about dating than they are in most cases today."

Scotty had never thought of that, but he figured it made sense, sort of. He'd never once talked to his old man about what girls he dated. His dad would have thought he was nuts. And KayLee didn't get that many dates. She was a looker—that was obvious—and talented. Karin thought she scared the boys off, and she was likely right. "I know this much," she told him one night, "when you were her age, you wouldn't have come anywhere near her."

Strange thought, but Karin was probably right.

"That's why I wanted you," he told her, grabbing her arm.

"And got," she said. They both smiled.

He turned to the back cover again to try to get the gist of it because he thought it was a strange to know that KayLee was actually reading stuff like this. It made so much sense too. So much trouble could be avoided if kids only got their heads on straight, if they avoided some of the things that had cost him and Karin so much grief. Times were so different. Just exactly how Scotty and Karin Faber got angels for kids, he never understood. He didn't deserve them. "By grace alone," some folks from church might say.

He was thinking about that book when he got out to the shed that night after supper. He stood inside for a minute, remembered thinking he really didn't know what to think of it, whether it was righteousness or just plain bullshit. Even though it was cold in the shed, at least he was out of the wind. He thought maybe sometime he could bring it up in Bible study, whether anybody else thought they ought to approve of their kids' dates.

There was one whole part on "What Gals Need to Know," or something like that. "Some psychologists maintain that every six seconds, a boy's RAM registers some kind of vivid sexual thought—every six seconds! Young men—even good Christian kids—are hot-wired for horniness."

When KayLee was a kid, he used to think about someday having to watch her leave the house with some high school hero who was all about trying to get into her pants. He'd hated to think of that day coming. Night would be worse. But it hadn't happened, at least not that he knew of, and KayLee wasn't the kind of girl to hide a relationship, pure as the driven snow.

After that quiet supper, Scotty looked at his watch one more time, figured he'd stalled long enough, then climbed in the truck and started it, hit the garage door switch, waited for it to rise behind him, then tuned in to that Christian station from Aberdeen because a few hymns on the way to Bible study might just help the cause along a little, he thought. He took a deep breath as if to clean things out inside, all the while telling himself that it was going to be a good thing to be with those guys after what had happened, a good thing to be with men he respected. Tonight, maybe, he needed them more than before, just like he needed the Lord, he told himself, because Karin was right about KayLee and that tough kid, his other daughter. Still hard to say that.

But some things were going to have to be faced. Karin was right about that too. The two of them had held a free pass for a long, long time—for sixteen years and more. *Who has to know?* he asked himself. *Really, who has to know? It's all dead and done and over.*

Except there was this girl, Dawn, a girl he didn't know, not at all, a girl that was actually his daughter, a girl, they said, who took a shot at her own life.

Tonight, he needed Bible study.

I'm the one who's singing

KayLee had found the two of them together, Mr. Dekkers, from next door, the old history teacher and all-around nice guy, and her mother, the two of them holding hands and praying in the sun room. She'd left the piano and walked into the kitchen in her stocking feet and seen them, their eyes closed. She had turned back immediately and walked away in silence.

Woody didn't remember thinking that the slight line of single notes from the piano a room away, KayLee's voice softly following, had stopped even for ten seconds during the few minutes he was there, certainly not while he was praying. When he left the Faber house, KayLee's music was still playing in his mind.

But when she showed up at their door a couple hours later, he and Tieneke found out the music had in fact died. He snapped on the light above the driveway door and saw her standing outside in her logger's cap, shoulders hunched, hands jammed in her pockets.

KayLee Faber had been a frequent visitor when she was a kid, but she hadn't dropped by all that often since sixth or seventh grade. Not for a moment did Woody Dekkers doubt why she was standing there, even though right off he dodged a little, tried to lead her astray.

"KayLee," he said. "Good night, come in out of the cold. You need a cup of brown sugar or flour or what?" He took her by the shoulder, then arm, and led her through the doorway, but the moment she swept that silly cap off her head he knew he wasn't dealing with a child. Her eyes were steely, crusty with frost from tears that had spilled on the cold walk over.

The phone rang behind them. Tieneke said she'd get it.

Later, he couldn't help but think about how instinctively one's systems create deceit, how practiced we are at lying. It would have been the takeaway his old man would have sermonized, which didn't mean the idea was wrong—story of Adam. The moment KayLee had appeared from the darkness, his imagination created a shelffull of age-appropriate deceit.

She unbuttoned her coat, her face red as a berry.

"Tell me you didn't walk," he said, "—all that way?"

She nodded.

"You must be out of your mind," he told her.

"I needed cold air," she said. "I wanted to use a phone."

It was impossible for him to believe she didn't have one. All the kids had phones today, and the Fabers were neither paupers nor Luddites. He pointed up over his shoulder. "Well, you heard it just now," he told her. "Yours is out?"

In thirty years of teaching, few of his kids, if any, had ever given him a look like she did just then, so full of darkness that whatever triggered it seemed far vastly beyond his power. She reached in her purse, retrieved her cell. "I said, I wanted to use *a* phone, not *your* phone."

Bitter as the December night.

"You want to come in?" he said, even though it seemed a foolish thing to say. And then, even worse: "To what do we owe this visit?" Flat out deceit was never his strong suit.

She tipped her head toward the kitchen and dining room, and he led the way, even though he knew he was the one doing the following.

Tieneke crept out of the kitchen when the two of them came in, the phone still to her ear. They'd talked about the whole story earlier, about Karin's sadness, about Dawn's injuries—whatever they were—about the cold, the car in the ditch, the miracle of somebody just happening by, spotting the vehicle—was it a Chevy, a Mazda? He couldn't remember.

"Some things just won't go away, will they?" Tieneke had said just before supper, her face up and out of that cookbook she'd been consulting.

It was the kind of statement on which he didn't care to comment.

"I didn't mean it that way," she said. "I just meant that I guess I always thought that whole mess was over, behind us, behind everyone. That's what I meant— 'some things just won't go away.'"

"She's not a *thing* either, I guess, is she?" he said.

"Be a ton easier if she was," Tieneke told him. "I'm glad we're out of it this time. I don't have the strength anymore for those kinds of things, Woody. You don't know her, do you?"

What registered in his mind was an answer he didn't give her: he knew Dawn Burnett because he would never forget her story. Didn't that mean he owed her something?

All of that before KayLee showed up at their back door.

KayLee Faber was her mother's child, as angelic-looking as any of the northern Europeans that sat in his classes—Germans, Dutch, Norwegian, Swedes—maybe more so. Her hair was neither thick nor luxurious, but cut perfectly to shoulder-length. It wasn't red, but auburn, unique enough to set her apart from the blondes and brunettes who sat in his classes and seemed clone-ish for a half a semester, until he got used to reading their papers. It didn't burn—her hair wasn't that kind of red. But it set her apart, and it was—as she was—almost always perfectly behaved. So much unlike her parents when they were her age. Remarkably unlike them. Shockingly unlike them.

He pulled out a chair from the table, offered it to her, and she sat stiffly, brimming with purpose. For a year or more she'd been singing in almost every church in a ton of neighboring counties, here, there, and everywhere, the national anthem at ball games too. Her voice was exceptionally fine, but her stage presence, for a kid at least, could have sold anything. You could not look away. Sometimes he thought selling Jesus was only her first item of business, even though she didn't know that herself quite yet. Soon enough, there'd be more places to get up on stage.

"You got an essay to write," he joked.

Not a line cracked in her face. Her cheeks had just enough childishness to make it impossible not to think of her as an innocent. She pulled both hands out front of her, then folded them. "I saw you praying," she said. "I saw you and Mom praying when you came this afternoon, and dammit, I want to know why."

The profanity shocked him. She stared so grimly it was impossible for him to think of her as a child.

"That was your mother," Tieneke said, coming back in the room after hanging up the phone. "And she's worried because you didn't tell her where you were going—that you were leaving." She put the phone back on the wall. "They're worried. I told them you were here."

"Great," she said, irony dripping.

"I told them we'd bring you home." Tieneke intoned clearly—emphasis on *we*--that she meant KayLee's parents were not coming after her, that, for a time at least, the three of them would be alone.

KayLee turned back to Woody but didn't repeat the question. She didn't have to.

"What did your mother say?" he asked her.

"Nothing."

"And you asked?"

"No," she said. "When she came back to the piano room, she told me she couldn't practice anymore—she said she had to talk to Dad." She rubbed her face with the sleeve of her sweatshirt. "I figured it would come out when it had to, but it didn't." If all of this had been rehearsed, she'd been able to put it to memory quickly. "And something happened to them too—after you came and she told Dad, something happened, and I want to know because I'm not a child anymore and I'm getting sick unto death of being treated like one, and I have my own suspicions."

What both Woody and Tieneke knew was that it wasn't their job or privilege or place to talk about it, to open up a story that likely had never been shared, never been brought up since KayLee was still, well, a kid—not a little girl anymore, but still a child.

"It's not about me, *is it*?" she said. She didn't mean it as a question.

Woody had no idea what he could say, or what she could know. But KayLee Faber, the young woman sitting there, was not to be trifled with. Ever since second grade—maybe before—she was a kid who was noted with jubilation by an entire community, among the cutest in the country. Like few kids her age, she'd only rarely tasted defeat. But it wasn't terror written on that otherwise angelic face. What was there was something else, something greatly darker.

She looked at Tieneke, who reached for her hand. "It's got nothing to do with you," Tieneke told her.

"Is it the business?" she said, tears forming at the corners of her eyes. "Are we losing money or something? —is my dad's business going under or what?"

Woody Dekker knew he couldn't tell her the story even if he'd wanted to, even if he were forced to. "It's nothing about the business," he said, smiling reassuringly.

"I'm not a baby," she said.

A pause—then, "I called the church where I'm supposed to sing—I called them on the road when I was walking over—and I told them I wasn't going to be able to sing next Sunday because I can't—I honestly can't."

"You have a gorgeous voice," Tieneke told her.

"Got nothing to do with that," she told them, her hands turning inward into fist. "I can't praise God when I have no clue what's going on," she said. "I go to the kitchen for a drink of water or something and there you are, Mr. Dekkers, holding hands with my mom, praying like the whole place is on fire." And then, without warning. "It's Dawn, isn't it? I know it is."

Woody had no idea KayLee Faber even knew Dawn Burnett, even though Cottonwood High was barely 250 kids on a good day. Neither did Tieneke, but he did not look over at his wife as if to beg some help. Instead, he played dumb. "Dawn who?" An idiot question.

"I'm not a child," she said again, and brought her fist down on the table. "They won't tell me—my own parents won't tell me. They're all broken up, and I can't sing because I can't help but think the worst right now."

Woody looked at Tieneke as if to find answers in her eyes.

"Talk to me!" KayLee said. "You're a good teacher. You know kids. Everybody says they like you. Mr. Dekkers, help me." Tears showed, not so secretly, wrung from sheer anger, or so it seemed. "My parents won't say a damn thing, and I know it's something big because I saw you praying—you and Mom. I walked in to the kitchen and there you were, in the sun room, holding hands. Mom couldn't even talk when you left."

"I'm sorry," he said.

"I want to know why because I don't think I'll ever get a straight answer out of my parents," she told him.

"It's not my job, KayLee," he told her. "It's not my place, not either of ours."

"It's not something we have any right to explain," Tieneke told her. "We're *not* your mom and dad."

KayLee took a huge breath, sat still for a moment as if she had no place left to go, then bit her upper lip. Her eyes wandered around the room, trying to find somewhere to rest.

"Can't you see?" she said finally. "I can't ask Mom because I know her and I know she'll break down. It'll kill her because if it wouldn't she would have told me long ago." She had to stop to pull in enough breath to go on. "I love her—we got this super relationship," she said. "We do. We're great together. That she can't tell me--" She tightened her lips. More words would break her, and she refused to be broken.

When Woody looked up at his wife, he saw a face as empty as his, because there were no words for so much story.

"I came to get your car," she said hurriedly. "I'm going into town to find Dawn because maybe she knows, and I think she'll tell me what's going on here—I think she'll tell me because we're sisters."

Suddenly there was music because there were no words—only piano, more piano, coming from the dining room, where Tieneke had on NPR while she'd been working on bills—something quiet, meditational.

"It's true, isn't it?" KayLee said. "I knew it." She was angry. "I knew it somehow—otherwise you'd talk, both of you. Otherwise you'd say something." She got up, pulled her jacket around her. Then she pointed, preacher-like. "I figured if you wouldn't say anything, then I'd be right, then I'd know for sure."

"KayLee," he said, getting to his feet.

"I just needed to know," she said. "And now I do—I know it's true."

"Where do you think you're going this time of night?" Tieneke asked her. "Blasted coldest night of the year, girl—you going out hunting?" All three of them were standing. "Even if it's true, you know? —what you're saying, even if it's true, really, what can you do?"

KayLee looked at both—at Tieneke first, then at him—as if the two were beyond hope. What she'd determined to be the truth was so deeply set within her that all the world could read it across her forehead—not to mention in her face, in her eyes.

"Can't you see what I feel?" she said. "Can't you understand how blessed I have it—and what a curse that is?" She jerked at the strings around the bottom of her jacket, sniffing back tears. "'KayLee Faber—ministry in music—come one, come all, Sunday afternoon, get inspired, get Jesus, get faith and grow where you're planted.'" She reached up as if there were a headache there. "Answer me this: would I have Jesus if I didn't have all these good things, everything Dawn--everything my sister--didn't have?"

Woody couldn't say anything. This sweetheart of a girl had locked him up in the heart of a story she'd created to try to understand the mystery around her, the mystery in a story she had, finally, every right to know.

"I think," she said, then swallowed, and swallowed again, "I think my faith is like a necklace, an accessory." She raised a hand to her forehead again. "I mean, like a purse, you know? —like pearls or some pendant. Like I went shopping and picked out something that would look good—I mean, because I had the money, you know. I couldn't have shopped if I didn't have the bucks, and I do—good Lord, I got the money." She growled. "And what does Dawn have? What did she get out of the deal?"

His mind thumbed through things to say. "You think you owe her something?" he asked.

"It's true then, isn't it?" she said again. "*You* know, Mr. Dekker, don't you? —because you've been here like forever, like when my parents were kids. You know what happened back then and I don't, and I can't ask because all I know is it kills my parents, just kills them."

And then she cried. She slumped back down into the chair and put her hands up to her face.

Tieneke got to her knees beside her.

"I'll get the car," Woody said.

Tieneke looked up at him as if horrified.

Whatever was going to happen, he thought—it couldn't start with parents. That was not the way to start things here.

The two of them weren't kids anymore. It was just as KayLee said. There was too much there, too much for a kid. The best way—that's how it came to him right then and there—the best way to start unraveling everything was to begin with the kids, the two half-sisters. She'd already had down how it happened, at least something of it, half maybe, if that. KayLee knew the bottom line.

"Have you ever spoken to her?" he asked KayLee.

She had to lift her face from Tieneke's embrace to answer, but she did and she nodded.

He looked at his wife. "I think it ought to start with them—the two of them—the whole business."

Tieneke looked back at the girl in her arms. "Did the two of you ever sit down and talk it all through?"

KayLee shook her head. "But I know," she said. "Somehow I know."

"Does *she*?" Woody asked.

Gently, KayLee took Tieneke's hand and pushed it away, then straightened herself as if she were embarrassed to have lost control. She pulled back her shoulders, kept hold of Tieneke. "In some ways, she's so much smarter than I am—I mean, she gets these awful grades and she hates school and thinks it's all so much bullshit and everything," she said. "But there's so much of her that I'm just blind to, like a baby."

"The two of you talk?" Tieneke asked her.

She shook her head.

"How then?" Tieneke said.

"A kid told me, years ago already, when I was—I don't know—years ago—a boy. When she came back here—Dawn, I mean."

"Four years?" Woody said.

"Middle school, I think. I didn't think much about it because the kid was like a jerk, you know."

"Who?" Woody said.

"Doesn't matter—I didn't take it seriously." She pulled the hair back out of her eyes quickly. "I couldn't even have guessed what it meant"—a laugh came out, self-mockery. "I mean, what do you know when you're twelve? You don't understand any of that, and the kid wasn't even that in-your-face about it. He just like suggested it or something and then laughed and ran away—I don't even remember. It was dirty—I remember that—I mean, what he said. But I shrugged it off almost."

"But you remembered?" Tieneke asked her.

"This year it came back," she said. "This year I remembered—you know, when Dawn had some trouble. Things like that, even though she's a junior, you hear the stories." She shrugged her shoulders. "And I could see it in Mom," she said. "That's what did it. I could see it in her—and then in Dad too. And then, you came today, and somehow, I just knew—you know, after school today and everything." She looked at Tieneke. "Intuition, right?" she said spitefully.

"In spades," Tieneke said.

"What do you want to do?" Woody asked her. "How can we help?"

"You can tell me why you came over," KayLee said. It was all supplication now, the fire almost abated. "Why did you come to our house this afternoon?"

He got to his feet. "Let's go find her," Woody said, "—the three of us. Let's go find Dawn. That's something we can do."

"And Karin and Scotty?" Tieneke asked.

"They're not going anywhere," he told them. "We'll stick KayLee here in some snowbank somewhere and sneak in a call when we can."

KayLee wasn't listening.

"What did you hear—about Dawn?" Woody asked her.

KayLee took a deep breath, clearing things out a bit. "It kills me to say this, but at school it wasn't a big deal. Nobody said much. She doesn't have any friends at Cottonwood. Nobody likes her, Mr. Dekker. She'd just as soon spit at you as smile. I'm the one singing."

It had not occurred to him that she wouldn't have known what had happened to her own half-sister. So, as they pulled on their coats and gloves and hats, he told her—they did, Tieneke helping out, softening things once in a while like a mother. He told her everything, even the part about some people thinking that maybe what Dawn had done out there in the middle of some snowfield somewhere was willful. All the while, she said nothing.

The moon was bright, the air insanely frigid when they stepped outside.

What he wanted them to know

That it all had happened just one night ago, and everything in one night—the fight between her and LeRoy and then the little fire in the machine shed and the way the two of them had ended up in bed together—all of it made Marcus Pritchard believe there were no questions in Dawn's mind and no stopping things once they got going. Not that it was a big deal. It just happened, and it was good. Damn right it was good. There was no second thought, it seemed, not for either of them. None at least for him.

Because it was all so fast and so good, he couldn't help wondering why she did what she did that night, threw back the blankets the moment it was over, pulled her things from the floor at the side of the bed, not in a rush but in a kind of silence he thought sealed up everything they'd just done. They hadn't said anything since they'd left the barn. Not really. She'd gone to the bathroom, and he'd waited. He listened for the door to unlock, and when it did he simply assumed she would come back. She didn't.

Instead, he heard her footsteps down the stairway of the back hall. Maybe she was hungry. He listened to the hall door's skirt scrape over the wood floor, heard her kick the boots out of the way to open the big door, then heard it close quickly, not as if slammed, as if to say she was pissed, but not whispered closed either, as if she didn't want to wake him. She was leaving. What the door spoke was a sad sound because it told him that he didn't matter all that much, that what happened between them had nothing to do with him, had only to do with what she thought might well feel good after the big rage with LeRoy or whatever, something Dawn wanted. He was just lucky enough to be what she needed.

He'd got up when she stepped out the door, and pulled back the curtain far enough to look outside and see her car backing out the driveway and into the road in front of the house. The dog, Roland, was gone, or he would have been there somehow.

Marcus stood there naked in the night, all alone in a place that was his and wasn't, a place where a wheezing old furnace had to struggle to fight off the press of a razor-sharp northwest wind filling a steely night outside. Damn place should have been tribal land anyway, his grandma had said, should have been and would be again if the tribe could only buy it back. Rat-infested old place, he thought. Who'd want it anyway but a bunch of Indians?

At the end of the driveway, Dawn had stopped, then put that Firebird into reverse and backed up just on the other side of the machine shed. He wondered for a moment if they'd actually burned all the drawings because she put the car in park and left it out there for a minute—he could see the interior lights because she left the door open. Just like that, she jumped out and, right away, was back in and gone. Made him think, just for a second or so, that maybe she still held out something for LeRoy because you just don't know about women. Everybody said that.

He had thought to help her, he told himself. He'd assumed what he was doing was the right thing—the fire, the sleeping bags, the hay bale, all of that was what she'd wanted. But it was what he'd wanted, too. When he saw her at the fire, her face so perfectly gold, a sculpture, a painting, he wanted her and he knew it. It wasn't her idea, their walking upstairs and getting into his bed. Once the blankets fell away in the back hall, they held hands up the stairway, through the house. He didn't pull her, didn't even try to talk her into something she never didn't want to do; and after all she was older, too: older than he was. He wasn't misreading her—that wasn't it.

After she had left last night, he went over every step and never once remembered a moment when she'd even begun to try to stop him or herself from going directly to that warm bed where it had ended. It wasn't as if she'd fought him or he her, not at all. No way. Wasn't something he shouldn't have done.

He remembered stepping back from the window last night and crawling back into a bed still warm with her presence, with her loving him—if that's what it was. But if it was, he couldn't help thinking she wouldn't have walked away the way she did, as if all that good stuff didn't mean a damn thing, meant nothing at all, as if what had happened—he'd actually put out a hand as if to see if she still might be there—as if what had happened really hadn't.

The winds were blowing spirits into the house from the frigid basement of the northwest, a hallway window screeching when the long branch of an old ash scratched it up just outside. He'd always liked being alone, LeRoy gone somewhere, the place to himself. Things were less complicated, always less complicated when you're alone, he'd told himself.

But then, he'd been alone a lot in his life. It was different now though, having been with Dawn, having watched those sketches flake with flame in the dance of the fire, having undressed, the two of them, having done what they did together.

She'd be back, he told himself. She'd said that she wasn't going home—he remembered her saying that, that she wasn't going to go back home again. She'd be back. Maybe not here either, but he couldn't really imagine that she could walk away like that.

He got back up himself then and pulled on his clothes, went downstairs, gathered up the sleeping bags bunched up in the hallway near the door, and threw them over the couch where the two of them had sat together, then sat down himself, reached up for the light and switched it off, pulled those sleeping bags around him, and grabbed the remote, turned on the TV to cover the voices inside him.

It was what she'd needed, he told himself. *He* was what she'd needed. He'd helped her do what she needed to do. It was the right thing. He'd actually helped her. After those things LeRoy said to her, after LeRoy took off, after he left her with the baby. Or even without the baby. After he left her with a dead baby. Burning all of that stuff was the right thing for her to do. She never gave him cause to see it any other way.

He turned the volume down on the television because he didn't need the sound, the voices. What came back to him just then, thinking about Dawn, was the sound of a girl crying long ago, a young mother crying in his grandmother's house, when he himself had lived there, the time a woman had come, some relative, with a box, in it a baby, a dead baby. He was maybe eight years old, and his grandmother had them all hold hands—the mother, and his grandmother, and his own older sister, and two other women—he didn't remember who. They'd come with the mother of the baby. He too.

They'd all held hands around that table in his grandmother's dining room. They'd been seated there, and his grandmother had called him from his room, called him to be a part of this circle, this little box, decorated with feathers, in the middle. What he remembered was his grandmother's tears as she held the mother's hand, something pulsing running through their joined fingers, something he couldn't begin to understand back then, but something that came to him now, alone in the cold night, because what he knew was that he hadn't cried with Dawn Burnett. He hadn't cried with her for what was gone, a child who would never be. He knew what he wanted when they were there together in bed, when they were naked beneath all that warmth and outside the killing cold. He knew very well what *he* had wanted. And there were no tears. He wasn't thinking of a baby gone.

It was an hour or so before he'd walked out the door last night, maybe more before it came to him as surely as the wind's dark moaning that Dawn Burnett had not gone home when she left the Brethower place—she had said she wouldn't and she didn't. But neither had she returned. She wouldn't. It took him some time to think that somewhere along the road her car may have well been parked along a ditch because she had no place to go. Maybe she went out to the middle of nowhere to die, because so many others had died just like that, out in the cold. And maybe she'd stayed out there because of what she'd let him do—or what she wanted to do herself, even though it hadn't been all that long since she'd let someone take away the kid in her, the baby she would never have. He looked at the microwave to read the time, figured his grandma was already off to sleep, or he thought maybe he would have called her to talk.

What all that shouting was about, she'd said, was how it was that the best part of her was lost. And then he'd gone and put it to her the way he did. She hadn't complained either, hadn't fought him on it because if she had he told himself he wouldn't have pushed. It wouldn't have happened. Once, when his own mother had a baby, she'd been a basket-case for months--never did get over it. Something happens to them—to women, he thought. Maybe.

It was a good night to die, he thought, as those words came to him. It was so cold that his old truck felt frozen solid. But the engine started, and he sat for a moment while it idled into a rumble. He didn't know where to go either really, where he might find her if she wouldn't go home and she hadn't returned. Nothing was open in town. There was nothing for her anywhere, and that scared him.

Among the buffalo it was the bulls, not the cows that walked away from the herd once they knew their time had come. But he couldn't help thinking that something had tripped in her mind, bullied her down, something sat on her so heavily it was impossible for her even to imagine life without all the shit. It was the baby and what she'd done because that damned LeRoy talked her into it. All of that was churning in her, he told himself.

He didn't go to town and didn't go toward the reservation. He went north, where no one else did; and he followed what tracks he could still read in the gravel and new snow until he spotted her car, some miles west of the Brethower place. It was her car parked in the opposite direction from her house, her lights still on in a long way into a ditch that was—if she chose it to die—not that good of a bet, not near steep enough to flip the car. He stopped on the gravel a quarter mile back and doused the lights.

He didn't pull her out of her car, because she'd left his place, his bed, the way she had, as if there were other matters of concern, as if she obviously didn't need him or want him to be a part of that. He had this sense that he had already given her all he had that night, and that now she needed something more than he could find within him, someone more, someone with more of something than he had. She didn't need him, didn't want him. That's why he didn't go after her himself. That's why he called 911.

He stepped out of his car and walked down the road toward hers, then ran to stay as warm as he could in the gusts that pushed him along. The moon was ablaze, the whole world lit as if the land itself were aglow, and it was.

She could not have heard him come up behind her, and she could not have guessed he'd be out there searching the back roads to find her. She could not have seen his lights unless she was actually looking.

He followed her tire tracks through knee-deep snow in the ditch she'd chosen, and looked in through the back window, saw her head slumped slightly away—toward the lean of the car. She seemed asleep, the interior lights on, still bright, the engine off.

He looked back up to the road as if someone might have spotted him there, then took another step or two towards the front door and looked in again, her face still painted bronze from the interior lights, not unlike that soft glow he'd seen the fire throw over her. There was no blood, couldn't have been—she'd chosen a soft landing, hadn't even tried to flip the car because she had wanted to die the easy way, in the embrace of the cold. She probably turned off the ignition, but then preferred the light to the darkness and snapped the interior light back on. Music. He could hear it, but softly.

He gave her life to the EMTs, gave them the rescue, even though he wanted badly to pull her from that car himself and take her home. He couldn't. She told him she wasn't going home, but she wouldn't want to go back to their place either, and he wouldn't have known where else to take her anymore that night. She really couldn't come back with him. Something had already been burned behind her. When he'd kissed her, he'd felt tears. What he knew was that she needed someone or something that was more than he could give because he'd already given her everything, given her himself—the fire, the love. There was nothing more he could give her, and when she left she was probably still crying, maybe because he wasn't.

For a minute he'd thought of Grandma's, but he figured Dawn needed the hospital.

He took two steps back, took off his gloves, and put both hands on the roof as if to bless the Firebird, and then said a prayer, silent prayer, before singing an almost silent song of life as he walked back through deep cuts in the snow and up to the road. There were no hills around, but she'd chosen a spot high enough on a rise to see for miles in every direction, so he stood there and waited, pulled his coat around him, his collar up high, his hands—even in his gloves—shoved in his pockets. He'd forgotten a hat.

It wasn't weather for a vision, even though the heft of the stars was just huge, the north sky lit with lights from afar; but it was far too cold, and he had no time. There were animals up there in the night sky, even Europeans could see them in lines your imagination had to fill. But none of them were speaking because it was way too cold to stand out there and listen. That's what he was thinking right then.

He stood out there anyway and waited until lights appeared two miles east, red circling lights. Then he ran back into the face of that wind all the way to his car, and he took off up the road toward the ambulance. He watched it turn up north from the blacktop, more than a mile away. He slowed because he wanted them to see him, wanted to be seen. Then he turned right at a mile road, his lights doused.

He wanted them to see the lights of whoever it was who called it in, someone who hadn't just run. He wanted them to know that he cared.

I got stuff I want you to tell me

When Dawn's mother came to the hospital to pick her daughter up, Coby had trouble believing the woman who showed up was who she said she was. Could have been prejudice too, the sense that this young girl—her drinking, her shipwrecked love affair, her late nights alone, the way she'd seemingly driven purposely into the ditch, her fake suicide—all of that had to be borne from some broken-down rez family's generational mess.

The woman who walked directly to her daughter's room, smiling politely as she passed the station, then slipped through the door and closed it softly behind her, was handsome, tall and square-shouldered. She was dressed in enough leather and turquoise to make a statement, her hair shiny silver at the temples, perfectly brushed back, long and heavy in a single braid, eyes dark as her daughter's. She wore jeans, a suede coat opened at the collar, a brilliantly colored handmade scarf around her neck. She'd come to take her daughter home. She thanked the nurses profusely.

Coby wheeled the girl out to the front door herself, where they waited for just a minute before her mother drove up in the SUV.

"Who are you anyway?" Dawn had asked her, and Coby had flashed the badge on her blouse. "You don't have relatives here?" she said. "There's some Ojibwa around."

"No relatives," she said.

"Then what are you doing out here in this shit-ass country?"

The car swung up and her mother got out.

There was still enough anger in the girl's voice to make Coby say what she did. She did not want Dawn thinking that she was just some gum-shoe disguised as an Indian rape counselor. Maybe it was the girl's good looks, and then again maybe she herself wasn't any different or better than a TV station might be right now, drawn into action by a face so pretty neither she nor the camera could quite get themselves to look away.

There was something in the girl that wouldn't let her go so easily. Maybe it was looks. Maybe if she were really butt-ugly.

"What on earth are you doing here in the middle of nowhere?" Dawn asked when they'd come out the front door.

"Came to say I'm sorry," Coby said.

"Sorry for what?"

"For calling you snakes."

It was clear the girl didn't know her history. "We're the ones that called you Sioux, you know—*Sioux*, as in snakes," Coby said.

The girl shook her head. "I don't even begin to know what you're talking about," she said.

"We put you out here—all of you Sioux people," Coby told her. "We're the ones that cleaned house up north and sent you out here to buffalo country—hot summers, cold winters, nothing but grass." It was clear she could just as well have been speaking in the Ojibwa language. "You need some old woman like me to teach you your history, girl."

"I don't care about all that Indian shit," Dawn said.

"We're enemies—you and me. Long time." Coby hit the ground floor button on the elevator.

"That I knew the moment you came in the room," Dawn told her. "So how come really you moved here from Minnesota?"

What Coby had said right at that moment was the plain and unvarnished truth. "Because I'm in mourning, all right?" she told the girl. No hitch in her breathing, no sourpuss line, no winks, no rolling eyes, straight-up honest.

Dawn Burnett turned around in her chair, her eyes more fully open than she'd offered at any time that morning. "In mourning?" the girl said.

"That a crime?" she said.

"Some guy?" Dawn said, pointing roughly. "Had to be some guy."

"Where does it say in the manual that I got to tell you anything?" Coby asked.

"I'll take her now," her mother said, and reached for her daughter's arm. "I can't begin to thank you." And at that moment, that mother almost broke—just a thin weakening in her lips, and eyes that quickly looked away. That sadness helped fill in some empty spaces in a much larger story. She was taking her daughter home from the hospital, from emergency, and she was in tears—not just grateful tears either. Tears because that mother had absolutely no clue how to deal with her own daughter. That was a look Coby had seen before.

Together they took a few steps to the passenger side, and Dawn pulled herself up easily into the seat. The girl would be just fine, on the outside, Coby had thought.

Her mother circled the car, got into the driver's seat, and drove off, Dawn raising a hand to wave, a smile that Coby knew would not have been there had she not said what she just had let slip about mourning. For whatever reasons, something got through.

She was startled herself by what she'd said—*in mourning*. But she also knew that it was the right thing for the girl the moment the words had been out there. What she'd said had been totally unplanned. If she'd have taken the time to think it over, she doubted she would have said it. But she did. She didn't even think of it as the truth—*in mourning*. Where did that come from? —words she'd never used about herself. Very strange.

And now she sat there over what remained of her packaged supper and told herself she had to start eating off of plates or she'd end up some fat old eccentric with a thousand cats, some mad village grotesque.

The television was on, somebody talking about women, about how, in the last fifty years, the time a woman spent making dinner had shrunk from a couple of hours to just sixteen minutes. She looked down at the empty TV dinner tray—wasn't cheap either. She'd stopped buying cheap ones years ago already. Sixteen minutes, she told herself, and remembered that this one was maybe a quarter of that.

Why *had* she left Minnesota? Why *had* she come way out here, out west? That was the question—and the answer she'd given that day, when asked, was mourning.

And it was true.

Some of it at least. She was running away from a vanished future. Jonathan was gone. There was nothing left for her in Anoka, nothing she could do but start over. She'd looked online for a job one late night, saw one in South Dakota, close to the rez. She knew she could get it—a nurse, after all, with genuine redskin blood in her veins, however diluted. She wouldn't have to worry about rejections. Slam dunk it was, and besides, it was something she needed to do. She'd asked God, who didn't write on her walls or anything; but when the urge wouldn't subside, she'd listened, even to the silence, and took the job, followed the call or whatever it was. In a way, she sometimes thought she had run away.

She picked up the empty plate and walked back in the kitchen, tossed it in the can beneath the sink. The cat whined as if disappointed. Sixteen minutes to make dinner, twenty seconds to clean up. You've come a long way, baby, no matter if you don't have time to toss up any decoration but that scrawny fake tree.

She went back to the phone because she hadn't erased Trent's note and—okay, all right—she wanted to hear his voice again; not the first man to come into her life since Jonathan, but a real someone. She wanted to hear it again because it comforted her, even though at the same time she could feel the press of a fear of something really huge, something she didn't know if she could beat because she liked him. She honestly liked him. She hit the button.

"Coby," the voice mail said. "Here's the deal. Got something every night this week—basketball, Honors Club, what not. Got to be the man, you know. Comes with the territory."

Just like that the phone rang, and his voice quit on a dime. It had to be him, she thought, so she let it ring again, let him wait just a bit, laughing at herself, flirting again after all those years. Three rings. Four. It's the right thing to do with men—play hard to get, they love it. She giggled at herself, then picked up the phone. "'Got something every night this week,'" she told him in his voice. "If it isn't sports, it's some kinda' music thing or whatever—parents' visitation or school board. . ."

She waited, but all she heard was a block of pure silence. She tried to mimic his voice. "I got a gym full of responsibilities, you know," she said, "—things I just can't break away from. I'd love to drop by, but oh, boy—am I busy!" She let that sit for a minute, then pulled on a tone that was deadly serious, no mocking: "And somehow you think this girl's going to wait? I'm going to sit here like some priss, waiting on my gentleman caller? Is that what you think, Principal Sterrett?"

Dead silence, except some thick beat coming up through the phone, music unlike him or his.

And then, finally, a girl's voice, familiar. "Is this the nurse?"

"Yes, it is—this is Coby."

Silence. Then, "You're really a first-class shit, you know? I can't believe I'm talking to you."

"Dawn," she said. "I thought you were someone else."

"No kidding," she said.

"Where are you?"

"At home," she said. "Right where you want me."

"First person to listen to me all day."

"No wonder when you talk like that? You and that new principal a thing—that what's going on?"

"Get serious."

"Think I'm an idiot?" Dawn said. "That was heavy duty tease, if you ask me."

"Where are you?"

"You asked me that already."

"Okay, so I'm asking it again—it's not a crime."

Dawn let out a disgruntled sigh. "Want me to turn up the cartoons or something, let my little sisters talk?"

"Mom there?"

"Sitting right beside me like the Brady Bunch."

"I don't believe you—not for a minute."

"How about I ask the questions for once?" Dawn said. "How 'bout you let me do the talking?"

The radio was on, hip-hop.

"Shoot," Coby said.

"Okay, here's what I'm wondering?" She waited, some serious hesitation. Tone change. What's this shit about mourning?" Dawn said.

"Mourning?"

"Mourning—just when I left, you said something about mourning."

"Next time you come in, let me have a look at those ears," Coby told her.

"Sorry—wrong number."

"Dawn, wait." All Coby could think of right then was that she should keep the child on the phone, keep her talking, keep her mind off whatever else was there, in flames. "Okay, sue me—go ahead. It wasn't in the best interest of patient relationships for me to gush all over you when you're the one. . .well, I mean— "

"When I'm the one with the problems, you mean— "

"Exactly what I mean. It was stupid and pushy."

"Pushy?" she said.

"For me to tell you about my life in the middle of whatever it is you're going through."

"So you're not lying, are you? I didn't think so."

"So what does it matter?"

"I'm coming over."

"Dawn, for shit sake, it's zero degrees. Less, I'm sure. Your car'll freeze. My goodness, you don't even have a car. It's ridiculous for you to think—" Somehow, Coby knew it was impossible to argue with this girl. "Now?" she said.

Pause. Hip-hop again, no other sound in the background. Coby didn't know where it came from, but the image she had was Dawn on a bed in her room at home, basement maybe.

"Sometime tonight. I got stuff I want you to tell me."

"What stuff?"

"Just stuff," she said, and the receiver clicked when Dawn put it down.

I can't be that people

The wind felt like a chunk of ice against Tieneke's face, even though at their place a line of pines someone planted years ago held back winds that came in like death itself from the northwest. Once the garage door opened, snow swirled in as if it been lying in wait for just such a moment. Such cold made her think it could well be the right night to try to put out fires; but it had been a while since they'd found themselves in heat like this, a blaze not of their own making. Cold as it was, she didn't question Woody's determination to do something. Already when she'd married him, she knew darn well this penchant for helping kids was drilled into his DNA from his old man the preacher long before he knew it existed himself.

Besides, they owed the Fabers some time to organize. She wanted no part of the action once they brought KayLee back home to her mom and dad. But giving Scotty and Karin some time to think was the break the two of them needed. She simply assumed she and Woody and KayLee would not find Dawn Burnett. She hoped they didn't, even if she did think Woody was right: if there was going to be any kind of healing, it might best start with the girls, the sisters, the half-sisters.

"You just sit in front with Woody," she told KayLee when they stepped out into the garage. "And for heaven's sake," she said to her husband, "turn on the seater-heater."

The Aurora was the most expensive car they'd ever owned, and they loved it, even though it was as old as the hills now, and maybe *because* it was. It was -20 at least that night, without figuring wind-chill; but as Woody liked to say, that car-seat warmer could fry bacon in six minutes. It wouldn't be long, and they'd have the shakes out of that child, although

Tieneke was sure it wasn't the cold that was giving sweet little KayLee the chills. The girl was possessed because she knew—at some level both of them thought she'd already begun even to understand—that the firmament beneath her was dangerously unstable. If in KayLee's mind her parents fell from grace, and at some level the child already knew they were going to, they'd take most of her then-known world with them, not to mention the bliss that warmed her soul and made her sing. KayLee had admitted as much herself—something about her faith being little more than an accessory, wasn't that it? That's what she'd meant, and she'd been dead serious. But then, she still wasn't much more than a child.

Five years ago or so, Woody and Tieneke had talked about the fact that kids today are amazingly close to their parents, how it may have been safer to grow up long ago when they had been kids, a time when, quite simply, if you were sixteen, you didn't trust ma and dad or their values. You distrusted them because parents were *all* stupid. Woody used to insist kids were growing up connected at the hip to Mom and Dad, which is okay if you would just as soon that they don't grow up.

They used to talk that way before Teresa's death; but the subject didn't really come up anymore, not because they didn't have opinions but because Teresa's absence made them wish they would have been closer to her themselves. Not that they weren't, Tieneke knows. That wasn't it. But it's hard to fault parents for crowding when you've lost your own precious jewel, when she's no longer there to crowd.

What she knew, regardless, was that KayLee Faber was, that night, already growing up, painful as that may be. But then, growing up is not one of life's electives, she thought, but something that had to be faced, often enough over and over again, even when you're almost sixty, as she had been. KayLee was going to get a whole lot older that night, and if not then, tomorrow. It was going to happen. There was no way of side-stepping what had gone on so long ago. The sad thing was, something's always lost in that transaction, she thought, no matter how inevitable or how important knowing the truth actually is.

They'd seen her sing in church a few times, enough to know that the child lived in a charmed world, as lots of kids do, trying to touch the spiritual heart of whatever blissful saint they believed God to be. Like so many others, KayLee Faber really wanted an all-over tan from the very face of the divine, some kind of life-changing experience she and so many others would just as soon have, maybe once a week or more.

Didn't matter really, but it did make Tieneke afraid of what the girl was going through. Tieneke was herself an ex-teacher, and she knew that watching kids fall—which is only another way of saying, watching them fail—is always scary. About the girl's intelligence, there was no question. Woody claimed she was a shoo-in for valedictorian. With respect to matters of faith, no parent could have hoped for more, radiant public testimonies every Sunday. No matter. But the school the child found herself enrolled in right now, for the first time, offered the toughest curriculum of all, a reason to be afraid.

Tieneke reminded herself that she was a mom who'd lost. Teresa was nothing like KayLee, really. Teresa had been a free spirit who died being just as reckless as she dared, tubing down a river swollen with late spring rain. KayLee Faber had far too much sense for such danger. KayLee was all-this, all-that, all-everything, a dream child, all-wonderful.

Still, they all had to learn, she thought, painful as that might be.

Their own grandson had come over on a day when the snow was melting. He was three. Woody leaned over just off the driveway and grabbed a handful of snow, packed it into a snowball, and smacked it up against the garage door. Eli thought that was best thing he'd ever seen and spent the next ten minutes, no gloves, packing snowballs and whipping them up against the house, all of which would be hilarious if he hadn't, when she came out, eventually taken a look at her as if she were altogether too good a target to pass up. Tieneke told Woody later that morning that teaching that sweet little boy to throw snowballs probably wouldn't lead him any farther down the paths of little-boy righteousness.

She had thought about grabbing a coat off the rack in the back hall and throwing it over KayLee's shoulders because the poor girl wasn't dressed for the cold. KayLee was wearing a cropped denim jacket when she walked into the house—khaki pants, a maroon turtleneck, rib-knit and cotton—just as perfect as she always looked and probably cuddly warm, if it were, say, early November. But it was late December and, in truth, January cold. She had thought about grabbing a coat, but she knew what KayLee had going on right then called for some degree of comfort in what was about to happen—and she wasn't going to be all that comfortable, no matter how cold, in a sixty-year-old neighbor's barn jacket. Besides, KayLee wanted to visit Dawn, not be mothered by anyone, even a neighbor.

The longer she thought it through—and it seemed they didn't talk much once they got out to the car—the longer she thought about what Woody was doing, the more confident she was that he had it right. Not that he always did. Karin and Scotty were a whole different story, even though their roles in all of this were major. Woody had it figured that taking apart this ancient story in some manageable fashion should begin by bringing the girls together, a first step. Start there—that's what he was thinking. Bring the kids together first, and all that awful history might just fall into place.

That dark curtain was going up faster than Karin and Scotty might have ever guessed, she thought. But then who could know exactly what they were thinking? Had they presumed their pasts could stay hidden from their kids, as if that history didn't exist, as if Dawn weren't real flesh-and-blood and their own war-torn separation way back then had been nothing more than a bad dream they'd blessedly sewn back together?

Maybe they'd assumed KayLee would simply never know, even though all of the characters in the old drama now lived a stone's throw from each other. She couldn't begin to presume to know how Karin thought about that history, but then that old Bible passage jumped back in her mind, how we're "fearfully and wonderfully made." No kidding.

Not only that, but we lie—all of us, she thought.

But the door was wide open, and ghosts were exiting the closet as if they'd been locked up for years, which they had. When KayLee simply announced that the cause of all the hush-hush Woody had tried so nobly to play with Karin was really Dawn Burnett, Woody was stunned. They both were, having never suspected that KayLee could have known a thing about all of that. After all, if Dawn, who was only a quarter Sioux, could keep herself clean and put that long hair in a headband, she'd be as good a candidate as any for a casino commercial. KayLee was a blue-eyed, paleface angel with hair that was daringly close to red. The two of them couldn't be more different.

Yet somehow, amazingly, KayLee knew.

If we treat kids as kids, and they're not, we're going to get smacked around ourselves when, finally, those pudgy little hands get pulled away from sweet little eyes. When she'd seen KayLee sing in church, she thought of her as a holy fool. But, some loose-lipped kid on a playground had let out a story line that had finally come to make sense years later at a moment her parents had gone into a strange and silent funk—and at Christmas, too. What KayLee Faber thought she knew was that somehow, someway, Dawn Burnett was her own father's child.

Tieneke could feel the distance stretching out behind her when they left the driveway and headed towards town. She would have loved to call Karin back just then and tell her exactly what they were up to, because she knew Karin had tried so hard with those little girls and done so well. That God-awful time in their marriage was so far behind them, or so it seemed. Besides, when does the Bible say anything about the sins of the mothers, as if that's a blessing? It's "the sins of the father upon the next generations thereof." Hardly reassuring.

Karin had no idea what had already happened at their house—what was going on at that very moment in her daughter's mind and soul, nor where she and Woody and her daughter were bound right now, for that matter. Karin's worry may have been more painful if she did. It was just another one of those things that had made Tieneke rethink the adage about the truth making you free. The older you got, she told herself, the more you begin to believe that sometimes it would be much better for some people not to know some things. She'd watched her own mother's world shrink, day by day as she'd aged; there were times now when she and Woody had giggled themselves into believing that such shrinking could actually be a blessing. Maybe, she thought. Maybe it's a gift of grace to be stupid.

The more they put on miles, the more she hurt for Karin. Just last week, Karin had opened her house up for the Chamber's annual holiday tour, and the gravel road past their place had never been as busy, tossing up unlikely dust in what was then a snowless December. Tieneke hadn't toured the place herself. Karin had way more house guests than she needed already. Besides, Tieneke had taught art for too many years, and had no hankering for Karin's endless array of holiday decorations—tedious silliness, she'd always thought. At the Dekkers, nothing changed during the seasons--well, precious little.

Maybe they should have taken the truck and sat three abreast, she thought, because she wanted to be close to KayLee. It felt good in the back seat because Tieneke knew she could reach around and hold the girl if she needed to, and she wouldn't have been able to do that if KayLee had been behind her. KayLee is a beautiful girl, she thought, so touchable too, even though that night she wasn't begging to be held by anyone. That night, maybe for the first time, she made it very clear she wanted to choose who could hold her and who couldn't.

In some ways, she and Woody were lucky KayLee wasn't talking because she could well have said, "Okay, you two—what the hell went on 17 years ago anyway?" She didn't, but maybe their silence only further convinced KayLee that everything she'd feared—and more—was undeniably true.

Tieneke's own mind was moving faster than the Aurora because she couldn't stop wondering what she would have said if KayLee had thrown that question at them. Woody would have simply turned the car around and headed for the Faber's house because telling the whole darn story wasn't their job, not at all—*if* they even had a job in this whole mess that is, and about that she still wasn't sure. They'd been drafted, and they were in the war because they happened to live down the road and because Woody had once promised to be a messenger, a job he didn't need to do any longer, now that KayLee was in high school herself.

For the most part, the car stayed silent. She reached around the front seat, and took hold of KayLee's arm, even though she had no idea if that was something the girl wanted or not. Sometimes you just have to do what you have to do, and she wanted to touch her because the girl needed to know that even in the silence she and Woody were there.

She looked out at the long, open snowfields and decided that if the moon wasn't full, it was close, the air clean and pure, the world lit so bright that Woody could have driven along the old highway without lights. Somehow, she'd come to love this broad world out here, even though so few did. Its endless open spaces could be spellbinding, even in winter, when the snow took on a wind-blown crust that shone like something pinkish and dream-like beneath a bright moon, more yellow than pink maybe, just a smudge of bronze. It was other-worldly in a way, the infrequent ranches like shadows against a luminous palette. In the eerie brightness of a dark night, the land spread out as far as you could see, so wide and far it seemed impossible to capture on a canvas, the great beauty little more than an endless expanse of pallid light.

"You already called them—the church?" Woody asked KayLee, when they were already a couple miles out.

Tieneke could see the outline of the girl's face in the glow of the dash lights. KayLee looked over at him as if what he'd said came packaged in a foreign language.

"You called the people at the church, and you told them you weren't going to sing this Sunday?" he asked again.

She laughed.

"I didn't mean it to be funny," he told her. "I'm just wondering if that's what you said."

Woody had a deft touch with kids, even though he claimed he'd lost it as he'd aged—that lately kids didn't even notice him in the hallways, as if he were invisible. It was his strengths that made her quit teaching, because she came to understand that she didn't have it—that talent, that heart. Furthermore, what little she did have was dropping off year by year.

"It's almost impossible for me to imagine standing up in front of people and 'ministering in music'," she said, spitting. "I take that back. It *is* impossible—it's not '*almost* impossible,' it *is*."

"People do it," Woody told her. "People do it all the time."

Tieneke would never have said that, she told herself, but she'd learned to trust her husband. Most of the time.

"I can't be that people," the girl said.

"Makes sense to me," Tieneke threw in.

"Makes sense to me, too," Woody said. "That's not what I meant."

Deathly quiet. The car felt tight to her, as it always did in frigid temperatures, as if they were rolling along in an ice cube that was heated inside, although far from warm. Not even when they got to town did it feel warm.

KayLee didn't follow up on what Woody said. She didn't say, "What did you mean?" and Tieneke didn't know if Woody expected her to either. The conversation was going nowhere anyway, and she had no intention to egg him on or set him up. But she also knew this about her husband—he wasn't a lecturer. He didn't have all those successful years in the classroom because he preached at kids or was in any way mouthy, so she didn't worry about where he was going because if Woody had been some yokel moralist, she would have left him so fast years ago he'd have never known she was there. She never would have married him.

KayLee said, "I can't believe my dad could be a--"

What? —a sinner? A womanizer? A gigolo? Tieneke had no idea what the girl was going to say, even though she understood where the assertion was aimed. She had hold of the girl yet, just her arm, and she rubbed her lightly from the shoulder down.

The silence filled again, broad as the prairie.

"So anyway, there was this woman," Woody said, as if out of nowhere, speaking in a whole new and gravelly radio-show voice. "And the whole town wanted to stone her because she messed around," he said. "And Jesus said, 'Okay, if you want to be that way, let the one among you who is without sin. . .'" That's where he let it hang.

For a while that too went nowhere.

"I had my chances," KayLee told him. "You think I didn't have my own good times with guys? —more than one. You think I'm a child?"

Yes, I really do, Tieneke thought, and what's more you're lying, simply swinging back at your old man.

"We're talking about my father, Mr. Dekkers," KayLee said. "Don't do the Bible thing. This is my old man we're talking about, okay?"

The fact that Karin wasn't there, Tieneke thought, was a great blessing.

They were coming up to the mobile home park at the edge of town. It wasn't late, and it wasn't really dark. Lots of

Christmas lights outlined the sagging roofs, Santas upstairs and down, so many lights that the town seemed like a carnival.

She told herself she would not have played the card her husband did, the Jesus card, and she was surprised that he had because so often he swore he wasn't his father. She knew he was trying to get KayLee to see her own father as the good man his daughter knew him to be, to suggest that not a single one of us is without sin, a tough lesson for the angel. Even if she wouldn't have gone there herself, she knew he was protecting Scotty, putting the whole thing in some perspective that little girl just didn't have, no matter how religious. Protecting Scotty was something he hadn't done when the whole mess happened years ago, when Celine got great with child and Dawn showed up as if out of nowhere.

To say Memorial Community Hospital had fallen on hard times wouldn't be totally true, but the new reservation medical facility put Cottonwood's to shame and regularly drew most of the tribal folks. There were a couple of lights out on the old Emergency sign: "EM__GENCY" it said, which was enough to get the message across.

She started to feel a bit nervous, not because she didn't trust Woody, but because they hadn't talked about what they were going to do. But what she'd come to understand—both of them had—was that you reach a point in life when such goings-on seem more abstract, more distanced, not a part of your life anymore; and that growing isolation, they both thought, wasn't all bad. Teresa's death only made them more distant. Woody's father wore a hearing aid, but often as not he had it turned off anyway because the old pastor had come to believe that so much of what people say is perfectly forgettable, by his standards anyway. And where two or three are gathered, for the most part, all you hear is noise, he might have said, but didn't.

Besides, on some days neither of them could keep their hearts or heads above the deluge of hurt in the world, she told herself. They heard stories—leukemia in children, young moms with ovarian cancer, men maimed in ranch accidents—that crippled them for hours on end. Not more than two years ago, a friend had taken her sister in for a cancer treatment. While she was there, she had a test herself. Two days later she had a mastectomy. Six months later, she was dead. Tieneke told herself she couldn't handle those things anymore. Sometimes she cried putting on makeup.

When they pulled up to the big front door, Woody said he'd go into the hospital himself and check about Dawn. She was likely no longer there.

That left the two of them alone in the car, and she still didn't know what to say.

You probably don't even know the half of it

Woody Dekkers was glad the Burnetts' place was on tar—as the old folks said, on blacktop, on pavement—and not on gravel, because the wind had shifted and clouds had come in out of nowhere to erase the stars. Earlier, the weather bug on his computer at school had warned about more snow, even though it seemed too cold for anything but flurries. Most anyone would think the frozen air would squeeze out every last touch of moisture.

He had no desire to get too far off the beaten path, even though the Burnetts, as it turned out, didn't live all that far from town. This time of year, it didn't take a blizzard for the whole world to be a dangerous place; ground blizzards could erase visibility in a flash, even though, up above, the sky might be clear as heaven all the way to the next galaxy, which sometimes didn't seem so far away on the plains.

The local public radio station had dumped classical music in early evening and gone to an international music format featuring cuts designed to bring in a much younger audience, not exactly the background music Woody wanted in the car. He disliked being perceived as some old poop trying to be hip. Too many teachers—or that's the way it struck him anyway—wanted to stay cool somehow instead of simply being who they were. Often enough, it tripped them up because kids could see right through the ruse. So, for a while at least, after they left the hospital and started west, he kept hitting the seek button, hoping and failing to find something apropos. Found nothing. Just turned down the volume.

"I really wish it was May," he told Tieneke, loud enough for KayLee to hear, once the silence had stationed itself inside like an enemy. Something had to be said. "Of course, it would be light then. It would be light as day right now out here. Prettier at least."

"And warmer," Tieneke said.

"Amen."

What he'd heard in the hospital was that Dawn had been released that morning. Sharlene Maanders had told him at the hospital's reception desk, and when he asked about nurses still being around—ones that might have treated her—Shar shook off concern. "Nobody's said much," she had told him. "What that means is that she's just fine—or they wouldn't have let her go."

"Off the record," he said, "what happened?"

She had looked a little sheepish. "You mean, what does the hospital know?"

"I think I know what the hospital knows," he'd said. "But you're not much older than she is. You got friends."

In high school Shar Maanders had been one of those girls who ran interference for the headline love affairs, managed them almost—always the bridesmaid, that kind of thing—and always the publicist. Sweet personality but had her share of trouble attracting boys herself. Back then, she would have known most everything worth knowing.

"There's this place—I've never been there," she said. She pointed west. "I'm not even sure where it is, just somewhere out there west of town, off the old highway, the Brethower place, people call it. Don't know why."

"Brethower?"

"These guys live out there—don't even know who or how many." She held up a hand as if something smelled offensive. "You know, one of those kinds of places? Always a dozen people and it's a wretched mess."

"There was a party?" he said.

"The word is *no*—not last night. But something happened, and nobody really knows, except the story goes that this guy—his name is Marcus—he's the guy people say called 911—I mean about her being in the ditch, you know?"

"Sheriff know that?" Woody asked her.

She shook her head, raised a hand, and fluttered it. "It's what I hear," she said.

"Good guy?" he said.

"He's a kid. Maybe not the problem either," she told him. "She's no angel, Mr. Dekkers."

"I know—I know," he said. "But there's a guy in this, Shar—there's got to be a guy in this."

"Probably more than one with her," she said, dropping her pen in the coffee cup on the desk in front of her. "She's had her share."

"You don't like her?" Woody said.

"What's there to like?" she said.

"That bad?"

"Sometimes kids feel sorry for her—I mean, lots of kids sort of know that her old man isn't her old man or something, you know?" She stood up behind the desk in order to see over his shoulder, as if worried about someone coming along. "But then, you can't feel sorry forever either—if you know what I mean. There's plenty of kids in Cottonwood High—white kids and Indians—who've got it lots tougher than she does. Sometimes you just gotta to pick it up and go on."

"She can't be forgiven?"

She looked up and down the hospital hallway. "She's pulled this suicide thing before already—you probably don't even know the half of it."

"All I know is we're supposed to believe them when they say it," he told her. "It's written in the book for teachers—and parents. You know— 'don't laugh suicide off.'"

"Yeah, 'wolf,' 'wolf,' 'wolf,'" she said. "And then lo and behold, there's nothing there. Besides, look what she's got. Her mother's got bucks and her old man's got bucks. Lots of Cottonwood kids come from really bad families, and they don't pull her stuff."

He nodded. "So this Marcus—he got a last name?"

She shook her head. "Don't know him—I just know they got this place where some guys, some losers, hang out—and maybe sometimes not, too. Girls too."

"And how do I find it?"

"I've never been there," she said. "I'm no goody-two shoes, but some places around here—it's just not smart to show up." She put both hands down on the desk and leaned over towards him. "What's in it for you, Mr. Dekkers?" she asked.

He laughed. After how much she'd told him, he figured she deserved the truth. "I've been in this for a long, long time, Shar, this story too," he told her. "I've been in this whole saga from the very beginning."

"So, who's her real old man?" Shar said. "Would I know him?"

He laughed—he just laughed. "I'm about to make you really mad," he said, "but the truth is, I can't tell you."

"Me?"

"Anybody—don't take it personal."

She pulled herself back from the desk and crossed her arms over her chest. "And after everything you've told me, too," he said.

She looked at him as if she were about to turn him to stone, then reached down beneath the counter space between them, picked out a peppermint in a cellophane wrapper, and gave it to him. "Could have expected as much," she said. "See if I ever talk to you again." She was kidding, and he knew it.

"Thanks," he said. "Who you going with now?" he asked her.

"Jack Stremler," she said. "Graduated about ten years ago."

"Old guy," he told her.

"*You're* an old guy, Mr. Dekkers," she told him. "He'll do."

He thanked her again, and she smiled. Running into her was a blessing he got, he thought. "Just in case," he said, "I mean, just in case we got to get out there for some god-forsaken reason, where about is that place in the country where her guy holes up?"

Shar shook her head, raised a hand and pointed roughly west. "Out there somewhere." She meant hinterland, he thought. "Honestly, I haven't a clue," she said. "I'm too good a girl." She didn't mean it. And then, right away, "If you got to know? --call me. I'll figure it out. It's just another boring night at the hospital."

Just like that, she scribbled out her number on a scratch pad for some unpronounceable pharmaceutical.

A couple of miles outside of town, the snow was coming down sideways, not heavily, but the road was clear, swept clean by that hard wind. He checked his speed. They'd be at Dawn's house in ten minutes, maybe less, and it was still early. It was lucky they'd started all of this when they did, because the farther they went down the road, the more he simply came to assume there was going to be more to this night than he'd ever dreamed of when he'd left school that afternoon.

"KayLee says she's quite sure that Dawn knows the whole business." His wife didn't know the right words to say exactly. "She says she thinks Dawn knows about the two of them—I mean, being sisters."

"You've talked to her?" Woody asked KayLee.

"Not about that," KayLee said.

"Then how do you know?"

"I don't *know*," KayLee told him. "Something I just feel."

"I think she's right," Tieneke said.

He had enough of world music. He slid down the volume and bumped the button so the radio quit.

"Kind of weird anyway," KayLee said, pointing to the radio. "Is that what you guys listen to?"

"My wife," Woody told her, pointing a thumb in the back seat, "real artsy-fartsy." But he was thinking that it was good to know KayLee might have been thinking about music. That meant that whatever was going to happen at the Burnetts wasn't freezing her up.

"You got senioritis?" he asked her, to change the subject.

"Terminal," she said.

"It's like a plague—worse this year than last, I think." It occurred to him suddenly—he had never thought about it before—that she had to know her father's sin was adultery because KayLee was older than Dawn, older than her half-sister. It struck him with such force that he had to grab the wheel tightly because it had not occurred to him earlier that she might have considered what her father did with Celine to be anything but messing around before he got hitched to Karin Sommers. Somehow that it was adultery upped the ante, shot a deeper sense of fear into his system, right through to his fingers, made the whole thing worse, he thought, harder for a kid like KayLee to take. She had to figure her dad had stepped out of his marriage. She was an honor student—she had to have figured it out. No wonder she hated the old man, he thought.

"Where do your parents think you are?" Tieneke asked.

"Ball game," she said.

"There's a ball game tonight?" Woody asked her.

"There's a ball game every night."

The Burnett's house looked just fine from the road, although had it sat on a residential street in Rapid City or even Mitchell, it would have been unremarkable. Out here, so close to the reservation, it wasn't bad, ranch style with an attached garage on a lower level, some part of the house above it, and a steel building—lights on—just north. No barn. Thirty years old maybe, he thought—maybe more. No split foyer. The house where Celine lived.

Celine.

If students gave of themselves somehow—if in the awkward courtship between teacher and student, a student, for whatever reason, saw fit to give a teacher something uniquely personal—then and only then would he not forget the kid. That's what he'd come to believe because he'd had so many students in his years of teaching and so many students had been almost completely forgettable.

But then there were those who forever after seemed your children, even though they never were and eventually got old enough to have their own—and did; even though they got bald as billiard balls, pudgy and triple-chinned, those students, the ones who gave you something personal, were the ones who remained yours. That's what he was thinking when they drove up to Celine Burnett's place, how strange it was going to be, now, to walk up to this house and to know that the woman inside had had two lives, three lives, maybe more, some of them monstrous—and yet, after all these years, to think even yet of her as still being the kid he'd once known, bawling and pregnant, sitting in the chair behind his desk while he sat beside her—not touching her, but trying to help along somehow, looking for the words and phrases to stick together to make her figure there was some kind of future.

"You go," Tieneke told him. She pulled herself up from the back seat as if to say it softly, even though KayLee couldn't have missed a word. "I think you ought to give Celine at least a minute to order some things in her mind."

Snow crunched beneath their tires as they came up the driveway.

"Only a minute?" he said, rolling his eyes.

"Well, she's already had a lifetime," Tieneke told him.

You got my name, you hear?

Marcus was surprised to hear Dawn's voice when she called him that night, because the way she'd left the night before got him thinking she would never again come out to their place, not only because of LeRoy, but also, now, because of him getting her into his bed the way he'd done, not to mention all of that other stuff—the fire in the barn—like some kind of come-on, all of it nothing more than a way to get in her pants when it really wasn't that at all, when he was just trying to be nice. God's own truth.

Last night, he told himself, there were moments when he thought she really shouldn't get naked like that, really shouldn't climb aboard as if he was just some other ride. But he kept going because there came a time when he stopped thinking at all. Once things got rolling, he couldn't get off the train. He was no longer thinking about her, not one tiny bit. That much he knew. He remembered every moment they were together in his bed, every last one. Most of the day those moments had played in his mind on a big screen.

"Come get me," Dawn told him when he tapped the phone he'd pulled from his jacket. "I'll be walking down the road," she said, "just south from my place."

"It's a damned freezer out there, way below zero," he told her.

"I'll time it. I know exactly how long it'll take you to get here."

"What about your old man and so?" he said. "They won't let you go again."

"Never mind them. Just pick me up—that much you owe me."

Then she hung up. Just quit.

She wasn't wrong. He owed her that much.

Sometime during the day, LeRoy had returned, earlier than Marcus had thought he would. Marcus had been gone, but when he got back LeRoy was entertaining some chick—he didn't know who, and he hadn't seen either of them. LeRoy's truck was in the driveway, and there were voices, one of them female, laughing.

Dawn had called Marcus when he was in the kitchen eating cereal, the last dish of a box of Honey-Nut Cheerios. The refrigerator was empty, as were the cupboards, but he'd always liked cereal anyway, ate more of it now that he was on his own than he had when he lived with his mother or his grandma, even though he'd eaten it often then, too. In the next room, the TV was on to some cartoons, but the place was a dump and he'd decided that he didn't need to spend another night on the couch in front of a stupid television. He'd just decided to clean the place up, and that's what he was about to do, when it was Dawn on the phone.

Hers was a voice he wanted to hear more than anyone else's because he couldn't help but hope for another sunrise with that girl. She had probably regretted getting into his bed because she hadn't planned it that way and it probably made her feel even more worthless—that's the way he had the whole business figured, even if he hadn't felt that way himself. Maybe he should have.

What made her drive off into that open field in the killing snow was that she'd just gone through all that shit with LeRoy, had an abortion and everything, and then, still pissed from her last words with the guy who'd talked her into it, she'd simply taken the next dick she had in her hands. Now it was his stuff in her making another baby she'd have to get ripped out of her, maybe. Made sense, he told himself.

Not that it wasn't his fault. He could have stopped her. Could have. It wasn't that he hadn't thought about it, but once it got to being just the two of them getting all warm beneath his quilt, even the hand brakes couldn't have slowed things down. He knew what she might have been thinking, but he knew a damn sight better what *he'd* wanted.

It just wasn't a good thing he'd done, no matter how much he loved it.

He'd spent time outside that afternoon, and his cheeks still felt burned from the cold air and wind. When he stepped out of the house again, he was surprised that the wind—strong northwest—hadn't bedded down once darkness fell. All around him, the old cottonwoods creaked and groaned as if at any minute they might lose a branch right over his head or drop like some dead missile on the roof of his car. Two cold, cold nights in December, a week from Christmas—very cold, wind like sandpaper.

That morning, he'd gone to his grandma's to fix a door that had blown out of its hinges, caught in that wild wind. It wouldn't close again, not right anyway, she'd told him over the phone. She was getting tired of its constant banging—and she didn't want the glass to break. Could he come over and have a look? "You're not in school?" she'd asked.

"Pick-up don't start," he'd told her, even though he hadn't been out.

"Then how can you get over here?" she said.

He told her LeRoy would jump him.

"Then you should go to school," she told him.

"My grandmother needs me," he told her.

"Who?" she asked.

"You," he said, and they both laughed.

She didn't let that school business go. After he'd pulled the door straight and tightened the chain so it wouldn't blow so far open again, he found some longer screws to hold the hinge into the door frame. Then he'd gone in for coffee, and she'd let him know again that he shouldn't be skipping school, that going was the very best thing he could do for himself. Maybe twenty minutes or so she'd kept telling him in a voice only his grandma could use, not all angry and snarly, just direct, on task. She didn't want him out doing nothing when he should be getting an education.

"Fastest way to zero is the path you're on," she told him. "It's all I got left to do is make sure my grandson don't just walk away from what he could be—hearing me?"

"They don't teach me nothing I don't already know," he told her.

"Don't be a smart ass," she told him and grabbed his hand across the table. "World's already got too many smart asses. No jobs there either."

"I'm serious," he said.

"Maybe you are," she told him, "and maybe you're wrong."

Nobody else in the world talked to him like that. He couldn't help but smile.

"And don't you laugh me off either, y'hear?" she said, squeezing his hand. "Your father I can't do much about anymore but pray, maybe. But you're a just a kid, and I got to do better or someday pay the price."

"To who?" he said.

"To whoever asks them questions we get asked when we leave the reservation for good," she said. She pulled her hand away quickly, even turned away from him. "That said, if you want to skip tomorrow, I'll look the other way."

"You need me?" he said.

"The riders are coming," she said. She got to her feet and pulled the shade up as if they were just outside. "Cold as it is, people here going to have to warm them up somehow."

Marcus had no clue.

She looked at him. "You got to go to school to learn things, to know history," she said. "Or should."

"What 'things?"

"Riders, going to Wounded Knee. Like they do every winter. You know that story. Big Foot—he was from right here. He was our people."

"They don't teach that stuff at Cottonwood." he told her. "That's just Indian stuff. I know something about it only because you told me a hundred times. My grandma's my teacher."

"How do you know they don't talk about Wounded Knee? —you're never there." No one was apparently outside the window. She turned back to him.

"I never heard Wounded Knee stuff," he told her. "Not at school. Never."

"Maybe that's your fault, Marcus—maybe you got to tell them."

It was just like her to make him the guilty party. She could do that in a flash. He just should have guessed he wasn't going to get anywhere anyway.

"Ought to be a holiday," she said.

"How come Indians don't have holidays?" he said.

But she didn't hear him. She turned back to the window. "Here they come, all the way from Standing Rock—way up north, snow and ice and winds that freeze your eyes open." She stopped, looked back at him, measured him. "My grandma told me when she was little that her Daddy packed them all up and brought them down to the river because there was going to be Ghost Dance, the last one ever, she said her father told her, and he wanted them all to see it because it was going to be the end of the old ways."

"I didn't know that," he said.

"Lots of things I didn't tell you yet, you mongrel," she told him and walked back to the table, grabbed his shoulder with her right hand as if she needed to lean against something strong. "Right down by the river it was, for a dance that went all night long."

"Cool," Marcus said.

"Don't be stupid," she told him.

She took her hand away and stood there beside him. "It was the end of the old ways because that's when we died, at Wounded Knee."

He knew he wasn't supposed to say anything. She'd created an empty place and made it clear he wasn't supposed to fill it up with words he might have thought worth saying.

"I'm making chili," she told him, "—a couple gallons, and I might just need someone to carry. If I had a dog, I'd make a travois."

That was a joke. "Plenty of dogs around," he told her. "Want me to pick one up for you?"

"Can't get a good dog anymore," she said, a little shaky. "Dogs don't care anymore, not like the old days. The whole works here is just spoiled, you know?"

"I know," he said.

"If you don't go to school," she said, raising that finger in his face, "then you come here for some home schooling, you hear, Marcus Pritchard?" She grabbed his hand again and then flipped his hair back behind his ears. "Your grandma cares, child," she said.

He'd nodded. And when all that talk was done, she'd asked him how he was doing out at that place, with that white guy named LeRoy whatever.

He didn't know what to tell her or how to explain it. He thought of coming out and telling her the truth, then looked at her the way he did sometimes when he came to the point where he knew, even though he'd not admit it, that this old woman was the only soul on earth who really cared.

"You wanta' hear?" he said. "You're not lying?"

"Not lying," she told him.

He pointed at the chair, wanted her to take it, and she did. But she kept her hands in front of her, just a couple inches from his, when he laid them down in front of him. "Sometimes it seems like I have to work really hard just to be," he told her.

His grandma let that sit for a while, sipped her coffee, didn't look at him, not at all. It was like her to do that. "And who exactly do you think you are?" she'd said.

He didn't like to think of himself as "LeRoy's friend," but that was just about all he could put his hands on out at the Brethower place. It felt like some kind of lie to answer that question by saying he was in high school because he wasn't there enough to qualify or whatever. Whenever he picked up a friend, it seemed like it was someone like Dawn, someone LeRoy had tossed away.

"I don't know," he told her. "I don't even have a last name—not really." He looked up and figured maybe he'd hurt her. "Well, I have couple, like maybe a choice, I guess."

"You got me," she said. "And I got you." She giggled. "Sounds like Sonny and Cher."

He didn't know what she meant.

His grandma was thin like a girl. Even though her face was not full of wrinkles, her skin still told the stories of her years. That was her wisdom, he was told by others out there on the reservation. She was an elder. She was something.

Up in the corner of her forehead, just in front of her ear was a small, deep scar so ancient it marked her face like something forever in the landscape. His grandma could never be fat because she moved way too fast for anything to get settled on her body or on her mind. But she was sick now, or told people she was. Her hair was cut short because she didn't want to spend so much time taking care of it anymore, she'd told him, even though her trailer was always neat. She didn't need men anymore, not at her age, she said, but if she did she could find a dozen of them anywhere. She could have found someone to fix her door too, he supposed, but then she'd have to be friendly or whatever. He'd driven over to the rez because he knew she liked to see him, her grandson.

"Let me just tell you this much, okay? --your name is Marcus, boy," she told him. "That's so hard to remember?"

She knew very well what he was talking about. Her own son had left him behind.

"You're all I got," he told her, "and what happens when you kick off?"

"You know something I don't?" she said.

"I'm not wishing it," he told her, "but sometimes I think I could just die myself and nobody would come around and bury me. Wouldn't even have a funeral up on the hill above the river. Nobody knows my name."

"I do," she said, and then, right away, "I'd have to be nice all the time, and that would kill me probably, but maybe you ought to come and live with me again." That she was being playful didn't mean what she'd said was a lie. She pounded lightly on his fingers. "What you need is a vision, like the old days."

"I'm only half-Indian, Grandma," he told her.

"Your best half—that's sure," she said. "You're growing up—nobody knows who they are when they're growing up. Not even God."

"You're the one used to say that God knows everything," he told her.

"Well, maybe he does," she admitted, "but He must be an Indian because he's sure not telling us much." She coughed heavily into her elbow. "Maybe we aren't listening, but that's not strange either."

And then she'd told him, again, the old story about how she'd married early and left with her husband for Denver, and how they'd lived for several years there, an old story that ended back on the reservation where she'd started her life--some of it at least--with a husband he had never met because the man was dead long before Marcus was born: a soldier, a warrior, his grandma used to say, smiling as if she got some joy out of using the old words.

"When I was 17, my head was full of voices saying all kinds of things," she told him. "Yours is too, I'm sure."

About that she was right, he thought, lots of voices.

"I'm serious, Marcus," she told him. "What you need is a vision."

"Too cold to sit out on some mesa right now," he told her.

"Never too cold for a vision," she said.

"Can't it wait until June?" he said.

"You just be ready, boy. You just make your heart ready."

All of that was what he was thinking about as he pulled out of the driveway at LeRoy's place, on his way to pick up Dawn, the old Dodge edging up the grade in first gear, whining in a pitch that always seemed higher in the deep cold of winter. Mostly, it was funny—the very idea of him sitting up on a mesa where some old guys waited like zombies for some stupid hawk or porcupine to tell them something profound or spiritual. Grandma was a Christian, his grandma. She'd gone to church pretty regularly for a long time, but that didn't mean she didn't believe in visions. She was still Indian.

He ought to tell Dawn about him doing a vision quest. Maybe she'd come with. But that wouldn't be official, he told himself. He could just about see Grandma if he told her he and a girl had done a sweat and then sat up on Sugar Mesa. It'd be desecration.

He turned right when he left the driveway and looked at his watch, then determined to hurry because he didn't want to think of Dawn outside on a country road too long in these temperatures—again. She'd time it, she told him.

There had been more at Grandma's this afternoon, more that spoke to him in voices, new voices added to the many already talking in his heart and in his head.

When the phone rang, it was one of her old coffee buddies, so she'd waved him goodbye. He got up and pulled on his jacket. She held the phone away from her face. "Tomorrow you go to school now, hear?" she'd said, waving a crooked finger. "Just remember you got my name."

"Tomorrow is Saturday," he'd told her.

She'd waved him off. "Well, whatever," she said, and started in on the phone.

All the way back to the house, all along the old highway, he kept giggling, thinking of his grandma wrapped in a blanket or a buffalo robe, having some vision on top of the mesa. She'd die for sure, he thought, and then who would come to his funeral?

Right then, he had actually felt tears welling up in him because there had been nothing for him to think about, nothing more than a long and lonely night at LeRoy's. That's when Dawn had called. She wanted him to pick her up out in the country at her place, along a road in cold so deep even the buffalo would have bunched up.

"Pick me up," she'd said. Wasn't a question. Wasn't something he'd had a choice about. "Pick me up," she'd said, and he never really questioned whether or not he should because it was like she said—he owed her that much. He owed her that much and a lot more.

When finally, the heater started to kick out something close to warmth, he told himself once again—just as he had a dozen times in this awful cold spell—that he had absolutely no idea how his people could live in teepees, buffalo hides or not, in dead cold weather like this.

But they did. Somehow, they'd made do. Somehow, they'd made a life.

A damned saint

For maybe three years, Tieneke had given the little sweetheart piano lessons. Then she'd told Karin it was time to get someone more accomplished for such a talented little girl. KayLee was extraordinarily dedicated. Her eyes begged for more and more and more, the tip of her tongue always protruding just a bit from the corner of her mouth when her fingers danced through arpeggios. So much delight, a perfect angel.

"I can't believe Dawn will be here anymore," Tieneke told her. They were sitting outside the hospital, waiting for Woody, who'd gone inside to check if Dawn was still there. Even though the heater was blasting out warm air, the silence was unnerving. KayLee seemed talked out for the time being. Tieneke could see a bit of a reflection of the girl's unmoving face in the passenger side window. What she said wasn't a question really, but she did expect the girl to say something.

KayLee grabbed the rearview and twisted as if to find Tieneke in the back seat, then, failing, she turned around as far as she could, far enough so that she almost faced her. "What exactly did happen, anyway?" she asked. "People say things—at school, I mean. You don't really know."

Tieneke didn't know how to answer.

"I think I deserve to know," KayLee insisted. "Dawn is my sister, after all."

"There was an accident," Tieneke told her.

"I know that," KayLee said. "On the rez?"

That question had baggage. Tieneke didn't know where Dawn had gone off the road. Woody had told her it was nowhere near town, out west somewhere, that's all. But she knew that if she said yes, KayLee's imagination would outfit the whole story with the Native horrors white kids are born believing.

So, she told the truth. "Honestly, KayLee," she said, "I don't know. Woody never told me where it happened, just somewhere west of town."

Once more, KayLee tried to get her in the mirror. This time, she did.

"He would have told me if it was on the reservation," Tieneke told her. "He would have mentioned it, I'm sure—and besides, if it had happened out there, Dawn wouldn't have been brought to town, right? They would have taken her to that new hospital."

"She tried to kill herself, didn't she?" KayLee said, looking down. "That's why Mr. Dekkers was praying with my mom. Dawn tried to kill herself, and they were praying for her." She laughed, almost scornfully. "I knew it in a minute," she said. "I knew it the moment I saw them because people talked about it in school, you know. And it's strange—if you want to know the truth—it's stupid strange to hear your friends yakking about it as she was a whore and all that, you know, and that she was someone who could have wasted her life and no one would give a shit anywhere, you know?"

"You heard that?" Tieneke said. The language surprised her, but she wasn't about to quibble.

"I'm by Sara Esselink's locker, you know, and Megan Anderson is there, and, I don't know, some others too, you know, and somebody says how they heard she was just gonna be another frozen Indian—that that's what she wanted, and that she was pregnant, too, she was pregnant with some loser's baby or something."

It wasn't hard for Tieneke to hear all of that being said in school.

"And there I stand, you know—and I'm thinking that Dawn Burnett is my sister. Not knowing it really, but it's hard for me not to think that maybe that kid wasn't wrong, the kid that told me that when I was still a kid. I mean, what do I know about my parents when they were kids? Nothing really. It's possible, isn't it, Mrs. Dekkers? I mean, anything is possible."

"Yeah, well, anything is possible."

Somehow, Tieneke thought, this young lady was going to make it. What was inevitably in front of her, maybe even this very night, was going to test her soul, but it wasn't going to break her.

"I don't know that I ever saw her mother," KayLee said. "Dawn's, I mean."

Some mothers had to drag kids into her piano room to make sure they'd get there. Not Karin.

"Not that it makes a difference, I guess," KayLee said, and then, "I don't want to think about it. I can't. Who'd want to think about her father fucking some other woman? Tell me that. I don't even know what she looks like."

Tieneke figured it was impossible to grow up and not hear that language. She hadn't seen Celine either, not in years, not often at least, which, at the moment, seemed almost ironic, because she and Woody had tried to do so much with her way back, when she'd been so full of promise, and when the two of them still thought they could change the world--if not the world, at least the reservation.

"You know her?" KayLee asked, looking up again into the mirror.

Tieneke had seen Celine once in a while in the years after she'd left Cottonwood, when she'd run off to Rapid City and then returned. Back then, she'd seen her in Foodland maybe, or at a gas station, where—she hesitated thinking about it, even if it were true—she'd been shocked to see how the Celine had changed, even though it was such a familiar story because young women aged so quickly on the rez, losing something dear in hard times. And then a change, something big, and Celine was gone, for years again, a decade at least, before she'd come back with a husband who wasn't from here, Native guy, Navaho, she'd heard, from somewhere Southwest.

"What does she look like?" KayLee asked.

Celine Burnett had become a beautiful woman whose accomplishments were notable. That she could have done so wasn't a surprise; that she did, given the shit she'd gone through in high school and out, was still remarkable. Tieneke couldn't help thinking that KayLee really didn't need to see Celine Burnett that night, not that night of all nights. She was gorgeous.

"You must have known her—you were teaching then, weren't you? Both you and your husband were teaching?" KayLee asked in a tone that seemed almost to predict that she would no longer abide Tieneke's silence.

"You know Dawn at all?" Tieneke asked. "I mean, you know what she looks like, right?"

She nodded. "She looks like her mother?"

"Lot of people would say that in twenty years she will," Tieneke said, and it wasn't a lie. And, it was enough to stop the questions, at least for a moment.

KayLee reached up and turned the mirror back towards the driver's side, then swung herself around in the seat, facing the front. "I just don't know how she can forgive him so easily," KayLee said. "I mean, it seems as if they're in this together, the two of them, Mom and Dad. I'd think she'd hold it against him—what he did. But she doesn't seem to."

"Give them some mystery," Tieneke asked.

"What does that mean?"

"They don't know you inside out, but you don't know them either—give them some mystery."

It wasn't the most elegant thing to say right then, but Tieneke didn't really know how to say it better. It was something she'd read in a book long ago, at a time when her own mother was getting difficult about something—she couldn't even remember what. "We're all mysteries," the book had said. "When you don't understand your own parents, give them their mystery." It was something like that, something she'd never forgotten.

"Maybe I'm just not old enough," KayLee said. "Do women just forget things like that eventually, just pull a Hillary or something—as if it never happened?"

"I don't think so," Tieneke told her.

"Do you?" she said.

They'd arrived at a point where no questions were really out of bounds. "I had nothing to," she started to say, then thought better of it. "Let me put it this way: Woody never once did anything I had to fight to forget," she said. And then she added, "that I know of." And she tried to giggle a bit.

"Well, maybe I'm just naive, but I don't know how my mom does it," KayLee said. "I think she's a stupid saint," she said, looking out into the dark world in front of her. "I honestly believe she is, because I don't know how she isn't forever pissed. And I don't know what I'm going to say to her except I'll hold her, you know? I know I'll just hug her because she really was what I said, Mrs. Dekkers. She really is—she's a saint, she's a damned saint is what she is."

Maybe she was, Tieneke thought, but she hadn't been, and there was more to the story, and it was going to be a long night for the little girl who used to sit beside her on the piano. What KayLee would have to learn was that she was more right than she knew. Her mother, just like most of the rest of us, was a damned saint.

I just want to see how she is

To Celine, it could be any of dozen kids coming to see Dawn, Woody thought. If someone was in the family room, he or she might have seen lights sweep up when the car turned in. Dawn had to have some well-wishers. Nobody else would go out on a night like this, he thought, only kids, only friends. They'd mean no harm. Celine wouldn't think it could be any danger. "Going to be shocking for her," he said to Tieneke.

"Was the windshield broken?" KayLee asked, still wondering about Dawn.

"I don't think she had any cuts and bruises," Woody told her. "All she hit was a snowbank. She went in the ditch and half-turned on her side. Maybe something on the top of her head—I didn't hear a thing about a seat belt."

"She get a ticket?" she said. They were sitting in the driveway waiting for the courage to march up to the front door.

"You're getting cold feet, dear?" Woody asked her. "We don't have to do this, you know? —not in the dead of winter, for pity's sake. No reason this has to be done tonight."

"I just want to see her is all," KayLee said, which both of them interpreted as a lie—or a half truth. "What time is it?" she said, pointing at the clock on the dash.

"We don't know how to change the dumb thing—it's an hour fast," Tieneke told her about the dash clock. "Not even eight."

"We've come this far," KayLee told them. "I'm not going back home yet because that's a whole different story right now."

The car rocked slightly in the gusts of wind.

"Just so you know," Tieneke said. When he turned toward KayLee across from him, he saw his wife's hand around the girl's arm again. "Just so you keep track of things here—

you know you're walking into a place with at least one locked-up room. It's one thing that you want to see how Dawn is doing, that you want to be nice or whatever—but it's a whole different thing for you to walk in there and meet her mother and you know why. Don't think her mother won't get it."

"I know, I know," she snapped. Then she cried, not hard enough to make a show, but enough to make her turn away. There were too many dash lights in the Aurora for her to be able to find darkness, and she couldn't have stepped outside if she wanted to just then, not in the snarl of a wind so cold it could kill.

"There are a lot of layers here that have got to get themselves unwrapped, maybe too many," Woody told her. "I mean, maybe too many for one night, is what I mean—one dang cold night on top of it."

Tieneke was leaning up between the seats, still holding the girl, who must have had the door handle in her grasp because just like that she slammed at the door with her shoulder and the interior lights flashed, but only momentarily because Tieneke pulled her back just as quickly, reached around the seat and jerked her back into the car, even though she hadn't really been out at all. It was a momentary thing, just a flash of light.

"Not by yourself you're not going," Tieneke said. "I won't let you."

It would be prudent, best for all concerned, he thought, if he just backed out of the driveway and left. There was no reason this whole story couldn't unravel in the light of day, the lead roles all together somewhere in a room with a couch, some professional counselor around to walk them through what had to happen, what had to be said. The girl's emotions were as volatile as the weather.

He put the car in reverse. "We don't have to do this," he said. "Nothing's going to change by tomorrow morning, and we'll all be better off if we get some distance, you know? —if we sleep on it."

"She wants to see her sister," Tieneke told him.

He stopped the car, slid the transmission back in park.

"It's not that simple," he told his wife. "You talk like we're bringing in a tuna casserole."

Tieneke kept hold of KayLee's arm. He could see it there. "What do you want to do?" she asked the girl, emphasis on *you*. "It's *your* sister we're talking about here," Tieneke told her. "It's not our call."

Putting the ball in the girl's court was the right thing to do, and he knew it, no matter what might happen, because for too long she'd been a spectator. If he'd simply have backed out and gone home, he would have made a decision for her once again. If she wanted things picked up, she was going to have to gather the pieces herself.

"I just want to see how she is," KayLee said. "I just want to check on her is all," she told them. "I just want to see that she's okay."

But simply saying sweet things to Dawn Burnett wasn't possible just then, he knew, because too many other sealed rooms would have to be opened. No graves—at least none that he knew of; but too many old stone walls would have to come down.

"Bundle up," he said. They'd already been in the driveway forever and a day; and he owed the girl this much at least: she'd come over angry and hurt because of the bad tidings he'd delivered. He owed her some peace of mind, even if what she was figuring on was altogether impossible. She and Dawn may never have talked to each other as sisters before. Now they were going to. And Celine—he had no idea how Celine had carried this whole story for all these years, how she played it herself in her mind. She was another one of those kids who had given him part of her soul, then grown up and left. Retirement looked damned good sometimes, if for no other reason than he would no longer have to carry those kids' disappointments and sadness—or presume he was. No high school teacher worth his or her salt could help being a parent too, he thought.

He pulled up his collar before opening the door. Purposely, he let the car run, not just to keep it warm but to suggest to KayLee that this visit wasn't going to be forever.

Tieneke was out before the girl. She was there at the door to take KayLee's arm up the driveway to the house, even though it wasn't slippery—far too cold for ice, the snow almost sand beneath their feet.

The front door light was on as if Burnetts were expecting company, and maybe they were. What he knew about the couple was that this marriage wasn't Celine's first, and he wasn't sure of the exact count they'd totaled between them. Celine had banged around in her early twenties, after Dawn, and her husband, Andrew, had some kind of past somewhere in the Southwest, a wife and kids—or so he'd heard. But the two of them, once together, had been good for each other, Andrew the administrator of the reservation's Head Start programs or something related—he never knew what exactly—and Celine doing well with her art work and what-not else. Celine had been one of Tieneke's real stars way back in those early years, so promising but so undisciplined—so much a stereotype that for several years Tieneke had simply considered her one of her own most memorable and complete failures. There'd been others too, too many others. There'd been bad blood between the two of them, even though today Celine was doing exactly what Tieneke would have wanted her to be doing—showing a lot, selling her things all over out East, the general public's appetite for Indian art significant, although interest did wax and wane. What his own wife should be doing, he thought, if she hadn't hung it all up after Teresa's death.

He took hold of KayLee's left arm so they walked three abreast up the sidewalk to the steps in the front of the house. Through the front window they could see no one, even though the television was playing, images flashing across a half-darkened room.

There wasn't enough room for them on the little front step, so he hiked up first and rang the bell, Tieneke and KayLee two steps down on the sidewalk.

The house stood east and west on the yard so the north side created a buffer from the wind, but even without the chill the temps had to be somewhere in the basement.

He rang the bell again, and then saw Celine, a rolled-up Kleenex in her hand as she made her way from the back of the house, through the kitchen to the front door. What he thought right then, when he saw her, was that the poor woman had already suffered enough in the last 24 hours, that she likely wasn't thinking at all of who might be there at her front door in this horrific weather, not guessing ever it would be KayLee Faber.

The light was on so the moment she looked through the glass, her eyes flashed when she saw who was there. The door was frozen shut against the sill, so she had to lean into it to get it open.

"Mr. Dekkers," she said, almost twenty years after she'd been in his class, and he knew the moment he heard it that she hadn't even seen two other figures a couple steps down and into the darkness. "What on earth?" she said.

And then she saw the girl.

My father was a shepherd

Marcus Pritchard found Dawn Burnett that night exactly where she'd told him she'd be when, as if out of nowhere, she'd called him. By the way she'd left his place the night before, stamping her feet out the door, not saying a word, not even goodbye, he'd guessed he was history.

Through the swirl of snow, his headlights picked out a ghostly figure a quarter-mile down the road, not all that far south of her house. She'd timed it as she'd promised. When he passed her place, he doused his lights, hoping to slip by unnoticed, even though his truck hadn't had a muffler since his year in seventh grade.

She'd snuck out. Again. Her parents were good people and they cared. LeRoy had told him as much, how she wasn't the usual Indian kid, he'd said, forgetting Marcus was half Lakota himself. But the point was that Marcus often wished he had parents like hers, wished, simply, that he *had* parents, that they were there somewhere, anywhere. Not just sometimes either. But what are you gonna' do?

He was surprised that she'd snuck out again, but when he came up behind her, there was only one voice in his mind and that one was telling him he wanted her to be right there beside him in the truck, out of the cold. He didn't want to be anywhere else that night, didn't want to be with anyone but her.

Still, he couldn't help asking. "What's your mother say about you're out again just one night later?" He pulled the truck into first gear and edged away from the ditch, the gravel sticking to the tires and cracking up into the wheel wells. "To town?" he said.

"I'm not going back home—I told you," she said. "I said that before—I'm not going home again because I know stuff." And then she told him how it was she'd decided to leave, how there was always hard feelings and shit between them, between herself and her mother, more so than her father, who was her step-father, and did he know that? Marcus said he did, that people did, that LeRoy did too, that lots of people knew.

She told him how she'd come back to her house after talking to this woman, Coby, in the hospital, and how she'd been crying—not because she was hurt or frostbitten. Her car was in for repairs, and she couldn't go anywhere if she tried, but that wasn't it. It was as if everything had come down on her head, and she seemed to have no one. "Seems like I end up in places I don't want to, and it happens to me all the damned time," she said.

"Like now?" he said.

"No, not like now," she scolded. "I wouldn't be saying all this shit if I didn't think you'd listen—I mean, if I didn't trust you."

He remembered what LeRoy always said about women—how you never know exactly what they were thinking because they had this thing about not saying what was really going on. It was just what women did. Even then they just expected a guy could translate, which they couldn't, he'd say, because women just don't think like men, not at all.

"You mean it?" he said.

"Mean what?"

"You mean it when you say this place isn't someplace you shouldn't be?"

"I mean it," she told him. "You think I'm lying to you?"

"I'm not saying that," he said.

She said she couldn't put all of the LeRoy stuff behind her yet, even though she'd burned those things, those drawings. And then she went back to her house that morning, she said, went and sat in her bedroom at home. Her mother didn't know what to say anymore, didn't know whether she could say anything. She told him how her mother had cried on the way home, tried to hide it from her, tried to sniff quietly so she wouldn't hear.

And how it was when she got home that her little sister had come into her bedroom, her step-sister, just 13 years old and everything she herself had never been, you know—almost like perfect. And how her sister sat there on the edge of her bed and then finally just exploded, as if she'd had enough and couldn't go on, spit it all out, how tired she was of getting shafted because Dawn was always making her parents mad and how Dawn was always getting in trouble and how Dawn made the whole house feel as if it was about to break like glass or something, and how they'd all be better off if she'd just leave; how all of them—Mom and Dad and little sisters—how all of them would have a good life instead of rotten one with her creepy sister always around, always doing awful shit and making everyone scared and ashamed, getting into trouble with drinking and weed and what not. "You ruin the whole world around you," her little sister had said. "You're a slut and a jerk," she'd said, and more too.

He didn't say a thing.

She had to leave because she had no place there, she said, because her sister was mostly right about how she was messing up things for everybody. She told him she wanted to say goodbye to her horses or something, so she'd marched out to the barn in the cold and wind anyway, just to tell them they'd be okay and stuff. By then, she said, she knew he'd be coming so she'd headed back to the road, quite some ways away from the house, and sort of waited, trying to keep warm, even though, she said, she was full of steam, mad as hell at the world.

"I didn't have anybody else to call," she told him. "I don't have a soul."

He didn't know what to say, but she left this open space he thought he was supposed to fill somehow. "You saying you want to be my friend?" he asked her.

"No, I want to steal your truck," she said, and both of them laughed.

And it went on from there, the two of them driving back to the blacktop, south of her house, and then turning east and heading to town, Dawn talking and talking and talking, and Marcus listening, not saying much but trying to turn down the volume of some sweet voice in his mind telling him that what he was hearing from her, just the sound of her voice, was the most beautiful music he'd ever heard.

"You know," she said once they got going down the road, "I didn't even think of whether you were doing something tonight." She pulled out the seat belt, but it didn't work. "Were you maybe going somewhere?"

"Got homework," he said. "Paper to write for history."

"No shit?" she said, laughing. "Little Big Horn?"

"Wounded Knee," he told her.

"You ever write a paper, Marcus?" she asked him. They were leaving her place far behind.

"My grandma doesn't have a computer," he said. "My grandma doesn't have electricity," he told her. "My grandma's got an outdoor shithouse and she lives in a wigwam."

"Seriously," she said. "You ever in school long enough to write, like, a whole paper?"

"I don't know if I ever did," he told her. "On what?"

"On anything."

"Uses of the buffalo," he said. "Once in grade school maybe, I wrote about uses of a buffalo."

"Lots of research time on that one."

"You going to get around to telling me what I'm doing here?" he asked her. "How 'bout this? --you going to tell me where we're going?" He glanced at her quickly because he didn't want to look, her presence alone making him nervous. She was so much of what he wanted.

"I don't know--just wondering what you were up to," she told him. "That's what I was asking."

"I was going to Winnipeg," he told her.

"Winnipeg?" she said.

"Always wanted to live in Canada."

"You were alone at your place?" she asked.

"Big party—thirty, forty people, a band, a pig roast out in the barn."

"You lie," she said.

"I was sitting in the kitchen and my cell was on the table. There I was, watching it, waiting for you to call."

"Will you tell me straight?" she said.

The snow, the loose snow was starting to billow, a bit of a ground blizzard, not bad enough to make them stop.

"If I didn't know better already, I'd say you were gay," she said.

"And just how far we going in all this snow?"

"It's not a blizzard," she told him.

"Depends on what you see."

She took a deep breath and loosened the zipper of her jacket from where it was locked just under her chin, pulled off her stocking cap, and held it over the floor before shaking off the snow. "'Where are we going'?" she said, as if he hadn't just asked that himself. "That's what you're asking?"

He tipped his shoulders towards her as if an answer might be nice.

"Would you believe me if said I wanted to thank you," she told him. "People think you're the one who saved my life."

He let that go.

"*You* must have called it in," she said. "But how did you know?"

"What you talking about?" he said. "You got news I don't know?"

"Don't be stupid," she told him. "You know what I'm saying. Somehow—I don't know how—you followed me when I left your place last night, followed me or something, figured out where the hell I was and called people or whatever, called emergency, called 911."

"It's an Indian thing to make up stories, ain't it?" he said.

"Stop it," she told him. "The way I got it figured, you were the only soul who knew I might have been out there that late."

"Somebody just came by is all."

"You're the one, and you just didn't 'come by' because nobody just comes by out there when the world's colder than an igloo—"

"Lovers."

"Ain't no lovers going to park on that crap road late at night—sheesh! It was you, and I know it was you."

"You pissed or what?

"Haven't decided yet. It's a damn cruel thing to stop someone from dying when it's number one on their minds."

"Sorry," he said. "You're serious? —you wanted to thank me? That's what this is all about? —I mean you calling me up and all that?"

"How'd you know to follow me? How'd you ever know I was on that road?"

"I can track stuff," he told her. "I'm an Indian. Once you're only a quarter, you lose all that somehow—all that white blood grabs all the good stuff."

"Will you shut up and tell me how you knew?" she said.

"You told me you weren't going home," he told her. "I took you at your word. I'm just a kid, you know? —I trust people way too easy." He knew, even in the dark and even in the cold, that he didn't want this to end. "But tell me this—last night, you really want to die out there like some fool?"

She let that sit for a long time, while he kept going up some featureless gravel road, darkness all around, swirling snow caught in the headlights.

"I'd off myself too if you'd have done it," he said. "I swear. After, you know. . ."

"After what?"

"You know."

"Don't be a kid, Marcus--that was no big deal," she told him.

He wasn't sure she could have said anything worse, but he was with her now. She was there in the pickup and she didn't seem to know where to go. He had her with him, even if it didn't mean anything that they were together the way they were last night—all that stuff, the dancing and the fire and the cold and getting warm the way they did—right now she was right beside him. He had that much at least and it was worth holding on to. They were together right now, right there.

"I got issues, Marcus Pritchard," she told him. "I got issues you don't know a thing about, see?" He knew she was serious because she almost turned away from him when she said it, as if there was a box around her or some kind of prison he couldn't even think of getting into. "How come you came along like you did?" she asked him again. "I mean, how'd you know what I'd do? —that's what I want to know."

All he knew for sure was that he didn't want it to end, their talking—he didn't want her to leave. It wasn't a question he knew exactly how to answer either. "My grandfather was a shepherd," he told her.

"Out here?"

"Okay, I lied."

"Really—did you really come looking for me?" she said.

"I was going to town for cigarettes," he said.

"You don't smoke."

"—for donuts."

"You lie."

They finally came up to the blacktop. "Which way are we going?" he said. "You're the one got me out of bed."

"You weren't in bed," she said.

"Which way?" he asked her.

"Just stay on gravel," she told him.

"Okay," he told her. "But I'm not going in the ditch like someone else I know."

"Don't be a shithead," she said. "That's not why I called." Then she reached across the seat for his arm, took it in her left hand. "I'm not lying. I wanted to thank you because, it's like people say, you saved my life."

"You tell them?"

"They just know somebody way outside of town on some lonely road called it in." Her hand moved to his leg. "I thought it must have been you—just had to be. There's this woman-- she wanted me to take a rape test," she said.

"Wasn't rape," he told her.

"I know," she said, but I got to thinking how easy it would be for me to get you behind bars." She laughed, grabbed him hard. "Honestly," she said, "I wouldn't think of it, because I like you, Marcus, but I could've had your ass in a sling, you know."

He looked over at her right then, maybe for the first time.

"That'd teach you a lesson."

They were barely crawling along, the gravel road straight as a razor in front of them, the lights from the truck out front in a blur.

"The whole fire and everything—it was nice," she told him. "It was. Now just pull over."

"Pull over?" he said.

"Just do what I ask for once in your life," she told him.

When they came to a stop, the wind was blowing so hard the truck rocked. She pulled both hands up to her face in front of her, blew in her fists, then folded them together in front of her closed eyes. He could see in the light cast by the dash.

"Now tell me," she said. "You couldn't have followed me. You'd have been way behind."

He let the silence sit there for a while, surrounded by the privacy of the storm. "You ever think how many people might come to your funeral—you know, if you die?" he asked her. "You would, I suppose—come to my funeral, right? I mean, I can figure on it? Well, maybe. If you weren't busy or in prison or whatever. But I don't know one other person in this world who gives a shit."

"LeRoy?" she said.

"I said 'human being,'" he told her and they both laughed.

"You're just a big cry baby is what you are," she said.

"I'm not kidding," he told her. "You got a mom and dad," he said. "At least you got them."

"You came looking for me last night, didn't you?" she said. "Your grandpa was a shepherd."

"I told you I made that up."

"It was freezer cold and it was late and you were sleeping—I swear you were sleeping when I got out of bed and got into my clothes. You had to be. So you actually came looking for me."

"You left pissed," he said. "You just walked out without saying a thing, not even good-bye or anything. I figured maybe it was at me, about what happened."

"Not at you," she told him.

"I figured--" he said.

"How did you figure? I mean, what were you thinking?"

"You didn't plan on screwing LeRoy's roommate. You weren't figuring on that, were you?" he said. "And I thought maybe it was my fault because it all went too fast, all of it, and you were pissed at yourself after getting rid of that kid and all of that, and here you just get in my bed the next night or whatever— "

"That's why you came after me?" she said. "Because you knew I was mad at myself? You got in the car and looked for me?"

"I figured I'd go get some donuts," he said again, but she didn't laugh.

She reached for him again and kissed him, quickly, on the cheek, like a sister, then pulled back on her side of the seat.

"Now you tell me the truth—so help you God," he said. "Did you actually really and truly want to end it, like everything?"

She held her arms out in front of her as if they were stiff from working or something, held her arms out in front of her and stretched, but she said nothing.

"I'm asking you," he said, "because if you did, then I'm thinking that you wouldn't be thanking me and you wouldn't have called me. You'd be pissed that I broke off your death song."

She spoke very slowly. "Maybe I don't know what I want," she said. Even though it was very dark inside the truck, he could see her lips tighten. "Maybe I would have walked away from that car—I don't know."

"You'd be one dead Sacajawea," he told her.

"I know, I know," she said quickly. "But even if I did want it to be over," she told him, "that had nothing to do with you."

"Thank you," he told her.

"Because you don't know what happened," she told him, "and I don't know if you could understand either. Damnit, you're just a kid. And you're a guy."

"True," he said, "but there ain't nobody else in this old truck." That she hadn't said *boy* was a joy he'd remember later, he told himself. He loved the way she looked at him just then even though it was a test, her eyes asking to see whether something in him was there to trust.

"What happened last night," she said, "—I mean you and me in that bed--that was my fault maybe."

"It was a bad thing?" he asked.

"Don't talk stupid," she said.

"I'm not a kid."

"I know," she said. "I know very well. I didn't want to do no rape test shit."

She stared out into the snowfields, as if she could see clearly, even though frost was already rising from the edges of the windshield. "I can't tell you everything yet," she said, "—I just can't." She looked away then because he could tell there was more that he didn't know, more that was in her, more for him to be afraid of. "And now you have to go because we can't just sit out here in the darkness and the cold all night. We can't just sit here like this or the darkness will come after me again or something—I don't know. . .like it did, and I don't want that."

"What darkness?" he said.

"We got to go," she told him once again. "Trust me, Marcus—we got to go."

"Where to?" he said.

He could tell by her tone of voice that it was like any port in the storm kind of thing. "For donuts," she said with altogether too much force. "You were going for donuts last night, and you never got there because of me." She took a deep breath, and he could just tell her mind closed in on the café downtown. "I'm so damn hungry, you know? I haven't eaten since that soggy hospital food. What I need a donut, Marcus. We can still get one, can't we?"

If that's what she wanted, he thought, that's what she'll get.

The two of them were on the same seat—no buckets, but right then, even though he was pulling away from the spot on gravel where they'd been parked, he felt as if she were right beside him. And she was. He'd known Dawn Burnett for as long as LeRoy had been seeing her, for months already. He'd seen them together at the house often enough, but he'd never thought of her the way he did just then because what he'd learned in the half hour she was in the truck was that she still needed him, just as she had last night in front of the fire in the shed.

"I'm buying," she said. "It's on me because you saved my life." That made her laugh. "You save my life—I buy you a donut. That's a deal."

"Biggest one I can find," he told her. "Not just some little fart."

"Biggest one you can find," she told him. "Two of them even. Three."

Workmanship

When Scotty Faber drove by Woody's place on his way to town that night, he couldn't help thinking of Dawn Burnett again, even though he didn't want to. The arrangement Karin somehow created with Woody—Woody as paper boy--wasn't something he liked much, but he couldn't kick because it was necessary. His old man used to say there are a ton of things in life that you just got to tolerate even though they're not pleasant. "In life, it's not what you want, it's what you get, fool," he'd say. Karin had told Woody a year ago that if ever things happened with Dawn, she—they—needed to know.

Once you come out of the river bottom, you wind around for a couple of miles before you get to the old highway that runs straight as a yardstick into town. If right at that point you grab the wheel, you could read a book and not look up again until streetlights start to parade. That night, he got lost, not lost really, but confused because he had this old Marshall Dillon feeling that comes over him every once in a while, this sense that maybe he ought to ride up on a white horse and take care of whatever he can all by himself—you know, visit this kid in the hospital and not involve Karin or KayLee at all, just take care of business all by his lonesome. The whole thing was his problem. He should just pick up the damned burden himself even though he'd never really spoken to the girl, never even seen her up close. Just go in and wish her his best, apologize maybe. No, apologize for sure, he thought. Yeah, apologize because there was no running away from the fact that he had made her life miserable. He was her father after all, and he acted like some jerk absentee landlord. Or worse.

Dawn wasn't really Karin's. He did the deed, more than once, too. No matter how hard he tried to deny it or forget it, there was no walking away from the truth. He was Dawn's father, who'd never been that because he'd pretended she didn't exist. It was something he'd done. She was a kid he'd made, he and Celine.

Years ago, when he and Karin got back together, they'd needed somebody to keep them from brawling. That's when he got church. They both did. It made all kinds of difference.

Verse 8 is what they were on that night at Bible study, second chapter, book of the Ephesians. "For it is by grace you have been saved, through faith—and this not from yourselves, it is the gift of God— not by works, so that no one can boast. For we are God's workmanship, created in Christ Jesus to do good works, which God prepared in advance for us to do." There's some smaller stuff around that one too, but the heart of things was those verses.

And how true is that? --he asked himself. Only a God could have pulled Scotty Faber's ass—could have pulled both of them—out of that shithole he'd been in that first year they were married. Well, not *married* exactly. Now he knew what that meant. Then, it didn't mean shit, quite frankly. Even their friends were sure the two of them wouldn't make it to their second anniversary, and look at them today, he thought.

Just had to clear this stuff up with Dawn, with Dawn and with KayLee, with his daughter, with both of them, both his daughters. Something had to be done, he told himself, and it was not going to be pretty or easy. Takes a lot of prayer, a lot of it. That's why going downtown—no matter how blasted cold—was a good, good thing. Bible study was something he needed, something he always needed, but more right now, today, tonight, he told himself, with the big mess going on with Dawn, who was his daughter, Dawn.

They met at the café, where there were almost always a couple other groups with Bibles open in front of them—men and women, old and young sitting around tables. Ever since he'd been into Bible studies, it seemed to him that everyone else had been into it too.

He goes because Bible study with a couple of guys is something like AA, even though he kicked the drinking thing without it years ago. He goes because staying on the straight and narrow is something he understands to be the kind of hard work that has to done. He knows firsthand what it's like to be pickled and half dead. The truth is he didn't go to Bible study because he loved it, because it's full of warm fuzzies, or because he left the café humming "Ten Thousand Reasons." Sometime the whole night was ping-pong: he serves, Alvin slaps the ball back on Larry's side of the table, and Larry arches one up back at him with all kinds of spin. But it's a doubles match because there's four of them, sometimes five. What they do is slap the Bible verse around a little, drink some coffee, eat a donut or two, talk about making a living, then pray and call it a night. Sometimes he's not particularly interested in leaving the house, especially mid-winter when the cold can freeze your eyes open. But he knows that when he does leave, he'll thank himself all the way home. That's the way it goes.

It's a little men's group from church, a monthly thing at the café. They'd started the year with maybe a dozen guys, but, mid-winter, when a bunch of cattlemen light out for a warmer climate, the numbers dwindle—ordinary attrition. Reading the Bible and talking about it is not for everyone, Scotty's always figured. Wouldn't have been for him either for a long time—and wasn't. Anyway, five guys are sure bets to show up and have been for almost ten years. That night, Larry was out of town—that left just four.

Barry, the youngest member, studied some religion in a Christian college because once upon a time he wanted to be a missionary. But when his dad's ranch was mostly his for the asking, he grabbed it because he'd always wanted to run cattle himself. While they're trying to get on their feet financially, he's doing some teaching, middle school. When the Bible Study doesn't quite understand where they're going, they look at Barry, even though sometimes Scotty thinks the kid is short on knowing how life really works. He knows the Bible and what's around it, you might say, but he sometimes comes up a little short on understanding what goes on around him.

Glenn never says a whole lot, but when he does, whatever he says pretty much ends discussion, not because he's pushy but because you can't help thinking that what he says is about right. End of conversation. Sweet man, and a wise man.

Alvin, the oldest, is living proof age doesn't necessarily brew wisdom. None of the regulars is in trouble—at least Scotty doesn't know of anyone—and no one yaps like they've got all the answers, which is why, or so Scotty tells Karin, the whole outfit has stuck it out as long as they had. Some men from church—you'd think they thought they were right there in the barn in Bethlehem.

Often enough, Glenn's got the kind of answers you can believe in, but he doesn't use an exclamation mark or stare anybody into thinking that if they don't agree they're dumb as a mud fence. Besides, he doesn't play his cards right away, doesn't say much until everyone else takes a shot at things, something Scotty, and the others too, have grown to appreciate. They're all married, have kids, although Alvin's are long gone and out of state.

They're friends, not buddies. They don't hang out together or as families because all this happens through the church. It's not like they go up to Canada for walleyes or Northerns, although sometimes Scotty thinks that might well be a plan.

By the time he got to town that night, he hoped that once he sat down with the others, put down a couple swallows of hot coffee, opened his Bible, and started with prayer, Dawn Burnett would plain disappear. She'd been gone for most of her life, after all. He hadn't see her bloody, hadn't see her hauled out of her car by the Jaws of Life, didn't see her drunk or beat up or whatever got her there in the middle of nowhere. When he tried to imagine her face, what came into his mind was a school picture that seemed stamped inside his glasses so that he couldn't see anything without her being there, just an ordinary, innocent school picture right in front of his eyes, dark-haired, dark-eyes, like her mom. Nothing at all resembling his gene scheme.

It was grace alone that stopped that image from killing him, he thought, and that's why he started that night the way he did. He was, after all, the leader. "You guys tell me," he said, rubbing the open pages of the Bible before him, "—you guys tell me how we can ever say enough about grace?"

After prayer, he said that, because it was his job, leading things the way he was. That's all he had to say, and just like that they were off. Didn't take long—maybe twenty minutes—before Alvin brought the whole Dawn business up because he teaches too, like Woody, only in the middle school, where he'd heard about the Dawn Burnett thing, as everyone had.

They were on "workmanship," an idea worth their time, Scotty thought, when he read through the chapter the night before. They were on workmanship when Alvin brought it up because, he said, he wondered about this girl who had the accident or whatever it had been, and what God in his almighty power was working out in that girl's life, or something to that effect. If we are God's workmanship, Alvin said, then what's he making out of Dawn Burnett? That was the gist of what he'd wondered, only he didn't use her name because not everyone knew the girl. She was the kid who tried to take her life in the storm. That's the way they knew her mostly.

Alvin knew the story because he always knows the hot news. Scotty sometimes thinks he comes to Bible study just to make sure the rest of them are caught up on what's been traded locally. He's not a particularly smart guy, Scotty thought, and he cries easy—and that's okay sometime. Not all the time, but sometime.

"What happened?" Barry said. "I didn't hear." Innocent as anything. He had no idea, so Alvin tells what he knows of it.

"She had an accident," Alvin says again, "maybe."

"Don't know her," Barry says. "What you say her name is?"

"Dawn Burnett," Alvin says, almost in a whisper; and then he says, "Her mother's the painter, the artist," and he looks around as if he might see one of Celine's paintings right there on the wall above them. "You know—Celine Burnett," he said. "She does these winter night kinds of things—moon and stars and warriors—sometimes wolves. They're beautiful." He shook his head quite miserably. "Poor woman's had her share of troubles with her daughter, I guess. You know Celine, right, Alvin? Drop dead gorgeous. Quite an outfit once upon a time herself, I guess."

"Some people think it was deliberate," Alvin said, holding that cup up in front of his face like he often did. "I was reading all of this today," he said, tipping his head at the Bible down on the table in front of him. "I was just going over things right after I heard what happened." He shook his head in disbelief. "You can't help but wonder, you know—if we are God's workmanship, you just can't help trying to figure out what the Lord is shaping this young lady into, what he's up to anyway."

"She did it to herself," Glenn said. "Likely as not, she drove in that ditch deliberate." He was deadly serious, didn't say it as if it was condemnation. "I don't know that you can think that God took hold of that steering wheel and drove her out into the ditch, can you?"

"Then it's her fault?" Alvin said.

"'Shit happens,'" Glenn told him. "Nobody should take blame for that."

"Not even her?" Alvin said.

"How old is she?" Barry said.

"High school."

"Drinking?" Barry asked.

Alvin shrugged his shoulders as if admitting as much. "Nobody knows, but the word is—well, you know." She had Indian blood after all. That's what he meant.

"You're the boss here, Scotty," Alvin says to him. "You're running this circus. What do you think? —God almighty working on this girl when she tried to take her own life? He behind it? What if she froze our there?"

Scotty Faber wondered whether this wasn't the time for him to unload a ton of shit on the guys around that table; but when he looked around it seemed that not one of them had the kind of look on his face that betrayed some sense of knowing who they were talking to right then. What he had in mind was the same thing he had in mind earlier when he thought of it—that maybe God was working him over right now with this whole mess. And the girl was okay. You had to remember that, too—this young girl of his, his daughter, she wasn't dying. "She's my daughter," he could tell them. That would shut them all down and put all this holy talk to work.

What they were wondering was whether the Creator of heaven and earth took a part in Dawn's unlikely excursion into the ditch—or whether what happened that night out in the frozen cold was only the girl's doing. Or something else. Or booze. Or snow blindness? Could have been a thousand things, and that's what he told the others. "They find her phone?" he said. "Maybe she was texting somebody—I don't know. Maybe she just screwed up."

"You don't think God is behind it somehow?" Alvin said.

Silence.

"Where's the pastor when we need him?" Scotty said, and they all laughed.

When he looked around the table, he knew that Glenn was the only one who could possibly have known the whole story—that's what he was thinking. And it wasn't like him to stay out of the conversation, not at all like him.

"Anybody know the girl?" Barry said, and he looked at Scotty, who was the leader, after all.

Scotty looked at Glenn, who shook his head, and then at Alvin, whose face never moved, not a twitch, not a bit, eyes down as if he'd rather not admit anything he wasn't saying.

"I can't say as I know her," Scotty said, slapping the ball back across the table. "I know she's Celine Burnett's oldest—i'n't that right?" He looked across the table. "You're the oldest one here, Alvin--you know this girl?"

Alvin sniffed a couple of times as if he was wanting to postpone an answer, as if he had an allergy, even though it was midwinter. He looked around the table, at each one of them, measuring something, then stuck the pen he had in his right hand back into his pocket, as if something had just then been decided. "I don't know a soul in town anymore outside those old timers in Pioneer Home," he said, and they all laughed.

"Why do we got to blame people anyway?" Glenn said again.

"It's either that or God," Alvin said.

"Maybe it's the frickin' ice—maybe it's what she was drinking, poor kid—maybe she hit a white out," Glenn said, shutting his Bible. "Maybe it's her mother—maybe it's Adam and Eve," he said. "Isn't this really all about just cleaning up the mess?" he said. "Why do we have blame things on people? —because it makes us feel better?"

"Good Lord, bad day at work, Glenn?" Alvin said. "Nobody buys cars in this cold, I bet."

Glenn pulled his chair back from the table almost as if he were going to leave, then he threw his hands back behind his head. "Just hits a little close to home is all," he said.

Things got quiet then because even though they met once a month and stumbled their way through difficult passages, they rarely cut themselves open that way. The whole conversation poked at some kind of scar Scotty hadn't ever seen. If Glenn wasn't going to say what on his mind, nobody there was going to push him. No one ever pushed anyone at the Thursday night café Bible study.

"You know this kid?" Alvin asked again.

"By parentage," Glenn told him, --that's all."

That's when Scotty got the feeling that Glenn was talking to him, squawking like that first rooster on Good Friday. He slapped back across the table, looked at Barry. "What were you saying anyway? Why don't you run that all by us again?"

"It's like he's got all of it figured out, the way I read this passage," Barry said. "It's like the whole thing is laid out for us and we just walk into it. The whole time, every last minute of our lives, he's working on us, sometimes maybe even working us over, like he did that girl."

It got quiet again.

"Got nothing to toss in here, Scotty?" Alvin said.

Sylvia the waitress came around with coffee and, as usual, filled their cups before anyone asked for seconds. "Answer me this," she said. "How come there's all this sin in this burg when there's so many people reading the Bible? That's one I can't answer."

"Sin?" Glenn said, as of mightily shocked. "Haven't seen any for a month now at least."

"You're looking the other way," she told him, pointed up at the tin ceiling above, and left for the next table.

Scotty normally thought he wasn't as smart as Barry or wise as Glenn, but he stuck in his own two cents' worth then, told them he thought it was sort of reassuring to know that the hands of God were constantly working us over because he knew from his own life—and the other guys knew about most of his drinking—that he had more knots in him than a scrub oak, and that sometimes we all bang around quite a bit before He finally catches our attention, even though all the time he was bending, shaping—that kind of thing.

All of that stopped the conversation, just as if they thought Scotty a whole lot wiser than he thought he was right then. He wasn't lying when he said it either, not by a long shot. But neither was he telling the truth, and nobody knew that better than he did himself.

It was his job to manage the conversation so that it didn't end up just yakking. That's what he knew and that's what he did. He had to keep control, keep things from wandering, which is where they'd go if someone didn't monitor things. "Well, all of that's interesting all right, but I think it's time for us to get back on task," he said.

When he left the café, he figured Karin was right on the money: something had to happen. They were going to have to take some other road altogether.

But for that he didn't have a map. He wished the Lord almighty would have equipped him with some divine GPS right out of the factory, although even if he had such a thing himself it likely wouldn't have mattered because he wouldn't have known how to get to some destination he hadn't even begun to locate.

And what if he stood in front of that girl now—somewhere in the hospital or anywhere? What if he stood there and wished her the best? He wouldn't have the words to know how to talk, what to say. Sometimes he wished he were still trucking and not just in the office sending out his drivers.

When he got back in the pickup, he figured that even though it wasn't the kind of night to take a drive in the country, he couldn't go home right away—which is not to say that he was thinking that maybe with more time he could figure things out. Meanwhile, he'd just ride around a little.

He needed time. He got this urge to run because a man always is thinking there's got to be a better place just off the horizon, he thought. Sometimes he still gets that feeling, even though so much is good about his life—his family, his business, his church.

Right then, the only thing he couldn't help seeing was that he didn't know the half of it.

I feel it in my bones

Marcus parked his pickup out of the wind because he wasn't sure if they would stay and he didn't want it not to start. It was that cold. He didn't know if he should or not, but when she climbed out of the truck—the passenger door wouldn't open from the inside, so she had to come out of his side—he took her hand. She didn't pull away either, kept it there in his when they walked together, quickly—it was cold—into the café. A kid from school was straightening the metal branches of a Christmas tree he was assembling near the door.

Right there, at the front stood a display case of cakes and muffins and donuts, all kinds of things, so he stopped, took off his gloves and pointed with his left hand at something cinnamon. She didn't say a thing, but grabbed his sleeve and pulled him along to the left, the old smoking section.

She pushed him along to a table and a chair, then slid out the one on the other side and took it herself. "It's my old man," she said quietly shifting her head slightly back toward the other side of the restaurant. "It's my real father over there," she told him. "I saw him."

The display case separated the sides of the café, along with the register, where a waitress was ringing up some customer's coffee. Marcus backed up slightly in his chair to see past the couple in thick winter coats getting change, but all he could see was the tops of men's heads above the half wall separating sides, two of those heads bald ones, two others.

"I bet he didn't see you come in," he told her. "If you walk out beside me," he pointed to his arm, "he probably won't see you walk out either."

"My real actual father," she said, through her teeth.

"You know him?" he said.

She shook her head.

"He know you?"

"I know who he is," she told him.

"And he knows who you are?" he told her, not a question.

She shrugged her shoulders. She didn't know.

"He knows you exist," he said. "He's got to know you exist." She looked at him with eyes so empty they made it clear she had no idea. "He knows he's got this daughter, right?" he asked.

She shook her head as if to say she didn't know, not for sure.

"He's a white man?" Marcus asked.

She nodded.

He'd never doubted the two of them were both mixed bloods, but he'd not considered the possibility of her father being a white man, even though he had to be, or probably was; but then even her mother was mixed blood. Still, when he saw the crowns of bald men on the other side of that planter, it seemed almost impossible to believe that her real father was just some paleface from town. "They having coffee?" he said.

"I don't know," she told him. "But I saw him." She told him how, when she was much younger, and she was with her mother—in some of the bad times, she said—that her mother had spotted him. Dawn was little then, and her mother wasn't always to blame for what happened, she told him. It was the grocery store in Mitchell or something. Her mother had too much to drink, and she was very angry, and it probably wasn't right for her to say it just then, but it wasn't a scene either, she said. She told him he shouldn't think it was some kind of big drama because it wasn't. Her mom pointed at the guy—Dawn must have been maybe ten, and they were back in the area for awhile for some reason—and told her that the man picking out grapes or whatever was her father and she should never forget his face.

"Out loud?"

"Yes."

"I mean," he said, "loud enough for him to hear?"

"Yes, loud enough to hear—that's why she said it. For him."

"And it wasn't a big deal?"

"Not *that* loud. Not like screamed it or anything. Just out loud."

"And that's him?" Marcus asked.

"I've seen him a hundred times."

"And he doesn't know?"

She said she suspected he did because she knew his daughter. She'd come to talk to her after a basketball game once when they were in middle school—a couple years ago, picked her out from the rest of the girls on the team. Really awkward sort of thing. "KayLee Faber," she said. "Know her?"

He said he'd seen that last name on trucks. "Cattle guy?"

Dawn nodded.

"Rich?"

She nodded again.

Marcus got up and went to the display case, told the waitress that they'd have a couple of the brownies behind the glass and two coffees. What was clear when he could see the table full of men was that each of them had a big flat open book—Bibles. It was cold night and a couple of them had work shirts on, and that's how it was he could pick out the man Dawn named as her father. His said "Faber Trucking" in fancy writing.

"Two dollars even," the waitress told him. "We're about ready to close."

He took the money out of his billfold and handed it to her, then lugged the two brownies over to the table where Dawn was still sitting, and went back for the coffee.

There was nothing—absolutely nothing—in the man's face to suggest that he was her father. They didn't look at all alike. Not a bit.

"You're sure?" he said when he came back with the coffees.

"That man is the one," she said. "I know. I feel it in my bones."

"Weird," he said. "Like some kind of magnet?"

"Don't be an idiot," she told him.

"People feel a lot of stuff in their bones," he told her.

"Don't question me," she told him, her eyes sharpening. "I'm going to the toilet," she said, which was on the other side of the café. "I'm going to walk right past him. I'm going to see if he knows me."

"You going to talk to him?"

She shook her head. "Just look in his eyes."

"I'll watch," he said. "Don't look at him—don't give him that much. Just let me watch. Let me witness the whole thing," Marcus told her.

"I want to know," she said. "If I look him straight in the eye, I'll know."

"And what if he doesn't look at you?"

"Then I'll know too."

"No you won't. What makes you think he'll see you?"

"I'm a girl," she said. "He'll look—especially with a table full of men. They'll look. Don't you know nothing?" She reached in her purse and pulled out a silver barrette, then shook her hair back, reached around her, and grabbed a handful of long bangs to pull and fasten behind her head. "All I got to do is walk past."

He reached for her arm. "Let me go with," he said. "I'll know better."

"No, you won't."

"I'm a man," he said. "I'll know."

She looked at him angrily, then reached in her billfold and took out another dollar. "Go buy another donut—that's why we came here. To go. Go buy that donut I owe you and watch too. We'll both watch."

She pushed herself back from the table, took off her jacket, and hung it over the chair behind her. She stood straight, then snugged up the sweatshirt, pushed her shoulders back, and stuck her fingers in the front pockets of her jeans. She was putting on, turning herself into something so sweet no guy couldn't look. Just like that he remembered last night, holding what was beneath all those clothes in his arms, his legs around hers.

They walked together to the front counter, and he watched as she angled around the tables to the right toward the restrooms in the back, walking tall, some kind of Vegas broad, a whole lot different from the kid on the road who'd jumped in his truck.

The man in the Faber shirt glanced up at her when she started walking toward him, but he looked back toward the man across the table, who was talking. He glanced at the Bible that was open before him, took a sip of coffee, and never again looked up at her, no matter how hot she pranced. Marcus knew—he was sure—that this Faber guy, her real father, had no idea what his own daughter looked like. If he'd seen her, he showed no sign. Nothing.

Marcus stood there at the cash register and acted as if he couldn't make up his mind about a donut as he waited for Dawn to come back out. When she did, she came up from behind the guy. Another man at the table looked at her in the way old men do—you could see that. But this guy, the rich guy, the cattle guy, wasn't thinking of her. She could have been naked as the day she was born and the guy would not have seen her, would not have noticed her walking right past him. She tried, walked like some hot chick, but he never saw her.

And it wasn't the Bible either—Marcus could see that. It wasn't as if he was buried in something like a holy man. It wasn't that, because his eyes—those same eyes that Dawn was sure would recognize her—were dazed, as if he was neither seeing nor hearing. He was not forbidding himself from looking at this girl. He'd seen her, after all. When she'd walked toward the back, he'd looked up simply because something moved. But he'd not recognized her, of that Marcus was sure.

Dawn put her hands down on the counter when she returned, but said nothing. She closed her eyes. "I hate him," she said. "I absolutely hate him. He wouldn't even look at me."

"He never saw you," Marcus told her. "You got that wrong."

"He looked right at me."

"Maybe so," he told her again, "but he never saw you. He doesn't know what you look like—if you'd ask him right now, 'Is that girl that just walked past, is she Indian or white?' he couldn't say one way or the other." The waitress was coming up from the kitchen. "He's not thinking about what's going on at that table either. Something else is in him." And then it came to him. "Maybe he knows what happened to you last night. Maybe he heard."

She reached for her coat and pulled it back around her, bundled herself up to leave. But her eyes had softened, almost in the way she would have liked this guy's to soften when he saw her coming towards him. "How could he have heard?" she said.

"They could be talking about it right now, you know? — 'this Dawn Burnett chick, you know, that young girl'—they could be saying how this Indian girl went in the ditch last night late and how it is people are worried about her because they thought she was drunk or whatever and how them Indians die out there in the cold, way too often, way too often. They could be saying all of that right now. They could."

She looked across the café, as if she might be able to pick up conversation. When the waitress came, Dawn pulled a couple dollars out of her purse and the waitress gave her three more donuts in a small brown bag, free—it was late, and they were trying to get rid of what they'd had left, she told them.

But Dawn kept staring at the men. Even though Marcus couldn't see what she was seeing, he was sure the man she'd called her father never once looked up—or if he did, he'd shown no interest. There was no recognition.

Finally, he took her arm with his left hand and pulled her out toward the door.

The pickup was cold even though they'd been in the café for such a short time, but that's when she bawled, not hard, just enough that she couldn't really cover it up. She made no move towards him, as if he wasn't to be part of this or as if maybe he'd been too much a part of it last night already. She tossed the bag of donuts between them and put her face in her hands for a moment, then took out her mittens, pulled them on her hands and put her face back in, as if they could soak up the tears.

What it was exactly that created those tears—grief or sadness or anger, or maybe all of those—he didn't know. Maybe it was just a broken heart.

The old Dodge Ram started up quickly, and the fan blew hard over a thin line of frost already forming like a horizon at the base of windshield. But there was only one voice in him just then, only one heart speaking; and that voice said to stay with this girl, no matter. No matter what, it said, you stay put now.

"You got your cell?" she said, reaching into the pocket of her jeans. "I have to make a call."

She's not here

Tieneke didn't think that Celine recognized KayLee. If she had, it certainly didn't show.

"Come in, come in," Celine said to all of them. "You gotta be a buffalo to love this stuff." She swung the storm door open, holding it with a forearm until all three were inside.

Nothing in her face suggested the faintest notion of recognizing the girl with them. She seemed perfectly on stage, Tieneke thought, far too composed for what she must have been going through, her daughter ambulanced off to emergency last night, having gone into a ditch on a road no one traveled in weather everyone knew was a killer. She smiled like a perfect hostess who'd been thinking just then of how she would greet her dinner guests.

"The Dekkers," she said. "It's been so long. And this is?"

Nothing in her eyes hinted she might know.

"--Our neighbor—KayLee," Woody told her.

"KayLee Faber," Tieneke said, quickly. "She lives just down the road."

Celine reached up to her face with her right hand as if to cover something, then slipped two fingers over her lips without moving her eyes from KayLee's own. The shine in her eyes seemed to vanish, her smile fading, then, just as quickly, it returned. Simply the introduction was enough for her to understand the story of the three visitors from afar on a night few took on the cold "You want to see my daughter?" She said it in a voice that didn't register at quite the same pitch. "You want to talk to her I suppose? --am I right?"

Tieneke told herself, hard as it was not to respond, that the time had come for KayLee to speak. She stood there beside the girl, waiting, then turned more deliberately toward her as if to make very clear that no one was going to mother her right now, that she was on her own. She was the one who insisted on coming out in the cold.

And—bless her heart! —she didn't hesitate. "I know that we're sisters—Dawn and me," KayLee said, chin high. "And I know what happened between you and my father," she told Celine.

Maybe a bit too self-assured, Tieneke thought, but she couldn't help but feel good about the way the girl was going after things.

Celine stared. Something fierce rose in her face, something angry.

"She wanted to see how Dawn is doing," Tieneke told her. "We went to the hospital to check on her, but she'd been released. She wanted to come out here." She nodded a bit toward KayLee. "She told us she wanted to see how her sister was doing—that's why we're here."

Whatever fortified Celine Burnett for just a moment, whatever it was that made Tieneke feel as if things might be spoken that shouldn't be—all of that disappeared. Celine's lips tightened. She never once took her eyes off KayLee, but they changed, softened. Her shoulders dropped a bit, and she took a deep breath through her nose, audibly, still biting her lips.

"Dawn left somehow," Celine said. "She's not here."

She seemed not distressed.

"Where is she?" KayLee said. "I just wanted to see her, to be sure she was okay."

Celine looked at Tieneke, then Woody, but said nothing. She turned back and looked into the house as if something there might give her words. She ran a hand through her hair, pulling it back behind her ears nervously, then bit just a little at her upper lip. Dawn had left. Again. Without permission. Helplessness was written all over Celine's face.

For what seemed the longest time, Celine didn't look at any of them, eyes flitting to places she didn't see—her hands, the ceiling, even the cold night. "I suppose I deserve this," she said, finally. "I mean, you know—what happened. You remember."

"Deserve what?" Tieneke asked.

"It's been a couple of years already—I mean, it's been a long time since I had much say about what goes on in my daughter's life," she said. With her left hand, she grabbed the two sides of her vest and pulled them together as if she were cold. "She may be too much my own daughter—I don't know. But it's worse to watch it happen in someone you love than to be, well—you know, than to be the one it happens to."

"Where is she?" Woody asked.

Celine shook her head. "I can tell you what she told me, but I know you won't find her there." She backed up slowly, tentatively, leaned against a bannister near the doorway. "I don't think she's told me the truth for two or three years—I don't know how long. Seems like a lifetime."

For reasons neither Tieneke nor Woody understood right then, it was KayLee who went to Celine, Celine the adulteress—KayLee the innocent, KayLee the gospel singer, KayLee the child. It was KayLee who walked through the silence to hug a woman her father had loved—*is love the right word?* Tieneke wondered--so very long ago.

She looked at Woody as the two women held each other, and Woody squinted back as if it made no sense because it didn't, except to say that KayLee Faber was responding to plain old sharp human pain, not her own but someone else's, in a way that showed she'd either begun to leave her childhood behind or else that she hadn't at all. Who could tell? Innocence or experience?

When the two of them pulled apart, Celine held KayLee at arm's length and nodded as if in thanks. Then she looked into the girl's face, into her eyes, as if making an assessment. "What happens in my daughter's life--" she said, then bit her lip again. "*I don't know* what happens in my daughter's life." She reached up and brushed KayLee's hair back from her face.

"Where is she?" KayLee asked her, the two of them still in a half embrace.

"Honestly," she said, "I don't know. We wouldn't let her use the car, wouldn't let her leave—the doctor's said. . ." Celine paused, looked back at Woody as if for help. "Someone must have called—someone must have told her she'd pick her up or something because she just wanted to be alone. She has ways of making that clear. She wanted to be alone, and when we looked in on her later, in her room, she was already gone."

"She couldn't have walked anywhere," Woody said.

"My husband went out looking in the car—he's out now, in fact. Our children are here."

"We'll find her," KayLee said, and she shook Celine's arms. "We will," she said.

Tieneke couldn't help thinking it was a shame to have to grow out of that almost shocking innocence kids came with from the factory. It was at least something of what Jesus found so blessed about them, even if there were times—lots of them—when she thought what he'd said about suffering the little kids was more than a little pie-in-the-sky.

"I'm sorry," Celine said. "I should have asked you in."

"I left the car running," Woody said. "We didn't intend to stay." The way he looked around, Tieneke knew he was trying to determine where Dawn's room was, how she could have snuck out of the house. "It's early," he said. "It'd be one thing if it was midnight or something, but it's still early."

"It's so cold," Celine said.

"You're right about that one," Woody told her. "It's really cold."

"You want me to stay?" Tieneke asked. "If you want me to stay for a while with you, I can—besides I'd love to see what you're doing." She pointed at the walls, where lots of Celine's things were hanging. It wouldn't hurt to get Celine's mind off of things, she knew. "It's too cold to be alone."

When Celine didn't hesitate, Tieneke knew she wanted her around, probably needed her. That would put Woody and KayLee back in the car—just KayLee and himself. She could see on her husband's face that he didn't like that somehow. Having his wife with, that was a good thing, the safe thing. And that's why he said what he did. "Maybe KayLee too," he told them. "Maybe she ought to stay here with the two of you."

This whole thing had started with KayLee's head of steam, and it wasn't going to play itself out until something in her got satisfied, some darkness dredged up and out and into the light, she thought. It wasn't in the girl to stay here now, in this warm house and out of the cold, out of the danger, not when Dawn had gone back out in the cold just a night after what she'd done looked frighteningly like suicide.

"Let me run around outside a minute," Woody told them. Then to KayLee. "You stay put or you'll catch your death of cold."

She was proud of him, Tieneke was. He was an old man, an old teacher, but it never once struck him as stupid to do anything other than what he assumed had to be done. They had to find Dawn. They all needed Dawn.

There's things I need to know

"I just want to talk to someone," Dawn told whoever it was she was calling. "It's about something I think I know the answer to, but you said you were a nurse once upon a time."

The two of them had just left town again, and Marcus felt his own nerves start to settle once the truck crept back into the darkness, which wasn't all that shadowy because the moon off the new snow lit up the world as if it were a half day. She wanted to call someone, she said, and she did.

"Where do you live?" Dawn asked.

Someone she'd met in the hospital, Dawn had told him before she'd called, some woman from Red Lake, in Minnesota, who'd got stung somewhere along the way. When he'd asked her how, Dawn said she wasn't sure because the woman hadn't said exactly, only that the woman was getting over something—or trying to, which Dawn said was absolutely not a lie because she could see it in this woman's eyes—her name was Coby something—she couldn't remember exactly but there was a saint in it, like St. John.

"You're shitting me," Marcus had said.

"Saint something—St. Mary. I don't know. But she wasn't lying, and I could see it."

"That's what we need right now is a saint," Marcus said.

"You can see those things," Dawn had said. "I can anyway. Didn't come off like the bullshit you get from people like her."

Not old—a young woman. Not a nurse exactly, but in the hospital. He didn't get that part so he asked her what she was doing there anyway, in Dawn's hospital room, and she told him how this Coby woman was like assigned to her because this nurse-like person was young and they—meaning cops or EMTs or whoever in the hospital—wondered whether maybe there was rape— "you know, last night," Dawn explained, sort of fumbling.

Marcus sure didn't think it was rape, but he let what she said alone.

"We're coming over," Dawn told this woman over the phone. "You there alone or what?"

"How young?" he asked her, but Dawn waved him off.

"I'm in this guy's pickup and we're just riding around—me and Marcus. Just riding. ... No, the heater's working fine. It's warm," she told the woman. "Sure, who doesn't like hot chocolate? Not long either, right? Just a quick visit because I got these questions. Well, just one really."

He pulled into a driveway and turned around by backing up onto the blacktop. Didn't even have to look for cars on the road because the two of them were the only ones stupid enough to ride around in the deep freeze. He could break every traffic laws in the state and no one would care. Hot chocolate, he thought. Maybe weenies over an open fire too or something. Sing Sunday school songs.

"I said, we'll be there," Dawn told this Coby person. When she looked at him she rolled her eyes. "Yes, I swear."

He wondered what she had to swear for because she'd just told the woman they were coming and he'd already turned the damn truck around. "She doesn't believe you?" he said, and once again she waved him off.

"Everything is fine," she told her. "I'm okay. Would you stop worrying? We came into town for a donut, you know? —and I thought I'd call because. . ." She waited as if the words had to appear on a monitor in front of her and weren't. It all had to do with truth, he thought. She's either going to lie or else she was going to talk. "Because you said I could," she said, which he thought probably wasn't a lie and nicely avoided her having to. And that was something for Dawn Burnett, he thought. Just not lying was something.

And then more waiting, that voice on the other end coming up as if squashed. "Christmas tree?" Dawn said. "—My mom had ours up weeks ago."

Hot chocolate and Christmas trees, he thought. Sure. Soon enough, holding hands or bobbing for apples.

"Not long—we're here in town." Dawn looked at him and he saw a smile for the first time since she'd left the café.

He shrugged his shoulders as if he didn't know where to go, and she pointed straight up the road.

"Maybe five minutes is all."

Nodded. Said goodbye. Stuck her phone back in her jacket. Looked straight ahead, out of what of the windshield wasn't blocked with frost, seeing nothing anyway, he thought. Wasn't like her to call this nurse or whatever, he told himself. Fierce as a warrior she was. LeRoy always said it was one of the reasons he liked hanging out with her because she didn't take any shit, and now she goes crying to this nurse. Made no sense.

"You talk like she's your sister," he said, then thought better. "Like she's your friend."

"She's a nurse I told you," Dawn told him.

"I thought you said she *wasn't* a nurse," he said.

"There's things I just need to know—I mean from her."

What he'd already begun to think about was that three was going to be more than this woman's house would hold, especially because he wasn't a girl. There wasn't much open in town anymore, wasn't anything open for that matter anymore—maybe Pic'n'Pak, but even they closed up when they went to card readers on the gas pumps. He could have read magazines if they were open. He didn't want to burn gas with a flat billfold, didn't feel like riding around town when the whole place was arctic.

"How long you going to want to stay?" he said, but she was going over something in her mind. "Dawn, you going to stay there, you think?" he asked.

"You mean like a sleepover?" she said as if suddenly tuned back in to him. "You wondering if I'm going to like stay there for a while?"

"I mean, you thinking you want me take off?" he said.

She looked at him strangely, then smiled as sweet as anything he'd seen all night. "Hot chocolate, Marcus," she said. "Geez, you don't even have a mom and dad. How long has it been since you had a warm cup of hot chocolate?" She grabbed his hand off the wheel, held it. "You're my savior, Marcus Pritchard. Don't you be leaving me now."

"I'm in this?" he asked her.

"You'll freeze outside," she told him. "There's things I just got to know."

He hadn't been around women that much, at least not in a friendly way. Once upon a time he had a sister, but she left when his mom did and that was years ago. He didn't really know where they went either, but his father used to think it was Albuquerque or somewhere down there where cactus grew or palm trees, or both. Otherwise, there were girls out at the place with LeRoy often enough. He'd bring them home on stringers like fish. Sometimes just one at a time too, like Dawn. But when they'd come in bunches they were there to drink and smoke and do whatever, and not really just to be girls, or women. Girls, LeRoy had in spades—white and red and every shade in between, lots of them, like coyotes and rabbits.

Once in school Marcus had stayed after because he was tardy, and he was in detention with three girls older than he was—he was eighth grade then maybe. When the teacher left the room to get a drink or take a leak, those girls started talking as if he wasn't there, as if he was invisible, started yakking about stuff that made no sense, about clothes and t-shirts and flip-flops and how much they liked magenta, which he'd never heard of. He'd wondered if that was the way they talked to each other all the time—which made some sense after all because when guys were together they talked in a certain way too.

"I can watch TV maybe," he told Dawn, and Dawn said this Coby woman must have a TV so that was something he sure could do if he wanted to. But he wasn't supposed to leave she said again, and she meant it. He knew she meant it.

"What you gotta' talk to her about?" he said, "—this nurse?"

Dawn shook her head. "Something I need to know," she said. And then she stopped to look at him, sort of purposefully, in a judging way, as if to see if he was worth what it was she was going to say, he thought. "About a baby," she told him.

Which he interpreted as meaning something women talk about. "There's got to be something on TV," he told her.

She put her hand on his again, reached over and squeezed his fingers. But when he looked up at her, he saw that she wasn't looking at him, which, in an odd way, a surprising way, he sort of liked, almost as if she needed him even though she wasn't thinking about it or him, about putting her hand on his. Like she just needed him to be him, not someone he didn't know how to be.

So, he did the old patty-cake trick. He pulled his right hand out of hers and held her hand instead, which didn't seem to change anything at all, which he also liked. All he saw on her face in the dash lights was tightened lips. That's all. But she kept her hand there, quit the game, you might say, and just let him hold her. And that was good, he thought, as they passed under streetlights that, off and on, made her face shine.

"How come you act scared of this woman?" he asked.

She shook her head. "I'm not scared of her," she said.

"Then what you scared of?"

"I don't know," she said. "I don't know about a kid."

"I thought you took care of that," he said, and she pulled her hand away and pointed left at the street where he had to turn. And then she looked at him funny, in a way he didn't understand. Not angry, just as if he could have been anyone at all, as if she'd heard the question he'd asked her in a cave.

"Don't be an asshole," she told him. "I don't need you to be an asshole, Marcus—I need you to be a friend. I really do."

She'd definitely left the house

"Let me just walk around the house for minute," Woody said. "Got a flashlight or something, Celine? —let me just check for tracks."

"It's snowing, honey, isn't it?" Tieneke asked.

Didn't matter really. If Dawn had left tracks anywhere they'd just be blown full in the wind, but a flashlight would pick them up—you could see them. That's what he told them.

Celine reached in the closet right there at the front door, pulled out a flashlight and a stocking cap. "You got gloves?" she said, and he told her he'd left them in the car, but that he'd be okay. She insisted, gave him a pair right there with the hat. "Just around the house," she told him. "No farther, you hear? You're not any younger either, Mr. Dekkers."

He smiled when, for the first time, she looked directly into his eyes the way she did so long ago. "If they go out to the road and disappear," he said, "then we'll all breathe a little easier."

He remembered not seeing any tracks when he came up to the house. He remembered thinking that if people ever visited the Burnetts, they likely used the door just off the driveway, which would mean they'd have to walk up the steps from the garage to the main floor of the house.

The beam from the flashlight ran out ahead of him like a pup as he walked back down the sidewalk toward the driveway, then took the driveway up to the door off the garage. That Celine's husband had left with the car was clear because stripes of snow lay across the cement. But no footprints coming out from the garage door.

To get around the north side of the house, he had to walk back up the driveway toward the road until the berm allowed him to get up to the next level. The wind howled. He was glad to have the stocking cap. He pulled the collar of his coat up higher, angry that he'd chosen looks over comfort when he left the house, something he should have never done, having lived on the plains for as many winters as he had. Stupid too.

There were no windows at all along the north side, must have been cleaning room or something on the far edge of the house, above the garage.

Then he saw the footprints and turned to follow them. Snow swirled and ripped at his face like a ratchet as the wind battered the side of the house. No boots either. It was downright stupid of him to leave with his school shoes on, even though they were chukkas. How many times hadn't he laid into his idiot students for their frigid weather carelessness, the way they'd come to school in shorts, the temps buried somewhere deeper than dead.

Dawn Burnett wasn't around, wasn't in the horse barn. The tracks said she'd gone inside, picked something up maybe—a jacket or something? —and then came back out, or so it seemed. He stood there puzzled, then looked at the house and realized the place was much bigger than he'd thought at first. Out back, much of the west exposure was glass, perfect for sunsets. Truth be told, Dawn Burnett hadn't had a really awful home life, but he had no idea that Celine and her husband were doing quite that well.

He flashed that light out in front of him as he slowly made his way back down the grade again toward a basement where there were doors. No lights shown from the west side of the house. If Dawn's bedroom were there somewhere—and that could have been true because there were two full floors of rooms—Celine must have doused the lights once her daughter had gone.

And how many times as a teacher hadn't he heard that from parents? —"I hope you can do something with my kid, because I can't." Made no difference either, Indian kid or white. The first time happened when he was a coach—it's exactly what the parent said, the father, when his son got in trouble with technical fouls. "Good luck. I haven't been able to handle him for two years"—something like that.

His cheeks were burning. He followed the tracks that had doubled back as if she wanted to get something from the barn and was now returning to her room—all of it from the back door so no one knew. He tried to pull the collar up even farther, but when he followed the west side of the house at least that awful wind was behind him. When he looked up, he realized the visibility wasn't encouraging.

Then he saw what he'd thought he'd find—a single pair of tracks out the doorway on the far end of the west side, small enough to be a woman's, going south. He looked around for another set, thinking he might have found her step-father's tracks somewhere, but there was nothing. They had to be Dawn's, and she'd definitely left the house. Snuck out. No question.

They were capped with snow already, but the imprints were clear, and he could follow them all the way around, up along the south side, where there were more windows, and then out to the front. There hadn't been that much snow with the last storm, so it hadn't been a problem for her to cross the lawn. The path was clear and definite, as if she knew where she was going, straight out to the road.

He looked back at the house and took a breath of relief because he knew that the worst possible outcome wasn't all that bad now because he could track her. He doubted that those tracks would disappear unless there was a ton more snow. As long as it was simply a ground blizzard, he could follow those tracks and find her, something he'd have to do.

He buttoned up the coat once more as he crossed their long lawn out to the tar, the blacktop. Because they lived where they did, some car would see her too, wouldn't just pass by—he was sure of that. And the tracks led out to the blacktop, not to the gravel on the other side of the house at the corner.

Once more, he looked back at the house. The wind stung him, with every breath took a bite out of his lungs. It would be smart now to get in the car, he thought. His taillights threw a red glare over the snow on the driveway where he'd left it running. He'd get KayLee and come out to where he'd followed the prints.

Just a bit farther, he thought. It would be like her to take off again in the cold—she'd done it before, walking this time. If all the speculation were right, she could have just walked away, but she'd have to have reason. He remembered what Shar had told him back in the hospital, how there was this place somewhere out west here, even farther, some place and some guy. Marcus was his name. The only Marcus he'd heard of was a kid who never came to school.

The footprints kept going. He had never tried to get close to Dawn. He'd stopped doing that intense stuff once his own kids had grown up, when it got to feel almost creepy for him to want to know more about kids' lives. The truth is, he got old, got less interesting to high school kids. The year she'd sat in his class hadn't been memorable because he had to wring assignments out of her just to get her through. Sometimes he wanted to tell her he'd been there at her baptism—he'd once said in front of a whole church that he'd do what he could to bring her up right, whatever the form said. He wanted to tell her he probably knew more about her than she'd ever guess.

But the kid never once made any kind of move toward him, no signal of recognition so he let her alone. Prudent, he thought. Maybe he shouldn't have. But then maybe he should have lived his whole life differently. Maybe he'd done it all wrong, staying out here, middle of nowhere.

Once more he looked back at the house, wondered what they were talking about now because there was so much to say and so much that would be hard to. The stocking cap was riding up on his head. With both hands, he pulled it back down, over his neck and under his collar and kept going.

Somehow the whole story of Teresa channeled into his mind and soul again as if out of nowhere, even though her dying happened midsummer, a time of year when the heat could be as deathly intense as the cold was now. It all came back in part because he had remembered then as he remembered just now how much he'd wanted his father to be there, his father who'd died just a year ago back then, his father the preacher because it was his father's story he remembered now, the story of forgiveness. We're closest to God, his father used to say—how many times hadn't he heard his old man say it, endlessly, tiringly—when we do what we know he does, when we forgive. And he'd given his father a bundle to work on. That was an understatement.

He was about 100 feet up the road when Dawn's footprints simply ended, south of the house, where it was clear she had gotten herself into some car and left. Someone had picked her up.

He turned back into the wind and followed his own tracks across the lawn and back to the door they'd come in. She wasn't out in the frozen cold. She wasn't trying to do what she didn't get done just last night. Somewhere, she was warm, he thought, and doubted that for her or for them the night was over.

I can't forgive him

"Why don't you two just sit down a minute?" Celine asked them, once Woody had gone outside to search.

They were standing at the door, scrunched uncomfortably into the corner, Tieneke thought, but she also understood Celine had lots to fear right then—they all did—from just a few stray words. She wasn't at all sure what KayLee might say. "He won't be long," Tieneke said, about Woody. "It's too cold for man or beast out there."

"I insist," Celine said, taking KayLee's arm. "C'mon—please?"

The two of them walked around the lattice railing set in the floor near the door and to the couch at the south end of the living room, where Celine offered KayLee a place, then looked back at Tieneke with the unmistakable frightened eyes of a child, like a high school kid who'd just determined that somewhere in her an actual baby stuck to her own very insides. She wore a hooded chenille sweat suit, dark and warm as flannel pajamas. By Tieneke's estimation she looked perfectly regal, queen-like, her hair straight back, then pinned into a single ponytail with a gorgeous beaded barrette she might well have made herself. Nothing of that beauty, even though there was lots of it, was enough to cover her fear.

"Maybe I could get you something?" Celine said, motioning her to sit down beside them.

"If you want to know, KayLee," Tieneke said, "Ms. Burnett here was just about the best artist I ever had during all those years I taught at Cottonwood." Tieneke pulled off her jacket, laid it over the handrail, and walked around the couch and into the living room, taking a chair beside an angular pole lamp, a touch of strict modernism, actually, in a room that was immensely attractive despite its almost overwhelmingly eclectic character, probably because of it.

From the look on KayLee's face, she seemed almost in love, no hesitancy whatsoever in her eyes. She was studying Celine as if somewhere in the lines of the woman's face she could read an answer to things.

Some doors had already opened. The moment KayLee had hugged Celine, it seemed to Tieneke that there could be no more pretense, no more questions about who knew what—which didn't make conversation any easier.

"KayLee sings," Tieneke told Celine, "she sings beautifully."

"I've heard her," Celine said, smiling. "I know."

KayLee seemed somewhere whole states of mind away.

"Two artists here I've got," Tieneke said, trying desperately to make conversation. And then, "I don't know Dawn," she said. "I've been out of teaching for five years already, so I don't know kids like I once did."

"You were a great teacher," Celine said. "If I were on the board, I wouldn't have let you quit." She smiled as if she were the one bringing comfort here. "And what are you doing these days?"

"Not much of anything, really," she said. "I should get back to it—I mean painting, not teaching. I'm past my prime that way."

Amazing, how time could alter things, she thought. There were times Tieneke had simply assumed that Celine Burnett—she was Celine Johnson then—thought her white art teacher was the scum of the earth. She didn't take criticism well, didn't finish assignments, got bored if a project took any longer than a few quick swipes on canvas. Somehow, over the years, Tieneke had come to recognize talent in a line, a stick-drawing. It was something no one could teach. Celine had it, a gift. Never had the girl shown any admiration or respect, even though Celine loved Woody.

"I can't believe you're not at it," Celine said. "I used to be intimidated by what you were doing—those landscapes? —they were stunning."

"Celine, you're just being nice—you used to think I was a clown."

"Not true," Celine said. "I swear."

The only memories she had of Celine Johnson were fraught with anger and disappointment, loss, save one, when she showed up at their place, pregnant. She was angry, her anger growing from the appalling recognition that finally something well beyond her was happening. Woody had asked about the father, and when she said Scotty Faber, her eyes flashed hatred. Neither of them were as surprised as Celine thought they would be. Hurt, yes—surprised, no.

"Don't ever be a teacher, KayLee," Tieneke said, playfully. "Takes way too many years to know you've done any good." All around her hung Celine's work, gorgeous. "Look at these things," she said. "If I had anything to do with them, my life has meaning."

"Enough," Celine told her. "There's so much more of you here than you'll ever know."

She tipped her head as if giving thanks. Celine's discomfort seemed to be easing in all the blessed small talk.

KayLee came up between them and stood straight as a warrior. "I want you to know," she said and then stopped, pulled things to a halt as she looked down at her hands and twisted the ring on her thumb. "I guess I don't know exactly how to say this, but I want you know, Ms. Burnett, that I'm sorry about what my father did so many years ago. I really am."

Celine sat perfectly still on the thick deep leather of that couch, just as black as Celine's sweat shirt and pants. She pulled her arm up over the back and swung around slowly. "You don't need to apologize for him," Celine said. "You can't really. Besides," she said, reaching for the girl's hand, "think of it this way--I have a daughter. I have Dawn."

"My father was married," KayLee told her, eyes specifically averted.

"I knew that," Celine told her. "Seventeen years ago, Cottonwood wasn't a whole lot different than it is right now."

"He was older," KayLee said.

"Three years— "

"And he was married."

"And I was stupid."

"And he was the one that shouldn't have been messing around."

"You don't mean to say that I should have?"

"He's my father," KayLee told her, angry now.

Tieneke knew there was absolutely nothing she could say at that point to moderate a conversation that belonged only to the two of them.

"You should be very proud of him," Celine asked her.

"But it's not the same—you and him," KayLee said.

"Because I was an Indian I didn't know any better?"

"No," KayLee told her. "That's not what I'm saying."

Sitting down beside someone who was breaking down just like KayLee was now was something Tieneke remembered all too well.

"I just hate my father," KayLee said, as if it made all the sense in the world. "Right now, all I care about is that I just hate him."

Celine let that one go. Tieneke started hoping Woody would find whatever he was looking for and make his snowy way back to the door.

"Not one thing that happened between the two of us was any more his fault than mine," Celine told KayLee. "If you're going to blame him, you need to blame me too."

"But he was the guy," KayLee told her.

"That makes it his fault?"

"He was older, and he was married, and you can't tell me that it was your fault—what happened. . ."

"Listen," Celine said, "I've got Dawn, and I love her."

"Well then it was a sin, wasn't it?" KayLee said. "You can't deny that, really—it was awful, what he did."

"What *we* did," Celine told her.

"Think of what he did to my mom," KayLee snapped. "I can't imagine what I'd do if my husband. . ." She brought her hands up to her face, drew her fingers beneath both eyes. "I mean, I'm not married or anything, but if I were, I just couldn't imagine what I'd do, you know, if he went out on me or whatever."

"I don't suppose anybody thinks about that on their wedding night," Celine told her, "—how all of that might end in some kind of misery." Tieneke could see that Celine wanted to edge closer to the girl, but she knew she still couldn't. "No married woman I know of anyway—know what I mean? Nobody thinks the worst until it happens." And then she looked at Tieneke, almost as if to beg her old teacher to get into it with her, to help the girl make some sense of things.

"Something in me just died when my Teresa did, and she wasn't even mine—I mean, not by blood," Tieneke told them both. "I don't care what kind of trouble she might be in, I'd take Dawn home tonight in a heartbeat."

KayLee looked up at her as if maybe it was the first thing she'd heard that made sense. "It doesn't change what he did to Mom," she said. "Nothing you can say changes that in the least bit, and I can't forgive him."

Tieneke knew very well that Celine knew why Scotty was out drinking back then, how things had fallen apart at home. She brought two fingers up to her lips as if to tell Tieneke that going that next step was certainly not her job, nor her prerogative, nor her wish. The only human being on the face of the earth who could finish the whole story was Karin—no one else.

Cautiously, Celine moved across the couch and put a hand on KayLee's thigh. "Sweetheart," she said, "take it from someone who really, really knows—'I can't forgive' is something you don't ever want to say, don't even want to think."

"Are you a Christian?" KayLee said, looking up at her.

"I don't know that you have to be a Christian to know that," she said. "If we can't forgive, I'm not sure how we can be human."

For a moment, there on the couch, it seemed almost as if KayLee got smaller, climbed into some small, dark place within herself. "You can't blame me for being angry," she said. "Honestly and truly, you can't blame me for feeling what I do."

"I can't blame you," Celine said. "But maybe we can slow you down a little. I just think 'I can't forgive' is too brutal."

"But I can't," KayLee said.

"Next July, we'll be way hot out here, you know? We'll be hoping for rain, but the world will be gray and tan and almost lifeless." Tieneke told her. "It'll be a whole different thing a year from now—and two years, nothing will look quite the same. We'll have forgotten about this infernal cold."

"Does she know?" KayLee asked, meaning Dawn.

Celine nodded.

"How come she never told me?"

"I suppose nobody knows exactly how our own stories are going to play out," Celine said, "not until they go the way they do."

"You tell her not to tell me?"

Once again, Celine nodded.

"Why do I have to be the last to know?"

Celine shrugged her shoulders. "Somebody always does, I guess."

"I feel so damned stupid," KayLee said. "I feel like the biggest fool of all, and it pisses me off. It just flat pisses me off, you know?"

Just then, Woody came in the door.

It took just a few minutes and the three of them were on their way. Both Dawn and Tieneke hugged Celine long and hard when they left, probably for the very same reasons, Tieneke thought. To her at least, it felt a little warmer in the car.

She told herself, in silence, that it was time for the child to visit with her father.

Another woman all together

Once they got in the old house where this woman named Coby lived, Marcus wished it was still afternoon because inside of a half hour he could find a ridge somewhere not that far away and cut the woman a real tree instead of the plastic piece of crap she had on her kitchen table, creepy thing with the price tag still wound with bare wire into the branches. Must have picked it up on sale at Pamida this close to Christmas, he thought. But he kept that to himself because right away he knew he was in a place he didn't know all that well. Once the two of them started talking, it was like he didn't exist, like being in that detention room, Dawn and that Coby really into each other, making him feel like somebody else's shadow.

This Coby was really fine for an older woman—short hair, really short, like a guy's short, and she was as tall as he was, half a head taller than Dawn. Not that old. Her eyes weren't dark brown. They were brighter, but she was an Indian all right. Dawn told him and he could see it.

The look on her face was all he needed to see to understand why Dawn wanted to talk to her—deep as an ocean, deep as a well, sweetwater eyes that took someone a long ways in. Sometimes you just knew who was good people, he thought—it's something you just get.

Still, when she looked at Dawn and reached out for her, it wasn't hard for him to pick up that he could just as well not have been there. So much of something strange there was in that look that it scared him for a moment. What did he know about this woman anyway? —not a damned thing, he thought. She was older too—I mean, he told himself, who knows these days? Maybe she's got other shit in mind here, is what he thought. He couldn't help it.

She turned to him. "And this is Marcus?" she said. Then she smiled, as if it was a planned-out second act or something. Then, "Got a last name?"

"Not that it matters," he told her. "Pritchard is what I go by." When Marcus kept his hands to home even though the woman reached out to take his, that sweet look on her face and those shining eyes didn't disappear.

"He's my little savior," Dawn told her. "And more too."

Surprised him.

"Where do you go to school, Marcus?" the woman asked him.

He pointed his shoulder as if the high school was next door. "Here," he told her.

"When he goes," Dawn added.

"Hey, listen," Coby said. "Me and the honcho are a kind of thing—you know, Sterrett?"

"A 'thing'?" he said.

She raised a leveled hand and shook it as if to say it was borderline. "No big-time commitments, but I can get you in big trouble if I want."

"I already am," he said, and Coby smiled. She meant it as a joke. He knew that.

"Marcus called me in," Dawn told her, pointing at him with a thumb, then hugging him, her arms around him. "He's the guy called 911."

Something went out from those eyes just then, something hit a switch, some joy fell.

"I stayed with her until I saw the EMTs," he told her. "The red lights. She don't know that—she wasn't awake."

The shine came back. What he said changed things.

"Well, don't just stand there," Coby the saint told them, "—get yourselves out of those huge jackets."

What he saw of her then—the way she talked to Dawn, the way Dawn minded her—reminded him of what an older sister might have been like, pretty much what he'd imagined her to be when Dawn was talking to her on the phone—more than a little older, someone you can trust. Coby took hold of

Dawn around the shoulders when she wanted them to go into the room with the TV, then reached for him with her right hand too, as if she didn't want to forget him. That was nice, both of them in tow.

He hadn't remembered seeing her around town, and it looked to him as if she hadn't been around long anyway—her pictures were sitting on the floor beneath the spot where eventually someone would hang them. He figured they were Indian stuff, but not stallions in the moonlight. No war paint, but the colors were Injun colors, he told himself. Her house was an old, low ceilinged place, all the rooms a half inch from square and tiny, cracker-box rooms. Reminded him a ton of grandma's, not unlike their place too, except maybe half as big. Little chicken coop of a house for one person maybe, a one-suitcase house.

Coby sat Dawn in the chair under the lamp, then took the rocker across the room, a tiny room. He sat on the couch himself, a fleece blanket over the pillows beneath him—for warmth, he thought, although a couple of cats could have kept the place steamy, he thought—it was that small.

"How come you're a nurse but you're not a nurse?" Dawn said.

"Long story," the woman said, looking at both of them but mostly at Dawn. Still, she was careful not to let him get out of the picture. "That's why you came here? —to hear me talk about me?" She meant that as a joke, but you couldn't tell it, he thought, not at least until she laughed to make sure they understood. "You said there was something you wanted to ask me."

Dawn looked at him in a fashion she never had before, in a way that made him think she wanted him out of the room, the only room with a TV. He wasn't an idiot.

"I really ought to get some gas," he told them. "That old truck keeps me poor."

"It's not about him?" the woman asked.

"About Marcus?" Dawn said.

Coby sort of shrugged her shoulders.

He felt naked. "I got to smoke," he said. "Dirty habit."

"He doesn't smoke," Dawn told her. "But I want to know how it is you're really a nurse when you aren't a nurse."

Coby sat back in that rocker and started moving just a little. She brought both hands up in front of her. "I got a license," she said, "but it's like I don't want to drive. I mean, I'm legal, but I'm not getting behind the wheel."

"You had some accident?" Dawn asked.

"You might say that."

It was like begging a cat out of a tree, Marcus thought. Good looking though, so much so that he just assumed there had to be a man in this story somewhere, someone she cared about. Pretty thing like her wasn't going to get away on any reservation he knew of.

"With some guy?" Dawn said. "You said you were getting over something—that's what you told me. Some guy in this somewhere?"

The woman named Coby took this giant breath and came up smiling, not as if she didn't want to say, didn't want to open something up, but instead as if she knew it was going to take something out of her to go there. "I should never have told you that, Dawn," she told her. "I don't know what got into me, but I shouldn't have said it. It's not my job to tell people what they don't need to hear, you know? It was very unprofessional." She tapped the arms of that rocker with her fingers, took another deep breath, as if she was ashamed somehow.

"But you did," Dawn said, "and now I want to know."

"I think I left my pick up running," he said.

"I know you didn't," Dawn told him.

"You can stay, Marcus," the woman said. She put on this face, calm and steady; but it was the first time since he'd come into the house that he got a sense that she was just another nurse or teacher, someone who knew when to pull on a mask--that sort of thing. Wasn't a mask. She was scared to say much—he could see that.

A cat he hadn't seen jumped off a stool in the corner across the room, stretched her front paws over the rug, and looked up at him as if he was a person of interest.

Coby leaned forward on the rocker. "There was an accident, and I was on—I was on emergency," she said. "Small town, like this—up north in Minnesota—a little bigger maybe. Three stop lights, you know?" She was trying to make a joke, but neither of them laughed. She stopped flexing her fingers, but kept them up front of her face. "And it was bad--it was a bad accident and I was there. I was working."

"Somebody died?" Dawn said.

And then Coby did something with her face, pulled it into a smile, then a frown, then a smile again, as if she were exercising, as if she couldn't decide which face to wear. It was nervousness, something Marcus couldn't help reading as this woman being plain-old scared. Her eyes fixed on something somewhere across the room—no, they fixed on something farther away than that, he thought, somewhere across time.

"Two people died and another one was badly injured," she said.

"And you saw it?" Dawn said.

"It was my shift."

Long ago already Marcus had told himself he could never be a doctor because he didn't think he could take that bloody stuff. Once when his father got into trouble, he was himself the only person around, and there was blood all over he'd never really forgotten. He was just a kid.

Things were starting to make sense. This story came out slowly, in an Indian way. This morning this woman had hinted at something Dawn had gone for, and that's why the two of them were here in this little old house, no bigger than his grandma's. Whatever this woman had said, it did something to Dawn because here they were, after all. Dawn needed this woman, this Coby the saint.

For a while, nobody said anything, and the silence settled in around them in a good way, the furnace a constant whirr as if the motor was right there beneath their feet. An old fan was spinning away from the ceiling, keeping the heat from pooling up there. The cat stood up again and walked over to him, as if he was the cat's only source of heat.

Nurses got used to blood-and-guts already in school, he figured, where they probably showed films like drivers ed, people without arms and legs and heads or whatever. That wasn't it. There was something else. Then it came to him--*she knew who got killed,* he thought. That was the big deal. *She knew that torn-up body in front of her.*

"I was a piece-of-cake patient—with what you've seen, I guess," Dawn said, feeling around for the bump on her head. "I was in good shape when they took me in. Just a little cold."

"Nobody's a piece of cake," Coby said.

"Two people were dead?" Dawn said, leading.

He couldn't help it. "She knew the guy," he told Dawn. "What happened is that she knew the dead guy." He pointed a thumb at Coby. "That's got to be it. Maybe it was a woman. Your mom or something?"

Coby smiled as if maybe he'd saved her from having to say something it just hurt way too much to give up. The room was so small she could have touched him across the magazine table. She had to reach a little, and she did—she touched his arm for a moment.

"You were seeing this guy?" Dawn asked.

She nodded.

"He was like your boyfriend?"

She nodded again.

"Not your husband?"

She shook her head.

"Boyfriend though—ring and everything?"

She nodded.

"Aw, shit," Dawn asked. "You loved him I bet?"

This woman named Coby looked away, a tiny fake smile across her face.

This nurse is in a nurse's suit, a white one—that's what Marcus imagined right then. She's watching an EMT pull this guy out of the back of the ambulance, and she goes to check his pulse or whatever and there's a river of blood already, so much that she doesn't think to look into his face because so much of him is leaking and spurting, and she's working to stop it until she looks up and oh, my Lord, it's him, it's this guy she loves. Aw, shit, he tells himself. He can feel it way down inside his ribs. It would have killed her. Just like that she's fighting for his life, fighting some part of him that wants to die or something. Fighting for her own.

Dawn said. "I'm so sorry."

That's where things sat for a couple of really long minutes. He had nothing to say and wouldn't have said anything even if he did because there are times when only silence makes clear what needs to be heard. When the cat jumped up beside him, she went first thing for Marcus's lap, did some circles like cats do, and then laid there, purred like a maniac siren.

This Coby had the radio on in the kitchen. He hadn't noticed it before, but it was on to some station with violins and all of that, just kind of soft but loud enough to be heard because just for a moment the furnace had stopped running and nothing moved and nothing was said and his mind was kicking out all these god-awful pictures. Christmas music. His grandma used to say that sometimes silence makes the finest quilts. Sometimes you just pull it in around you.

"When all this happen?" Dawn asked her in a voice that didn't seem like hers.

"Long ago," Coby told them, trying to smile again.

"How long?"

You don't trust it when a woman like Coby waits to answer a question like the one Dawn asked, because she damn well knows how long it's been and therefore she's just figuring she has to find the best way to say it to whoever wants to know. And when you're a kid you get lied to often enough, too, as if you aren't old enough to know the truth—that kind of thing. What you get is some cooked-up lie or some kind of spin. Never the truth.

Still, if he had to describe the smile she wore just then, it would have to be something sincere, even though it locked out what he figured she was probably feeling in bringing up all that sadness. She sat back a little, started rocking again, just a little, drew in a good-sized breath. "I went back to school, Took me a year or more, I guess, to get a teaching degree because I didn't know if I ever wanted to do that again, didn't want to be anywhere near an emergency room." She blew on her hands as if they were cold, which they couldn't have been—not really. "I always thought I'd be a teacher, and when I decided to be a nurse I didn't know if it was the right thing." She took hold of both arm rests of that rocker. "And then I looked for a job—and this one came up."

He felt cheated. "You're a teacher?" Marcus said.

"Third grade," she said. "And it's been almost three years—I mean, since the accident." And then she said really quickly. "And now I'm here."

"Then he died?" Dawn said.

Coby nodded.

If he ever found Dawn that way, messed up or dead, he'd kill himself. Right then and there, he'd swallow a bullet.

He would. He wanted to leave, to go out and cut that woman a real Christmas tree—he didn't care how cold it was, how dark.

"You loved him?" Dawn said.

"I did."

He didn't know why Dawn had to ask her that because it seemed perfectly clear--else why all the shittin' agony? —he thought.

"What was he like?" Dawn said.

He didn't want to hear, and he didn't want this woman to have to go through everything—like what color his hair was and whether or not he was a good dancer or whatever, what a great guy he was, what an angel, which all dead people are. Marcus had always figured that everybody had a sadness tank and a needle somewhere that made it damn clear when you shouldn't have to have anymore because you just had enough. Like Dawn, really. There she stood at the café trying to get her father's attention, and it was like the asshole didn't even know who she was, didn't care, didn't even look. Kills a person.

Coby the teacher took a deep breath. "I don't know what to say exactly—how to describe him, except that I loved him."

He wondered whether or not she saw that guy die, whether he was dead when he got to the hospital already, already gone—or if she had him in her arms when he breathed his last, that she actually felt his very, very last breath. He'd never felt that. Someday maybe, he thought. Maybe this boyfriend of hers died three days later. Maybe not. He didn't know whether to hope she was there with him. He stuck his fingers deep in cat fur.

"I had to get out of Dodge," Coby told them. "You know what I mean? Too many memories."

"I know," Dawn told her, and then looked up at him for the first time in a long while, just for a moment as if to be sure he was still there. And then back to Coby. "I want to go to Seattle, maybe," she said. "Someday maybe, to Portland or somewhere up there in all the trees."

"I like trees," Coby told her. "There are lots more in Minnesota." She looked at him. "How 'bout you, Marcus?" she said. "You like the Pacific northwest?"

"Never been there," he said.

"So where do you dream about?" she said.

He didn't have dreams--not about *where* anyway, just about *how*, about living easy and having people around him who were there most the time. Maybe do some woodcarving or something—he didn't know. He'd like to make things with his hands. "I don't have no crystal ball," he told her. "Or at least I don't see nothing in it. No pine trees anyway, except those in the ridges around here—you know." He thought about that Christmas tree again. "I could show you some," he said. "I could cut you something really nice that would fit just perfect in that corner there with the mirror." He pointed across the room. "I mean a Christmas tree. You wouldn't have to put up that ugly thing you got in the kitchen."

"Got it on sale," she told him.

"They should have paid you," he said.

"This is maybe your first Christmas alone?" Dawn asked her.

She shook her head. "A couple more already but I don't remember much because mostly I was," she pointed at her temple,
'because mostly I wasn't thinking about anything other than what happened and what was over. Silent night if there ever was."

"His name?" Dawn asked, and Coby told her his name was Jonathan, which Dawn said was a great name. "He have a family?" she asked, and Coby nodded again. "They loved him?" Dawn said.

Coby hunched her shoulders as if to say yes and why do you ask?

"He was Indian?" Dawn said.

"Like me, just partly."

"Me too," she said. "And Marcus."

"You?"

"Yes, me," he said. "All of us then?"

He'd never seen Dawn look like she did right then. It was as if she was another girl altogether because something almost poison had emptied, something ugly she seemed to have left behind. She was looking at Coby, but not seeing her, imagining what had happened in some Minnesota hospital, putting herself there.

"It was hard going, I bet," she said. "Must have been."

"Still is, Dawn—just that the pain isn't quite so sharp." Then she got to her feet. "I promised hot chocolate, right? Some kind of Indian giver if I don't."

He could see why Dawn wanted to stop over and talk to this woman.

"But you're the one wanted to tell me something," she said. "You didn't come here to hear all of my troubles."

He didn't need to be in on the conversation that was about to go on. "Got to be an idiot not to be able to make hot chocolate," he told them, getting to his feet. The least he could do was clear out of the room. "You got powder or syrup?" he asked Coby.

"Packets," she told him. "I steal them from motels. Can you boil water?"

"Sure," he said. "So what's the cat's name as long as we're friends?" he asked her.

She smiled. She did a lot of that, this woman the saint. "Lexi," she told him.

Okay name for a cat, he thought. He told himself he'd get them each a cup of hot chocolate and then head out to the ridge to cut Coby a real tree. That's the way he had it figured.

Did my dad not love her?

What Scotty Faber did that night was done with the very best of intentions, intentions he thought to be the course of action God almighty in all divine wisdom wanted his servant to take, or so Tieneke thought. That was exactly where he went wrong.

Scotty Faber never questioned what he considered the paths of righteousness. He thought himself so blessed with the mind of Christ that he forgot his feet of clay, or those of his precious daughter. That's the way Tieneke saw it anyway.

His first reaction to the news Woody had delivered that afternoon hadn't been all that upsetting. That he was Dawn's unacknowledged father is something he'd known for 16 years, and it wasn't the first time Dawn had been in trouble. He had come a long way from the mess he'd been in when he and Celine created that beautiful kid, so far that this new, born-again Scotty Faber, their neighbor, one of the most successful businessmen around, was barely recognizable as the same guy who'd spent entire weekends on binges that barely slowed by Tuesday.

Scotty Faber had been, in every sense—even in identity—reborn. If the man carried guilt or sadness, she'd not seen it. For years, she'd simply assumed he truly had been forgiven. That he was, didn't mean Dawn Burnett was any less a real human being. And if that was true, she thought, then a man like Scotty probably couldn't help wondering what forgiveness was anyway?

But this time—maybe it was the way Dawn had ditched that car last night—this time something changed in him, Tieneke thought; maybe he'd simply assumed the whole story had been stowed blessedly away somehow.

Sometimes the knottiness gets simpler to parse when you've got a ton of it behind you, she told herself now that she was retired. Scotty Faber would say that Dawn's ditching her life the way she did was part of some divine plan; but Tieneke wasn't so sure. When they buried their own foster daughter, they stopped attributing everything to God's divine will.

What happened to Karin and Scotty *after* the disaster of those first two years of marriage could only be seen as a miracle, two people groping through darkness only to be brought by divine hand into abundant new light, as miraculous as any hard drinker putting it all behind him, as Woody once did.

But Dawn had been out of sight and out of mind for years. When Celine came back with her new husband, Scotty's child came with, a girl who became a young woman whose troubled soul wobbled along beneath burdens those who knew her story—even her father—could feel but not still.

Most frightening, Tieneke thought, was what might have happened if some kid had not called 911 and Dawn Burnett had simply fallen off into sleep and death like so many others, kids, far too many, most all Native. Her death would have ended everything. She and Woody wouldn't have been out here, trying to run down a story that would have simply ended in a ditch. Scotty would have been home free. Even with KayLee in the car with them, Tieneke couldn't help thinking how easily we fool ourselves into seeing lollypops where there aren't any, delusions that make us believe the world is or could be just honky-dory.

"Did my father *not* love her?" KayLee said as they left Celine Burnett alone in that home in the country.

It was too blame cold to talk it through. That KayLee still blamed him was understandable. She had seen Celine Burnett broken, and had never seen anything like that in her own father, in Dawn's own birth father.

KayLee had not seen Celine the way her father had on the night Dawn was conceived either, a gorgeous young chick drunk and footloose, begging for love as passionately as she'd been doing just in that country home of theirs, but a whole different genre.

Once they were back in the car and all was quiet again, what came to mind was a hidden camera in a bank office in a mall, a camera that had caught two kids, bank robbers, as they demanded cash. They were wearing celebrity sunglasses, but nothing else in disguise. Dozens of kids who went to high school with them could have ID-ed them in a moment, and did. They were girls, young women; and because they were, their faces appeared on every cable news station in the country that night—"hotties in a heist." Had they been boys, the story would not have made local news—man bites dog, girls rob bank. Two high school girls as bank robbers is just plain startling because unthinkable.

It was even more unthinkable to KayLee that Karin, her mother, could have played a leading role in a line from a third-rate country-western song, as it was difficult for people to believe a couple of high school girls had tried to knock off a bank. The whole mess simply had to be started by a man—her own father—who couldn't keep his tools in the box in the back of the truck.

Celine was striking in a way that older women can be, and KayLee could not help but see that. Even with a daughter out of control, Celine still seemed on top of things. She seemed to gain in strength and composure so that even if she was hurting, she seemed to be suffering in dignity.

"You think my dad loved her?" she asked once they were on the road back to town.

Neither she nor Woody knew how to answer. KayLee was in the back seat then, which maybe made it easier for Tieneke—not having to see her face.

"You could ask him," Woody told her, softly—no edge. "But I wouldn't. It's no fun digging something out of the landfill."

"You were both there," KayLee snapped back. "You were both around, Mr. Dekkers, weren't you? You've been in school forever, and they both went to Cottonwood—both Mom and Dad. I know they did."

"What do teachers know?" he said.

"A heckuva a lot," she said angrily.

Once again, the car got quiet.

January cold in the middle of nowhere can rob the landscape of its spacious glory. At night, it gets so cold that nothing, Tieneke thought, not the hills or the bluffs or the snaking rivers even get on the map. All you do is stay down and out of bitterness that kills everything but buffalo, like Celine said.

Nothing was moving anywhere. Nothing. Up above, the moon lit up the world, so what you could see all around was little more than emptiness in swirling snow that makes things scary, she thought, even though they'd been living there in the blasted bosom of all that naked openness for years. She didn't know why exactly. Maybe only this—that the land is bigger than they are.

"Where are we going?" Tieneke asked sweetly. What the girl still needed to know, at least with respect to her dad and mom was a story that was not theirs to explain. They'd tried to bring the kids together—what KayLee wanted. No one knew where Dawn was.

"Time to hang it up," Woody said, flipping a hand toward her. "Somebody picked her up. She's not out walking, so we don't have to worry about her freezing or anything. I just don't know if there's much more we can do." He reached for the radio, but kept it off. "Nothing about this is going away, KayLee," he told her. "All the drama will still be here in the morning."

"I still want to talk to her," she said.

"It's not the looking that bothers me," Woody told her. "Car's warm, we got lots of gas, I can turn on the radio—we could look all night. That'd be fine with me."

"Won't be fine with me," Tieneke said.

They'd already taken this whole thing as far as the two of them could—they were not the principals in this drama, bit players at best. The whole rotten business had fallen into their laps, and Woody'd been right in thinking that if they'd just bring the two girls together, if they could get that much accomplished, the rest of the story's telling might well have taken care of itself. But Tieneke had no desire to lie. If KayLee were to ask them, flat out, some of the questions she had to have in her mind right then, she knew she'd lie through her teeth. This young lady needed to hear the truth from her own mom and dad.

"What do you suggest?" Woody asked her. Tieneke reached over to grab his arm as if to tell him she had no plan. What she wanted to do was go home. The girl ought to make it a sleepover at their place, stay around for a couple days and wait for things to melt.

KayLee pulled out her cell phone and started punching numbers. "Dad?" she said when he picked up his cell.

Neither of them could hear him.

No, she told him, she hadn't been to a ball game. She wasn't sure who won, she said, and the ball game was the farthest thing from her mind right then, because she wanted to talk to him— "I *need* to talk to you," she said, not *want*.

He must have been in his truck because she said something about not going home right then because she told him she wanted to talk to him alone, not with Mom around and that he should meet them at their house, at the Dekkers'.

The child had always been so deferential—sweet and unpresuming. She'd taken off her shoes when she came for piano lessons even if it hadn't rained and the yard was crying for moisture. It was so much *not* like her to force herself on them that Tieneke wasn't so much shocked as simply obliging, maybe from fear.

"I don't want Mom because this is something between you and me just," she told him. "No, you can't call her—you can't tell her—because if she knows, she'll be there," she said. "She loves you—I know that."

She told him they were west of town somewhere and asked Woody where.

"Fifteen minutes maybe," he told her, and she told her dad as much.

He must have told her that he'd had Bible study because she asked him if it was any scripture verse in particular that night. The way she said it had an edge that could have come up out of that phone and opened a wound across his face. He said something and then she boiled over. "Never mind what I know or don't know!" she told him. "I'll tell you this—I don't know my own father." End of conversation Tieneke didn't want the girl going into things with her father as if he was the Devil incarnate.

"He was at Bible study," KayLee told them, laughing. "Makes sense," she said. "Just right, don't you think? I'm getting my heart loaded up to here with his damned lies, he's got his nose in a Bible."

KayLee was in the back seat, but Tieneke swore she could just about hear her spit. "You get it, don't you?" she said. "I mean, like, you know what's tearing me up?"

"We get it," Tieneke said.

And then a ton came out in raw-boned curses Tieneke thought totally unbecoming but greatly understandable on this cold night. A torrent. Words swarmed out like bats from a harrowing cave of passion and anger, a blizzard in gusts that screamed around the corners of everything that wasn't simply blown away. And all about her dad— "the son of bitch—this," and "'the fucker' that." Just so much bile.

Woody reached for the radio when she quit, punched a couple of buttons, and ended up with something sort of bluesy, which he turned down low enough so that it wouldn't interfere. "It's a good thing you got that all out, girl," he told her, "because now it isn't inside, and you can get on with life." He said it with just the right spin. "And you know what else, girl?" he said. "Now it doesn't have to be said again."

"I just started," she said.

"Not in our house," he said, "—not in our house those things aren't going to be said, you hear?"

"What?" she said, sharp as glass.

"I'll throw you out if you want to talk like that to him," Woody said. "Nobody deserves that."

"You're a man."

"And I'm a woman," Tieneke said, "and I'm with Woody." She reached around the seat and grabbed the girl's arm. "We open the doors and all that shit will spill out into the cold and freeze and fall apart like thin ice." With that, she cracked her window. "If people wonder what you said, they'll have to thaw out the chunks." The window came all the way down. "There," she said, "good riddance. It's gone."

They came back into town from the west, drove up to Main Street, turned left, and headed north past the car dealers and trailer courts and the Farm Supply, nothing but street lights and businesses, and those Christmas lights the town puts on light poles every year, most on, a few off. Hardly a car on the road, or truck for that matter.

They were down in the river flats when, in all the silence, she wished she could grab that girl's arm again, as she had when first they got into the car. Maybe it could calm her.

She was alone

What Coby hadn't told Marcus was where he could find those motel packets of hot chocolate, which cupboard or whatever. And besides, it wasn't the best hot chocolate in the world either, that cheap motel stuff probably. Maybe there'd be some choice, he thought, maybe one of those Hershey plastic squeeze bottles for pouring over ice cream. He opened the fridge and looked around. Wouldn't take all day to hunt a little. She didn't have that many cupboards.

"Listen, Dawn," Coby said—the front room was all of twenty feet away. "I wish I hadn't told you all of that because you didn't come here for me, you came here for you."

Didn't take a moment for Dawn to say what she did. "I wasn't raped," she told Coby.

"That's over," Coby told her. "I started to believe you this morning already. We just passed that one up. But that's not it, is it?"

Soup, lots of it, even boxes of mix. This Coby must love soup, he told himself. Women do, he figured. He was surprised, no shocked, when Dawn said what she did next.

"I just saw my father," Dawn told her. "Just now I saw my old man."

He hadn't thought it was all that scary or whatever.

"I just now saw him, and he didn't even know me," she said.

"Your father?" Coby said.

Nothing for a while. He opened the fridge and looked for milk.

"Maybe a half hour ago I walked right past him, and the bastard never saw me," she said. "Right here in town—at the café."

Half-and-half she had. He waited to move because it was all quiet out there until finally Coby said, "I'm sorry." And then, "He's a white guy?"

"You don't have to be sorry," Dawn told him. "I never once spoke to him in my whole life. I never felt anything for him at all, not one shittin' thing."

Marcus let that one go, even though he had just seen her angrier than spit. It wasn't *nothing* that she felt.

"What about Marcus?" Coby asked.

He couldn't believe that they'd forgot he was just in the next room. He shrugged his shoulders.

"His mother lives somewhere southwest—in Arizona, maybe—maybe New Mexico," Dawn told her. "Where's your old lady, Marcus?" she yelled as if he was like out somewhere on the reservation.

"New Mexico," he said, just as loud.

"His father—I don't know where he lives but sometimes he comes around."

"Not so often," he added, still staring into the fridge.

The whirr of the furnace started in again, and he could feel the draft from the vents behind him coming up in swell of air just a couple of feet away from the door. He shut the fridge. The music from a Bluetooth speaker had a really heavy sound. It was on a shelf in the corner above the kitchen table, parked right there beside her iPad.

"You've been alone mostly, Marcus?" Coby asked him from the other room.

He really didn't want to be part of this. "My grandma says I ought to go live with her," he told her.

"You live where then?"

He figured he'd let Dawn answer that one because it included LeRoy and that was a whole different tale. He waited, but Dawn wasn't talking.

"Out in the country—on an acreage with a guy," he told her. "Don't matter really."

He wanted to leave, to disappear out whatever back door Ms. Coby had, to go somewhere and hide, to be by himself. But he was trapped in a kitchen. There Dawn sat in a room so small not even six people could sit down without taking out the television, which was turned off just then, an old one. She didn't even have a flat screen. He didn't think that was even possible anymore.

"You told me there was a question you wanted to ask," Coby said to Dawn, and she was right. Dawn wanted something from Coby, something he figured she wasn't about to tell him, for whatever reason, but probably because he was a guy who'd just last night slept with her. There was that in it somehow too, he knew. Didn't understand really, but it was female stuff.

But you couldn't expect a guy not to listen in either, he thought. If he was going to make hot chocolate just a room away, she couldn't expect him not hear whatever she couldn't otherwise tell him. Besides, he'd already begun to think that it was going to be hard for him to take if Dawn really up and took off for Washington or Portland or whatever, someplace with trees, for shit sake—without him. It rained a lot up there, and you had to really get used to living without the sun and what it was going to be like for a chick named Dawn to grow gills?

He cranked up the volume just loud enough on the speaker to try to cover the conversation next door, but what he heard was a lot of nothing. It wasn't easy for him to imagine what Dawn wanted to tell Coby. It was about what had happened between her and LeRoy—not that exactly either because she wasn't bawling about LeRoy's dropping her. That wasn't it. Their breaking up was something he really didn't think mattered to her all that much, maybe because he had burned that out of her last night. It was this baby that was the problem, the one she got rid of.

"I was going to have a baby," she told Coby.

Here it comes, he told himself.

"I was going to have a baby I didn't want. I was stupid and silly because I know about how girls get pregnant, but I just figured it wouldn't ever happen to me because I'm not that regular, you know—never have been. I'm a mess." She stopped for a moment. "I'm flat out stupid."

That wasn't news and it wasn't the whole story.

In the cupboard above the fridge, of all places, sure enough, he found a box full of the free stuff: sugar, creamer, hot chocolate, tea. Plenty of bags.

"Funny thing," she said. "I just sort of knew it maybe a week before I took one of those tests, you know? —maybe more. I just sort of knew it. That happen much? You're a nurse."

He could hear Coby laugh. "'Course it happens—not always, but sometimes."

"You ever get pregnant?" Dawn asked her.

He felt as if he should deliberately make some noise to remind them he was there.

Coby laughed. "No," she said, almost as if he were supposed to hear it.

"You a virgin?" Dawn said.

She didn't say, but Dawn went on.

"I just sort of knew," Dawn told her. "Weird, huh? So when I took the test I wasn't surprised, you know, to see those two lines. Wasn't shocked. Maybe I should have been, but I wasn't." She didn't wait for Coby to say anything. "This guy—LeRoy," she said. "He knew someone who knew someone who knew someone—it was that kind of thing."

Coby must have looked at her strangely because Dawn filled her in.

"He was the guy," she said. "He was like the father."

"*Like*?" Coby asked.

"*Was*," she told her.

He cranked up the gas on the stove and fire popped, then pulled out a pan from the drawer beneath the stove, put enough water in it for a couple of cups, and stuck it on the fire.

"He knows," Dawn said, and he could tell she meant him, Marcus, in the kitchen.

"Won't be long now," he said from the other side of the wall.

"All of this is over?" Coby said, very slowly. This was it, he thought. She had the operation and everything and she felt like pure shit now that there was no baby in her. That's the way he had it figured.

No response. Dawn didn't say a thing, but she must have nodded.

"I'm so sorry," Coby told her.

Quiet.

More quiet.

Bubbles started to rise in the water, flames rising around the sides of the little saucepan he'd pulled out of the drawer beneath the stove.

"I had friends," Coby said. "I know it's not easy, no matter what people say."

He couldn't hear a thing, but he wondered if Dawn was crying, which wouldn't have been like her. Having a baby inside, he thought—it was something he couldn't imagine. And then all of a sudden gone. That too.

And then Coby said, "But you and this LeRoy guy—you're now over with him too? —is that right? No more?"

Dawn must have nodded.

"And now you've got this new guy, like you said—you got Marcus here?" she said.

"New squeeze," she said again. "Yeah, new squeeze."

Somehow the way she said it, the angle, didn't make him feel good. When the water was boiling, he poured the hot chocolate mix into two cups, then followed with the hot water.

And then she told Coby something that he hadn't expected—not for a minute.

"I didn't go through with it," Dawn told her.

He wasn't sure he heard that right. LeRoy himself told him how he'd told her to get it done, how he'd lined it up for her, how he'd taken care of it, even promised to pay the bill or whatever. It had never dawned on Marcus that it wasn't a done deal.

"I was going to," she said, "but I didn't. It was harder than I thought—I mean actually going in. I guess I just kept thinking maybe it would go away or something. I don't know."

He grabbed both cups and started out of the kitchen, then waited just around the corner.

"You're not pregnant, Dawn," Coby told her—it wasn't a question either. "That would have showed up this morning. We would have known. I mean, in the hospital."

He stood still just behind the door.

"I know that," she said. "I lost it."

He wasn't sure what that meant.

"Oh, Dawn," Coby said. "Oh, my dear. Oh, sweetheart. Oh, honey. Oh, child."

He didn't get it, didn't understand, but when he turned the corner into the front room of that little house, Dawn was already in Coby's arms, hugging, holding on, Dawn crying, bawling out real tears. Lots of tears. He'd never seen her that way. Couldn't believe it.

He could have been a servant or a waiter in a café because what they were doing, how they were holding on to each other, it reminded him of that movie about the ocean liner that went down, the big one, the *Titanic*. That's what he thought of. He didn't remember seeing two people hold each other like that, as if waves were already coming up and the two of them were already sliding away.

He put the hot chocolates on coasters Coby had in place on that coffee table, pictures of some city skyline. Neither of them looked up. He was an outsider. He wanted to be there for Dawn when she needed him, but right now he wasn't supposed to be stuck in this little room in this little house, and no matter how cold it was outside he knew dang well that what he needed to do was get lost somewhere. He knew where he could cut a decent tree out of a pine ridge along the road just up from the river valley, and he had a hatchet in the tool box behind his seat in the truck. It was time for him to go. There were things he just didn't know, didn't get. What he knew is that these two didn't need him, and that maybe he wasn't supposed to be there.

"I can't stand it," he told the two of them. They weren't looking at him. "That stupid tree has to go." He pointed at the lame excuse on the floor but didn't look up to see if they were watching. "I know where there's a great one," he said. "You ought to have a better one."

They didn't argue.

"Oh, sweetheart," Coby said still holding tight when he pulled on his coat. "Oh, my dear—you poor, poor girl."

He didn't get it, didn't get it at all.

The interior of the old truck probably still held a little warmth, he thought. And he was sure that hatchet was still behind the seat. What was going on between those two was intense, he told himself. When he slipped out, it was as if they didn't even see him go.

Because I'm forgiven

KayLee didn't speak again until her father walked in the door at the Dekkers' place. Neither did Woody or Tieneke.

Scotty Faber looked pretty much like he always did, an eager man who can eat almost anything, anytime, anywhere, and still look half-starved--thin, gaunt, wiry, overactive, the kind of man who burned calories simply by stepping out of bed, maybe even by dreaming, a hard worker who would, if Karin wouldn't insist otherwise, do nothing more than work. Not high maintenance, Tieneke thought, but super high energy, his eyes crystalline blue, almost radiant. Even when he was a cocky high school kid he was the kind of man some women fear, not because of what he does but because they're scared of what they might do themselves for him. That's what she remembered.

His bright eyes brimmed with confidence, which is not to say he was looking forward to what was coming—he wasn't. But he didn't look defeated. She knew he thought of himself, these days, as a man of faith—not a saint, but someone forgiven for what he didn't really want to remember, lots of things, not just Dawn Burnett. He'd probably just finished a prayer, probably told the Lord that he was figuring on a blessing, she thought. He came walking into the neighbor's house expecting hellfire, but confident that something good would rise from the embers. The purity of faith was all over his face.

Tieneke took his jacket, hugged him in the hallway, didn't try to whisper a thing. "I'm making coffee," she told him. "They're in the front room."

They live in an old, turn-of the-century Sears farmhouse far too costly to heat and maintain for a couple of cutters-and-canners like the two of them, at least that's what she tells people. They really ought to get a condo in town like sensible people their age, but both of them have come to enjoy living out in the open. They've got a room for what was about to occur, a room her very Dutch father used to call the *mooie* room, the pretty room, reserved for important guests and preachers. Sometime after Thanksgiving, they close the sliding oak doors. Even if they'd have opened it earlier, it would still be far too chilly for what needed to be said.

Instead, KayLee and Woody sat in the family room, which was really, long ago, some kind of master bedroom--nothing more than a couch and a chair. Woody had put KayLee in the chair, then sat on the couch himself. Scotty sat on the opposite end, as good a place as that room was going to afford. Tieneke pulled the hassock across the room from the couch and sat, with her back against the wall. The heat from their new furnace kicked up more warmth than any of them needed just then—or so it seemed to her. With four bodies in that small space, she could have turned the thermostat down, no matter how frozen it was outside.

Woody let them alone. He didn't try to intervene. He let the silence sit there until finally Scotty looked at his daughter and said, "You probably want to know some things."

"No kidding," KayLee said.

Tieneke wished Scotty would have let his daughter talk first, but she knew it was going to be hard for him to let KayLee be. The man felt called, too. They both did. By different voices.

"I don't know that we should be here," Woody said to her, and she couldn't have agreed more so she started to get to her feet. But it was KayLee who wanted them there, told them, angrily, to stay.

"This is between you and your father, honey," Tieneke said, her hands down on the side of hassock. More than ready to leave she was.

"But you were there," she said. "I mean, there's nothing new here for you two, and besides I just want you to stay—I want you here."

Tieneke looked at Woody, who nodded.

That little prelude was, for the next ten minutes or so, the only moment of warmth. Tieneke had no desire to stay in that room, but desire, she'd long ago learned, is more than occasionally fickle. Like it or not, they were there.

"What I can't understand is how Mom could stay with you," she said. "I can't begin to imagine how bloody bad you hurt her."

What scared Tieneke was that Scotty had no idea exactly what his darling daughter knew about things back then and what she didn't. He'd come into this whole event blind, full of the spirit, maybe even the Holy Spirit, but blind as a bat to know much about what was roiling in his daughter's soul. She wasn't who she had been that afternoon when she came home from school and parked her car in driveway.

That old chair in the family room is a beast she should have gotten rid of years ago already, she thought, and would have if it hadn't belonged to her mother. It was built at an angle, the back sloping back farther than you might see on chairs today, so that if you're sitting there in it, you simply look at ease—and that's what KayLee looked like when she delivered her first lines, perfectly at ease, even though she wasn't. Just the way she sat there, the almost banal tone to what she said just then—it had to scare Scotty, Tieneke thought, and it did. Something burned up in him. He looked down at his hands, painfully.

"I've known for a long time already that she was my sister—my half-sister," KayLee told him smartly. "I've known like forever."

Tieneke thought that was bullshit. Scotty didn't look up.

"You think I didn't know anything, but I did," she told him. "Maybe I just didn't believe it, but believe me, I knew."

Scotty Faber couldn't look at his daughter. He was fully and completely broken, probably to a depth he'd not before fallen—not even when he discovered—when *they* did—that Celine was going to have his baby, as was Karin. "I'm sorry you had to find that out like you did, sweetheart," he said, "but you have to know that I'm forgiven," he told her.

Wrong, Tieneke thought. Wrong, wrong, wrong.

"I confessed already years ago, and your mother and I got back together. . ."

"Will you shut the hell up with that damned Christian stuff?" KayLee said. "I can't stand it."

Scotty looked at Woody and then at her. Nothing good was going to happen in their house that night. KayLee Faber had just then destroyed the whole strategy by which her father had determined to speak. He had no back-up plan because he simply wasn't bright enough to guess that what had already happened had opened a wound in his sweet daughter's otherwise unblemished heart. It might close. It might heal. But not now, and there would always be a scar.

It wasn't going to be easy.

"What good does it do me to know you're forgiven?" she said. "You think that's going to solve anything? What about me? What about her? What about Dawn Burnett, Dad?" She stopped to reload. "How about this, Scotty Dekkers? —how about you never asked me or her to forgive you?"

Tieneke felt tears start at the corners of her eyes because she knew that Scotty was not up to what was going to happen. Way back he'd ruled the hallways of Cottonwood High, toughest kid in the senior class, but he'd been converted to something grand and sweet. Now, years later, he'd been told off by a child he'd loved, beaten up by a child who was no little girl any more but probably forever would be in this bad-ass guy's mind. What he was learning, sadly, was that spilling what he thought was God's love was going to be useless, and he didn't understand why.

KayLee stepped it up. "I want to know exactly what happened," she said. "I've got a right to know—I'm your daughter, and I've lived for all these years with what you never once gave to her, to Dawn."

It was going to get even more ugly. It already was awful, but there was going to be more. She looked at Woody, wondered how long they could let this go on without this wounded daughter killing her father right here in the family room.

Scotty looked at her, maybe the wrong thing to do. He let the silence go for some time, didn't try to counter or turn this into debate. And he was serious. Good Lord, he was serious, she thought. He was coming after her in the only way he could right then, confession. "I did a lot of stuff I'm really, really sorry for," he told her in a voice that wasn't shaky or tenuous, pathetically sincere. He was trying to be a Christian, but he was facing something far worse than a pride of hungry lions.

Even Tieneke felt knifed when KayLee went after him again. "I want to know exactly what happened," she told him. "I want to know how often and where and why and what you felt when you did it with her. I want to know everything because I never really knew my father—I never did."

Woody looked at Tieneke, and she shook her head at him as if to say that they had to let this go. Something had to come out, some damned poison had to be drained.

Scotty looked at Woody, and Woody nodded.

"We were at a party," Scotty said.

"How often?" she interrupted. "How often did you and her--?"

Scotty was beginning to realize he was looking into a face he didn't recognize. "Once," he said. "At this party. It started at this party."

That was a lie, another lie. It had to be a lie.

"Just once?" KayLee said. "How stupid do you think I am anyway?"

Tieneke felt fear rising. She had no idea what Scotty would do, how he'd act, what he'd say.

"Four times maybe—six—I don't remember," he told her, but she knew that he'd already lost. There was no going back because nothing was back there anymore. He wasn't going to be believed.

"Maybe it isn't all that important for you to know how many times," Woody told KayLee. "Does it matter?"

"Damn right it matters," KayLee said. "I need to know what kind of monster he was. Can't you see that?"

She didn't mean it for him. Tieneke understood that she and her husband were barely recognizable right then by either of them. Everything had collapsed.

KayLee sat up, flipped her hair back behind her ears, and took a deep breath like some prosecuting attorney. "And where was Mom during all this? —was she home sick with me? Is that it?" she said. "Home with morning sickness or whatever—post-partum?"

He didn't respond.

She kept pounding. "I can't understand how you can just go and let your own wife alone with a new baby and all and just go out partying and get yourself laid," she said. "I'd have left for sure. I'd have taken a bus to Omaha—I don't know. I can't understand how she could take you back. We're almost the same age, Dad. You were fucking both of them at the same time?"

"KayLee," Scotty said in a voice that felt like a reprimand.

"Don't you dare tell me what I mayn't say." Her bottom lip quivered a bit, maybe for the first time. "Sometimes I need to know how on earth Mom could forgive you because I sure can't, and I don't think I ever will either because I had to find out who my father was on the damned street—you hear me?"

Tieneke kept thinking the child could break.

"You just did what you did with Celine because Mom was too busy taking care of me? —is that what happened?" she said. "You had to go somewhere to get your little jollies or whatever?"

How Scotty Dekkers answered that question would determine where they were going or whether they were going anywhere at all, and Tieneke was afraid he would lie because he really couldn't understand that his daughter wasn't a child anymore.

"Explain," she said. "Just explain to me so I can understand—I feel like a.. ." she didn't know what word to choose. "I feel like a toad stool or something. Dumb as dirt. Here I am doing the Jesus stuff when my own father. . ." She rolled her eyes. "How can you even stand to be in church?"

"Because I'm forgiven," Scotty told her again. "Because I know God has forgiven me."

"Well, I haven't," she said, the first words in a while Tieneke thought she should have guessed were coming.

Scotty pulled at his ear, at his nose, even wiped a bit at the corner of his eye but never stopped looking directly at KayLee. He seemed just then to be gaining strength. "I told you what happened," he said. "Your dad walked out on his wife—that's the way it went. That's what I've had to live with for the last 16 years," he told her. "That's what I did to your mother." He stopped as if to gather his breath. "You can be mad as heck at me, KayLee," he said, "but I know she's not. She loves me and I love her and maybe that's something you're just going to have to live with."

What she said next made Tieneke wince, and Woody reach for her hand. "You're a fucking liar," she told him, and more--a torrent of darkness.

Scotty stood there and let all that vulgarity go. "It's all my fault, sweetheart," he told her. He sat at the edge of the couch. "You have every right to say every last thing you've said and more." He shook his head as if he could shake something loose, lips tightly held together. "If you hate me," he told her, "you got cause."

He was still lying, still making things up. From the moment Woody had come in that afternoon, through their talking with Celine and her own earnest chatting with KayLee, Tieneke didn't remember another moment when she felt so close to bawling as she did just then because she knew Scotty thought he was doing the right thing, picking up the cross for her mother, becoming the lamb, the sacrifice.

"You see what I feel like?" KayLee said. "I mean, Dawn is as much yours as I am, and look at her life! She tried to kill herself because of you, and I'm out making people happy to love Jesus. Did you ever think of that? Look at the difference. How is that fair?"

Nothing he could do would help him sidestep the pounding he was taking. In his mind, he had no choice but to keep his wife from suffering the same blood-letting, she thought. That's why he didn't tell KayLee the whole story.

Scotty's sweet martyrdom gave him new strength. He was protecting his wife, taking the blows himself. The beating he was taking, Tieneke thought, protecting the love of his life and even his daughter from the whole rotten story.

He stood up from couch and told them all he was going. There was nothing more he could do that night, and he seemed to clearly understand that.

"I'm going to check into the motel, KayLee," he said. "I'm going to go to town now and I'm going to stay there tonight because I don't think you can sleep in a house that's got me in it—maybe tomorrow too. Maybe not until you say I can move back in. Sometime, we'll talk about it."

KayLee looked at him, some of the flames not so much doused as for the first time brought under control. She straightened her back, sat upright, took a few deep breaths.

And then he left. He didn't try to hug or kiss her, which was probably the right thing, no matter how hard it might have been not to.

Tieneke got up walked him out while Woody stayed with KayLee. He pulled on his boots. There were tears. She helped him button the coat up.

"So much I wish I could do over," he told her.

"Sure," she said. She knew exactly what he meant. "You got to find your own way," she told him. "All of us do. We'll take care of her."

"You going to be there when she tells her mother?" he asked.

She told him they'd do what they had to. "And you're going to the motel?"

He nodded. She didn't for a moment believe the night was over.

She shut the door behind him and watched his headlights sweep over the snow outside and line up north, taking him down their lane to the gravel road. When he got to the end of the driveway, he turned west, away from Karin, away from his home and his business, just as he'd promised.

Got a license on that pickup?

When Scotty Faber left, he could have walked all the way to town, all the way to the motel, and he would have never felt the cold. Shafts of snow slid over the road like flames out front of the truck, even though the sky was clear, neither moonless nor sinister, and alive with stars in a way that only country skies can be.

The pickup was still warm when he got back in. He looked at the clock on the radio and realized he hadn't been at the Dekkers' place for more than twenty minutes. But his hands were shaking in a way he didn't remember them ever shaking before. He'd looked in the face of a child he thought he knew, his own little girl—but hadn't seen her there at all.

Gravel crunched beneath his tires as he hit the pavement and turned left. Not in years had he felt so alone. There was no going back, not ever really, he told himself. Something was going up in flames.

He pulled his cell from his belt and tried to rehearse a call to Karin. *I'm on my way to town*, he would tell her. *I told her it would be better for me to stay away until*, and then he didn't know the words himself, *until, well, until things calm down, until she'll have me*. Karin wouldn't say anything. *To our daughter right now, honey, I'm a monster*. That's what he'd say—then there would be silence.

Not until that moment, on his way to town, in his truck, his cell in his hand, had he really considered just exactly what he'd done. When he thought about talking to Karin, about what he'd say, he knew he couldn't tell her what he'd not told their daughter. He knew he couldn't say that he'd done everything he could to protect her—Karin—by lying and taking the whole shit on his own shoulders. And while it had been very easy to keep the truth from KayLee, he knew damned well he couldn't slide a lie past Karin, not even with the best of intentions, not even if he tried to explain that he wanted to save her from grief and guilt and what not else. It wouldn't work.

The fact was--and he pulled over to the side of the road right then because the realization was that pointed—the fact was, he'd set Karin up for a battering even worse than he'd taken because there was no way Karin would let her daughter think her mother was a saint. Another lie would have to unravel, and that one could be even more painful.

I didn't tell her anything about you, he would say. He'd have to. It had seemed so much like the right thing to do. *I screwed up*, he would have to tell her. *Good Lord, I did the whole blessed deal wrong even though I was trying to do it right—the best I could.*

Prayer came as instinct right then because he knew there was no place else to turn, and how many times hadn't he said it himself—how the Lord God almighty wants us on our knees. Well, he was on his knees. *Shit*, he told himself, *he was sure as anything on his knees.*

"Good Lord, help me." There he sat in the swirl of snow from a ground blizzard, his truck lights cut and fractured out front, heater fan roaring. He shut off the radio, put his head in his hands because it came to him out of heaven or hell itself that he'd sure as anything done it all wrong for the best of reasons, and he knew it.

He thought about going back—right then and there, turn the truck around and head back to Dekkers. where Woody and Tieneke were likely trying to talk to his daughter, to soften the blows she'd already suffered. He could storm in again and apologize up and down, but what would he say? Would he tell that child of his that her mother was no saint, that there was more to the story she didn't know, more she couldn't ever have known? How on earth would the damned truth set her free? —he asked himself. *I'm so sorry, KayLee*, he'd have to say. *I'm so sorry for lying, because nobody helps anybody by just lying through the teeth the way I did.* And then, *Your mother was screwing somebody too.*

He couldn't say that. He couldn't say anything.

This whole business was something he couldn't handle, even though he had the Lord. Some things were just beyond him. He looked up ahead at the road, still visible, even though snow was running over it as far as he could see. He couldn't go back. What he'd done was line them both up for more misery, even though protecting Karin had seemed to him so clearly the right thing to do.

He pulled back into the right lane on his way to town, the lines in the blacktop making the frame of the whole pickup jump as if everything beneath the hood was frozen. There was no good way of dealing with all of this, he thought. There wasn't any way out of there for awhile. Someday, maybe.

Maybe she was already there, back at home. Maybe KayLee was already talking to her mother. He couldn't call, shouldn't.

Some guys who'd seen all kinds of horrifying stuff in battle came home and locked the door behind them as if what had gone on hadn't rattled them, he thought. Sometimes they'd go ballistic for no good reason, just blow up. He knew guys like that, men older than he was who'd been in Vietnam. All of sudden—boom! —and what they'd locked up busted out of a stall like some bull never ridden. All of that anger KayLee had burned him with, all of it, had come from something he'd honestly thought—with God's own permission—was behind him, locked away. He wondered, honestly, what might happen to him.

Dawn Burnett wasn't from some rez disaster, he told himself. Maybe it wasn't so easy those first years, but Celine had given their kid a good life, a good marriage. He read about Celine in the papers all the time, showing paintings and what not in Albuquerque, in Rapid, in Bismarck, lots of places. Maybe getting filthy rich, who knows? The kid grew up with advantages, lots of things others didn't have—Indian or white. Lots of them—shoot, more than he had himself.

But all that muttering was nothing more than self-defense, and he knew it. He was doing everything he could to squirm out from the cursing his beautiful daughter had laid on him. The fact that Dawn Burnett had a father, a stepfather, a good man, did nothing to change what had happened 17 years before, nothing—and it meant nothing to KayLee, who at this very moment was marching over to their house to cry on her mother's shoulder, only to be told—Karin would not keep up the lie—that there was more to the story, still more ugliness because her mother was not for a moment innocent.

An uncle, from Washington or Oregon—couldn't remember which exactly—once came out to visit and said he couldn't live out there on the Plains because there was no place to hide. That's what he said, and maybe he was right. Seemed like an odd idea when the guy said it years ago, but even in the darkness and cold, even though the streets in town were empty as an early Sunday morning, he felt as if he couldn't go anywhere without being seen.

He had no desire to spend the night at the motel firetrap, but he had no choice, less choice than he'd had even ten minutes before. It had been the one good thing he said right in those moments of pain—that he would clear out until KayLee thought it okay for him to be home again, under the same roof. That was the right thing, the only right thing.

When he passed by, he saw Starlight Motel still had a neon "vacancy" sign from the days before the interstate, a time when people used to cross the state on the blue highways. Starlight wasn't new even when he'd used the place years and years before, and not alone. The couple that owned it back then moved out in the eighties, when almost everything went bust, and he hadn't bothered to keep up with the new ownership. Likely as not, it was somebody's wife sitting behind the desk—or some kid, some member of a ranching family trying desperately to make a buck and somehow cling to the land. Somebody he'd know.

He turned around and pulled up at the end of the sidewalk on the north side of the line of rooms that probably hadn't changed much from the days when, on good nights, he used to haunt the place. His mind kept running out images of what might be happening in his house right then, Karin denying what he'd said to KayLee, Karin taking on the blame herself in the way he absolutely knew she would. He had no idea how KayLee might react, what she might do, but he'd already seen someone other than the daughter he thought he knew for the last 17 years. He'd already heard her fly into cussing he had no idea she'd ever learned well enough to repeat. He'd already felt her anger, and he couldn't imagine she would sit still for anything her mother would tell her, once she opened up the whole story.

He didn't have a thing along—not even a toothbrush. Still, he got himself pushed back into the old days, when he never had a thing either but a woman, a girl at his side, sometimes someone he didn't even know, sometimes Celine.

He pulled his gloves on and pushed up his collar, then stepped out of the truck on the crunch of snow beneath his boots and walked up to the place marked "Office," even though he could see through the front window it would take some kind of bell or something to get whoever was on duty to the front to give him a room.

Inside, an ancient rack of Black Hills tourist brochures leaned out from their separate compartments, their faces faded from an afternoon sun that poured through the windows west. He'd come in in silence, so he waited before hitting the doorbell duct-taped to the surface of a desk so full of notes and faded instructions it would have required half a day to read. Strange, to come back here now, where one could probably simply assume some of the whole mess had first begun to take over a life that seemed such a hoot back then. He remembered how much he hated Karin, hated having married her, hated himself, although he hadn't thought about that until later, how all of that drinking and partying got done by the wrecking ball something in him had become.

For a long time when it was over, Celine remained a kind of shadow that could come over him so easy it was scary, whenever he and Karin were the least bit on edge. Not that he loved the woman—never did. Celine was as careless and messed up as he'd been, probably worse, just as faceless, he thought. If there was one thing about all of that mess that was somehow a relief, it was the fact—he was sure of it—that to her, Scotty Faber wasn't really anybody in particular. Everything they'd ever done together got done in a mist, a fog. Fog of war, not love.

When the door opened, he hadn't even rung. Somehow, the old woman who walked out must have heard the pickup door, maybe his footsteps on the screech of cold snow.

"Didn't even ring the bell," he told her.

"I wasn't sleeping anyway," she told him.

He didn't know her.

"Need a room," he said, but she was already searching through the cubby holes on the desk between them. "Just for tonight," he told her. She looked up at him strangely. "Cold out there," he said. "Saw a buffalo dead on the road."

"You're lying," she told him, dropping a key on the desk, then turned the book around so he could sign it. She pointed generally in the direction of the blank spaces at the bottom of the ledger. "John Henry goes right there," she said.

"Got my stuff out in the truck," he said, picking up the pen.

"Sure," she said. "I gave you a room down there on that side of the place. Shouldn't even have to move it at all."

It was a game he hadn't played for years, getting a room like this. Wasn't new to lie. He put the pen down on the ledger book and wrote in a name he made up of a customer in Gillette, Wyoming. "Jared Eliot," he wrote—and then made up an address somewhere in Everett, Washington.

"Got a license on that truck?" she asked him, pointing at another empty space.

"Don't know it," he said. "How about we let it go right now? I can't bet I'm going to live through another walk down your sidewalk and back in this cold."

She hunched her shoulders as if she'd let it go this time. She was wary—that much he could see. But it struck him that she'd have to be because there was no telling what the cat might drag in this time of night, even here in Cottonwood, where you probably count the strangers in town on one hand most nights of the year. She was not thin, not young, not pretty, but she was a woman, after all, and he wasn't, and that was reason to be wary.

"Don't know your game, Mr. Faber," she told him, "but I been working here long enough to tell my customers that what happens here, stays here—like Vegas. You seen them ads."

His insides buckled. He looked into her eyes, and she looked away as if to reassure him that he didn't need to say a thing because someone who worked a motel desk in a town like Cottonwood sure as nuts understood sin. "Family problems," he told her. "Nothing big either—not that can't be conquered."

She nodded as if she'd already heard every last excuse she could have.

"I'm serious," he told her.

"So am I," she told him, and then she pointed out the door toward the room she'd assigned him.

Is she alone?

There really wasn't anyone Marcus Pritchard could talk to but his grandma. Even if he thought about it, he couldn't think of a single someone he could ask. He didn't catch on to what was going on. But then, Dawn didn't either. That's why they had to stop at Coby's, because Dawn said she didn't understand something she should have or really wanted to. Neither did he, and he wasn't a girl and that made it all that much harder.

Once, when he was little, a woman had come to Grandma's. He was on the floor in the living room of her trailer, playing with those plastic monkeys Grandma had in an oatmeal box. The two of them ended up—three of them, for the woman who came by to visit had a friend along—the three of them ended up sitting around the table a step up on the far end of the trailer so that they figured he wasn't in a position to listen in. He was a kid. And he was a boy. But he did listen.

He'd been around white people enough to know that they were always hugging and holding hands. Wasn't that way on the reservation. But that afternoon Grandma had held that woman's hand across the table, rubbed it the way she'd rubbed his when he was little, soft little strokes across the palm as if there was something to read there, something important.

What did he know about what was going on? Not much. What did he remember? Not much either, but what he'd always associated with that moment was that there'd been a death, maybe of a teenager, he wasn't sure. But the woman and her friend had come to Grandma's trailer because Grandma was Grandma, because she knew what to say, what to do; and while he didn't remember much, what he did remember was his own pride because it was his grandma those two women came to visit, his grandma who said things or prayed or touched or shared tea or smudged or something—his grandma who did something that made that woman feel stronger.

That's what he remembered, and that too was a reason why he got on the phone as soon as the truck started, as soon as he was down the road and on his way out of town to get a tree. He pulled the phone from the little pocket on the sleeve of his jacket and told it he wanted to call Grandma.

It was getting late, but Grandma was a night owl who could exist on just a few hours of sleep. One of the reasons he didn't stay with her was he always felt lazy when he stayed in bed, as if he was some old agency injun'. He wasn't, never was. It's just that Grandma didn't need sleep.

"You here?" she said when she picked up the phone. "Marcus, you coming to my place tonight? Awful cold outside. I'd like that."

He told her no. He told her he wasn't looking for a bed because he had one out there closer to town.

"I'm driving your way," he told her. "Right now, I'm coming straight west towards your place."

"Not going to stop I bet," she said, chuckling. "Who'd want to stop for an old woman anyway?"

He let that joke sit to tell her that he got it, and it wasn't as funny as she thought.

"What's this all about?" she asked him. "It's not every night I get a call from my favorite grandson so late."

"It ain't late, and you only got one."

"I didn't raise my kids well," she said. "I ought to have a couple dozen like every other old woman in the trailers here."

He told her he'd been in town with Dawn Burnett—"You know, the artist's daughter?"

"The one they found out in the cold?

He told her yes. "She's okay," he said. "She's no worse for the wear."

"What she go and do a fool thing like that for anyway?" she asked him. "People die, you know."

It wasn't inky dark out in the country. The wind had slowed, easing the cloudiness that had obscured what now seemed the moon's almost shocking glow. When he hit his lights to see for himself how bright it was, he knew he'd have no trouble finding a tree on one of those hills close to the river.

The moon was a ball that was a good deal brighter than shiny silver.

"I don't know how to say this, Grandma, because I don't know the words."

She waited.

"Let's say there's this girl and she's going to have a baby."

"Aw, Marcus," she said, "You didn't go and knock that girl up, did you?"

"Course not—I'm just a kid."

"You're old enough to diddle around." She cleared her throat. "What're you saying again?"

"I'm saying there's this girl, an imaginary girl, and she finds out somehow that she's going to have a baby, and she's all cranked about it you know, all excited and everything—and then all of a sudden she isn't."

"Isn't all cranked?" Grandma said.

"Isn't pregnant," Marcus said right away.

Whenever he had Grandma on the phone, he couldn't help but remember her age because she wheezed a little, as if just drawing breath was getting to be a chore.

"I'm maybe not hearing so good," she said. "Lenore tells me most every day I got to get a hearing test. They're free you know, down at the clinic."

"Grandma, I don't know shit about girls, about women, and I'm just a kid. I don't know."

"So, what is it then?" she said.

"This girl—Dawn Burnett. I think you know her mother maybe— "

"This child's not pregnant anymore—that's what you're saying?" his grandma said. And then a low voice as if someone might be standing outside her trailer listening. "She get an abortion?"

"No," he said, "she says she lost her—I mean 'it' or whatever. She lost the baby." It was as if right then the two of them sat there listening in, Coby leaning over Dawn, all arms and legs in a hug and all of it twisted together as if maybe if they held each other tight enough they could stop the tears. "Dawn says she's lost that little baby, Grandma. She do something she shouldn't have done or what?"

The silence between them made it clear that what he said got home. He waited, then waited some more because Grandma was thinking hard, thinking deep. And what if it was *him*? What if *he* did it? What if *he* was the one did something last night in bed?

"You *love* that girl, Marcus Pritchard," she told him finally, her voice become a machine gun. "You hear me? —you *love* that girl." She didn't mean it as a question.

"What you mean anyway?"

She grabbed a breath from some place deep in those old smoke-filled lungs of hers. "I mean, Marcus, you love that girl now, y'hear, because maybe it woulda' been one thing if she got that baby taken out of her—I mean by a doctor. Abortion, Marcus. But it wasn't, right? She didn't have no abortion."

"No abortion, she said." He told her just what Dawn had told Coby. "She said she lost him. That's what she said exactly."

"Oh, heavens to grace--she miscarried," Grandma said and then, right away. "Now you just go and love that girl, Marcus, because if she's just a young thing like you, and she lost that child like she says she did, then she's going to need all the love you and me and the rest of everybody can give her."

"She do something wrong? —she drinking or something?"

"No, no, no—don't go thinking that, honey. She didn't do nothing wrong," Grandma said. He swore he could hear something cut out in her voice. "It's just that the baby didn't work."

"I don't get it," he said.

"Sure as anything she don't either." She let that sit for just a second. "She miscarried, Marcus. It just plain didn't work out—who knows why? She got herself all pregnant but some switch in her got flicked or something and her body, something in it, decided that that baby wasn't going to be this time around."

"She didn't mess up?"

"No, no, no—and that makes it all worse, honey, because she doesn't know a thing, see?" Often Grandma's voice got all airy or something when she thought she needed to bear down. "Poor girl probably doesn't get it, and truth is there ain't nothing to blame. She just lost it, like she says. Things inside didn't work out."

It made him want to cry, just to hear the way his grandma couldn't stop talking about it.

"What can I do?" he asked her.

Three or four or five wheezes came up through the phone. "She with her mother now?" Grandma said, finally.

"Won't hear going home."

"You're not letting her alone, are you?"

"She's not alone, not right now."

Three wheezes, four, five—maybe more.

"You bring her out here, you hear? Your old grandma been through enough to know at least a little bit about what the poor girl needs," she told him. And then, "It's love what she needs, Marcus—you hear what I'm saying." She drew in a breath as if it was about to be her last. "You love that girl, hear? You just love her. Don't need to say a thing right now when you're with her. Just keep your mouth shut, but love everything about her, give her everything she wants, listen to her every word." It all came out in a tumble. "Marcus Pritchard, you need to love her or maybe she'll try to do some stupid fool thing like she tried last night. You listen to your grandma now—you just love her to death, you hear?"

She meant a different kind of love than what they did together last night. Not that he didn't love her then—that wasn't it. Not that that wasn't love either. When the two of them sat together around that fire, that was something of beauty, he thought, something he would have loved more of, still did.

He told his grandmother that he'd go back and pick Dawn up, if she wasn't going to stay with Coby. If she needed a place, he told her, he'd bring her out to her place. He'd call for sure. "You still a night owl, Grandma?" he said. "You going to be up?"

"Don't think about me, Marcus—just think about that little girl. She's the one needs you."

It was something inside, he told himself, something that somehow explained Dawn's wanting to kill herself. He hadn't considered any of that before, the possibility that she deliberately drove into the field last night, deliberately put herself in a place where no one would find her, out in the middle of a snowfield where she'd die slow, as sweet a death as a person could have, some said. He told himself he hadn't believed that because he simply didn't want to, didn't believe that Dawn Burnett could be that depressed or dark or whatever.

Grandma seemed to think that what she did, she did because that baby didn't work—because Dawn had miscarried, she said—there was cause for her to try to end it all.

He needed to get back to Coby's now, but he also needed to get that tree because he didn't want the two of them to know he was just a kid who didn't really understand what it meant to miscarry, or to know, as Grandma said, that having one was enough to make some people wish away their lives. He needed to get back to Coby's and find out what was going on, but he also needed that tree. He needed it for cover. He needed it because Grandma said that his job right now was to love. "You *love* that girl."

She didn't mean it like a question.

I didn't notice?

Scotty didn't have to lie, didn't have to try to hide from God or whoever, hadn't really been forced to it. But he had, and there was no turning back. He looked at the woman behind the motel desk and held up the key as if it were something to treasure, a toast to their complicity, then leaned against a door so full of frost it required most of his weight to swing open.

He felt different when he left, as if he was someone he hadn't been for a long, long time. Walking out of the motel and into cold air didn't affect him because it was as if all that time between visits to this old place wasn't recorded anywhere. His body seemed to soften and rock more when he walked, the way it had in the old days, when most of Cottonwood thought him bad ass.

But he had no stomach for some motel bedroom, for sitting there and waiting out what might happen, watching TV, his cell out in front of him as if at any moment some Lone Ranger would call in or ride up on a white horse and deliver all of them from evil. He didn't want to sit still and hated being alone. But there was no place else to go. He'd promised KayLee he'd stay away from her.

And he had nothing along, nothing at all. "HBO," the sign said. He pushed through the door—it was terribly light, made of balsam, he figured, and walked in, snapped on the light just around the corner and the place lit up. All paneling, new light fixtures on the walls, cheap ones. The picture above the bed was a team of horses blowing steam, some stage jockey trying to get them up and out of a river bed, water splashing all over. Wild, wild west. The TV was ancient, but cable anyway, or satellite.

He wasn't really running away, he told himself, but no other course of action was open because he could not go home. He had to give his daughter space to process what had gone on, even what she was learning right now, right at that moment in the sun room of the house in which she'd grown up. She'd stared him down in a way she never had before, his own child, his little sweetheart. She'd cut him up because the old man wasn't who she had thought he was.

He picked up the remote, sat down on the bed, and slapped buttons, surfing through murders, detectives, comedy, History Channel—until he came to classic football, where Denver, his team, was handing it to Green Bay in the '98 Super Bowl. He watched as John Elway did his famous helicopter spin to get a first-and-goal late in the game—a 37-year-old man putting himself on the line to get a win. He'd been watching at home back then, and he came up off the chair in a way that scared KayLee, who was just a little girl.

The only thing he could keep on the screen was that old football game, not because it offered him any surprise, not because he needed something to cover his grief or hurt or sadness, but because it was background music that wouldn't take him anywhere he hadn't been before. He watched but didn't see. The game rolled along toward an end he knew very well. The Broncos took home the win, and for a while he simply sat on the bed and stared at the old Magnavox on a creaky table full of little stains he could have left himself years ago. Wormy cigarette burns.

It was going to get worse. All that darkness was going to turn to pitch once his daughter understood that she'd been lied to again, that her mother—a saint—wasn't perfect. If all the smoke could sometime clear, he'd have to get to know his own daughter all over again because something was forever lost.

When the phone rang, he reached for the cell.

"You talk to her?" Scotty said.

"Scotty? —is that you?" It was Glenn. Bible study seemed like another lifetime.

"I thought you were Karin," he told him. "I'm expecting her to call me."

"You still out?" Glenn asked.

"Haven't been home," he said.

"Way too cold to cat around, brother."

"Got that right."

"Listen, I don't want to hold you up or nothing, but I just thought I'd tell you something you didn't catch."

"When we were talking?"

"There was this girl—and it was Dawn Burnett. I know it was her, and she was there with this kid, this boy—I don't know him. Don't know his name."

"What you talking about?"

"At the café," he said. "I'm saying she was there when we were, this girl we were talking about, this Dawn Burnett."

"She was there?"

"I'm sure. Not that long ago her old man came in with her and bought a car," and then he said, "—her step-father."

"When we were there sitting in the café, she was there?"

"She walked right past us," he said. "I thought it was like—it seemed like she wanted us to see her--*you* maybe."

"And I missed her?"

"Must have."

There was this other girl, this other child, he told himself. He'd almost forgotten that all of this was about that other girl who'd tried to kill herself, his own flesh-and-blood daughter. "I didn't see her when she walked by?" he asked Glenn. "I didn't notice? You're saying she was testing me or something?"

"Seemed like it at the time, but I was figuring that maybe I was the only one there who knew the whole story because it wasn't something you forget all that easy, you remember?"

He tried to picture it—the girl coming by while he had his nose in the Bible. He tried to imagine what he must have missed, what she might have thought. "You should have said something to her."

"Being as nobody else seemed to notice, I figured we'd just look like a bunch of dirty old men, so I didn't." And then he waited as if more needed to be said. "You were into it just then," he told Scotty. "You were like in another world and you never saw her."

"You say she wanted me to see her?" he asked.

"Seemed like some kind of test is what I'm saying," Glenn told him. "And that made me wonder, you know—about whether this girl knows. . .well, everything. And you don't have to tell me either. I mean, I didn't call in order to get the gossip or whatever. I called because the way she walked by made it seem like it was planned. Even when she was on the way back from the john, it was like she didn't look up at anybody except you." He took a deep breath. "I know it's all behind you and everything," he said, "but I just thought you ought to know because that girl is sort of dangerous too, you know? I mean, I wouldn't have said all of this either except for the fact that you all were talking about possibilities—I mean with that accident, as if she was trying to go off the road and all of that, as if it was deliberate. You know as well as I do, Scotty—you lived here your whole life—you know that we got way more of that than we should."

For a while, nothing was said.

"I just thought you ought to know," Glenn told him. "Didn't mean to tie you up for so long."

"No, no—I appreciate it," Scotty said, and then he just blurted it out. "I don't know if that young lady knows, but my own daughter does—just tonight. KayLee knows. Just now, in fact. Just now it all came out." And then he couldn't talk anymore because he thought maybe he'd already said too much, drawing Glenn into the whole thing when the guy didn't have to be.

"Scotty?" Glenn said. "Where are you?"

Even if he tried, he couldn't talk.

"Scotty—you need some place to go?"

"Dawn Burnett just walked right past me you say?" he repeated, measuring breaths. "Walked right past me tonight when I'm going on and on? I'm not even sure I know what she looks like."

"You weren't looking," Glenn told him. "Nobody can blame you for not looking. You were leading the Bible study."

"Where is she? She still there?" Scotty asked.

"They left—she and some guy, some kid."

"Who?"

"Don't know. My wife says that it's a Van Camp—you know him? Wife's got her ear to the ground and there was a lot of talk about it today, about whether the girl really tried it, you know? —suicide. And why. Anyway, she's been seeing this Van Camp kid or that's the word—what's his name?"

"LeRoy?"

"Yeah, that's it, I think."

Glenn pulled the phone away, but the question he yelled across the room came up through the phone anyway and he heard Glenn's wife say that was the name—LeRoy. "That's the one," he told her. "That's it, I guess—and maybe it had something to do with him, at least that's what's being said."

LeRoy Van Camp worked for him not that long ago and not that long.

"Maybe it was LeRoy—I don't know."

In the background Scotty could hear laughing on television.

"Too cold for man or beast," Glenn said. "Get yourself home now, hear, Scotty?"

That his own daughter had walked right past him, looked at him, tried to get his eye—that she had done all of that meant very clearly to him that he had to find her, if for no other reason than to apologize. If Glenn was right, the girl had tried to see if he would see her, and he didn't, which must have made her feel what? --invisible, made her feel as if there was nothing between them, even though she must have known better.

"Scotty, listen," Glenn said, "—you still there?"

"I'm here," he said.

"Listen, it's way too cold to do anything—way too cold and it's getting late. Don't do stupid stuff, right? It's been years now since all of that, and it'd take a miracle to bring some kind of peace in one night—it ain't going to happen, Scotty. You hear me?" He waited again. "You come over here to our place if you need a place to crash, okay? Stop over, and we'll talk this through, what we can."

"Sure," he said, but it was a lie. "Let me think a bit," he told Glenn as pulled his jacket back around his shoulders, one hand on the phone. "I'll call you, all right?" he said. "I got your number in my phone. I'll call you." And then he hung up.

LeRoy Van Camp—sure, he thought.

Sometimes you just have a feeling about people

Marcus Pritchard wasn't thinking about trudging through snow because most of the time the snow doesn't get really deep on the plains. Way too much wind. It blows and blows and ends up, well, nowhere, he thought. Well, not *nowhere* because it can fill valleys and woods and railroad trestles, drift things in like a fortress. He was wearing boots, always did really, expect summer. But if he was going to get that tree he'd promised this Coby woman, he was going to have to go down by the river and into the trees, where there was bound to be snow.

Sometimes you just had a feeling about people like this woman, Coby the saint, he told himself. Sometimes you just had a feeling that she was going to be okay, and he could tell Dawn had the very same feeling, had it already since morning because it wasn't like Dawn Burnett to warm up to a woman like that or anyone for that matter unless something in that somebody's face or eyes lets you in to find a place. Coby Saint Something had that kind of thing. Right now, Dawn was spilling her guts, telling her things he thought weren't meant for him or any other guy for that matter. The tree would be a blessing. Everybody deserves a Christmas present, he told himself—the tree would be a Christmas present this Coby woman deserved. He'd bring it back, be Santa.

He was tempted to let the pickup run while he went out after the tree—it wasn't far down the slope, not far at all from the road; but his gas gauge told him he didn't want to risk running out. It still wasn't all that late, even though the night had already been way long, he thought, even though he'd have trouble trying to figure out when it had all started with the call--Dawn called him, told him to pick her up out in all that wind and snow, along the road like a fool. That was it. Told him exactly where and when. God almighty, was he happy about that.

The temps were somewhere down in the basement, but at least the wind had blown itself out. He cut the engine, kept the lights on for a minute just to keep his bearings, opened the door, stepped out, then reached down behind the seat for the hatchet, reached down for where he had tools wrapped up in an old shirt. He felt the heavy cord of the jumper cable—just had it out last week, but he had to feel around beneath the seat to find the old t-shirt around those tools.

Gloves he had between the seats. He pulled down the stocking cap on his head, then realized that it wouldn't be dumb to find that one his grandma had bought him from some Salvation Army store in Sioux Falls—had a tassel and braided straps. He was sure it was a woman's. She'd thought so too, she told him. But she told him it would do the job better than that black beanie she thought made him look too much like a gang-banger. He was surprised she knew that word, but then, tons about Grandma was surprising. It was a Broncos cap. He wasn't that much of a fan, really. Beggars can't be choosers, he told himself.

He unwound the tools and grabbed the hatchet, an old thing he'd taken to the emery wheel just to de-rust not that long ago. It would do fine. He'd cut Grandma's tree out there just last week. If the snow hadn't blown so hard in the last few days, he could have followed his own tracks, not that he needed to.

I lost it—that's what Dawn had told Coby the nurse or whatever. *I lost it*. She didn't have an operation, an abortion—she'd lost it herself. He still wasn't sure how you cut the difference there. Six of one, half dozen of another. Either way, she was home free now, right? No more baby. She wasn't carrying a kid nobody wanted. That was done away with somehow. Sometimes he told himself he didn't get being female. What he knew—all he knew--was that he loved her. Or thought so. What'd he know about love? he asked himself. There was so damned much he didn't know. Made him sick sometimes to realize how much he didn't know.

He pulled down that Broncos cap over his ears—great ear flaps! —and slammed the door of the truck, stepped over the guard rail at the side of the road and started down the hill, just as steep as ever but a lot slicker with a glaze of that frozen snow.

He tried to imagine what it would be like to have a baby inside you, to be carrying something that was eventually going to be a real live human being, a somebody. In your stomach yet, carrying it along day after day, this huge belly. He'd seen pictures.

He pulled the zipper of his jacket up higher around his neck. The cold was a wearying enemy, sapping strength. But it wouldn't take him all that long.

And then that little child finally comes out, rips you in half almost. He remembered how this kid once told him—that was years ago—that for a woman having a baby is like taking hold of your upper lip and jerking it all the way up to the top of your head. He just didn't know how Dawn could be so weepy if she didn't have to suffer all of that pain for something nobody wanted.

But then, you lose something, and you always feel bad. Once upon a time his old man had given him one of those knives with a thousand blades, even a scissors. Wasn't Christmas either. He'd just come back from wherever and pulled it out of his pocket, told him he picked it up for him on purpose. Six weeks later, no more, it was gone. He had no idea where. Broke his fucking heart, he told himself. He lost the stupid knife and it wasn't even all that good. But he still could cry about that, even though it happened three years ago already, maybe more.

What happens if you've got this baby in you? He was down off the bank and marching across the field toward the woods. What if you've got this baby inside you, this life, and you lose it? It like disappears and you don't know a thing about where it went or where it is? What happens then?

What happens to it? What happens to you? Seriously.

It was real, he thought, even though she didn't see it and neither did he. He actually held that Swiss knife in his hands, in his fingers, in his pocket. He fiddled with it a ton, even tried to carve a bird with it once—didn't work all that well because it wasn't really a carving knife. But right now, he remembered it so well he could have sat in the truck and drawn it. And he lost it. Just frickin' lost it.

Dawn hadn't seen that baby, and besides that baby wasn't a baby at all. Wasn't alive really. Not ever. Just some little thing the size of a quarter or something. How big, he didn't know.

Or was it alive? Of course, it was. It was alive in her stomach or wherever babies hang out. If it wasn't alive, she wouldn't be over there with Coby right now telling the whole damned story. Dawn wanted to know some things, she'd told him. That's why she wanted to talk to this woman, to Coby the Saint. She wanted to know some things he didn't know because he was just a kid. And a guy.

There was a whole stand of spruce on the side of a hill not all that far from the road. Ranchers hated them. He was helping whoever owned this ground by cutting a couple of trees out, couldn't get in trouble for doing work he'd otherwise, come spring, get paid to do. Coby and Dawn would love it—they both would. He comes back with a tree that's worthy of Christmas, and they'd both think he was a great kid.

The moon wasn't full, but it was big, and it hung up in the black sky so monstrous he thought it shouldn't even be there, so big, so shiny, so bright. The moon gives us affection, he remembered some guy saying, some Indian guy teaching them about Native stuff. Lots of moon tonight. If a crowd of deer were anywhere close now, he told himself he could see the whites of their eyes.

When a set of lights pulled up behind his truck on the road above, his first thought was the sheriff or some state trooper; it wasn't hard to see that the truck wasn't a car.

He tried to imagine why it would be against the law for him to do what he was doing. This was someone's pasture land, but every rancher west river got rid of spruces on these hills or wanted to because he didn't want those lousy weeds to take over—and they would. Maybe it was LeRoy, he thought.

He got to the stand he'd thought about, looked for something with a shape, then stood there and looked back up the hill to where that pickup stood. It wasn't LeRoy. LeRoy would have yelled. LeRoy would have seen it was his truck, stepped out and yelled. "You idiot!" he would have said. "Get your ass back here." Something like that.

He wondered what LeRoy would say about him sleeping with Dawn. She wasn't his anymore. They'd burned all those pictures she'd drawn—seemed like a year ago already. That was all done. Still, you can't help wondering what he'd say. Probably "Good for you, kid." Probably.

He got down his knees in the snow—it wasn't that deep— when he determined which one he was going to cut, then looked up at the road again. More than enough moon there was for him to see that it wasn't LeRoy, too big a cab, way too big a cab.

He took a couple whacks at the trunk with the hatchet, sound echoing off everything in the valley, almost as if he was doing the work in a cave. With his left hand, he held the bottom branches up and away to get a clean shot. Every whack could be heard miles away, he thought, except he was the only fool outside in this freezer.

"I got a saw," a man yelled, the guy in the truck. He was tall. You could see him silhouetted against the interior lights, tall and thin, a big guy. "You need it?"

A saw would be better.

He could see the guy open the back of the pickup and grab something.

"I'm coming down," he said. "I need a tree myself, didn't buy one yet."

Marcus didn't recognize the voice either. It wasn't anyone from the reservation. He could hear that much. The guy didn't talk like an Indian.

He whacked away again, let the sound of his hatchet carry what he would have otherwise said. The guy was coming down the hill. Cold as it ever gets, and the guy was coming after him.

Didn't seem to matter what he said or how close he got, Marcus had no idea who was toting that saw, but he told himself he had the hatchet himself. All he knew was that the guy was white and he was bigger, a good deal bigger than he was. And older.

"I need to bring that thing back to Coby because I'm the guy trying to be her boyfriend," the big guy said.

Long jacket, orange beanie—one of those glow-in-the-dark things almost.

"You do what you can, right?" the guy said, coming closer. And then, "Light as day out here, isn't it?"

Still, Marcus didn't know him.

"Here's the way it is," the guy said. "I told her that tree she bought was a loser. I told her too, just like you did. I said I'd get her something else myself, but I didn't, and now you're going to make me a fool if you cart that thing back there and make it a Christmas present. You gotta let me do it."

Ten more whacks with the hatchet and he had it down. By that time, the guy was right behind him. He wasn't a fool. The guy was finagling something.

"Gorgeous," the man said. "I may have to build her a new living room just to find a place for it." He stuck his hand beneath his arm as if he weren't wearing gloves. "But then she can use the extra space." His collar was up high to keep out the cold, and he wore mittens, those gray ones women darned out of heavy wool. "Listen," he said, "you can't fault me for trying to get on her good side, right? You've seen Coby—she's really fine, right?"

"My girlfriend likes her," Marcus said, standing up, the hatchet still there in his hand.

"I was just over there," the school guy said. "I don't think you know me, but I know your grandma."

That pissed him off. "You're the big man at Cottonwood," Marcus said, "--the principal? I remember now because she said something about you." He pulled the tree up from the snow, stood it beside him—it was a little taller than he thought it was, but he could saw off some trunk. "You know my grandma--how?"

"Can't say," the guy said sort of sweetly, not a put down. "Legal stuff and all."

"You just over there?" Marcus said.

"At Coby's," he said. "I got run out of Dodge like you did." He hunched his shoulders. "What's going on over there isn't for the males of the species. They told me to go find you." The guy looked back up the hill where his truck was still running, lights on. "I think we ought to clear out before the Sheriff comes along."

"Not doing nothing wrong," Marcus told him.

"Yeah, sure—but doesn't do my reputation any good, hanging out and stealing a tree with some wild kid." He pointed at the tree. "You got it?"

Sometimes you just kind of knew when you were going to like a person, Marcus thought—he was just now telling himself that. Sometimes you just knew. "How you know my grandma anyway?" he said again.

"She can't help herself," he said. And then, "Look, I could get in big trouble telling you this, but the plain fact of the matter is, your grandma loves you."

You can be wrong about things, too, Marcus told himself. He'd been wrong plenty often in his life already. You can be dead wrong about what you might guess about people. But you can be right too. Sometimes you just got to trust what your insides tell you, and his insides were telling him this guy was going to be okay. Wasn't pushy. Wasn't mouthy.

So, he just asked. "What's it mean when she says she 'lost it'?" he asked the guy. "What's that mean anyway?" he said because it was on his mind. "All I heard Dawn tell this Coby girlfriend-of-yours was that she lost the kid."

"Take two of us to carry that thing up and out of here?" the principal asked him. "Or you got it?"

He stuck his hand inside the branches, took hold of a good handful of trunk, then picked it up. "I can drag it if I get tired," he said. "I can just drag it through the snow."

"She isn't going to have a baby," the white guy said. "Name is Trent by the way, and your grandma is a queen."

"Indians don't have queens," Marcus told him. "In cartoons we got princesses, but we got no queens and no kings either."

"Whatever," Trent said. "What she means is that her body didn't do what she thought it was going to do, just didn't. Sort of refused." He looked around. "I got my truck running," he said. "You mind if we talk this out where it's warm. I'm going to die out here."

"That hurt bad?" Marcus said, "that *refusing*?"

This guy named Trent stuck his hands under his arms. "You're asking the wrong person, Marcus," he said. "But I'm told losing a baby that way hurts in ways you and I are never going to understand."

Marcus didn't, but he somehow knew that when Dawn lost it, whatever happened was so awfully bad you felt as if your heart got jerked out of your chest. "I hate that," he said. "I can't stand it."

"That's good," Trent said. "That's very good. I'm glad to hear that." Trent pointed at the tree. "Why don't you let me give you a hand with that thing? Be easier," he said, bending down to take the trunk. "You lead."

Marcus stared for a moment, then nodded and lifted his end. It was so bright out that you could see the outline of the town, the buildings, like an shadow. It was almost Christmas. On top of everything else, cold as it was, it was almost Christmas.

"Seriously," Trent said. "You a Broncos fan?"

"Got it from my Grandma."

Getting their footing on the way up the embankment demanded more than either of them had—it was that slippery.

"Ha," Trent said. "Got it from your grandma, huh? I should have guessed."

And up they went to the pickups.

Please, let me get you something

By the time Tieneke came through the door, KayLee had already tossed her vest over a chair, slipped her feet out of her shoes. She fell into her mother's arms, her admiration and love on just as vivid display as the hate had been when, a minute ago, she wouldn't hear the word *forgiveness*. Her eyes may have been edged white with frozen tears from the walk home, but they were full of love.

And nothing could stop Karin right then from grabbing her daughter and holding her so tight that for a moment Tieneke wished they would keep holding each other all night long in the kind of silence that covered them both and everything else, silence she knew perfectly well wouldn't continue. And couldn't.

"I love you so darn much, Mom," KayLee said, first words, babbled.

Tieneke let the two of them stand there for a long time, swaying slightly as if dancing, Karin's hand up behind her daughter's neck to press her face into her shoulder. When Karin looked up at Tieneke, her face was pale, weathered by pure fright despite the tears, probably because of them.

"Everything is different now," KayLee told her mom without letting up on the hug. "It just changes everything. Nothing seems the same. How can it be?"

For Karin, not having to look into her daughter's eyes had to be a blessing.

"I can't stand to be in a room with him. I won't be," KayLee told her mother. "It's just so fricking awful—just to think of it. It makes me sick. I don't know that I can ever look at him in the same way again. I can't." With that she pulled away slowly, brushed at her eyes with the sleeve of her sweater, looked into her mother's face, then returned into her arms. "I was thinking just now, you know—I was thinking how happy I was that it was dark outside just now, pitch dark." They were still in the clinch. "Then I looked up and saw the moon's glow over everything, over the snow. It's bright as day outside, Mom," she said, "it's not that way in my insides because it's so damned dark in my heart right now—that's where the darkness is."

Karin brought her hands up to her daughter's cheeks, wiped her eyes.

"I am not going to school," KayLee announced. She took her mother's hands in hers and kissed them, then let them go. "Tomorrow morning, I'm not going, and you can't make me because everything has changed. I can't look at anything the same because I'm not the same."

"Let me get you something," Karin said, still clinging. "Let me get you some tea. Would you like some nice hot tea?" She pulled herself away and brought KayLee to the dining room table, pulled out a chair and got her to sit. "You must be freezing—it's terribly cold out there."

"You were married!" KayLee said. "The two of you were married because she's younger than I am—Dawn is younger. You two had to be married."

"We were," Karin said, walking over to the stove across the room and in the kitchen. "Please, let me get you something," she said again.

Tieneke was near the front door. KayLee seemed oblivious to her presence.

"How could he do that, Mom? --and how on earth could you forgive him, and how come you never told me?"

Tieneke wondered how Karin had prepared herself to answer. She had to have prepared—or tried.

"Don't just blame your father," Karin said, seriously, pointedly.

She wasn't going to stall. There could be no more concealment, no more left unsaid. Karin had determined to have it all out, quietly but clearly. "Don't just blame him because there's plenty of blame to go around." She turned on the burner beneath the tea pot, reached into the cupboard for a cup.

"I was just there, Mom. We were just at Mrs. Burnett's. Karin turned slightly.

"I met her," KayLee said. "Was it her fault? --'the other woman'? And how come it's always the woman's fault?"

Karin turned around, leaned against the counter top, tried to look calm. "I don't know where you got that idea," she said. "Maybe that was true once upon a time, but not anymore. You think, Tieneke?"

"How come she's here?" KayLee said.

Tieneke thought she had that coming after taking KayLee on the way she had in the car.

"I asked her to be here," Karin said. "I need her, honey."

"Why?" KayLee asked.

She didn't stop for breath. "Because it's a long story, and it's not nice, and I wish it hadn't happened—Lord almighty, I wish it hadn't happened—all of it, any of it, every bit of it. It's a long story that we never told you, not because we left it all behind but because we figured you just had to be older, mature or something."

What her mother was saying didn't quite register, but in an instant, her face changed. Something tipped. The room, everything in it, pitched sideways to avoid a head-on that could not be avoided. A realization she'd never come close to considering, crept in. "You mean, you too?" she said. "Don't say that, Mother. I won't believe it."

"Let me get you some tea here—just take it easy, honey. Just let it alone so we can take this all slowly because it's a long story," Karin said.

KayLee turned to stone. She absolutely could not have imagined her sinned-against mother, sainted for taking back the son-of-a-bitch her father had become, suggesting what she was. "I can't handle it, Mother—you mean, you too?"

Somewhere in the house two little girls were sleeping through this, Tieneke thought. That one of them might be hanging around the stairway listening seemed a horror.

"Tell me I'm wrong," KayLee said. "You too?"

"Honey—"

"No, really. You're out screwing somebody too?"

"Don't use that kind of language."

"Don't 'language' me, Mother. Words don't mean shit here, do they? 'Sticks and stones,' lady—'sticks and stones can break my bones, but words will never hurt me.'" KayLee sat back, brimming with raw arrogance. "Maybe you'd like me call it 'making love,' is that it? Sounds worse to me. I'd rather have my mother screwing someone than making love to some jackoff male she's not supposed to be in bed with. 'Making love' is worse, isn't it?" She didn't mean to give Karin an chance to answer. "My father made a baby at the very same time you were pregnant with me, Mom—do I have all that right? I mean, a minute ago I couldn't get my mind around my mother's own undying Christian strength in hanging on with my asshole dad. I mean, she forgave him. Takes a miracle. I don't believe in miracles."

"KayLee," Karin said. "Let's try to take this slowly."

"I don't even want to sit here, Mother," she said. "Everything smells—every little damn thing stinks in this house. It's a lie. All lies. You understand?"

"You're talking about *my* life," Karin said. "Of course, I understand."

KayLee stopped, tried to become the lawyer, affected calm. "Mom, you too?"

Karin came back to the table and tried to hold her, but KayLee would have none of it.

"I can't believe it," KayLee said. "Both of you." She looked at Tieneke. "They sit here every night and pray and read the Bible or whatever. And there was a time—am I right about this? —there was a time when both of you were out fucking other people?"

"Hear me out, honey," Karin said.

"Him I can understand," KayLee told her. "He's a guy. Guys can't help it almost, but you were sick--morning sickness maybe? Did I make you sick, Mom? I hope I did." She couldn't focus anywhere. "I get it. I'm not a kid anymore. I can figure this out. You were sick as a dog, and Dad had to go somewhere else to get his jollies—is that it? That's the story, Mom? You were out of commission in bed, so he had to take his love to town or something? But you too?"

"You don't understand," she said.

"What's there to get?"

"One person, KayLee. One person is it. The sum total is one man."

"That makes a difference?" she said. "*One* is hardly a slip-up, right? Shoot, who can't look past one little hot time in somebody's bed?"

Karin pulled a chair away from the table and sat. "You don't understand."

"What's not to get here, Mother?" she said. "What's not to understand? It's sophomore biology, for shit sake."

"It's not either, KayLee—we're talking about real people, real live human beings."

"Then tell me. Talk to me. Tell me it isn't true. Tell me this whole thing is a nightmare bad dream."

Karin waited. There were no simple answers, only a story her daughter would not understand. Woody was wrong, Tieneke thought. Maybe forgiving would be easier than understanding. Is that possible?

"This whole house," KayLee said, "this gorgeous place and all its cuteness—you should hear kids talk about it, Mom—'oh, KayLee, I just love what you mom did with your place—it's so beautiful. It's like a dream place, like a magazine.' But it's all just so much bullshit, you know?" She seemed to gain strength, fueled by her pride and anger.

"I wish you wouldn't say that."

"Then tell me," KayLee said. "Give me some way to understand."

"I want to hold you," Karin said, and took her daughter's hands in hers. "Our lives are not some kind of show, sweetheart. They're not. We believe what we say we believe—maybe even *because* of what happened, because of this whole ugly business."

KayLee stared straight ahead, arched her eyebrows as if she were picking up some transmission. "Oh, shit," she said. She looked straight back at her mother, then at Tieneke, then at her mother again, and then at Tieneke. "Mrs. Dekkers, tell me this. Right now, I don't trust my mother saying anything." The look on her face was dead serious. "Am I who I think I am?"

KayLee Faber's sharp mind had wandered a place no one, not even Tieneke had thought of, because the girl had every reason in the world to ask the question she just had. If she and Dawn were the same age, and Dawn was her father's daughter, and Karin Faber was sleeping with some other guy at the same time, then maybe KayLee herself was actually someone else's.

"Just hear your mom out," Tieneke told her.

"Who am I, Mother?" she turned to Karin. "Am I my father's daughter?"

A pause was all the answer KayLee needed. This discussion was dead in the water.

"Dawn Burnett is my sister, my dad's daughter," she said, "my stepsister—aren't we a lot alike?" She pulled her hand away. "We look so much alike—don't you think? And we act so much alike too? This daughter's never taken drugs, and my half-sister is strung out most the time. I work hard in school and sing solos in every church imaginable. She hangs out with assholes." All of this in a high-toned Pharisee voice. "I never once attempted suicide; this half-sister makes a habit of it. We're like twins, aren't we? --Siamese, in fact, I bet. We were connected at birth and you guys got us separated at some fancy hospital."

"Don't," Karin said.

"Then tell me how the hell I'm supposed to be some kind of saint right now," KayLee told her. "I don't have a clue because the saints I thought I knew sure as hell aren't."

"It was my fault too," Karin told her. She wanted badly to reach once more for both her daughter's hands. "KayLee, please," she said, "let's go into the sun room or something. This is no place to talk."

"My own mother?" KayLee said. "You're making this up, right? Don't protect him, Mom," she said. "That's what women do, but don't." It was costing KayLee great effort to stanch tears. "What you want me to believe is that my mother was in some asshole's bed?"

Karin nodded.

KayLee took a few steps back toward the door. She shoved her feet into the shoes she'd just removed, then pulled the vest back around her shoulders, took it off again, read the "Faber Trucking" label on the back, hung it up again methodically, and took her own jacket off an adjacent hook.

"Where you going?" Karin said.

Tieneke thought about standing in her way, but KayLee wasn't a child anymore. She wouldn't be restrained, and it would be wrong to try to hold her there like the child she wasn't.

"Don't go," Karin said.

KayLee pulled a stocking cap from a basket high up in the vestibule, pulled it down over her head, then jerked on a pair of gloves from the pockets of her jacket. "Got to dress for the cold," she said, mocking her mother. "If you're going to go out, you've got to dress for the cold, sweetheart." And then. "Who knows where you might get stuck on a night like this?"

"Please don't leave," Karin said.

But KayLee was on her own.

Even Karin had to grow up. "You wanted the truth," she told her daughter. "Now you have it. You're the only one who can decide what to do with it. Some assholes," she told her daughter, "are just human."

When she left, KayLee did so with a step that seemed emotionless. She closed the outside door behind her politely, latching it gently, as if she were comforted at having found a place to stand.

We're going to go get it

Dawn Burnett wasn't so much broken as tormented, Coby thought, beaten up by her own end-of-the-rope bewilderment, not so much brittle as deathly uncertain of what it was that had happened. Poor thing didn't understand her own body, even though every last voice in her soul was telling her the baby was gone. Maybe her body too. She lost it, she said.

What could Coby say? The child had lost a baby.

Whole clouds of useless words came from all kinds of people back when Jonathan was killed—parents, the pastor, friends from work, old roommates, Jonathan's own family. None brought healing. What substance there was in all those precious moments barely made it into her ears, her heart and mind and soul building a wall against billowing sentiments—"He's in a better place." Lines like that filled ditches in her memory. Words didn't count, meant nothing or very little. They just dirtied the world, litter. There was nothing to say.

And now here. A child lost a child.

She couldn't send the girl back out into the cold. The two of them—the boy too but he'd just stepped out--had to stay with her because there was plenty of room, plenty of warmth in the little rental place that just about turned her stomach when she realized it was the only place in town. The boy would stay too. They both would stay. They had to.

This morning she was confident this beautiful kid who'd taken a shot at ending her own life had been abused, raped and angry and lost. But she hadn't been angry at someone else, and hadn't appeared to hate anyone, not even this LeRoy jackass who'd put her up to an abortion. When she lost the baby, its death—her miscarriage--had carried her beyond hate. Her open wound grew from the place where, just for a month or so, a child had found a place, a child no more.

"I don't know," Dawn said when Coby asked exactly how long ago all of this went on. "Maybe two weeks, maybe more. I don't really know." She drew back for a minute. "Is it what people call 'post-partum'?"

Coby could have cried; we mature physically before we mature in almost any other way. "Do you mean," she asked, "is what people mean by postpartum what you're feeling?"

"All this cold—all this snow, all this damned cold, you know?" Dawn said. "I just got stuck with this awful feeling that it's always going to be this way, always." She pulled away slowly so she could use her hands. "It was such a bloody mess." She shuttered visibly. "I mean it. It was awful."

Coby's own heart bled to imagine the girl that way, sitting in her bedroom, more alone than she'd ever been in her life, nothing around her but her blood and the blood of a baby she'd already lost. "At home?" She grabbed Dawn's hand because she didn't want to let her feel alone.

"I'm not pregnant," Dawn said. It wasn't a question, but it really was. She wanted an answer.

"Lots of blood?" Coby said. "I'm a nurse."

Dawn's offered silence.

"It's likely that you're right--you're not pregnant," Coby told her.

"It's gone then." Not exactly a question.

So tough, so hard, so damned streetwise, but she was a child. "Dawn, honey," she said, both her hands on the girl's, "maybe you ought to tell me about it."

She pulled herself back, jerked a sleeve of her sweatshirt up to her eyes, but didn't look at Coby, didn't look into her face, stared up and into the next room, vacantly. "Well, that's good then," she said. "I was kinda sure, you know, but I didn't know really. Not super sure." She nodded, tried a smile. She seemed to want to unfold that news in her own mind, even though it wasn't news. She tried a smile. "Makes me happy, you know? I hoped that all of a sudden it wouldn't just start growing again—you know, like something in a garden. It's a miscarriage, right? I mean, that's what it is?"

"You maybe should tell me what happened," Coby told her.

Dawn looked into Coby's eyes. "It was a baby, wasn't it?" she said, poor kid. She needed to tell the story, Coby thought. "Wasn't fun," Dawn said. "I'll tell you that much. Maybe an abortion would have been better because what happened was really awful."

"You were alone, honey?"

"If my mother would have been home, I would have called her, I swear it—that's how much it hurt—I mean, inside." She pointed. "I would have asked her for help."

"In bed?"

Dawn nodded. "The first time."

"More than once—the blood?"

"Four times, maybe five if you count the last one."

"In the bathroom?" Coby asked.

"The first time in bed."

"Mom was home?"

"I figured if that was all there was to it, I could do it myself—"

"And she doesn't know—your mom, I mean?"

"Know what?"

"Know any of this? Does your mom know what happened?"

Dawn rubbed at her eyes, even though there were no tears. She held her strength by wetting her lips, biting them. "We haven't been all that close," she said, turning away towards the front window. "Mostly it's my fault, but there's so much shit there now that I don't know if it's worth redoing."

"There's never that much, honey."

"I just know I'm never, ever going back to LeRoy. Too much shit on that dead end, I'll tell you."

"I'll give you that one," Coby said. "But your mom's your mom. That's a different story."

"I would have called her the next time—the time in the bathroom," she said. "I was alone, and it hurt so bad that I would have tried to get her to help—I would have."

"There," Coby said. "Never say *never*."

"It took so long, like all day maybe." She closed her eyes, drew her fingers through her hair, then held her head as if it was throbbing, as if she had to keep her hands there to keep things from falling. "There I was on the floor—I wasn't on the toilet, so the bathroom floor was flooded."

"Pass out?"

"Just pain like nothing else I ever felt." It was a question she hadn't considered. She looked at Coby. "From the pain maybe, just the pain."

Dawn Burnett had miscarried. She might well have been pregnant for more than a couple of weeks. Coby knew very well what that meant.

"I don't know what to think," Dawn said. "Sometimes, you know? —sometimes I start to wonder about stuff, like who would my baby have been?"

"That's natural," Coby told her.

"I was like that once--little tiny something." She looked down at her hands. "I could have just bled out too, couldn't I?" she said. "I mean, God could have slipped me out down the tubes, just like he did with. . ." Where she was going there were no words. But then it came—what Coby had feared. "There *was* something there."

Dawn looked down at her hands again and spun the ring on her finger. "I was that kind of little thing myself once, and maybe it would have been better if I--" She stopped short. "My mom didn't want me, and my dad still doesn't."

"Don't say that. Don't even think it. You're here," Coby told her. "You're right here and you're a beautiful young woman."

"I saw it--that thing, that baby," Dawn said finally. "I'm sure I saw it, and it wasn't a baby."

That there was something in all that blood did not come as a surprise, given what this child had already described. It would be a horrible shock to see that little fetus, smaller than her thumb maybe, right there on the bathroom floor. That could have happened.

Dawn got up from the couch, and Coby let her stand there on her own.

"When I could breathe again, I kept telling myself that this pain and shit was a really good thing—that it meant that it was over, and I wasn't going to have a baby because that was even what I'd planned, what LeRoy wanted, and it didn't cost a thing or anything." She walked away to the other side of the coffee table, closer to the door. "I didn't want to have it pulled out of me or flushed out of me or whatever the hell else they do. I really didn't look forward to that, even though he told me it was something I could do. I thought a lot about it—about me, too, you know? —about how I bet my own mom wished I'd get washed out or whatever, I mean when she knew I was in her, how she probably thought that would be a blessing, too, I mean a blessing for it to be over."

"Don't say that, girl," Coby told her. "You don't know what your mom felt like. None of us do. We're all puzzles."

"Puzzles?" she said.

"I mean, we're all more than meets the eye, you know?"

"Puzzles?" she said again.

"I mean, we're like poems sometimes, you know?" Coby told her. "You know what I mean?"

"I like poems."

"You read them one day and they mean this, and the next day things change—they seem different or something. It's almost like they mean something else."

"Poems are puzzles, aren't they?"

"So are we," Coby told her. "And we can't know, you know? —we don't know what your mom was thinking when you were going to be born. We don't know."

The girl thought about that for a minute. "Well, I'm like a freak over there anyway," she told her. "They don't know what to do with me because I'm not like them at all."

"Your family?"

She nodded.

"And the father—this LeRoy?"

"Who cares?"

"Does he?"

"LeRoy," she said, twisting the name as if he were a mule. Just like that she came back to Coby again, eyes piercing. "I wanted to be happy about it, you know? —I did—because what happened wasn't something I just went out and did, went out and bought, you know, like new jeans. I didn't have it done to me, but it got done anyway. I didn't just get rid of it, God did." She ran her fingers through her hair again and shook it over her shoulders. "It was the worst pain I ever had, and then it was over, and I was sitting there on the bathroom floor in the middle of the day, nothing but blood all around."

"Listen, honey, I know married women with kids, who cracked up," Coby told her. "I'm not lying. What happened to you shouldn't happen to anyone."

"But it did."

Coby stood and walked over to where she was standing, took Dawn's hand and pulled her back to the couch beside her.

"So I took all of it—I'd wiped up a lot of the blood with the old shirt I was wearing and a towel and my stupid old t-shirts." Her voice fell away on her for a moment. "I honestly think I saw her," she said. "I don't know why I call it 'her'—I can't help thinking of it—I mean, I think of the baby as a girl for some reason. I don't know what babies look like when they're so tiny." Tears came in abundance, but she kept on talking. "I pulled on my dad's jacket and I was bare legs and it was cold, but I took it out to the burning barrel because I wanted everything to be happy and good again, you know, and after all there was no more kid. She was in my hands."

She looked up at Coby again, mimicked striking matches. "It was too windy, just like with me and Marcus, and I couldn't light the damned fire and soon enough I was out of matches, and I didn't know what the hell to do and my legs were freezing." She reached out for Coby's hands. "I couldn't burn things up because I couldn't even light a match, dammit. And I couldn't have been out there very long either because it was so cold that almost right away I couldn't even a hold a match or light one—I mean, my fingers were freezing and shaking and the wind was blowing and all that shit out there at the barrel behind the house, and I couldn't do it. I don't know why."

Jonathan's body lay in that coffin on those cold aluminum poles at the cemetery, and she remembered how the light in her own mind went dead. How many times she hadn't told herself now that she should have watched that whole coffin go down, should have watched *him* get lowered into the ground because some things are more important than we might believe at the time. She probably needed to see that body get put away. What was keeping her in this grief prison was that something hadn't ended. It needed to be over. You can tell yourself that forever, she thought, just keep saying and saying it, but it doesn't happen. It just keeps hurting.

"So, all that stuff is still out there?" Coby said, "—still out back? It's not burned?"

She shook her head. "I went out that night. When my parents were sleeping, I went out and hid it in the garden shack out back. Nobody goes out there in the winter—and it was so cold. I didn't want coyotes to get it or whatever—I don't know."

"How long ago?"

Dawn looked right into her eyes. "A couple weeks," she said. "Maybe a month."

"Still there, you think—all those things?" Coby asked.

Dawn shook her head. "I had in my mind to carry all those bloody things over to LeRoy to show him—that's what I was thinking. I just got to hate him, you know? So I put it in the trunk of my car."

"Did you?"

"When it came right down to it, I didn't bother because I kept thinking about it, kept thinking about him and his little operation, he called it. 'It's no big deal,' he'd say, as if it wasn't—and I bought it, Coby. I'm not at all proud to say I bought it."

"It's still a baby," Coby said quietly.

"That was bullshit, and he was bullshit too. I started to think that I didn't love him anyway and I was a total piece of shit myself, and somehow my body had killed my baby or something—I didn't know. I didn't get it, you know? I didn't understand."

She never seemed quite as strong as she did at that moment, Coby thought.

"I told myself he wasn't worth it anymore because what was wrapped up in all those old towels and t-shirts is so much better than he is—and she's dead—my baby, I mean. My baby's dead."

"Oh, child," Coby said, wishing there was more room in her arms.

She didn't try to stop the tears.

Dawn twisted herself around the corner of the coffee table, sat down beside Coby, reached out and around her with her arm. "I don't know what to do with her," she said. "I still have her."

"Oh, girl," Coby said. "Where is that stuff?"

"I don't know what to do."

Something plain-and-simple had to be done. That child had to be relieved of the burden she carried. They'd have to do something with whatever she'd wrapped up in those rags.

Something had to be done yet tonight. It wasn't just an it to her—it was a she.

Dawn had no car. She'd come with the kid, Marcus. "Where is it now?" Coby asked her, her arms around the girl.

"At the Brethower place."

Coby shook her head as if that line had no meaning.

"—Where LeRoy and Marcus live, way out in the boonies, an acreage."

"Inside?"

"In the cold," she said. She looked down at her hands as if to check them for stains, then shook her head. "It's been an icebox, you know."

Those rags and what was inside them had to be put away tonight, if Coby could just figure out how. They'd have to be buried in ground you couldn't break with a jack hammer. They'd have to be burned or something. She didn't know what could be done with them. They'd have to bury all that stuff above frozen ground like her Ojibwa people might, build a house around the body. She told God she needed to know what to do, even though she knew he didn't do special favors.

Dawn was not alone anymore with that tiny body and those bloody things. But something had to be done.

She ran in her bedroom, thinking about something soft and loving, a slip maybe, a wool sweater, something that would suggest the dignity that that frozen pile of bloody things demanded. She slung open her drawers. It couldn't simply be just any sweater, some odd print or the wrong color. Whatever it was she was looking for had to have meaning. She opened her closet, looked through her things. A blouse wasn't right, something that slight. What she needed was a blanket. She looked at her bed, but the down quilt wasn't right either, then thought of the blanket—the Pendleton on the shelf above, a gift from Jonathan. What he bought for her last birthday was the Pendleton because he knew it was something she wanted, a bright Navajo print.

"We're going to go get it, honey," Coby said. "You and me—we're going to go get it because it can't just sit there anymore. We need"—she honestly didn't know the right words— "we need to put it away."

You got to love that girl

Trent pulled his phone from his jacket pocket.

"Not smart," Marcus told him because he'd been around enough drivers ed stuff to know that the old guy teaching it at Cottonwood High—the ex-football coach—always told them getting out the smart phone was like asking to die. "Not supposed to use that thing," he said.

Trent looked at him as if he was little more than a brother. "This is an emergency." Flashed him the phone as if it was proof of something. "We're on our way back. Got a tree, a great one," Trent told Coby when he got her on the phone. "We both think you'll like it."

Marcus knew this Trent guy snuck "both" into the line because he wanted to tell her that the two of them were in Trent's truck and that this was turning into a team thing.

That was it. For five minutes at least, or so it seemed to him, Trent the principal sat there with that phone at his ear listening to Coby go on and on. He drove up the road far enough to find an old driveway across the ditch, backed in without taking the phone from his ear, pulled forward to turn around and headed back to town, all the while listening to Coby's voice coming through in little more than a buzz.

Marcus wanted to hear. Whenever he'd look across the seat, Trent nodded quickly as if whatever it was he was hearing was nothing at all and he'd tell Marcus right away, soon as he put the phone down. But all that time, the school man said absolutely nothing, nothing at all. They drove up to the next intersection, and Trent turned right, away from town, away from Coby's house.

"Where we going?" Marcus said.

"Your place," Trent told him, taking that phone down from his ear for once. "But you gotta show me where."

"My place?" Marcus said, but Trent was not into answering questions. He brought that phone back up to his ear, put his thigh up against the wheel, and pointed west with his other hand. It was meant as a question.

For the first time, this guy was being a big man and telling him what to do instead of playing cutesy. Something major was going on, some change in plans. The whole time they'd been moving, Trent hadn't hung up, hadn't talked either, just a grunt now and then, a "sure, sure" maybe, but that's it. Coby was telling some story.

"What's going on?" Marcus said.

Trent gave him a hundred quick nods, as if to say, *just a second, just a second.*

"I got an idea," Trent pulled the pickup off the road. "Maybe I'm crazy, Marcus Pritchard," he said, "but where's your grandma?"

"What's she got to do with this?"

Trent took that phone and put it between them, eye to eye, as if to say that it had everything to do with what he'd been hearing. "You care," he said. He seemed almost angry.

"That a question?"

"I know you do."

"Sure," Marcus said.

"I know she lives out here somewhere, but I don't know where—somewhere on the reservation."

Made no sense.

"Trust me," Trent said. "Just for now. You can tell me I'm flat out nuts, and we'll turn around when I'm done talking to Coby."

Fair enough, Marcus thought. As long as he could say no, it was fair. Barely an hour ago he was calling Grandma himself. Made him proud that this teacher guy believed—for whatever reason—that Grandma could be helpful. He pointed for Trent to keep driving west down the gravel.

"Listen," Trent told Coby, "Me and Marcus are going to pick up his grandma— "

Marcus couldn't hear Coby's words, but he could hear her surprise.

"Because I know her, and she's a class act. You're going to have to trust me on this, but I think we know what we're doing." He looked up at Marcus, and Marcus nodded. "She's an elder. She's like a judge."

Coby asked some question.

"Because she came in about Marcus," he told her, looking across the seat. "Not so long ago she came in because she wanted me to hunt him down." He broke into a smile. "Like tonight," he said. "I just got this feeling, you know? – she's going to be someone who'll help." He pointed out the windshield when they came to an intersection, and Marcus nodded, telling him not to turn. "She's a lot smarter than I am," he told Coby. "I don't know why—I just think I'm right on this one."

He should call her. He knew that. His grandma would be in that Chinese housecoat. Sometimes she was in her pajamas like really early, but that didn't mean she went to bed early. He should call her because she'd be ready. She'd be ready. "You got to love that girl," his grandma had told him not an hour ago. "Marcus, you just love that girl, hear?" He knew what she meant.

"All right—twenty minutes or so," Trent looked at the clock against the dash. "Maybe a half hour. Meet you there, deal?" Coby said something, and then, "'Without ceasing' the Bible says," Trent told her. "Sure," and then quit.

He stuck the phone back into his jacket, then took the kind of deep breath that, on a cold night in December, almost fogged the windshield when he let it go.

"My grandma?" Marcus said.

"You wanted to know what she meant by 'I lost it.' That's what you told me, Marcus," Trent told him. "I remember you asked. 'What's that mean?' you said." He looked back up at the road, grabbed the wheel with both hands at the top. "I know now," he said. "Your girlfriend had a miscarriage."

"I know that," he said.

Trent looked at him as if he were just another naughty kid.

"You thinking it was mine, I bet?" Marcus said. "—That I was the father?"

Trent said nothing.

"You do, don't you?" He didn't know what it was, but something started to pinch somewhere behind his face at that moment and he worried for a second about losing it right then and there. "Well, it's not, you asshole. It was LeRoy's, my roommate's. It wasn't mine."

"She didn't tell me that—Coby didn't." He slowed down. "I'm sorry—I really am."

"You mean all of that you were listening to was just Coby bad-mouthing me?"

"No, no, no. Nothing of that. She just didn't mention that it wasn't yours, didn't say that— "

"What were you talking about all that time anyway?"

And then the story came out, the story Dawn had told Coby and Coby had told Trent. How Dawn had started to bleed and didn't stop for a long time. How sometime on a Sunday she'd gone into the bathroom and left blood all over the floor in horrible pain, how she'd actually delivered something, something she saw, something she couldn't just flush away, something that wasn't a baby and was—something that probably looked bad, but she couldn't help but love because it was a kid, somehow it was a kid, Trent told him.

"Something like a baby?" Marcus asked.

Trent pulled over again because he didn't want to drive and tell the story at the same time. There they stood along a country road not all that far from where Dawn had thought about ending her own life. "It's not like a baby, really," Trent told him. "It doesn't, you know, look like one exactly."

Grotesque, bloody shapes wandered into his imagination.

"It doesn't just drop out. It takes more pain than you and I can imagine."

"Even if it's a miscarriage?"

"Trust me, my wife had two."

Nothing made sense.

"I'm divorced," Trent said. There was enough light from the dash lights for Marcus to see that it wasn't anything he was proud of. "I can't blame it totally on miscarriages, but they had something to do with it."

Dawn had lost it—that's what she told Coby. It wasn't like an abortion. Maybe in some ways it was worse because it was something that happened to her all alone.

"How come did it happen?" Marcus said. "LeRoy do something? Shit, I'll kill him."

Trent shook his head. He pulled down his jacket zipper. It was getting warm in the truck. "I used to think—I don't know if it's true, Marcus, but I used to think that what made it worse is the fact that something in them, something in their own bodies failed them. She can't blame somebody who took it out of her. She's only got herself to blame."

"You mean your wife?"

"And Dawn Burnett."

"Why?" Marcus said.

"Probably a thousand reasons," Trent didn't even look at him. "And because there's a thousand lousy reasons, there's no single good one." He shook his head. "That's what hurts—you know, you want to shoot somebody but there's no target."

"Hurts them?" Marcus said.

"Me too," he said. "But it's not the same. That baby, that little fingerling thing we called Adam once upon a time, of all things, that baby is inside them, and it grows inside their own insides, and they know it, even in the first couple weeks. Even if they never had a baby before, some of them get this sense that something's in there that never was." Trent looked up and turned toward him. "And it's life--and when it's gone—I couldn't help thinking this, really—when it's gone and no one's actually taken it away, she started to think of her own body as a killer. Not really, but something like that."

He wasn't talking about Dawn. "You got to love that girl," his grandma had told him. "Listen to me, boy—you got to love her." That's what grandma said.

"You think Dawn too?" he asked Trent.

"I think Coby knows."

Just like that, everything that happened last night replayed in a moment in his mind—that dance around the fire, their getting warm in bed, the sex, Dawn leaving without saying a word. "You think she drove into the ditch because she lost that baby?" he asked Trent.

"Coby believes it," he told him. "Wouldn't be the first time either— "

"You mean, your ex?"

"No," he said immediately. "But it changed her. She was someone I hadn't married—and maybe I was too, I don't know." He looked at Marcus. "Your grandma told me about your mon and dad, about all of that. Shit happens, right? It just does."

"That's what Coby was telling you?"

"Dawn was with her, so I had to sort of put the pieces together, but Coby knows I can do that because Coby knows about me."

"You love her?" Marcus said.

"Shit, yes," he said. "Can you blame me?" He put that pickup back in gear and pulled away from the side of the road. "Now which way do I go to your grandma's?" he asked.

"I better call her."

"Smart," he said. "And we're going to meet at your place."

Made no sense. "Why?" Marcus asked.

"Because that little thing, that little tiny, tiny baby, is wound into some blankets or sheets or something, and it's out there somewhere in a machine shed."

When she left the house last night, she must have stopped out there, Marcus thought. She must have left it there where they had the fire.

"You didn't know that?"

"I didn't know shit," Marcus told Trent. "I had no idea. I thought she had an abortion. That's what she told LeRoy—that she had an abortion."

"So, this LeRoy didn't know all of this either?"

"Lots of people have abortions," Marcus said.

"Lots of people have miscarriages," Trent said. "But you never saw this bundle of stuff? That's what you're saying? You were with her that night, and you didn't see it?"

He shook his head. "When she left, she must have ditched it out there."

"In a machine shed?" Trent asked if it was hard to believe.

"We did this thing—had a fire out there, you know, burned up some things that she'd done for LeRoy when they were together, some pictures, some drawings. I thought it would be good, you know, to do something special because she and LeRoy weren't a thing anymore, and she was all crying and stuff. She didn't want him to have them, so she came by and grabbed them and we burned them up, had this ceremony sort of, like a couple of blanket Indians."

He let that sit for a minute.

"There was more too," he said.

Trent never said a thing or asked a question.

"That's where we're going eventually," Trent said. "I don't know what Coby's got planned, but something in me said your grandma might know what to do—she's one wise old woman."

"I called her, just tonight. Before you showed up, I called her." Whatever this guy was up to, it was good. "I called her because I didn't know what Dawn meant when she said she lost it. I just didn't get it."

"She's like your mom," Trent said.

"I never had one—what do I know?" Marcus told him. "Far as I'm concerned, she is my mom." He pointed up the road. "Her place is maybe a few miles up—we got a ways to go."

"Am I right about her?" Trent asked him. "You think I'm right to go get her?"

He nodded. He did.

The Brethower Place

To say Scotty Faber had plans for LeRoy would be pushing it, but when the kid first started working for him he'd honestly thought there were some possibilities for something good because LeRoy had this high-voltage personality everybody noticed, even the drivers. For a while Scotty had thought about what he might do with that big, showy personality, what LeRoy could sell, how the whole company could grow with a slick talker who really knew how to hold a crowd. Yeah, he remembered LeRoy Van Kamp.

He grabbed the key off the desk in the motel room, put his billfold back in his pocket, and zipped up his jacket. He wasn't about to camp out in some sleazy motel room too full of memories he wasn't interested in refreshing.

Dawn Burnett and LeRoy Van Camp, he told himself. He could have cried. His own daughter. Suicide. That's where she'd be.

The kid lived on the old Brethower place, maybe 15 miles out and pretty much straight west. Little wreck of a house with a couple of bedrooms, a machine shed out back, and four or five steel grain bins—maybe an old tractor stuck back in the weeds. A pond—something dammed up just behind the house, untended. Nothing really to keep the place from being torn down except some family somewhere—didn't know who, probably somebody named Brethower—so attached to the place they couldn't torch it, having grown up there. Had been a rental for 20 years already, which always meant disaster.

Even if there was nothing he could do about KayLee, maybe he could make some things right with Dawn Burnett, keep her from this kid LeRoy, who had trouble keeping himself zipped.

The woman in the motel office would hear him leave, just the same way as she'd heard him drive up, probably the only customer. He crept out slowly as if to keep down the noise, got into the truck, backed around the flagpole in the middle of the parking lot, and headed back down Main. He knew where LeRoy lived.

He wasn't flying when he hit the gravel because he wasn't a kid anymore and Glenn wasn't all wrong—it was stupid to think this whole mess would up and leave if he pulled this chain or pushed that button. Sometime down the line, morning would come, and night would slip away the way it's supposed to. Things were going to get better.

Glenn calls, tells him about how Dawn Burnett walked right by him as if to test him or something; and she's hanging out with a kid he knows, a kid who quit on him less than a year ago. There's a path there, and it leads right to the Brethower place. Maybe he could keep her from LeRoy. He reached for the phone and turned it off.

When LeRoy quit, Scotty thought all the kid needed was just a little tending is all. Most kids do, boys anyway. Takes some time for them to cool down. Did him.

He knew about that, and that's why he'd hired him, even though he wasn't needing any drivers just then. There were things to do around the shop, keeping trucks up, and LeRoy was born on a ranch, even if it was a third-rate operation; at least he knew about cattle. It was taking more time than he had himself to keep up that little herd he just didn't have the heart to get rid of. When he wasn't cleaning trucks or whatever, LeRoy could do chores—that's the way he had it figured.

Wasn't a bad kid either, just too much wind in him and just a little out of control. But friendly? —no kidding. Everybody liked him, more or less, this Van Camp kid.

It still wasn't terribly late, he told himself, and he knew it was the Brethower place and he knew roughly how to get there. He was never more than an hour from home maybe, and he had the phone. Maybe if he went out there, talked to the kid, found the girl too maybe—who knows? It was time for him to take hold of some things with respect to this Dawn

Burnett, time to introduce her to her sister. If he could right it with Dawn, maybe KayLee, you know? —that's how we figured.

Straight as an arrow west out of town on the old highway, then south a ways, but nowhere near the river—the Brethower place. He could see lights from three miles off because the snow had quit now and the place was down in a low spot.

It was something he could do instead of sitting in that firetrap and watching old football games. Try to say something to this girl who wanted him to do that, just tonight, who walked right past him to get his attention. He owed her that. Try it anyway, and then things between him and KayLee might just be different somehow. Might be. At least I'm doing something, he told himself.

Not long before, in the pickup, he was bawling like a newborn, trying to figure what to do and where to go. And just like that, it's Glenn who calls and tells him the news that's just about exactly what he needed to hear, the whole works too, not just that the girl had come walking by the way she had, but that she's seeing LeRoy Van Camp. And just like that, he's on the way out to the Brethowers. Just like that. Hand-of-God sort of thing, he tells himself. No other way to account for it really. Nothing he's done at all, but what's been done for him, this yellow brick road to steer him somewhere through the mess, to make sure he knew that Jesus wasn't sleeping under some river valley cottonwood.

She'd tried to walk right past him in a way that made Glenn think it wasn't just a quick trip to the washroom. There was more to it. She wanted him to see her. It was like she was asking for what he was about to give her, something of himself, of the man who was her father.

That's the way he could start it, when he'd get there. That's what he could say to start up the talk. He could start by saying that
it was a time for something to be healed. Maybe there was something he could do about her life. Didn't matter how cold it was, he told himself. It was something he could do, something he could do yet tonight.

But what did he know about her? Some bad times—that much he knew. But people got over bad times once they grew up—her mother had, Celine. For that matter, so had he.

They'd both come up strong after crap that had nearly killed them.

So much of what he'd been back then was hazy and beyond memory. Drink was part of all that—all kinds of booze, whole weekends gone. He'd didn't marry Karin to get himself over the mess his life had become, and she had never tried to put a ring in his nose. Often enough, she was as smashed as he was, before and after they got married. Even his wedding night was gone. Not nightmareish, just a fog.

But Karin had come out of it before he did. If something didn't change, they were both going to crash—and they'd already had KayLee, a darling kid who had come out whole. That she'd come out in one piece, everything fully there, was something.

Celine was little more than an old picture whose color has faded so badly that the outline of her face is just about the only feature distinguishable. She was young, she was eager, and she was easy. And she wasn't the only one.

He and Karin were in their trailer back then, and it was Super Bowl Sunday. Every last Super Bowl since then put him in mind of that day. Super Bowl Sunday, and he'd been drunk out of his mind. He'd flipped the van early that morning, or late that night, New Year's Eve. They bought it because of the baby. He'd flipped the van on gravel somewhere a mile or so from where they lived, and that night—after closing every last bar in two counties—he was on his way home, loaded to the gills, when he fell asleep. He didn't remember the accident or the hike home, just remembered trudging down the road thinking it was a blessing that he'd flipped the van that close to his own bed.

None of that he remembered all that well.

It wasn't as cold that night, he told himself as he looked out the frosted windshield of his truck, wasn't as cold or he would have never made it because all that alcohol in the system, people said, isn't any kind of preservative. He'd likely have died. But it was a night *like* this, he thought—the fields bright with snow, something that doesn't always happen where there's so much wind.

Karin was standing at the door when he opened his eyes. He'd slept that night—that morning—on the couch. She was holding KayLee in her arms—maybe four or five months old—two suitcases behind her, and she was telling him that she was going to her mother's because there was no way she was putting up with it anymore. It was like he'd come to consciousness with some TV show blaring, Karin talking at him.

She wasn't really blaming him because she hadn't been a homebody herself in those days before KayLee came—even after a bit. She just stood there at the door, winding a blanket around her baby, and announced that she was moving out, taking KayLee with, and that she'd be at her mother's because there was no way she was doing life in this kind of madness.

She'd told him that she'd gone out to find the van because when he stumbled in he'd told her it was flipped somewhere; and when she'd found it, on its roof and in the ditch, she'd climbed inside, through a window after breaking out the shards, and then tried to find every last bottle or can she could because sooner or later the cops were going to be out there looking themselves, once they'd heard about his van being there, ditched the way it was. And then it would start again. They'd come by asking, and sooner or later they'd take his license away and she'd have to taxi him all over again and who knows how long for this time?

There were tears, from both of them—from KayLee too—who had no idea what was going on. She was just crying. And Karin wasn't sad—that wasn't it. She'd simply come to see that life in the way they were living it, offered nothing anymore, and she wanted no more of it, she'd said. She wasn't pitching righteousness either. She had no right to judge him. But she'd said she was crawling around in a frozen, upside down van trying to save her husband, the baby at home with no one there to care for her, her husband sleeping off another damned bender, when she just broke out in tears because it was clear that something had to change. She couldn't go on, couldn't do it anymore. Once in a while a sniff or two, some fingers up to her eyes.

He was on the couch, smelling like a brewery, his coat still on around his shoulders, a bag of chips emptied in front of the coffee table, where the cat had decided to get what he could from what Scotty had left open once he'd checked out.

Then she left, just as she said she would, and that day he hadn't even watched the Super Bowl, because that day, a

Sunday, he'd never once questioned whether she was stringing him or whether she was dead-on serious, because he knew she wasn't bullshitting.

That was the bottom floor. It wasn't him crawling out of a flipped van that he saw in his imagination, it was Karin crawling in, not in darkness either because it was morning when she'd gone out that Super Bowl Sunday, but in the darkness of a life that that very day he'd begun to see was getting him nowhere. Something had to change.

Celine was part of that life he'd left behind, as was this girl, Dawn. Once they had moved away, she was out of sight, out of mind, while in their lives forgiveness became the clear and open road out of storms. He and Karin had come out of all of that, marching along like onward Christian soldiers, radiant the new start the Lord on high had given them. Scotty had never even gone to AA once he'd determined that what he saw before him in the empty trailer that Sunday morning was not a way of life he really wanted for himself—or for his wife and daughter. He knew some guys who'd done it all themselves too, who'd simply quit and didn't go back. If they could do it, he could—and he did.

Dawn, his daughter, was with LeRoy. His child was the one he went on and on about. There was the time he and somebody—was it Alvin? —were in the shop going on and on about women. Christy Aalberts stopped by. She stood there in the office and the two of them, Alvin and LeRoy, were out back with the trucks, talking way too loud, and it grated on him because who knew when one of his daughters might come running for a Tootsie Roll Pop he kept in the drawer?

"You know, I'd rather screw than eat," LeRoy told Alvin, volume way up, something like that, probably worse; and Karin's coffee friend right there in the office beside him and all the while he's trying to cover the chatter from out back.

He pulled off the road again for a minute, just slowed down and came to a stop because what had been running in road gear in his mind just about shut down. He reached up above the visor as if there were cigarettes there, but he'd stopped smoking years before. All around, the world was dark, the interior lights shining full in his face, so he dimmed them and sat there, the engine humming softly, the truck rocking gently from big gusts of wind that simply wouldn't stop, the heater fan throwing out what he needed to survive.

It had never occurred to him before that when LeRoy went on and on about what he was getting off his girl, that girl was his.

He would have done something, fired him.

Or would he?

He'd never once put a face on that girl, not that other parts of her hadn't shown up in his own imagination when LeRoy went on and on about what he was getting. He never saw a face.

Taking the pickup west, heading out to the Brethower place, where the two of them were probably holed up on the couch, or in bed, to stay out of the cold—it was the right thing to do. Maybe he could still be the father he never was. Forgiveness is real.

What happened years ago was coming out of cold storage, or wherever it had been ice-jammed. The way he figured right then was that it was probably past time to start making peace. Something had to be done, *had to* because his own KayLee had strung him up. It was time for something closer to peace.

He pulled away from the side of the road. If two kids were buck naked, he was going right into that bedroom and tell that child what he'd planned to say—that he knew she'd tried to make contact with him that night, that it was wrong of him not to notice, that he'd spent too much of his life telling himself that she wasn't his daughter, when she was *very much* his. He'd say how there had to be amends, and that process was going to start right now. All of that was something that had to be said and had to be said tonight—he didn't care how cold or how late or how he found them.

Then KayLee. He'd have to do something about KayLee.

He saw the lights from the Brethower place. Someone was home all right. The old place stood on the broad expanse of open land like some square cloud against ground that was only partially covered with snow, two lights, like cats' eyes--one on the barn, one on the house. Whoever was home wasn't alone. They were a thing, Glenn said, the two of them, LeRoy and a girl who was really his own daughter.

He wasn't about to stand in the front of that house—there was no porch there—and beat on the door. Not anymore. That wasn't the point. He was going to beat on the door for ten seconds and march right in.

Karin was going to be calling him soon, bawling, he was sure, bawling her eyes out. He reached in his pocket and held his phone, then put it in the console because this was something he had to do himself. He didn't need to talk to Karin about it. Something about all of this was purely his, not hers. She had a story she was likely telling KayLee right now somewhere, maybe at Dekkers. Karin didn't know Dawn Burnett walked right by him tonight, walked right by and he hadn't even noticed. He needed to do something about that.

Jesus had a plan here, a plan he'd fallen into, had to be guided into. They'd just been talking about his workmanship, God's workmanship.

It just so happened he knew where LeRoy lived, *just so happened*. Glenn's wife knew the kid's name. *Just so happened* Glenn decided to call when he was sitting there waiting for life to happen in that shithole motel with too many memories he had to choke to forget. God wanted him to talk to this daughter he'd not even thought much about. It was something that had to happen, finally had to happen.

It was God's will.

Twelve west and three or four south

Woody didn't need a play-by-play to determine what had gone on at the Dekkers between mother and daughter. It had all been set in motion last night on some country road halfway to nowhere. Tieneke's voice wasn't broken when she called, but it was stiff and unyielding in a way that wasn't like her. That tone was all he needed to understand that what had to happen did. Sweet little KayLee, everybody's choice for Miss Cottonwood, had finally heard the whole story.

"Come over right now," Tieneke told him.

When he walked in, the two of them sat where he'd sat with Karin not all that many hours before. Dark of night now, and Karin's eyes were overflowing, a box of Kleenex sitting awkwardly in her lap.

"She left," Tieneke said, trying her best to be calm. "She took off. I left the keys in—I always do. She just took off."

"Where?" Woody said. He didn't bother taking off his jacket.

Karin shook her head.

"Some friend's place maybe?" Tieneke said.

"I don't know that right now she has any," Karin said. "'It's all different,' she said, remember? 'It's all just different.'"

There was only one option. "It's Dawn, the only one who knows," Woody said. He looked at Karin. "My money says she's going somewhere to find Dawn. That's all she thinks she's got left."

"Where?" Karin said.

Sharlene Maanders had told him how there was this place out in the country somewhere, an old house where who-knows-what went on, a guy living there—she hadn't said who.

It was Dawn's boyfriend or something. The name of the kid was gone, but he had the number she'd given him in the pocket of his jacket. He stepped back out of the room, grabbed it and his phone.

"Shar, you got some directions for us?" he said when she said hello.

"You already owe me big time," she said. "You know that, right? Can you change my grade anymore, or is that written on stone a decade later?"

"You can take the class over," he said. "I love non-traditional students."

"It's twelve west," she said, "on its own road, Brethower Road, and it's the Brethower place, the Brethower home place. Know any Brethowers? —I don't."

"They're gone, I suppose— "

"It's twelve west or something, and my sources say like three or four south—little place, just a house and machine shed and a couple of old buildings, middle of nowhere. Maybe a chicken coop."

"You got your sources with?" he asked her.

"Too cold a night to for a girl to be alone," she told him.

"I got a job for you."

"Too cold to leave this nest too," she told him. "Way too cold."

"Babysitting."

"What?"

"You heard me—babysitting. Not an option. I'm serious, Shar. You're needed."

"You and the missus? —did I miss something?"

"Scotty Faber's."

"Oh, no—you kidding?"

"I'm not kidding," he told her. "Honestly, Shar, you're needed. Take the hunk along. No sweat. But you're needed."

"Oh, no," she said again.

"Big bucks in it," he told her.

"We're on our way," she said. "But I think you should know. Me and Jack—after work, we sometimes just stop by the café, you know? Lots of times I don't pack a lunch at all, so I'm hungry." She let that sit. "You going to let me gossip here, Mr. Dekkers? That okay?"

He could hear her pulling on a jacket. "I owe you big time," he said again.

"She was there, in the café, with this kid—and it wasn't LeRoy, but it was this kid, this Indian kid—I don't know him."

"She drop LeRoy?"

"I don't know about that—we think the kid lives with LeRoy." She waited a minute, as if what she was a burden. "She was there, at the café—Dawn Burnett, I mean—and I spotted her because you were looking for her." There was a voice behind her, a man's voice. "It's not like I keep track of who's eating what or anything, but I looked around tonight and I saw her, and I thought of you out looking all over the country—and there she was. You ready for this?"

"Now what?"

"Scotty Faber was there too. They were both there in the café, Mr. Dekkers."

"Not together?"

"No, no, no—he was doing his Bible study thing, but they were both there."

"Oh, Lord," Woody said.

Woody knew Tieneke was in no frame of mind to figure out what could be done. She'd wandered to the couch beside Karin, who couldn't stop crying. The three of them had no choice right now but to try to find KayLee. They'd spent most of the night trying to find her suicidal half-sister and hadn't been able to track her down. Now it was Dawn's perfect half-sister.

"We got to go," he announced.

"Where?" Tieneke said.

"West of town some place—I got the directions anyway--some woebegone place out in the middle of nowhere, not all that far from where Ms. Burnett," he looked at Karin to see if the name created any reaction and it did, "to where Dawn Burnett's boyfriend lives, kid named LeRoy."

"LeRoy what? —he used to work for Scotty? —LeRoy who?" Karin said.

"KayLee's still got Dawn on her mind. Who else now? At least Dawn knows what she's feeling, you know? Dawn gets it." It felt hurtful to say that, but he told himself almost anything he could say right now would be. "We know Dawn's not home—at least she wasn't. I can call Celine just to make sure." He felt for the phone. "It's so blasted cold they couldn't have gone far, you think? —she and this kid who lives with LeRoy. They've almost got to be there." He stepped over to the couch and got down on knees that were getting too old to bend, did it anyway. "KayLee wanted to talk to her," he told Karin. "Earlier, she wanted to be with her."

Karin was still dizzy. "You think it was wrong of us not to tell her?" she asked. "She was just a girl. I can't believe we did it all wrong. Oh, child."

"You didn't," Tieneke told her and pulled Karin into her arms. "I don't think anyone would blame you. She wouldn't have begun to understand."

"But I can't leave," Karin said. "The girls are here—I can't leave them alone. Holly's just fifth grade—they're all three of them in bed."

"I got a sitter," Woody said.

"What are we going to do?" Tieneke asked.

"—Whatever the Lord almighty lets us, I guess," he said. "But we're going to stay with this thing for a while anyway because there's too much that's got to work itself out yet."

"I don't know how to thank you guys." Karin stood up. "I don't know what I'd do right now if you weren't here."

"You'd find a way," Tieneke said. "Remember how you came over when Teresa died?" She clamped down her lips quickly. "Right away you were there."

They'd lived too long out here, Woody thought, lost far too many kids—most of them Lakota. But once it started, it could just get away from you. "Get your coat on, Karin," he told her. "I'm sure they'll be here any minute."

"Let me just check on the girls," Karin said. She had wounds, Woody thought. Good Lord almighty, she had wounds.

"Shar says they were both in the café tonight," he told Tieneke Karin when went upstairs.

"Both?"

"Dawn and Scotty—both."

"You're kidding—something happen?"

He listened for Karin, heard nothing. "She didn't think anything of it until I mentioned coming here, to Scotty's place." He stepped back to the French doors just to be sure

Karin wasn't coming. "Not until I dropped his name into the conversation did she put it together."

"Does she know?"

"She didn't set the world on fire in Western Civ, but she's all there. You remember what KayLee said about Dawn—'in some ways, she's lots smarter.'"

The back doorbell rang, before anyone could get it, Shar and Jack let themselves in.

"Could be a while," Woody told the two of them. "There's no telling when we'll be back." He looked at Karin, as if to warn her, then turned back to the two of them. "Tomorrow morning you'll both be sportin' halos, I swear—maybe even tonight yet." He didn't know Jack, had never seen him before—big tall guy with busy beard and no hair on his head. Huge shoulders. "We'll stay in touch."

He had no idea really if Shar Maanders knew Karin Faber, but in Cottonwood people knew each other without being friends.

"We got to go," Woody said.

She's my own flesh and blood

Way out in the country, Scotty slowed down for the intersection, looked both ways as if there might be someone else coming down the pike. Super cautious.

He could feel how shaky he was, how unsure of how this was all going to go down. He'd never spoken to the girl, his daughter, seen her only a few times, then from afar. He was determined to excuse himself—no, not *excuse*, he was going to ask her forgiveness for not seeing her, not acknowledging her in the café. But that wouldn't be all of it. Maybe if he could patch this thing up some, he'd be putting something back together at least, something that will make the morning break in that lousy motel room.

What was about to go on was something that should have occurred long ago. That, he knew. It had to be done. He'd never backed down from those things that simply had to be done.

He remembered picking up cattle from the Brethower place years ago, just after they'd got things back together, he and Karin. He didn't remember who kept cattle out there anymore, but he knew the place was a rental and a wreck. Somebody couldn't burn the place down, someone who grew up there and just couldn't raze it, absentee landlord, somebody with more heart than brains, and more money than they likely ever dreamed of when his great-grandparents' family lived out here, snugged up close to the reservation.

He would try to love her because that's what the Lord required. It shouldn't be hard. The girl needed it badly or she wouldn't have tried to do what she did. He could deliver on that score, he told himself—loving her.

Two cars stood in the driveway. She had to be there. He didn't know her well enough to guess where else she might be, but he knew enough to think that if she was going to be anywhere, she'd be with LeRoy. She liked him.

He pulled over at the top of the hill to rehearse exactly what it was he was going to say when he knocked on the door, how he was going to hope LeRoy would let him in because he planned to tell the kid that he really needed to apologize to Dawn for something that happened. LeRoy, he thought, would let him in.

It was LeRoy talking that one time when Karin's friend Christy was in the office. The kid was always talking about sex, but he'd gotten himself stoked up for the other guys, who were all married and envious.

Dawn Burnett kept the guys occupied when they did their work in the shop, as if she was there on stage for all of them to see, as if the shop was some strip club. He had no idea the girl was his daughter, his own daughter. Made him want to cry.

He doused his lights. He didn't want them to look out the front window and see his truck standing there at the corner. His own flesh-and-blood. What if LeRoy had been talking about KayLee that way?

He needed to talk to her, to apologize. He switched on the lights and started idling down the hill toward the driveway.

She was just a kid, but it made no difference because he knew he had to do what he had to do, even if she told him to go to hell, just like KayLee had. Something had to be broken, and it didn't matter what the outcome was. He had to figure that no matter what happened, it was going to take a long time to heal, forever to forgive.

There were bales up against the side of the house to keep out the wind. He got out and shut the door softly, even though he thought it might have been better to let him know he was there. He looked upstairs—no lights. Doesn't matter what they're doing, he told himself. They were there, and something had to happen because something had to get healed.

Doorbell looked to him as if it hadn't been used for forty years. He hit it anyway. The screen door wasn't latched, but the storm door was shut tight, no windows. He'd rather not pound on the door because LeRoy might just assume it would be cops. He pushed the ancient doorbell again.

He figured he could walk around the house and look in through windows, just to be sure she was there. But the thought of him window-peeping that way was like a pervert. Banging on the door would put a halt to whatever they were up to.

He thought through what it was he wanted to say. "I want to talk to Dawn," he'd tell her. "I need to speak with her."

LeRoy will get it. He had to know.

"She's my daughter"—that's what he'd tell him. "She's my daughter. She's my daughter. She's my own flesh and blood."

There was a window just to the right of the door, so he stepped off the cement porch to see if he could see anything, and he did. Two of them were on the couch in the flickering glow of the television. There were clothes on the floor. If he was to pound on the door, he'd better do it before things marched along. So, he stepped back up on the porch and knocked—not with the heel of his hand, but with knuckles, a sharp rap that would sound less threatening than a beating.

No sound. "Give me the best words," he said, and then "get me through this."

He knocked again, and the door opened. It was LeRoy. His hair was messed, and his face looked red, but that wasn't strange—what was odd was the shock. The two of them stood two feet apart and stared. The guy who was never without words seemed to have none.

"Scotty?" he asked, as if he had to scramble through a file to get the name.

"Can I come in?" Scotty said. "It's late and all, but I got some things that I gotta say because for way too long, they didn't get said."

"Don't know if this is the right time," LeRoy said, and then he nodded, as if her being there was some kind of secret.

"I know she's here," Scotty said. "Just let me in. I just got to talk to her."

"LeRoy." The voice came from behind him. somewhere, something inaudible, but enough for Scotty to know the girl he'd seen on that old couch wasn't Dawn Burnett. It was KayLee.

"I don't know that you want in," he said. "I know she don't want you around, Scotty, that much I know."

"You and KayLee?" Scotty asked.

"Not my doing," Le Roy told him. "Nothing of this was my doing—I didn't ask for it."

"LeRoy," KayLee said again.

"You let my daughter alone," Scotty said, "or I'll kill you. You so much as touch her and I'll come after you."

LeRoy sniffed, wet his lips a bit, and looked down at his bare toes.

"Who's there?" KayLee said from across the room.

"Okay," LeRoy said, and he opened the screen door.

Just about every morning she got up for Rice Chex because she had to have a bowl before anything else, and her hair was always a mess. Not here.

"What the hell are you doing here?" she asked him. She had a blanket around her. Her vest was lying over an overstuffed chair beside the couch, clothes on the floor.

Nothing was said, but something made her stand there and let that blanket down from her shoulders and slip down to her waist so she stood there before him, making it very clear what she was up to.

What could he say? What could he possibly say?

"I'm looking for Dawn," he told her. "I thought maybe she'd be here."

"We broke up," LeRoy told him. "We aren't a thing anymore."

"Go home," KayLee said. "Leave. You're not wanted here."

There was nothing he could do or say, absolutely nothing, and he knew it. He couldn't tell her not to do what her old man did, but he could wrestle her out of there. He wouldn't worry for a minute about LeRoy. LeRoy didn't care, but what killed him was that she would. He'd have to carry her, kicking and screaming.

He shut the door behind him, stood there in the room, because he wouldn't let himself leave.

LeRoy went back to the couch and sat beside her, didn't sit back or anything, just sat there, arms up on his knees.

"Where's Dawn?" Scotty said.

"Don't have a clue," LeRoy told him, "but the last place she'd be is here." Then, to KayLee. "For shit's sake," he said, "pull that blanket up."

"I didn't see your car," Scotty said. "I mean, I saw a car, but I didn't know it was yours—I didn't see it, I mean."

"Lots of things you haven't seen, Daddy."

There they were—the two of them on the couch. What she wanted had nothing to do with LeRoy. "Don't do it," he said to her.

"Do what?"

He just pointed.

"She comes out here and says she wants to talk, you know—because she says she knows what her old man is like." LeRoy stopped. "She says she knows it all, about Dawn, about her being her sister and everything, and she says she needs to talk to somebody who knows her, you know?"

"She's my daughter," he said.

"Doesn't a mean a thing right now," KayLee told him.

"You're coming with me," Scotty said, and he walked across the rug and stood there in front of them.

"I'm not finished," KayLee told him.

"I love you," he said.

"Like shit," she said, and she pulled that blanket around her.

"Go home. This ain't no time to play hard ass with her," LeRoy said. "She's made of steel, Scotty. I swear, just like her old man."

KayLee put her arm around him.

Everything went silent. He stood just beyond the door, looking at a girl who acted as if he wasn't even there, raised a hand in front of her face as if she wanted him to see it, and pushed it down into LeRoy's crotch.

"Dammit, woman," LeRoy said. He turned toward Scotty, his hands up and off KayLee. "I swear I won't touch her," he told Scotty. "You always treated me good—when I worked for you, you treated me right. I won't touch this girl, but you got to get the hell out now. You got no place here. You gonna have to let me tame her. I won't do nothing to her—I swear."

LeRoy was right. Scotty knew he couldn't have wrestled her out of there.

He walked out, drunk, it seemed. His mind went blank, completely, terrifyingly blank.

We're all in this together, Mr. Principal

Coby needed to tell Trent she was in her car with Dawn and therefore had to be guarded. So she said nothing when he answered his phone, hoping he'd get the message about what she could say.

"You there?" he said.

"Yes," she said quickly.

He waited, thoughtfully. He was not difficult to like, she told herself

"She's with you?" he asked her.

"Yes," she told him. "Where are you?"

"We're in the driveway in front of Marcus's grandma's trailer. She's just now pulling on her big jacket—I can see her through the storm door."

"Here's what I'm thinking, Trent," she said, using his name because it just sounded like something she should say for Dawn, who sat across from her staring at the road. "I'm thinking you two guys"—*keep it familiar, keep it upbeat*—"that you two guys, you know, when you get there, head out to the machine shed."

She let that sit.

Pause. Long pause. "You're serious?" he said.

"Sounds weird, I know, but yes, I'm serious."

"You been in that hotbox little house too long," he said. "It's mean cold.

"Get a fire going—Marcus knows where to get the wood."

"She thinks we ought to build a fire and do marshmallows in the machine shed," she heard him say to Marcus. "The woman is crazy. Don't know what I see in her."

"Marcus'll know," Coby told him, then waited.

"You do sing-a-longs out there, Marcus?" he said. "You're both crazy," he told Coby. "I'm surrounded by nutcases," he said.

Coby looked over at Dawn to see if she was picking anything up. She didn't seem to be. She held the phone away from her for a minute. "I told him the two of them ought to go out to the machine shed and start a fire like last night," she said, "and Trent says, he's surrounded by nut cases." Dawn smiled, Coby thought it was a major victory.

"You're the one going by hunches here, my dear," she said. She'd already told Dawn she loved the guy. "Going to pick up somebody's grandma, right? Whose idea was that?"

"Machine shed in this December seems way nuts to me, but I'm going to lose the vote if I bring it up," he told her.

"They did something last night—the two of them, Marcus and Dawn. Whatever they did out there together, it was good," she told Trent. "I just thought, you know, maybe—"

"Maybe what?" he said after yet another too lengthy pause.

She didn't want to sound frivolous—*marshmallows, hot dogs, s'mores*. But neither did she want to just lay out what she thought they could do, what had to be done with that bloody mess, what the child couldn't toss. "I don't think Dawn cares to go back in that house right now," she said. "It's just going to hurt, and anyway they had this little fire thing last night out in the shed, just the two of them, and it was good, she says." She looked over at Dawn, who smiled again, wonderfully. "I'm thinking if you guys start a fire out there, like last night, then by the time we roll up it'll be going, and it'll be all right—it's out of the wind."

"Lord a' mighty," Trent said.

"Trust me," she told him.

"You and Marcus got this all planned or what?" he said, and she recognized immediately that what he said was meant for the kid in his truck. "I'm the only sucker here."

"We're in cahoots," she told him. "We're all in this together, Mr. Principal."

"That we are."

"Got it then? —make it roar. It's cold outside."

"Your faithful servant," he told her.

"I love you," she said, again, for the second time.

"You say that to all the boys," he told her.

"Maybe, but it gets me where I need to go," she told him.

"We're both suckers—you and me, Marcus," he told him—for her. "We're just another couple of suckers, a couple of carp they pull off the bottom of some muddy river—or spear. That's all we are."

"I do love you," she said.

"I'm not running back to town for wieners," he told her, "and Marcus says they don't keep 'em on hand in the house."

"We'll have to make do," she told him.

Dawn pointed out in the field. When Coby saw the headlights' glare, she snapped the phone off and stuck it in the cup holder.

You did the right thing

In some ways, pushing forward right now was easier than it had been all night long, Woody thought, because sitting beside the two of them—right there in the passenger seat where her daughter KayLee had been no more than a couple of hours ago—was Karin, an ever-loving mess. He could have simply driven off to Fargo or Butte, Montana, right then, because he doubted Karin had little sense at all of where they were going or what was coming. All she knew was that just about everything was in pieces.

So, Woody didn't tell her where he was going. He told Tieneke, talked to her as if Karin wasn't there, even though she was.

"He's probably in the motel if he's anywhere," he told her. "I think we got to check anyway because who knows what's going on in his mind right now?" He hit the defrost to keep the windshield clear. "You heard him, right? —he wasn't coming home, he said."

Tieneke was in the back seat again, her left hand rubbing Karin's arm in front of her, just like she'd done only a few hours earlier with KayLee.

"They always got each other," Tieneke said.

He knew Tieneke meant to remind him that the two of them had already lived through something awful in their lives. "My guess is everything else is closed up," he said. "He could be with some friends I suppose--" He deliberately left the comment open as if to check on Karin, whether she heard him or not, how she might respond. "He had Bible study, right?"

"Yes, he did," Karin said. "He had Bible study, and it was his turn to lead."

She was with them. Thank God, she was with them, he thought.

Whoever it was that ran the motel had already doused the lights. Dark as night in the office, too, just a run of lights up and down the sidewalk in front of all the rooms. Two cars stood there in the cold, no trucks. Neither belonged to Scotty.

"I got to check anyway," he told Tieneke. "I want to know if he's here, at least—I mean, checked into the place."

"Whose place might he stay at, Karin?" Tieneke asked her. "If he left Bible study with somebody, who might it be?"

"Glenn, maybe," she said. "Maybe of all of them, Glenn. They've been friends the longest probably."

When Woody walked into the office, lights went on automatically, maybe the only thing that had changed in this flea-bitten place in years, he thought. Went through owners as if they rode the wind. He had no idea who owned it this time, who would come marching through the door any minute once he whacked the doorbell taped to the desk.

No once came, but a voice descended from above.

"You looking for a room?" A woman's voice, hard and raspy from too many Camels.

"Not looking for a room—who am I talking to?"

"Owner is who," she said.

"Got a name?"

"Evelyn."

"Evelyn who?" he said.

"You don't likely know me anyway."

"Okay, Evelyn," he said, "what I need is information. I'm looking to know whether there's a man here, registered and all—guy named Scotty Faber. You tell me that?"

"Not supposed to."

"Ms. Evelyn, I got to find Scotty Faber." He waited. Waited some more. The woman had the world's worst handwriting. Signs all over the counter ran through do's and don'ts, all of them in purple magic marker.

"What you want to know for?" she said.

"Because we got to save his life—it's that simple."

"What happens here stays here," she told him.

"Evelyn," he said. "I respect that, but you listen to me now because I'm sure Scotty Faber is a good man, a fine man, and he's got a wonderful family. I can get you a picture—a beautiful family; but he's in trouble because of something that happened a thousand years ago now. And I got to find him, and I got his wife in the car with me, too, and I'll take her in here."

"I don't say nothing about my guests."

"Ms. Evelyn," he said. "Scotty's not got a girlfriend, but he's got a huge headache that won't go away and it came up quick and he told his daughter— "He was telling her everything, he thought, this disembodied voice. "He told his daughter that he'd come here and stay away while she worked things out—that's why he's here. He doesn't have some girlfriend, Evelyn. He's not that way."

"Lotsa people say so," she told him, "--talk one way and do something else altogether. You get that a lot in the motel business. I seen a lot."

"Is he here?" he said.

"He come in a truck, right?" she said.

"Yes, he did, ma'am."

"And who are you?"

"I'm his neighbor—and like I say, his wife is in the car, and I'll take her in if you think I'm just another jackass lying to you to hide his iniquities."

"He's here," she told him. "Don't know if he's in his room or not, but he's here. He's registered."

"Evelyn," he said, "just now you did the right thing. You go back to bed now and sleep good, cause you did the right thing. I thank you."

When he got back to the car, he figured all he'd have to do was drive by Glenn's place to see if the truck was there. He didn't know Glenn's number, had no phone book in the car, didn't know how to call him just then; but it wasn't necessary to talk anyway, because the question was really where Scotty was right now, and if his truck wasn't there in Glenn's driveway, then he had to be out there at the Brethower place, looking for Dawn.

"What took you?" Tieneke said.

"Had to sweet talk," he told her.

"You're too old for that," she told him.

"You know better," he said. "He's here, but he's not," he told them both. "He's signed in all right, but he can't be here unless somebody stole his truck. He's gone."

Glenn lived just off Main. They could be there and gone in less than a minute. He told them he was at least going to check as long as they were here, so close. He backed out of the motel parking lot and took an alley in order to get to First Street, then turned left and drove just a couple of blocks. Beneath the street lights he could see up ahead there were no trucks anywhere in sight. But once he got close, he couldn't help noticing that the light was on out front—odd, he thought, because there weren't any others. Glenn was expecting someone.

"Why don't you ask?" Tieneke told him, thinking the same thing he was.

"You got Karin?" he asked, looking across the seat. "How you doing, Karin? You doing okay through all of this?"

Karin nodded. That was about the best he could figure on getting.

"I'm going to ask Glenn if he's seen Scotty since Bible study," he said. "You with us here?"

"Thanks, Woody," she said. "You're a godsend."

"Yeah, well, I hope so."

Glenn came to the door quickly, a good sign. Most people up the street were already in bed or thinking seriously about it. Glenn was fully dressed, even wore a sweater as if expecting to leave.

"Woody," he said when he opened the storm door.

"You got any sense where I might find Scotty Faber?" Woody asked him. "We're trying to find him." He tried not to seem too worried, but his being here was reason enough for Glenn to dream up major trouble.

"He's at the motel," Glenn said.

"No, he's not. I'm worried," Woody said. "We got Karin with us."

"It's the girl, I bet," Glenn told him.

He acted as if he didn't know.

"The Burnett girl--she was in the café when we were there at Bible study—this girl of Celine." It was clear that Glenn didn't know exactly how to handle it. "She was there, and she did this thing, this dance."

"Dance?" Woody said.

"Not a dance, but she marched right in front of us at a time when Scotty wasn't looking up and down or at least wasn't seeing what was right in front of his face. He was in a kind of torture all night long because we talked about what happened—all of us. And you know, I'm maybe the only one who knows that story, who's been around forever like you."

"Oh, to be young again?" he said.

"She came by walking right in front of all of us—I swear it was a test, Woody."

"He never saw her?"

"I called him later because I figured he ought to know, just in case of something."

"What'd he say?"

Glenn took a giant breath. "I think the whole day had him in a mess, Woody, the whole blamed business coming back to haunt him." Another breath. "Is there something I can do?" he asked.

"Pray," Woody said. It's what his old man would have said.

"You been a great help." He held out his hand as if shake it, then thought it was strange really—but the touch was what he wanted to feel, to give. "What's your number? —just in case."

Glenn told him. "Don't hesitate."

It didn't make much sense to tell Karin what had happened at the café. Tieneke would want to know, but when he got back to the car he decided that what Glenn had said about Dawn dancing by them would just have to wait. Karin had way too much on her plate already.

That's him

When they were still a few miles short of the gravel where they would turn to the Brethower place, Coby couldn't help thinking about how Dawn had deliberately taken the ditch the night before and whether the two of them were anywhere near the place she'd left the road. It could be risky to ask Dawn about it—or for them to go out there; but ever since Jonathan, she'd told herself she should operate more often on instinct and will, more on what her insides begged her to do than what she'd ever before. Life had become too precious to waste on indecision or fear or whatever it was that so often made her gun shy.

"Where'd all this last-night stuff go on?" she asked Dawn. "They're picking up Marcus's grandma now. We got some time. Around here somewhere?"

"Nothing to see," Dawn said. "Just pastureland all snowy."

"Whatever," Coby said, not about to push.

"You're not going to get stuck, I'm sure." Dawn pointed to the side of the road. "Ditches are full, but out there where there's no trees and no barns—flat land, no drifts."

"Show me?" Coby said.

"It's no big traumatic thing, if that's what you're thinking."

It didn't appear to be, Coby thought.

"Take a right at the next gravel road," Dawn told her. "Maybe I can find it back. Everything out here looks the same at night."

"We don't have to— "

"It's no big deal," the girl said, waving her finger when they got to the road. Rochester wasn't exactly a metropolis, but Coby couldn't help thinking that once upon a time she'd had no idea that real people lived in such isolation. All around them was simply nothing; a crisp edge of snow at the side of the road made it clear that sometime today a plow had come through, but other than a razor-straight road disappearing into the night beyond the reach of the headlights, there was nothing but darkness anywhere and everywhere.

"You weren't really trying, Dawn?" Coby asked.

That the question went unanswered was scary, she thought. Dawn only barely understood what she was asking.

Finally, "Trying what?"

"Sorry." Coby sat up straight in the seat. They were just crawling along. "I mean you weren't honestly trying to take your own life?"

"I didn't want to live." She said it right away, no doubt.

"I guess that's not the same as saying you wanted to die, is it?" She didn't want Dawn to sense that she was trying to pin her down. "What I'm saying is, I'm betting that even if you didn't want to live, that didn't mean you wanted to die."

"I was deadly serious," Dawn told her, then a giggle. "That's a bad joke, huh?"

"Bad joke." But a giggle felt healthy, after everything the girl'd been through. "It's called despair," Coby told her, not really worried. "It means you got no faith that the sun's going to come up." She waited. "Ever."

"Spare me," Dawn told her. "I could still feel him, you know—Marcus, I mean. I could still feel him in me, and I couldn't help feel that I'd used him."

"Used?"

"I mean, not like guys *use* girls—that's not what I mean. But that I needed him, his whatever--his warmth. I'd used him."

"I suppose you did."

"And I'd been through too much shit already, all the blood and the not knowing, and the emptiness, and this god-awful feeling that I'd done it myself, you know? —that I'd ended it, that I wasn't good enough, or something in me was broken and let the life flush right out of me as if my whole body was a toilet." Another giggle, less convincing. "It wasn't Marcus—I love him, I really do. It was me. He's like a brother. I don't have a brother."

Coby let that sit for a minute, told herself she must have been getting used to life on the plains because she wasn't a bit scared of being swallowed by all the nothingness around them. There was some swirl, but snow blindness was behind them now, that part of the storm laid to rest.

"I shouldn't have done it," Dawn said. "That was part of it—people don't sleep with their brothers, you know?" Then quickly. "It was stupid of me after all that crap I'd gone through—I just felt like I was nothing but a piece of shit, an idiot."

"You needed somebody," Coby said. "Somewhere here? —or where?"

"Another mile down maybe," she told her. "Then left."

"This is all so nuts," Coby said. "Here we are in the deep freeze, way out in the country where there's more cows than human beings, and nothing's going away. Everything's going to be here tomorrow."

"Not *cows—cattle,*" she said.

"What's the difference?"

"Oh, geez," Dawn said. "It's something how much you still got to learn." She turned to look out front. "You're the one who insisted," she said. "You're the one who said we got to go back there and start a fire, us Indians--have a powwow in that machine shed. It's not air-tight, you know? Ain't no furnace either. Drafty as a screen porch. And we got no drum?"

"Milk cans?" Coby said.

"Ain't no milk cans. Ain't no dairy. Ain't no cows."

"But we can have a fire."

"Yeah, but can you rub a spark out of string?" Dawn said.

"What kind of question is that?"

"I mean, your people up there in cold country—there was a time none of them had a match or a lighter, you know?"

"Rub two sticks together?"

"That's Boy Scouts, lady—you know how to do that string thing?"

"I grew up with a Dairy Queen on the end of the block," she told Dawn. "Are we on a goose chase here or what? I want to know where you took the ditch." Maybe they ought to turn back, turn the car around, she thought. All the way from town, more than a dozen miles now, they'd not met a car or a truck, nor seen anything move.

As near as Coby could figure, they were still five or six miles south of the Brethower place, a couple miles east, when way up on the road—the snow wasn't swirling anymore, not all the much anyway—way up off the road in front of them, maybe a mile and a half north over all that flat land, something bright flashed, enough to make her think, right away, that it was her, Dawn, parked along the road in her car, some goofy Twilight Zone flashback.

"Your car is still there?" Coby said.

"We're still a mile away." Dawn sat up from the seat and swept her glove across the glass as if maybe it would give her a bit more of a vision. "I don't get it."

"Where's your car?"

"In the shed at home."

"Then what's that?" Coby said.

The gravel road was speckled with the snow, but road wasn't slippery or dangerous. She flew through a crossroad then went up a slight hill. A pickup, parking lights on, but it wasn't in the field exactly, just off on the other side of the ditch.

"Call the principal guy." Coby shoved her phone at Dawn. "Tell him where we are."

"I don't know."

"Then guess," Coby said.

"Who is it?"

"It's a pickup."

It took no time at all for Dawn to see it clearly. "It's him," she said. "It's my father—my real father. I saw him leave the café."

"Your what?" Coby said.

"My birth father," Dawn told her again. "My real father."

Coby could barely remember the guy had been mentioned a millennium ago, long before all the miscarriage stuff, long before the tears. Dawn had seen her father in the café. She didn't know her real father, but she'd seen him that night—something about her walking right next to him and not meeting his eyes or something.

She pulled along the side of the road, while Dawn tried to tell Trent and Marcus where they were. The lights were only partially out—just dimmers. She pulled beside the pickup, then stepped down the parking brake, got out, and walked over.

"It's him," Dawn said, above the considerable hum of wind. "It's like I told you—it's him." She pointed at the door panel. *Faber Trucking*, it said.

Coby didn't have the slightest idea who this Faber was. All she knew was what Dawn had said that when he should have, he seemed not to have noticed her. The address on the door said *Cottonwood.* He was from town.

She opened the door, and the interior lights lit up the emptiness. No one there. She looked in the back seat, thinking maybe the guy'd decided to sleep it off--who knows? Nothing. He had to be somewhere out here, somewhere.

Dawn pointed down at footsteps already filling with the snow sweeping along the ground. "Scotty Faber," she told Coby when she asked for a name.

"Trucker?"

"Rich," Dawn said. "Real rich."

Coby stepped back slowly, closed the door to douse the lights, and checked the footprints leading away. A single track around the front of the pickup led into the ditch, where there was no ditch, where the grasses stood maybe two feet tall. She looked up at the open sky and thanked God for miracles, because the whole dome was lit.

They'd have to find him. This guy couldn't last all that long in the cold, and if he left the way he did, he must have wanted to. He wasn't just walking home because he needed a breath of fresh air. She ran back to her car and grabbed the hat she kept in the back seat and the gloves packed inside, then gave the gloves to Dawn who pulled her hood up over her head and zipped her jacket all the way to her chin.

"He can't be far," Dawn pointed down at the open tracks.

"You know him?" Coby asked.

"He's my father," she said. "I don't think I ever said a word to him in my life."

Emotionless. Totally emotionless. "Well then, child, tonight that's going to change," Coby told her. "It's you and me against Mother Nature and this old man of yours you don't know."

"Would 'a been easier in the café," Dawn said.

"You ready?"

"We're first responders," Dawn said. "Think I should call 911?"

Coby determined he couldn't be that far away, and they weren't just hauling somebody out of the snow and cold. The jerk was Dawn's father. "That'll do right now," she told Dawn. "I don't think we'll need a crowd."

She thought about a flashlight, but she knew better than to think that there might be one that actually worked in the glove compartment. How many times hadn't she told herself she'd better get one going before winter? Besides, there was this much at least—the night was bright. She looked across the field, amazed at how far she could see now that her own headlights were out.

"Well," she said, "let's go meet this guy."

They started out on a pace she soon realized they couldn't stay with, even though the path of his footsteps was like some silver sidewalk--bright with the night sky, the stars, the moon--once they were actually out in it. So much open field in front of them, she thought she'd spot him right away, his silhouette sure to reach out from the snow. How far could he walk anyway? And why did he leave the truck? He couldn't handle the thought of his not talking to his own daughter, his daughter who just the night before had attempted suicide? Guilt, maybe.

She had no idea about time. She stopped, looked down at the tracks. It wasn't bright enough to determine if the man was in boots. "You okay with this?" she asked Dawn.

"I'm not staying in the car alone."

Coby tried to walk faster. The snow was ankle deep, at best. She knew they couldn't stay out long themselves without risking frostbite. He couldn't be far. He just couldn't.

They were moving fast enough so that she didn't get cold, but she couldn't help feeling the pinch of cold in her face, the frost already forming around her eyes and mouth. The hustling kept her warm, kept the circulation moving through legs and arms and into hands and feet, made her oblivious to the frozenness. She came up a rise and was sure she'd see this guy in a bundle just on the other side. She didn't.

There were trees in a draw, small ones, not all that terribly far across the field, the tracks leading in that direction. She didn't need to look back for Dawn because she kept up without breaking a bit. So they kept moving as fast as they could. Soon enough they'd be wet from the inside. You can lose toes. Those things happened. There was no blood. Yet.

When Coby thought the worst, it scared her. All Dawn would need was to come on her birth father with a hole in his head, snow soaked with blood.

"Maybe you ought to call," she told Dawn. "He's out here a ways."

"Oh, shit," Dawn said. "I left the phone in the car."

"And yours?"

"In my purse," the girl said.

"First responders, all right," Coby said.

"You're a nurse at least."

Snow was just a crust, not even all that much, not enough to make them stumble, so cold it crunched beneath her feet, even though it was all pasture-land.

The footsteps were like bread crumbs in the old story, she thought—that clear. The two of them stopped when they got to the draw at the bottom of the hill, watched those shadows disappear into the longer grass at the edge of a creek bed. She brushed back the grass with one hand, then pulled some low-hanging branches back and found him there in the long grass beneath a canopy formed by a couple of fallen limbs from the cottonwoods.

There he was.

"That's him," Dawn said. Then, slowly, "That's my father."

She came out of nowhere just then

Scotty Faber had no place to go. Glenn had offered, he remembered, but he couldn't talk to anyone, not even Karin, because what he'd done in not telling the whole truth only made everything worse. He could not go back to LeRoy's. He'd have to wait—God only knew how long—until KayLee would agree to see him again. A week? A month? No way of knowing. In a single night, she'd begun to hate him. In one night.

Maybe the best way out of all of this was running into a ditch here out in the country and wasting away in the deep freeze. Why not? All he had left was the business, and who really cared about the damn business? He couldn't go home, couldn't go back to that motel, couldn't go anywhere. A girl who was actually his daughter had walked right past him just a few hours ago, and he didn't even notice. KayLee was laying herself out like she was because she hated him. For good reason.

Scotty believed in heaven, believed he was saved by grace, not by anything he'd done, and he believed—he really did—that God the Father and Jesus the son wouldn't keep him out if he simply and calmly and determined that everybody else would be better off if he would not return. God's love was unconditional.

He turned off the blacktop and took the gravel east, back towards town, not because he could draw a bead on anything back there but because it made no sense to go farther west. Maybe he could find the place Dawn had driven herself off the road. Maybe her tracks would be there. Almost felt some comfort in that, a place to go.

But there was enough suicide, more than enough. There was Gerry Sullivan a couple of years ago, out in the garage; the tube in the exhaust—hardly anyone knew about it—

had been unmistakable. And every time he'd seen Darlene, he'd thought of her going out there and finding her husband slumped over the wheel. When it happened, he and Karin agreed there was hardly a more horrible legacy. "What you do to your family is kill them, too," Karin said. Every winter there was one, it seemed, more if you counted the reservation.

It seemed to him a hundred years ago now that he'd decided to go out to LeRoy's and see if he could find Dawn Burnett, a thousand years ago since he and the others were sitting around a table with their Bibles open. He couldn't even remember what they were studying, even though it was his turn to lead. What had happened with KayLee blew everything else out of the water. They'd never, ever determined that she shouldn't know that stuff way back when. That wasn't it at all. She was just too young. She was a kid. She'd been a child.

Somewhere in their family pictures there was a single snapshot taken long ago, when she was tiny enough to fit in the kitchen sink. He'd taken a shot of her getting a bath, less than a year old but old enough to know she was getting her picture taken. She was naked as a jaybird, her little legs outstretched, sitting straight in the sink, huge smile, as if she had the world by the tail. It was a time when they'd just got back together, he and Karin. He'd stopped drinking. They were going to church. Somewhere they'd got the strength and courage to go on, even though they'd been off to such an awful start. There she sat getting a bath in the kitchen sink, wholesale smile over that chubby little face.

She was so much better than they were, than he and Karin. Never in trouble. Honor roll. Music. Everything. Nose in books, not because she wanted grades but because she wanted to learn.

That same daughter who'd told him just now to get the hell out of her life.

It came out of nowhere just then—a doe, a big one. Came out of nowhere so that he didn't see her until she ran into him. The way he thought of it immediately, a second after it happened, was that the doe had run into him, hit his truck. He didn't hit the deer. She hit him. Hard.

It happened so fast that it seemed an impossibility a minute after he'd pulled over. That his mind was half gone was something he understood, and he actually wondered if it had happened, until he pulled over, stepped out of the truck, walked around the front and looked at the passenger side fender to see if—yes, there was a dent there, sure as anything. It was dark, but the light of the moon off the snow was enough for him to make no mistake. He'd hit that doe.

He walked back up the road to where it had happened, to see if he could spot it by his skid marks and the deer tracks down through the ditch on the right where she had kept walking, not running. The way he read the tracks, it looked as if she was lame, maybe broken a leg. No blood that he could see. He had a flashlight in the truck. He could look for blood, he told himself.

He ran back up the road to where his truck stood waiting, its lights still glowing over the snow. He jerked open the door on the passenger side—she'd hit him farther forward on the fender—then opened the cubby hole. Interior lights were bright enough for him to see inside. He grabbed the flashlight, switched it on—it worked. He ran back down the road again to where he'd hit her, climbed into the ditch to look closely at her tracks. Somehow it seemed that when she'd run into the truck—and clearly, she had, he never saw her—when she'd run into the fender she was too tall to hit her head. She'd taken some hard blow to the body, he told himself, but he figured she could live.

He had nowhere to go. His work jacket was heavy and hooded. He had four or five pairs of gloves—some of them singles—in his truck, and was even wearing boots, leather boots, but boots anyway. It was cold out, but there was this pact in him, an obligation. When a deer went down, you had to go after him--had to. It wasn't really a question. He had no idea where he would have been going anyway.

He had a .38 beneath the driver's seat. He was licensed to carry. The only thing keeping him from tracking that doe was pure cold, and that wasn't a good reason. Once more, he went back to the truck, turned off the engine, reached under the seat for the .38, grabbed it, strapped it around him, switched on the parking lights, pulled on gloves, flipped up his hood, then stood there a minute, waited. He had no idea why, really. He had to put her down. For the first time since he'd left LeRoy's place, he wasn't choked with what had happened, wasn't obsessed, didn't see his daughter half-naked in a nightmare, didn't hear her spew her hate. He had no idea why, but he stood there beside his truck, just stood there for a minute, collecting his breath, and cried. The tears came wringing out of him as if his soul was a wet chamois. He couldn't stop. He couldn't help himself. No one was anywhere near to make him ashamed, so the tears came like rain he had to wipe away to keep from freezing down his cheeks.

It was KayLee and it was Karin. It was Dawn Burnett, who he'd just plain forgotten. It was a memory of himself crawling out of that van on New Year's Day early in the morning, some place like this, crawling out drunk and laughing about it, taking a leak right there at the spot where he'd flipped it, giggling because he'd walked away. He was crying for being who he'd been.

Tears. He pulled the glove off to wipe them away with his bare hand. They didn't stop.

He reached down for the .38 and told himself it was time to go. He had to find that doe.

The flashlight out in front, he followed her trail, once in a while stopping to look closely down at the snow to see if she'd left any blood. She hadn't. He swore he could read the tracks clearly enough to determine she'd broken a leg. She was the one who ran into him, he told himself. The tears wouldn't stop. He kept using the sleeve of his jacket to wipe them away.

At the top of a rise, he hoped he'd see her slumped in the snow because he couldn't chase her all night, not dressed like he was. He'd have to go back home and get out a coverall and some good boots. He couldn't go home.

He believed LeRoy. LeRoy promised he wouldn't touch her, and he wouldn't.

Something good could come of all of it. Something had once already. Something had delivered them from what they'd got themselves into long ago, in another life he could barely remember. He'd walked home that night, still drunk, the van flipped on a country road. Walked home on New Year's Day, and he didn't even remember. Three miles at least. No memory.

What he did remember was Karin saying—no tears—that she'd had enough. She had a suitcase and KayLee in her arms, and she'd said it clearly, that her parents were coming to pick her up because she couldn't live like that anymore. The tone he remembered. It wasn't hate, wasn't that she was mad even. What made it worse was that what she'd said was offered in a temperature that made this night seem almost warm. That's what he wouldn't forget.

Down the slow incline he walked quickly, still following the tracks. At the bottom was a river or stream, at least enough water to sprout a stand of cottonwoods. The tracks led down into a thicket beneath a stand of a half-dozen trees leaning like matchsticks in every which direction.

And that's where he found her, lying down, so much fear in her eyes that he felt almost afraid to come close. She was exhausted and couldn't move, her front leg at a horrible angle. He'd done it before, a dozen times at least in the days when he used to hunt—mule deer, white tail, antelope, even caribou. He'd killed before, often. But when he pulled out that handgun, felt its heft in his hand, for a moment once again he thought of going with her, of taking her out the way he knew he needed, and taking himself along because even if he hadn't seen her just ten minutes before, hadn't spotted her coming up out of the ditch or over a fence, he'd hit her and now she had to die. Had to.

When he did it, every last shot like it replayed, every death, every one of them. The tears, which had not stopped, kept coming. He didn't put the gun back, kept it in his hand, and then slumped to the ground beside the doe, blood now seeping slowly all around her head and on to the fresh snow.

There he sat, the loaded gun still in his hand, when they found him.

She's going to be good

Scotty was down on his knees on a thin carpet of snow beneath some scattered trees along a creek, a gun in his hand, John Wayne kind of gun. Coby couldn't reel it all in—that this guy way out here was Dawn's dad; that the two of them had never talked, not once; that here they were, all three of them out in a snowfield; that the guy had a gun. Thanks goodness he wasn't aiming it at himself. All Dawn would need was to watch him, her father, kill himself in the middle of all this snowy grassland. She'd never find her way home.

There he sat, that gun in both hands, aiming down the side of the bank. Three shots in rapid succession thudded quickly into a something Coby couldn't help thinking was human. Dawn seemed perfectly still. She nodded as if to tell Coby things would be all right. This guy had just unloaded three shots at something just off the bank of the creek, the man she'd already identified as her dad, and it was nothing to sweat?

He had no idea they were standing there. He bent over to pick up the spent cartridges, then jammed the gun back in his belt.

What did she know about this guy? That he was rich. That he was Dawn's father. That he had a business in Cottonwood. Didn't even know what.

Dawn was on her haunches beside her, the two of them crouching. Coby tipped her head, pointed at the guy. Dawn wouldn't go over there or say a thing. She wasn't going to talk. Coby pointed again. Dawn shook her head convincingly. The coldness in the girl's face had nothing to do with temperature, and it was new.

Coby grabbed Dawn's collar and pulled her up with her. The guy was still unaware of them being there. He climbed down the bank and for a moment they lost him.

"Say something before he shoots us," Dawn told her, giggling.

"He's your father," Coby told her. "You talk to him."

The dead deer came up the side of the bank sideways, back feet just a bit out front of the forelegs and head. A doe. He heaved her up on the bank.

"Must not have been dead," Dawn said.

"Did you know?"

"Didn't you see the tracks?"

"What tracks?"

Dawn raised a hand to stop talking, then pointed at the man, who reappeared just then and was having some trouble climbing back up the side. Finally, he stayed on his belly and slid his weight up top until he lay there beside the deer. The whole thing, the climb had cost him something, she thought, because he didn't get up right away. Steam put a halo around his head, his staggered breath trumpeting from nose and mouth.

As if completely exhausted, he laid down beside that deer, one hand on its neck. She and Dawn sat in the perfect silence all around. That's when it became clear that the guy was crying, bawling, as if out of control, his own kind of death song, Coby thought.

She pulled Dawn close. "He's crying about the deer?"

Dawn shrugged.

Scotty pulled himself up until he could get his legs beneath him, then got to his knees. Didn't take his eyes off the deer.

"What his name?" Coby asked.

"Scotty—it's what people call him. Scotty."

Scotty sat there on his knees and pulled that gun from his belt, then slumped down once more, pulled back his stocking cap as if trying to make a tribute, all the time crying in a way she'd never heard a man do outside of Emergency. She had no idea why.

"Scotty," she said, not loud.

He didn't hear her.

She turned it up.

Still nothing.

He raised that gun up in front of his eyes, looked at it as if it was something totally new, as if he'd never seen before.

"Don't let him," Dawn told her. "Don't let him think about it."

When that gun went up to his face, Coby ran like she'd never had before and hit the guy so hard both of them tumbled over the deer's body and down the embankment. He didn't try to fight. The two of them hit the creek bottom, Scotty on top of Coby, and what she felt right then was something she'd never experienced, even though she knew very well what it was. She'd come down hard on the small of her back, got herself knocked out of wind.

The man called Scotty rolled off her, still crying. She couldn't breathe, but she couldn't help worrying about the gun--where it was, what he'd been about to do.

"You think I don't know," Dawn said. It was there in her hand now. She was standing there over her father. "You think I don't know, but I do and I know who you are and if you think I'm going to let you kill yourself, you're dead wrong, Charlie. You hear me?" Dawn stuck that gun in her coat, and then grabbed Coby's belt, pulled it up and back and up and back until Coby felt her breath return.

"This woman here just saved your life is all," Dawn told him looking down at Coby. "You coming around?" she asked her. "Talk to me, will you? You just got the wind knocked out of you."

Coby nodded.

"And what are you crying for?" Dawn said to him. He didn't respond. "I'm talking to you," she said. "You got beans in your ears? I said, 'what the hell are you crying for'?"

He couldn't talk, it seemed.

"This woman just saved your life, you know?" she told him. "This woman here just lost the guy she loved not long ago and here she is out in the middle of all this snow and cold and shit, saving you when you're about to swallow a bullet and God only knows why when you got the freaking money you do. What is your problem, anyway?"

"He's your father," Coby reminded her.

"He's never once been my father," Dawn told her. "Maybe he stuck his dick in someplace he shouldn't have, but that's all there ever was." She swung over to look at him. "Isn't that right? You never were my father, not for one day of my whole life were you ever my father."

He said nothing, just got to his feet, looked at the young woman, his daughter, Dawn Burnett, and kept on crying. He didn't try to say anything. He didn't even look at Coby. He just stood there, then turned towards the deer, grabbed both pairs of legs, and lifted just to see how much that doe weighed.

"I'm not giving this back." She padded the gun in her belt.

He took hold of the deer's back legs once again and started dragging her out of the trees and into the open field.

"Where you think you going?" Dawn asked him. "What you going to do with that thing?"

"Venison," he said. Then, "Somebody'll need it."

"You're my father, you know," Dawn yelled. "You know that, do you? I'm your flesh and blood."

He took both pairs of legs in his hands, lifted the carcass up and over his head, and carried it across his shoulders. He stood there, looking up toward the road and the car and his truck.

"Got a knife?" she asked. "You're going to have to gut that thing."

He stood there like a pillar of salt.

"Go to him," Coby told her. "Be bigger than he is. You already are. Go on."

"I hate him," she told Coby.

"You don't even know him."

There were tears in Dawn's eyes, too. "I got a knife," she yelled at her father. "You got one in the pickup?"

He never turned around, but he seemed oblivious.

"We're going to the Brethower place," Coby told him. She started to walk back toward the road herself. "We're all going to the Brethower place because there's things that need to be done, Scotty."

He straightened his shoulders.

"There's things that we need to get done, and we're going to do them," Coby told him. "Your daughter is part of it, too, part of the whole thing. You have to be there. We're counting on you being there, Scotty." Some things had to be said and some people had to be loved, she figured. There's others comin' too. They're on their way. It'll be a healing."

There he stood, wordless.

"Stuff's going to be cleaned up some," Coby tried to tell him. "There's so much brokenness—don't you think? In all of us. All of us walk on a carpet of broken glass it seems."

Dawn walked up to him then for the first time. She had a knife. God himself only knows where she kept it, Coby thought, but there it was. She didn't say a thing, just pointed it at him as if to say he could use it. That doe had to be gutted.

But Scotty had no hands. He had that doe up around his shoulders, so she reached into his jacket pocket and stuck her knife there, then slapped him lightly right there as if to seal it.

"I've done it myself," she told him. "More than once, I done it myself."

He nodded, and then smiled, the first smile Coby had seen.

"That's it," Coby told him. "Dawn says it too—you're coming with."

"She says I got to gut this thing," he said.

"We'll do it," Dawn told him. "We'll do it together."

"I know people who could use all that meat," he told them. "She's pretty young. Too bad, huh?"

What just happened out there could have been awful, Coby told herself, but instead it wasn't.

Amazing. Instead it wasn't.

Five years ain't a big thing when you're 75

Marcus stood just outside Trent's pickup and waited for his grandma, who took her good-natured time coming down the steps outside her trailer after locking the front door up good and tight. "You get that back one too, Grandma?" he asked her.

"I never open it—you know that," she told him as he watched her step across the thin mask of snow over her front yard. "Get here and help me, Marcus—didn't I teach you manners?" She had a long-handled purse stuck up on her shoulder, and she was wearing that Northern State stocking cap, the colorful one she bought for him from St. Vincent de Paul in Rapid. Cost her a quarter maybe, he figured. It was the thought that counts.

"And where's that child?" she said before she got in the open door of the passenger side. "Where's the girl anyway? We going to meet her somewhere?"

"We're going out to our house, Grandma—we'll meet her there." Marcus thought about giving her rear end a heave to get her up into Trent's truck, but he let her alone because he knew she'd darn well tell him she wasn't some kind of handicapped. "She'll be there in just a little while," he told her.

"Mr. Sterrett, I think I told you what I thought of that place, didn't I?" She plopped down in the front seat and reached for the seat belt right away. "My grandson would do a whole lot better if he lived here with me—I mean, it's not the White House, but I can about guarantee I'd get him to school."

"We got to talk about that, Mrs. Pritchard," Trent told her.

Marcus shut the door slowly and safely, sealing Grandma in, then took the back seat of the pickup.

"As long as we're out there," she said, "I think you and me ought to check the place out. I don't want to think of what we'll see."

"Boys his age, Mr. Sterrett," she told him raising a finger and a thumb, "they're just this close to being reservation dogs, and I'm being unkind to four-leggeds." She squared her shoulders against the stiff seat she was in. "Just a phase, but it can wreck 'em. We've seen enough out here," she told him.

Marcus couldn't help thinking that whenever she said things like that, she was talking about her own son, his father. Occasionally—maybe at Christmas—he'd get a card and a promise that wasn't worth the stamp.

Trent's lights swept over the trailer when he backed out of the driveway. Her calico stood in the window, big eyes.

"You got to love that girl, Marcus honey," his grandma told him," because sure as anything she thinks she's a waste of time."

"She drove out here into the fields last night, late," Trent told her. "Out here somewhere, just went right off the road."

"I know women never recovered," she told him.

"His wife didn't," Marcus told her. "Did she, Trent?"

"Might have been better if you'd have let Mr. Sterrett tell me that news," Grandma told him.

"It's not news," Trent said. "Almost five years ago already, but I just told him, just now. I'm glad it stuck."

"Five years isn't a big thing when you're 75," she told him.

"She always says things like that," Marcus said.

"She has you to worry about," Trent told him.

"You darn right I do," she announced.

The whole thing was weird when Marcus thought about it. It was Trent who wanted her—he was the one who told Coby they were going to pick her up to come along. Coby the saint didn't even know her. Dawn maybe knew her a little, but not much. For the life of him, he really had no idea why they'd be going out there to their place anyway, or why Coby had told Trent that when they got there he ought to light a fire in the machine shed.

Truth be told, he liked the idea because if LeRoy was in the house, he knew Dawn wouldn't want any part of it. If they'd meet in the machine shop—for whatever insane reason—LeRoy might never know they were there. Besides, whatever it was that went on out there between the two of them—between him and Dawn—it was just right, just something about that fire out there in the middle of the cold, about being huddled up in those sleeping bags, something about sitting on that straw bale—it was good. Maybe Dawn had ordered it up, he thought. Maybe she was the one who'd told Coby they ought to do a repeat thing out there.

"You got some Lakota blood in you somewhere?" Marcus asked Trent.

"I'm a mutt." Trent had both hands on the wheel, drivers' ed style. "Lots of roots, but none of them Sioux—not that I know."

It was Trent who told Coby they were going to pick her up.

"Why you ask?" Trent said. They were going straight east now, on the blacktop. "I got blonde hair, for pity's sake."

"Maybe he dyed it, Grandma."

"He eats lutefisk, I bet," she said.

"What's lutefisk?" Marcus said.

"Don't ask," Trent told him. "Truth is, I don't."

Then Marcus thought he'd just come out with it, with what he couldn't quite determine. "So how come we got Grandma along?"

She was sitting over the console from Trent, seat belt strapped over her the way she always did.

"Me and Coby—we just got here," Trent said. "What do we know? Only people we know are kids." He looked at Grandma. "I'm going to make her blush, Marcus—that okay?"

"You can't make my grandma blush."

What Trent said came out slow and deliberate. "We need an *old* woman," he said, just like that; and he reached up over the seat to put his hand on his grandma's shoulder, "a wise old woman with a lot of life, a lot of living, behind her. And maybe some death, too."

"How come?" Marcus said.

Trent took this breath as if going down the road in this conversation was going to take some heavy lifting. "You didn't see Dawn cry," he told Marcus. "You'd already left, and Coby's doing her best right now, I'm sure. But when your grandma came to school to talk about you –" He didn't finish that thought. "I don't know what to say except you and me, Marcus, we got no real clout here except by way of support." He stopped to think through those words. "What made Dawn Burnett cry," Trent told them, "what made her take the ditch, what made her do everything she did that night is something your grandma knows more about than you and me ever will."

"Happened to your wife."

"Dawn needs a grandma," he said sternly, as if the case was closed.

Made sense to him. Made sense that once they'd get together, he'd keep his mouth shut.

"We got to love her, Grandma—right? That's what you're telling me," Marcus asked. "We got to love her."

"You aren't lying," she said, "we do—all of us. You got any wine?"

"Probably do—in the house," Marcus said.

"Know where to find it?"

"How much you want?"

"'Nuff to go around," she told Marcus. "You go grab some when we get there—and a couple of glasses or something, too."

"What for?" he said.

"Because I'm an old woman, child," she said. "You heard your teacher here."

"I told you she wouldn't blush, didn't I? I told you as much." It felt strange to feel what he did just then. But he liked it. It was something other people had, something like pride. Not just showy pride. He was proud of her, the old woman. He was glad his grandma was along.

I was looking for you

On top of everything else, on top of a blizzard and colder temps than Coby ever felt in Minnesota; on top of a child who didn't understand her own body and had just—Lord have mercy—lost a child, she thought; on top of whatever happened in that machine shed later; on top of all of that, Coby St. James came to know that night that she loved a guy, that she didn't want him to leave ever, didn't care to go on out here on the plains without him.

When she thought about it later, she determined that she could have explained exactly when it was that she knew. It wasn't when she'd announced that she loved him to those kids. She probably did then already, but when she said it to him the way she did—and he'd been shocked to hear her say it—when she said it that time, it was mostly because the answer she gave was something she had to say for Dawn's sake. It was not a lie. Her heart was in it. But in all truth, that answer was strategy. They were in a deadly game, and she had to play cards she wouldn't have otherwise. She had to remind Dawn Burnett there was such a thing as love, as happiness.

The moment she knew for sure that she hadn't been lying about him occurred during what had to the most freakish drive through the blizzard country she'd ever taken. There she was in a car with a girl slowly coming back to life after what had to be three weeks? five weeks? A beautiful girl who'd been through things that forever alter the lives of women twice her age and a dozen times more at home with who they are. Dawn was a girl. Somewhere in that machine shed, she'd deliberately hidden what she hadn't totally recognized as the mortal remains of the baby her own body had rejected, for reasons she didn't understand. Few ever do. It had taken Coby a whole day to believe it, but she came to realize that the night before, Dawn Burnett had meant to go into that ditch for keeps.

Just one day later, this kid sat in the back seat, her father—a man who had not once in her life acknowledged her, not once—beside her in the front, that man wan and beaten into an emotional pulp that left him unable to open up at all. She had no idea why. An accident? A deer?

The two of them had seen him take that handgun up to his head as if he were about to use it. They'd heard him bawl, hadn't seen him without tears in his eyes. They'd seen him sit in the snow over that dead deer as if she'd been his beloved.

When they got back to the car, Coby had signaled to Dawn that it might be best if she took the back seat. She didn't know if they'd have to take him back to town, to the hospital. He'd suffered no physical injury out in the cold, but his stony, frozen silence suggested some heavyweight emotional trauma.

They left his truck out there on the road. Coby didn't want Dawn alone that night, not right then, and she didn't want to separate her from her father anyway. The two of them helped him into the front seat, then Dawn jumped into the back, and the first thing she did—Coby saw it with her own eyes—the first thing Dawn did was lean forward and grab his arm with her hand to let him know that she was in the back seat, something of a seat belt for him. She'd done it herself. Coby didn't need to make Dawn a hero. The child had done it. She touched him, held him.

Dawn recognized mutual pain in a man she had every reason to despise, a howl of human emotion whose sources may be legion, as the Bible says, but whose intensity speaks a common language to those, all of those, who are suffering. That night, Dawn Burnett saw a wound in her father's soul, a wound not unlike her own. Whether or not she forgot hers, no one could know, Coby thought. But when she saw the girl's hand on her father's arm, she told herself she didn't know how to describe that moment except to say that she understood some story had turned a corner out there on those interminably straight roads.

"Mr. Faber," Coby said, "you know Dawn, don't you?"

He couldn't speak, as if there were no words.

"We'll take you where you want to go," she told him. "Can you tell me where we should bring you?"

He'd returned to even breathing, a stocking cap pulled over his ears so low that his eyes were deeply shadowed. "I have no place to go," he told her.

She didn't know whether he was aware of Dawn's hand on his arm. That's how broken he was.

"We can bring you home," she said. Then, quickly, "You know where he lives, Dawn?"

Dawn said she thought she did.

"We can bring you home—would you like to go home?" She was talking to Scotty Faber the way she might have spoken to someone deaf or drunk, maybe a lost little boy.

"I can't," Scotty said.

That's all they got out of him for ten minutes. Nothing more. And in that time, in that bizarre silence, even though Dawn kept holding him, Coby found herself searching for someone to try to think through this mess. The only person who came to mind was Trent Sterrett, and when that happened, she knew she wasn't spinning him earlier, saying something only for the benefit of the kids. That's when it was clear she loved him.

"He's coming along, Dawn," she told the girl. She couldn't see Dawn's face, so she didn't know how she'd react, but that she kept holding his arm the way she did made her think Dawn wouldn't be angry about what she'd decided. "It's his, too," she told the girl. "You know what I mean?"

She turned far enough back to see Dawn nod her head.

Coby turned toward him, then spoke as if the two of them were communicating in a different dialect. "We have something that we have to do—me and Dawn, me and your daughter, Mr. Faber," she told him. His determined silence made her feel like someone only partially in command. "I'm a nurse," she told him. "I'm going to stay with you for a while now, and so is Dawn." He seemed oblivious. "We're going to take you with us. Is that okay?"

He reached over with his right hand and took Dawn's, brought his arm all the way around and took hold of his daughter's hand, where she had hold of him.

"I didn't hit that doe," he said. "It just came out of nowhere, I swear it hit me."

Coby couldn't help thinking it was beyond strange for him to be obsessed with a dead deer. She looked down and saw their hands piled up on his arm.

"It was good of you to go after her," Dawn told him.

And then, finally, he said it. "You're Dawn Burnett." Not a question.

She said she was.

"I was looking for you tonight."

"Where?"

"LeRoy's."

"That's where you were?"

He nodded.

"I don't go with him anymore," she told him. "We're done."

He nodded, as if his mind had been forced to translate the news into some foreign tongue.

"You didn't find Dawn out there then, did you?" Coby asked him. "You're saying you were looking for Dawn, right? but when you got out there –"

"Did you find the house?" Dawn said. "Did you actually go there?"

He nodded.

"No one was home," Dawn said. "You got there, and the place was dark."

He shook his head.

"No?" she asked.

Harder. He shook his head harder.

"Who was there?" Dawn said. "Was anyone there?"

"My daughter," he told them, and when he did, it was the first time he seemed to wonder what she might have thought. She could have been just anybody in the café before that, but with that answer, something was coming back, something that made him conscious of being in a car with a girl he knew, a girl who was really there.

"You're shitting me! --KayLee?"

He nodded.

"KayLee Faber was at LeRoy's?" she said. "Oh, no. With him?"

Nothing. No movement. No answer.

"Your daughter, Kaylee, was with LeRoy?' She didn't ask that question as if she were jealous. "The two of them were together? They were making out or something?"

The slightest nod.

Coby was back on blacktop. She could hear rustling from the back seat as Dawn scrunched herself forward as if to get closer to him.

"Let me get this right, Scotty," Dawn said. She didn't know what to call him—you could hear it in her voice. "You went out to the Brethower place to find me—is that right?"

"I don't know why," he said.

"Because she's your daughter," Coby said, trying to keep him with them.

"Because you're my daughter and I didn't even see you in the café," he told her. Things were coming more clearly to him. "You walked by me, Glenn told me, and everybody saw you except me. I didn't see my own daughter."

"You came to apologize?" Coby said.

"I was lost," he said. "I can't go home."

Why would this man's wife throw him out of the house? Made no sense, Coby thought. What possibly could have happened to make her to put him on the street?

"So, you went looking for me," Dawn said, "but you found KayLee and she was with LeRoy? Oh, shit."

"I don't know these people." Neither of them heard Coby.

"And they were in bed maybe?" Dawn said.

Coby pulled over and stopped the car.

"She hates me," Scotty Faber said.

There they sat in the middle of a country road a hundred miles from anywhere, lights blazing, but nothing showing up anywhere around.

"Your daughter hates you?" Coby asked. "Why?"

He kept hold of Dawn's hand on his arm, but he flicked off the seat-belt and shifted to look more fully at Coby. He pulled off his stocking cap and dropped it in his lap. Coby could barely see his face in the darkness, but there was enough visible for her to believe that his eyes held something gracious, something kind. She wasn't afraid, but she was happy that gun of his was beneath her seat.

"I'm way out of town here," Coby told him. "Let me get this straight." She tried to get Scotty's attention. "You're way the heck out here because you wanted to find Dawn at the Brethower place because you thought she was still dating LeRoy—do I have all right?"

He kept looking at her as if he'd missed his cue.

She turned to Dawn slowly. "He doesn't know a thing about you?"

It was all too strange.

"Mr. Faber goes out to LeRoy's," Dawn says, "goes out there to find me and instead finds his perfect daughter in bed with LeRoy—holy shit."

"'His perfect daughter'?"

"She must be royally screwed up. She hasn't ever *been* with a guy, I'm sure."

"And she picks this LeRoy—your Leroy, your ex?"

"Something happened to her."

"You got no clue?"

"I'll tell you this much, Coby, this guy does. You can bet he does. He knows what happened."

"She's out there too right now?"

"LeRoy said he wouldn't touch her," Scotty Faber said. "He told me he wouldn't."

"Then he won't," Dawn said. "He can be a son-of-a-bitch, but he's not evil." She said that as much to him as to Coby. "We better get there. We're not far."

Somewhere in the car there lay a cell phone—Coby's. She didn't know where. All she knew right then was that there would be a fire in that machine shed, and Trent would be there. Marcus too, and the Grandma.

"I don't know what to do," Mr. Faber said. "I'm just so lost. I can't go home. I don't know where to go."

Coby wished she could wave a magic wand and fix it all.

The car, at least, was warm.

A bottle of wine in each hand and another under his arm

Trent Sterrett had seen worse. When he and Marcus and Marcus's grandma finally got out on the acreage, the Brethower place was lit but the machine shed was black-cat dark. His first reaction was surprise at how small the house was, even though it had sprawled on two sides because families who'd lived there had added on rooms when children came along. The place was misshapen in ways lots of old farm houses are in the country, where making a living was no given.

Nostalgia wasn't what was keeping the place standing, he figured. What kept it from being plowed under was bargain-basement renters. The owner, who probably lived in town, were fine with two kids who weren't about to improve a thing.

They left Grandma Pritchard in the pickup and ran in the house for the wine. As long as Trent was already aiding and abetting, he thought it only right that he go along with Marcus and pick up her order--go whole hog here, put his whole career on the line. The truth was, he could not imagine the law coming after him for a kid with a glass of wine in a machine shed when it felt like 87 degrees below zero or whatever. Besides, Grandma Pritchard had to be pushing eighty. Who, pray tell, would take her on?

You can't help loving old women, he thought, but then, his own grandma was a saint, whose all-time favorite story from the Bible was the one about not throwing stones if you weren't more than a little guilty yourself.

Trent wanted Marcus's grandma along because he trusted her. When she'd come to him, she was deferential in ways most parents could never even fake. She wanted him to know Marcus's story, and she'd told him she was plain scared of what might happen now that he'd moved into that place with a white boy people said was trouble.

"I don't know if I can get him to school much anymore," she'd told him, that afternoon. "He's on his own now, and even though he's got good sense, and I can't help but worry. He likes to read, but he never did like school."

"I'll keep an eye out," he'd told her.

She nodded. "When my son left, and his mother took off and got lost, so did he, I guess. It's been all me for awhile, and I'm way close to the grave."

"I can tell that all you is not nothing, Mrs. Pritchard," he told her.

"And he's just now growing, too," she said. "He was a little guy for such a long time—that ain't easy either, not if you gotta be a warrior." I was a bit of a joke. "I'm serious," she said.

"I'll do what I can," he told her.

"That's not what I'm asking," she said. "I'm asking for more. I need special favors."

That beloved fortitude in her eyes made it clear to him that he was dealing with someone special.

He followed Marcus in the door, walked in without knocking because it was the kid's house after all; and there sat KayLee Faber.

Good Lord, he told himself, KayLee Faber.

If you'd have asked him who might be in that rat hole, the very last kid he could have named would have been KayLee Faber. But there she was, just as fierce and driven as always. He'd never seen that child be anything but a teacher's dream--throw her out in the pasture and she'd find something to read and come back with some thoughts about string theory.

She held a blanket up to her face as if there may have been tears, but her eyes looked hard, angry. She'd been in his office a hundred times—class officer, student council, this award, that award. He didn't know the kid beside her—the guy, maybe Marcus's roommate. She looked mad as sin, but also beat up.

Marcus went downstairs so quickly that he hadn't noticed KayLee. He said later he'd seen plenty of girls on LeRoy's couch, plenty of them.

Trent didn't say anything. He let KayLee sit there and think, maybe worry. She was probably as surprised to see him as he was to see her, but she was the one who owed him the story. There was too much to suggest that if he and Marcus hadn't interrupted some kind of sex, then it a had already happened earlier, some kind of wrestling match anyway.

"What do you want?" she said finally. Phony toughness, paper- thin. The blanket was pulled up over just about all of her. It didn't look good. Neither did she.

"He's the principal," she explained.

The guy told her he'd seen him around.

"I'm not coming back," she announced brazenly.

"Coming back where?" he said.

"To school."

"Because you two are getting married?" Trent asked, "—is that it? Let me get this straight. You're quitting school because you want *this* life—that's what you're saying?" It was a smart-ass answer, and he said it as if he knew better. "You want to live on that couch? You two got a garage band you're going to tour? What are you talking about?"

Welcome to another blizzard, Trent thought. Dawn had just broken off with the same guy last night, the guy who'd made her pregnant. What was he, some kind of juggler? And she wasn't his type—good Lord almighty, KayLee Faber wasn't his type.

"You know," she said. It was meant as a slap in the face. He could feel it, but he had no idea why.

Marcus came back up from their basement with a bottle of wine in each hand and his finger hooked in the plastic wrap of a six-pack of Miller Light. "She's Scotty Faber's daughter," Marcus told him, pointing. "Scotty Faber's real daughter. She lives with him. In his house."

Trent felt strung up. He could feel it in his stomach, that line. He had no idea what was going on, and he hated to be the last one to know.

"This girl here is Dawn's sister," Marcus told him.

"You are?" Trent asked.

"Half," Marcus told him, not wanting to get too comfortable.

Every inch of KayLee's face hardened. She let that blanket down and buttoned the front of her blouse, swallowed something huge, squared her shoulders, and nodded.

"Dawn Burnett," Trent said, "is your sister?"

She kept nodding.

He wouldn't have guessed it in a thousand years. Dawn was on her way, if she wasn't already parked out in the yard somewhere or getting warm around a fire. "She's coming," Trent told her. "Dawn'll be here any time—your sister. She may be here already."

Poor girl had no idea. She looked around, apprehensive. Some of that pluck gone.

Marcus opened a window shade. "Not yet," he said. Then he looked back and said something Trent figured was meant for the guy. "He's not stringin' you. She's coming. I been with her most the night. She's on her way."

The guy on the couch had to be the jerk who got Dawn pregnant, who wanted her to abort.

He always told brand new teachers that what you learn quickly is that under the sun there's nothing new, that sooner or later you'll see almost everything flesh is heir to. He'd walked into that pig sty these guys lived in, thinking he was going to make sure Marcus didn't overdo the spirits. He thought he needed to control things. That's his job. Once inside, things got odd fast.

"We're going to start a fire in the machine shed," he told the pair on the couch. "There's more folks cumin'." It seemed only reasonable to say what he did. "You might want to join us," he said.

He'd seen a change in KayLee Faber that he thought he liked. "Your sister's going to be there, and Marcus's grandma—she's out in the pickup, keeping warm. She's the one needs a glass of wine."

He couldn't help thinking that something he'd said changed something in KayLee. She pulled that blanket up to her face as if to hide.

He told Marcus to get out to the shed and get a fire going for our guests. Then he turned to the guy on the old couch. "You mind if the two of us have a few words?" he said.

Kid smiled and left, walked upstairs to what Trent assumed was his bedroom. Trent listened until the guy's steps stopped above them and the shriek of an old box spring made clear he was out of earshot.

I wasn't about to argue

What Woody saw when he and Tieneke and Karin drove up to the Brethower place was Starrett's Ford 150, a pickup he wouldn't have recognized without that silly Eddie Bauer two-tone package. Had to be his, and it was running, lights on, parked up in front of the doors of a machine shed out back, its headlights the only light—or so it seemed—anywhere near the shed.

"We're not alone," Tieneke said. "Party or something?"

"The kid is here," he told her. "He's probably shining for truants."

"The kid?" she asked. "You mean your new head guy?"

"That's his truck."

First glance said the party was ending, a couple cars running, lights on as if someone was getting the innards warmed for a ride home. Woody drove Karin's Toyota toward the cars up near the house, and when his headlights swept over a Honda, he saw someone inside. Someone was inside that Honda, someone was inside the machine shed, and the house was lit as if there was still someone in there too. One of those old porch lights stuck out on an arm shaped like a shepherd's crook over the back door, a big dark hood over a bulb so old what it cast over the cement was the color of oleo.

"Somebody's in that car," Tieneke said, just about crawling up into the front seat. "I see somebody in there."

"It's Scotty," Karin said.

Woody had no idea how she recognized him. The three of them had just come from the motel, from Glenn's place, from a quick trip around town trying to spot his pickup. Nothing.

"You think Scotty knows Trent Sterrett?" Woody asked.

"The new principal? --" she said.

"That's his pickup."

"I don't think so," she said. "But that's Scotty. I know it's him." And just like that she was half out of the car.

"She right?"

"Trust her," Tieneke said.

When Karen opened the door, a moment's hesitation passed before Scotty got out, before the two stood there in the blasted cold and hugged. The hugging went on and on, but Woody figured he and Tieneke had some rubbernecking coming after what they'd put in all night long. The Fabers were not out of the woods, but at least they were together after taking separate beatings neither of them could have imagined.

"Time to quit," Woody said. "We're done here."

Tieneke stretched her arms. "Been a long night for a couple of old people."

Some slight woman came up out of the darkness, walked up to Scotty and Karin. She was wearing an old Cottonwood high school letter jacket, black leather sleeves, way too big, a jacket that had to be a hundred years old. Stocking cap was pulled over her head, over her ears. Short hair. She was a tiny thing, hands in her pockets. She said something they couldn't hear, then came right up and took them in her arms just long enough to let them know she was there, and then aimed them like an usher into the machine shed, of all places.

"Something's happening here," Tieneke said. "Something's going on. We got to stay. It's not over yet." She took an audible breath.

He knew she was right.

Will you come with?

Not until the kid named LeRoy had left the room did Trent notice that somewhere beneath that mess of unzipped sleeping bag KayLee Faber pulled over her, her jeans lay pooled on the floor.

Didn't matter. The only voice he'd ever used to speak to KayLee was respectful, a mentor's voice, even though he wasn't, and she didn't need a mentor, ever. He told himself it wasn't a time to pull out some other voice, so while he asked the salient question, he didn't use the back of his hand. Not at all.

"You want to tell me what's going on?" He looked down at his watch. "This place isn't exactly where I would have put you on a Friday night."

KayLee looked at him warily, not as if she was afraid—he wouldn't have described her that way at all. She looked at him as if he were speaking some lost dialect.

"Look," Trent said. "You want me to leave while you get your jeans on? It's not my policy to talk to honor roll kids in their underwear."

She sniffed, but she wasn't crying.

He turned around and looked out the window. "There's a crowd out here," he told her. "If they're not here yet, they're coming. You're going to need to be dressed."

Not a word.

"Marcus—you know Marcus?"

She shook her head.

"He lives here." He knew at that moment that KayLee didn't frequent the place. She wasn't lying. "Kid that was just here?—that's Marcus," he told her, pointing as if he were still there.

Silence.

"And his grandma—she's here too."

More silence.

"He doesn't have parents," he said. "Well, he has them—everyone has them—but they aren't mom and dad exactly, because they're really not part of his life."

She looked down.

"That's why his grandma is here," he said. "There's more too, but maybe I ought to inch into that."

The silence was starting to soften her. KayLee Faber was a smart girl, he knew, and maybe for the first time in a while, her mind was actually operating.

"There's Coby St. James—she's a new teacher in the grade school—school nurse too, sort of, whenever we need her. Maybe you've seen her. She's here too."

No movement.

"I don't know if she's here yet," he told her. "Tell you what, I'll look through the window here and you pull those jeans on. This ain't a good scene."

He walked back over to the window near the door, looked out again and saw Coby's Honda, its passenger side door wide open. A couple, hugging, was outlined in what little light spilled from the interior. He didn't see Coby, but he sure enough recognized her car. The swish of clothing behind him made him think KayLee was getting dressed.

The real story right there on the yard was Dawn Burnett. If he had all of this right—and he'd heard it in multiple ways in the last couple of hours—the two of them were sisters. He stood there at the window to make sure she had enough time to get the job done, waited, and then, without turning, told her what he guessed would be most noteworthy. "And Dawn Burnett is here," he said, didn't really underline it. "I know she's not big buds or anything. Maybe you know her from around school."

He turned around to see that the stone face was still there. The faintest twists in her lips made it clear something was broken, but when she still said nothing, he dropped the deception.

"Marcus tells me Dawn's your sister, KayLee," he said. "Marcus tells me that you two never really talk— "

"Not *never*," she said. "We talked."

"About him?" he said, pointing upstairs.

She looked repulsed at the suggestion.

"You knew that this kid is the guy who got her pregnant, right?"

KayLee Faber did not know that—she did not know the two of them were a thing, and she certainly didn't know that her half-sister was going to have a baby. All of that was written in shock all over that stone face.

"That's what the suicide thing was all about, KayLee. He's the guy got her pregnant—the guy you were with here." He stopped. He didn't know how much KayLee could take in one breath. "That's why I didn't really get it, you and him together." He pointed at the sleeping bag on the floor. "Still don't."

"Dawn is going to have a baby?" she said. First question.

"Sit down," he said. "You need to know what's going on."

It took every bit of that nightmare to break her, he thought, every bit. The baby was one thing, this LeRoy wanting Dawn to get an abortion was another. Their breakup made her eyebrows arch a little and some of the steel in her eyes soften. The little fire Dawn and Marcus had built out back last night made her curious, but when he told her about the miscarriage, the demon in her stubbornness departed as if the story itself was an exorcist.

"I don't know the details, but my wife—my ex," he told her, "had two miscarriages."

She looked into his eyes in a way she hadn't before.

"I could probably list a dozen reasons why that marriage failed, KayLee," he said, "but those two babies who were never born have to be somewhere at the top."

"Where is Dawn?" KayLee asked. First time she spoke the name.

"In the machine shed."

"Why?"

"Honestly," he told her, "I'm not sure. Something's planned out there—Coby's got something planned to help, to end--you know, to start over."

"Some party or what?"

"Don't be a jerk. Put it this way--I trust Coby," he said. "Don't ask me to explain." He leaned towards the door. "There's a fire out there—at least, I hope it's going." Marcus had made a fire out there last night, and Trent figured he could do it again. He turned to look out the window. "It's going, I think," he told her. "I don't know what's going to happen, but I know what's not happenin' in here."

"People are out there?" She didn't know what to say, how to feel. He was sure of it.

"I'm not lying."

"And she's here? —Dawn's here?"

"Came with Coby just now. The Honda's out there." He pointed as if she was right there beside him.

"I'm sorry," she said, just like that. It wasn't full of feeling, but it was the right words.

"He wanted Dawn to get an abortion?" she asked.

"Before the miscarriage," he said.

She looked around as if there were no places for her eyes to focus. Something fierce was working its way out of her heart, out of her soul. She didn't look at him. Couldn't. "Mr. Sterrett," she said, her eyes looking somewhere over his shoulder. "What happens when a baby doesn't come?" she said.

What he knew was what it had done to his wife, and Coby had told him at least something of what it had done to Dawn. "There are a couple of women outside who could answer that much better than I could," he said.

She shook her head.

He looked back out the window to see if Coby was around, but he didn't see her. Another car rolled into the yard.

"And they'd be happy to. You got a jacket?" he asked with his back to her.

She didn't say anything, but he took her silence as an answer.

That's when he saw Dawn's mother and step-dad get out of the SUV that had just rolled up. He assumed Coby had called them—that would be like her. She hadn't told him as much, but he had no doubt that she'd talked it over with Dawn before doing it. The two of them walked over to the machine shed.

"Will you come with?" KayLee said. "I mean, when I walk over there?"

He nodded.

She pulled on her vest and came up behind him. He smiled at her. She didn't smile back, but it was clear she was as ready as she would ever be. He pulled up the zipper on his jacket, grabbed the old worn doorknob, and opened the storm, then pushed the screen away with his elbow.

She stepped over the sill and onto the concrete outside, turned toward him, because he knew she didn't want to face anything out there alone right then. He closed the door behind him, and the two of them negotiated the icy steps down to the ancient sidewalk running out toward the gravel driveway.

What she said right then is something Trent Sterrett would have liked to forget if he could. He had no idea who it was she saw out there, but he saw them too, had seen them from the window before, a couple in each other's arms. She recognized them immediately.

She bolted, climbed back up the porch stairs and ran into the house, that screen door slapping shut behind her.

He had no idea what had happened.

She's your sister

Marcus told his grandma that he'd forgotten to grab glasses for all that wine, that he'd go back into the house and see if he could find some, but that she shouldn't think they were going to have enough to go around. The fire inside was going by then, maybe three feet high or so. But he knew it was still cold out there, even though he was sweating from hauling bales from the back of the place, a whole circle of them. He remembered the sleeping bags last night, but his truck was somewhere out in the hills where he'd grabbed that Christmas tree.

"I don't need but two or three," his grandma told him. "This in't no party."

"Then what is it?" Marcus asked.

"Well, maybe it is," she told him. "You just pray a blessing here that that's what it'll be."

He had no desire to talk to Dawn's parents when he saw them come in, so he hightailed it for the back corner of the shed to get two more bales of hay for them, and as he did, he stumbled on something that shouldn't have been there, a bunch of blankets that—he had no idea how—he immediately recognized as Dawn's, not because he knew anything about what kind of blankets she had in her house or room or whatever, but because they had no dust on them, nothing. They were simply lying there in the back of those bales as if someone had dumped them off there just today, just last night, just last night. He knew somehow that they belonged to Dawn. There was more, whatever it was that ended her having a baby. Whatever it was that happened was in those blankets. He didn't look. He didn't have to.

He stood one of the bales on its end on the other one, held it there, and looked over the crowd of people in the shed.

There was a teacher there, an old history teacher. Didn't remember his name. A woman, maybe his wife, beside him. Didn't know her. They were talking to Coby and Dawn. Not Dawn. really. Dawn wasn't talking. When she spotted him over on the other side, and when she turned slightly to see her parents coming in behind her, she came over to where he was standing.

"I think I'm going to go in my pants," she said.

There he stood like the Statue of Liberty, bale of hay balancing in his hand. "You know where to go," he said.

"LeRoy's home, isn't he?"

"You and him are done with," Marcus said.

"Doesn't make it any easier," she told him. Then she looked down behind him, not a bit of surprise in her eyes—then up at him as if to see if he'd seen it.

"That's it?" he asked her.

"What?"

"I don't know what to call it, Dawn," he told her. "But that's it, isn't it? You put that something in there, left it there last night, right?"

What he saw in her eyes right then was just about the best thing he'd ever seen because it asked him to love her, to be there.

"It's what she wants," Dawn told him. "It's what Coby wants. It's why we're here."

He didn't really get it, not at all. "What's going on?" he said. "Some kind of powwow?" He pointed with his left arm. "And your parents here, too."

She nodded. "Stay with me, Marcus?" she said. "Promise you'll stay with me."

"My grandma'd whup me if I didn't," he told her. "She says I gotta love you—exact words."

"She did?"

"Cause of what you been through, she said."

Dawn shrugged her shoulders. "Lots of folks here, and I don't know really what she's cooking up."

"This Coby's idea?"

She nodded.

"You like her, don't you?" Marcus said.

"You and Coby's all I got," she told him.

"I ain't leaving," he told her. "I swear it."

She hugged him.

"How about I take you to the toilet?" he said. "I'll go with."

"I don't have to go," she said. "I was just saying that."

"You need out anyway?" he said.

"Yes," she told him.

"Then let's just pretend," he said. He pointed at the bale. "You take this other one here and bring it over and put it next to the circle."

Maybe it was the people, maybe it was the fire, maybe it was the work, but he was starting to get comfortable in the middle of things, he thought. Wasn't exactly the time for marshmallows, but the wind had calmed a bit and it seemed easier—more light, more heat. He pointed at the spot where he wanted Dawn to put down the bale he'd asked her to bring over, then kicked two of them together.

"Got a job," Trent said. He hadn't even heard the guy come up, but he wasn't talking to him. He was talking to Dawn. "Got something only you can do, I think," he said.

Coby was beside him. That old history teacher and his wife were talking to Dawn's parents, closer to the door but close enough to pick up some warmth from the fire. His grandma stood just behind Coby. He hadn't even seen her walk over.

"I can go with," Trent told her. "But nobody else can do this."

Marcus could tell Dawn had no clue.

"KayLee Faber is in the house," Trent said. "Her parents— "

And right then, the Fabers came in, as if they'd been waiting to be announced. The history teacher and his wife walked over and took both of them in their arms.

"She shouldn't be alone in the house," Coby said. "She and her parents aren't speaking."

Dawn rolled her eyes.

"It's serious," Coby told them. "It's difficult—trust me, please."

"She not getting enough for Christmas or what?" Marcus said.

"She just found out about you," Coby told Dawn. "Just tonight."

“I tried to take her out of the house,” Trent said, “but she freaked when she saw them.” He shook his head. “This is all new to her.”

“Not true,” Dawn said. “She knew before.”

“Not everything,” Coby said. “Not the whole business—not about your mom and her dad. Not all of that. Besides, she never had a choice to believe it until just now, tonight.”

The machine shed was full of gunpowder, and all kinds of battles, so many you’d need a scoreboard to keep track, Marcus thought.

“KayLee needs to be here, Dawn,” Coby said, “—not alone inside that house.”

“I’ll take her,” Marcus said. “I promised I’d go with her. I just now told Dawn I’d go along.”

Trent looked at Coby. Grandma stepped up toward Marcus, grabbed his arms, both of them in her hands, looked straight into his eyes, said nothing, just nodded, then smiled. What Marcus knew inside his soul was that right then, he was her son. He was her grandson, but he was a whole lot more than that.

“Bring KayLee here,” Coby whispered to Dawn, reaching for her hand. “She’s your sister. Just remember that.”

The way it's supposed to be

Marcus figured he'd need to go along back into the house to get rid of LeRoy, too, because the last thing he wanted to happen was LeRoy butting in somehow and making everything go shitty again just by showing up. LeRoy wasn't a bad guy, and Marcus wasn't worried that he'd have to run him out or something, only that LeRoy didn't need to be there when the two of them, these two sisters, finally got talking to each other.

Dawn had hold of his arm when they left the shed and started to walk toward the house, and that's when she told him that maybe he'd have more to do once they got inside than just play bouncer, should LeRoy stick his nose back into what he shouldn't.

"I don't even know this chick," Marcus told her, halfway to the back door. "I don't know what she looks like and I don't like her."

"Frickin' angel," Dawn told him. "Cute little white girl angel—big frickin' eyes, green or olive or whatever, maybe blue, I don't know—a beak that's maybe a little too pointed, and these fatty white girl cheeks, too, you know?"

"Dark hair?" he said.

"You kidding? —blondish or red or something, long and straight and curly on the bottom." Dawn fussed with her fingers as if curls dangled on her shoulders. "Amber, maybe, you know? Magazine queen."

"You hate her?"

Dawn stopped, as if she had to think. "Last year, maybe. Too much other shit in my head right now. I got no time for that."

"She ever a friend?"

"The Queen of Sheba?" Dawn laughed. "Maybe Snow White's more like it."

"You're serious?"

"Perfect little white girl," Dawn told him.

"What you got to give a shit about her for, just another fancy-ass."

Dawn didn't miss a beat. "She's my sister," she told him.

"Half."

"Still."

"I know."

She kept hold of his arm, like they were together, he thought. He remembered what his grandma said. "What's she doing here anyway?" he asked.

"Damned if I know," Dawn told him, and started marching off towards the cement steps.

Just didn't add up to him, all this tough stuff and still her hand on his arm. Everything Dawn said made him think this white girl wasn't LeRoy's type either, no way. Besides, he knew LeRoy's party friends, and there were no KayLees. Didn't make sense that a girl like her'd be out at the Brethower place.

"I wonder if she was looking for you," he said, trying to slow her down. "Maybe she thought you'd be here, you know? You'd be sitting here watching something with LeRoy." Made good sense really. "Why else come out here? Why else she come out to this hole than to see you?"

Dawn looked away, hunched her shoulders.

"You didn't ever talk to her before?"

"Bits and pieces—maybe three times is all," Dawn told him. She stopped and looked at him. "I think she knows," she said. "I think she knows who I am and that I'm her sister. I think she knew it awhile already—the way she looks at me. I'm thinking she does, but there ain't no way she'd admit it."

"Cause you just a piece of shit or what?"

"Who'd want me for a cousin?" she said.

"Me," he said. "Not hot on the *cousin* part."

He loved the smile she gave him.

He remembered thinking about chunking the ice off the back steps, but he hadn't got around to it, so the two of them climbed up to the door a little gingerly, holding to a hand rail so old it barely stayed in its worn cement sockets.

"You ready?" he asked her.

"Look," she said, "Sterrett says she freaked seeing her folks, remember? It's not us—it's not me that's a problem. If she's sitting behind the door with a 12-gauge waiting to blow somebody away, it's not some half-sister."

"Thank you."

"Enough blood around here," she said.

He'd not forgotten what Trent told him had happened to Dawn, and he didn't want to hear really, didn't think he had to know all the gory details. What bugged him was that he had to hear it from Trent. "How come you never told me about all that ugly stuff," he said, stopping her again.

"About what?"

"You know—about that stuff that happened to you, about the miscarriage." He asked it in a hushed voice, as if that other girl, her sister, might be just inside the door, waiting. "I think things would 'a been different last night," he said. "You know—if you'd told me what happened. I didn't know any of that. Nothing."

She reached over and hugged him. "Wasn't what you were thinking about, you asshole," she told him, then leaned up and kissed his cheek.

"Lot of blood, Sterrett said," he told her.

They were standing on the porch, just outside the door. She pulled her hand from his arm, grabbed both his shoulders with both hands and squared him around. "I didn't know shit, Marcus Pritchard," she told him. "I was just a kid and I didn't know what the hell was going on."

"Then it's Tweddledum and Tweddledee," he told her.

"Tweddledum and Tweddle-dumber," she said.

"Let's do it," Marcus said, facing the door. "I'm dying of cold."

"What a puss," she said.

"One thing yet--way back there in the shed there's this bunch of stuff, an armful." He let that sit, let it be there in the cold air just outside the house. "That's your stuff, in't it?"

The way she looked at him just then, into his eyes, was intense. "That's why Coby dragged me out here—all that stuff back there. 'Something's got to be done,' she said. "That's what she thinks." She looked back at the shed as if whatever part of her was wrapped up and parked right there outside the door.

"Maybe she's right—I don't know. Maybe, she just made me think she's right."

"Like a funeral?" he said. "Too cold to bury anything, and we ain't even got a preacher. Hope they don't want me to try to dig in this frozen ground."

"I don't know," she said. "Let's just get this over with."

He nodded, tried to smile, even though she didn't seem all that worried. "My grandma said I had to love you," he told her. "'*Got to*! Hear me? —*got to*.'"

"She didn't mean that other way," Dawn told him.

"I'm no fool," he said.

"Your grandma was a man, she'd be a chief," she said, and opened the door.

"*Chairman*," he told her. "We call 'em *chairmen* now if you're wondering."

"Whatever," Dawn said. She took a breath, turned to him once more, grabbed the handle, and shoved with her shoulder.

Kaylee got up from where she was sitting at the end of the couch, pulled her hair back behind her ears, trying to look on top of things, Marcus thought.

The two of them stood across the room, neither moving an inch, like gunslingers facing each other down on Main Street. They didn't seem mad or angry. It was just weird, two of them, sisters, just staring. He could have slipped out and nobody would have noticed.

It was the white girl who talked finally.

"My dad," she said, but didn't keep going.

"I know," Dawn told her. "I know the story—you don't have to go there, not for my sake."

"I'm sorry," KayLee told her.

"Don't need to be," Dawn said. "Nothing you ever did. So long ago, could have just as well forgotten the whole sorry mess, right?"

KayLee looked like she had so much to say, she didn't know how to start. She pulled her hair back again, shook her head, as if something was stinging her. "I still feel like I got to say 'I'm sorry,' and I am."

"Tell you what," Dawn said. Marcus didn't have to look to know she was smiling—he could hear the smile. "You just get over it. You don't owe me nothing, no sympathy or nothing like that."

She still had hold of his arm. He had figured to get away from the two of them and head up to LeRoy's room the minute he got in the house, but Dawn didn't want him gone. She wanted him here.

"You knew, right?" Dawn asked the girl. And then, she pointed back and forth between them.

"Well, yeah," KayLee said, in a whispery way nobody'd ever believe her.

Marcus sure didn't. "You two sure don't look alike," he said.

Dawn backhanded him in the stomach. "Don't be stupid." She pointed at him. "This is Marcus Pritchard—he lives here, actually. He's my body guard."

"Nice," KayLee said, but nothing really showed on her face.

"My ma told me years ago," Dawn said. "I was a kid and we were in a grocery store, and I think she was drunk—I couldn't always tell, but back then, most often she was." She took a deep breath. "She pointed right at your dad—I don't know that he saw her. She pointed right at him and said, way loud, 'That's your old man, Dawn.' She did. I never forgot."

Marcus listened for any sound from upstairs. If LeRoy came on down just then, everything would get into deep shit. "Why don't you two sit down?" he said. "My foot's sleeping."

Dawn didn't let him go. She listened to what he'd said, but she pulled him along to the couch, set him down on the far end, and just about fell through when she sat herself down in the middle.

"Sometime I'm going to put some plywood beneath those pillows there," Marcus said. "Thing is worn-out and gone." He pulled his arm away from Dawn's grasp and sat up, then hunched himself up on the arm of the couch. "Can't get rid of it, though," he said, "on account of the wildlife."

Neither of them got it. "Regular zoo in there," he told them, pointing. "Saturday, I pulled a rabbit out."

"Did not," Dawn said.

"Who cares about rabbits? Damned weasel was scary though—I'll tell you that," he said. "You know they kill for sport?"

"No weasel inside this couch," Dawn told him.

"How do you know? You don't live here."

"Marcus Pritchard, you lie." She slapped his thigh with the back of her hand.

"You two, like 'together'?" KayLee asked. She'd sat down when Marcus said to, sat on the other end of the couch.

"He'd like to think so," Dawn said.

"Look who's holding on here," Marcus told KayLee, pointing down at Dawn's hand.

When the white girl smiled, it just seemed to him that something might work here.

Then, it got quiet between them. Marcus listened to see if he could hear LeRoy upstairs, maybe his music. He slid off the arm and stood, then grabbed Dawn's hand the way she'd grabbed his. He pulled her back to her feet, held her in front of him like a human shield, both her arms in his hands, steered her over to the other side of that old couch, and stood her there in front of her half-sister, then grabbed the white girl's hands and pulled her to her feet so the two of them were close.

"Let me take care of this," he said. "Whyn't you two just hug each other and be done with it, all right? You're sisters, for shit's sake."

He liked that Dawn was the one who started it. He could have kissed her right there and he would have, but it was time for him to make sure LeRoy was out of the way. She reached for KayLee's hand, almost as if she was going to shake it; but when KayLee gave it up, she rubbed it the way his grandma used to rub his when she'd take him along to church, just stood for a couple seconds and held her hand. And then they hugged, the two of them, the Lone Ranger and Tonto. Sisters. Kinda.

Later on, he told himself he'd have been surprised if they hadn't cried a little, like girls do, both of them, not a bit embarrassed and not reaching for the tears or trying to hold anything back either, both turning all wimpy and weepy, wrapping arms around each other as if they'd spent altogether too many years in opposite corners of the world.

I'm going to have a story to tell you

LeRoy had his earphones in. "What the hell is going on?" he said when Marcus showed up in his doorway. "There's, like, a hundred people on the yard."

"When this is all over," Marcus said, "I'm going to tell a story that you're not going to want to hear." There LeRoy sat, like a cat curled up on his ratty bed. "Right now you best leave."

"You're serious?"

"Take off in that truck of yours for a couple hours. It ain't all that late."

"My place here, too," LeRoy said.

"I don't mess with you, LeRoy—never have," Marcus said. "But right now you got to stay out of the way."

LeRoy pulled himself up. "I didn't ask that bitch to come out here. I didn't even know her. Chick like that doesn't hang around with trash like us, Marcus. I didn't ever talk to her before in my life." Marcus didn't want to hear any of it. "Girl just shows up," LeRoy said, "walks in the door and takes off that vest and then keeps right on going, takes off her sweater next and stands in a bra. I'm not lying. There she stands in front of me and off comes that bra—like you see in the movies. She like wiggles herself out of it." He was proud of it, of course. "What's a guy do when that happens? —tell her to get out?"

"What happened?"

"Her old man comes in and the two of them piss and moan and bitch until he leaves." LeRoy shook his head. "She like to beat the shit out of her old man, that girl. She gave him a blow upside the head that had him down—and then he left."

"With her hand?"

"Worse," LeRoy told him. "She went right for his heart."

"You screw her?" Marcus said.

He shook his head. "She didn't give a crap about me." He put his feet on the floor, sat up. "I didn't even know her. Seen her around when I worked for Woody, but she's nuts. She just comes in here and flips off her clothes, I'm telling you. Never seen anything like it."

"Look," Marcus said, "you got to stay away from what's happening out there. Don't come around downstairs, and don't come outside either. I don't know what's going to happen, but once it's over and done with I'll tell you everything—I swear."

"Somebody die or what?" LeRoy asked.

"Maybe you could say it that way," Marcus backed up toward the door. "Just stay the heck out of the way—that's all I'm saying. You got to promise me you're going to stay away."

LeRoy pulled his legs back up on the bed, put his head on his pillow, pushed those ear buds back in place, and shut his eyes. That was a promise.

When Marcus got to the bottom of the stairs, the two of them—the sisters--were still holding on, shuffling around as if they were dancing.

"You gotta love her, Marcus," his grandma had said three, four times, at least. Maybe more. "Just love that girl," she said.

After the three of them had walked back to the machine shed, Marcus stayed outside alone and let the two of them go in by themselves, holding on as if they needed each other to walk, because that was the way it was supposed to be. They were sisters.

Something Changed

While he waited for the girls to return, Trent was tending the fire, although flames were coming up just fine. Celine's husband came over and stood there with him. The two of them seemed to know each other. They'd probably spoken before—probably about Dawn, always about Dawn.

Scotty and Karen stood in the corner at the door, while Celine seemed unable to mingle, waiting, like they all were, for the kids to return. Celine hadn't seen her daughter since late afternoon, but someone must have told her Dawn was okay. She seemed very tense.

No one knew everyone, Tieneke thought, and no one knew everything.

Just exactly what that Indian woman knew about anything wasn't clear, but she seemed least affected and most determined in all that slowly warming darkness. Why she was here, wasn't at all clear. Woody's boss had brought her. She looked innocent almost, but engaged, an ancient Cottonwood jacket around her, way too big, unbuttoned in the warmth cast by the fire. Might have been an old crone maybe, but not a bit ugly, not a bit. Tieneke was quite sure the woman was older than she was, but aging didn't always leave tracks on Indian women. She was maybe the only person in the shed to wear a smile. Not big. Not sentimental either. Just confident.

The woman Woody called Coby decided something needed to be said. She stepped into the middle of things, in front of the fire. Woody had mentioned a budding romance, something that didn't really have to be whispered, like most of the affairs that went on during their quarter-century in Cottonwood. A new teacher and new head guy becoming a thing. Legit, too.

Coby stood up front, grabbed Trent's hand to get him beside her. Like training wheels, Tieneke thought. Cute. Right then, *cute* was a momentary blessing.

"Two sisters," Coby said. "There are two stories, I guess, isn't there?"

"Three," Trent said, looking at the Indian woman and reminding Coby of Marcus.

"Two kids I hope are looking at each other as sisters, because they are." Coby braved a smile she meant to pass along to the rest of them. Nothing phony. She wasn't running for office or selling anything. Besides, after what Tieneke and Woody had been through that night already, they were in a good position to buy some good news.

Coby's dark eyes made her seem Native, but her short black hair beneath that stocking cap made it hard to know what she was. Square face, strong jaw, she seemed a darling whatever she was. She pulled her mittens off with her teeth, then stuck them into the pockets of her jacket. "I don't know what's happening inside the house right now, but it's probably a good thing if we all know what we can of the whole story."

She waited, let the silence roam around the room a while. "I don't know that we have a lot of time. I hope they'll be back shortly, but we all need to talk a bit here."

Tieneke knew that someone was going to have to speak for Karin and Scotty because neither could have stuck together a sentence. After she introduced herself as Woody's wife, she pointed with her head, leaned a bit in the direction of Karin and Scotty. "I'm going to speak for the Fabers," she said, and then walked over beside them. "They're our neighbors. Their daughter is KayLee." She looked at Woody, because she didn't think she knew how to say what had to be said.

But it was Celine who filled in the blanks. "Scotty and I, long ago, had a relationship," she said. "Dawn is our daughter."

Got quiet again. People looked at each other, then away.

"Dawn knew about it?" Coby asked.

Celine nodded. "I'm not proud of what—" she stopped to tighten her lips. "She knew--" she said again.

Coby looked at Karin.

"KayLee didn't," Karin said, two words she could barely get out.

Speaking for the Fabers was an act of mercy, Tieneke thought, so she went on. "KayLee figured it all out, the whole story, just tonight." She didn't know how long those kids would be gone—no one did. She kept going. "She told us she kind of knew before, but she didn't—not for sure. We thought KayLee came here looking for Dawn," she said. "That's how it is we're here—Karin and me and Woody. Ever since late this afternoon, we were with KayLee, looking for Dawn."

Coby waited for all of that to settle. And then, "And when she found out about her sister--?" she looked at the Fabers as if maybe it were an affront for her to ask Tieneke, "--she reacted how?"

Scotty and Karin still weren't speaking.

"We were there," Tieneke said, and she looked at Woody, who nodded. "Can't blame her. It was no picnic for anybody."

Deliberately, it seemed, Coby looked slowly around the room. Maybe someone had a question.

"And Dawn was with us—she wasn't here," Coby said, then pointing at Trent first, and then at Scotty.

"She was with a kid who lives here," Trent said, "with Marcus."

They were standing in a broken circle around a fire that hung about three feet off the floor.

"With LeRoy?" Woody asked.

Trent nodded. Scotty tried to talk, but got out only something recognizable as an apology. "I'm so sorry—"

Trent laid an arm around the old woman's shoulder. "This is Marcus's grandma—this is Mrs. Pritchard," he said.

"Priscilla," she insisted, like a schoolmarm.

"Marcus came out here with me," Trent said, "and Marcus is a good kid. Doesn't come to school often, but he's a good kid."

"Better than that," Coby said. "He's a hero. He's the guy who called 911 last night. Marcus lives here too." She looked at the Fabers and then at Celine and her husband, and then turned to Priscilla—and hugged her. "Marcus saved Dawn's life," she told her. "Seems long ago."

Right then, everything had meaning

Sometimes, people ask Woody what it was like to be inside that wheezy machine shed in sub-arctic cold with a dozen people late at night, most of them beaten up, the whole gathering sitting in a circle on ten-year-old bales of dust, out on an acreage with a farm house that should have burned down sometime after Korea. When people ask, he tells them flat-out, it was one of the greatest moments of his life.

What kept the two of them there at the ramshackle Brethower place had been pure nosiness—nothing *pure* about it, either. They weren't needed. They could have been back home in less than an hour, Tieneke in her pajamas, Woody in his sweats, feet up in front of the tube watching *The West Wing* on Netflix.

Once they got Karin out to the Brethower place, it wasn't their story being told in that machine shed. What had happened in their presence that night broke their hearts, not only because of what had been said, what had been screamed, but also because what they witnessed was crafted out of beginnings they'd been a part of seventeen years before. Tieneke claims it was Woody's fault they got involved that night, because he was trying to be young again, the teacher he once was in a time when kids needed him. What drew him into the mess was a resurgence of old activism, otherwise mostly gone to seed, she says; and he mostly agrees. But then, she's usually right about such things. He just doesn't admit it.

How could they leave that acreage that night? The yard was full of vehicles. What's more, they'd come in Karin's car, and Karin was a mess. She'd been forced to tell her perfect daughter that her dad had been screwing another woman because she had been unfaithful, too.

Scotty looked diseased. He could have profited from a visit to the hospital. In his life, the man had suffered nothing close to what he had that night, begotten in part by the guy's own spiritual expectations— "the Lord is good to those who love him" --that kind of thing. Years ago already, he and Karin had rebuilt what had broken down in their marriage, erected faithfulness by hard, hard work; and because they had, he'd come to assume abundant blessings.

Right then, Woody and Tieneke had no idea what had happened to Scotty or what he'd seen when he walked into that old house, looking to love another daughter, the one he'd spent his adult life trying to forget.

When Dawn Burnett had walked into that machine shed that night, she was someone he hadn't seen before. She'd been too bitter to ask her mother anything, too estranged to talk to someone at school, too mad at the world to trust anyone until she'd opened up to Coby St. James, who'd insisted they make this blind pilgrimage to the Brethower machine shed.

There they stood, the adults—Tieneke and Woody, rubberneckers; Karin and Scotty, alone; Celine and Andrew, dumbstruck; and Coby, Trent, and old Priscilla Pritchard, standing closest to the fire, the youngest and the oldest and the strongest.

Coby had hold of a Pendleton blanket—a beautiful thing. She spread it out over a bale, opened it, then found a bundle of bedding in a corner of the machine shed, a bundle she looked for deliberately and seemed to know was there. She picked it up in her arms, put all of it into her blanket, and wrapped it up, that Pendleton over and around everything. Then she stood, straightened her jacket over her shoulders and stuck her hands in her pockets to warm them, even though it wasn't that cold in the shed. There were bodies all around, lots of them. Woody honestly didn't think anyone was cold right then. They were all far too apprehensive, waiting for the sisters to come back from the house.

Coby looked down at what she'd done, then picked up the whole bundle and put it down a couple bales away, not out of sight, just not in the middle of things.

That old shed right then was overflowing with hurt, Woody tells people when they ask, and he couldn't help feeling that whatever Coby had done with that blanket had meaning, because the silence all around told him everything did.

She told me she didn't want to live

Coby's heart told her that she'd done the right thing, taken more on than she ever might have guessed when she'd walked into Dawn's hospital room earlier that morning. Something had to be done with that bloody stuff Dawn simply couldn't leave behind. It was haunting that girl.

She took Celine's hand and led her and Andrew, her husband, closer to the fire, closer to where she'd been standing herself beside Trent and Mrs. Pritchard.

"What I am going to tell you is going to be very tough." She looked over at Grandma Pritchard beside her and read in the woman's smile some unmistakable reassurance. What she saw in the old woman's eyes told her to keep going.

"I wish all of this weren't true, Mrs. Burnett," Coby said.

"*Celine*, please?"

"I wish it weren't true," she said, had to, because it needed to be said, "but maybe a month ago, I don't know, some time ago at least—your daughter, Celine, lost a baby." It should not have been told so publicly, Coby thought, but it was part of an awful package now, a mess of things that had to be pieced back together somehow or there'd be even more risk to the girl.

"I'm not laying any blame anywhere here—all of this is really about all of us." She reached for Celine. "It was early in the pregnancy—I'm a nurse," she told her.

Celine nodded.

"She suffered a miscarriage--something no woman should ever suffer, least of all a child."

Celine's husband put his arm around his wife's waist. There were tears, but they were managed.

Scotty seemed in shock. Coby wasn't sure what was registering, or what could.

"The boy who was the father wanted her to abort the baby, but she didn't," Coby said. She felt the old woman's hand on her elbow. "And then, through no fault of her own, it just happened."

"Here?" Celine said.

Coby shook her head. Dawn would not confide in her mother, wouldn't tell her what had happened, wouldn't come for help or for love. Why not? —because shit happens, she told herself.

Andrew kept hold of Celine.

"And the ditch? —last night? My daughter deliberately drove in the ditch because—"

"She told me she didn't want to live," Coby told her. "But she didn't say, wouldn't even, that she wanted to die."

Coby pointed at the bundle in the blanket. "What's in there is what Dawn cleaned up," she said. "Your daughter believes what's inside that bundle is what's left of what was in her."

Celine pulled away from her husband and sat down on one of those bales, beside that bundle of blankets, and stretched an arm over them to lay her hand there.

"She couldn't just throw it out," Coby told her. "Too cold to bury."

Old Priscilla Pritchard came out from behind Coby and sat beside Celine, didn't touch her, just sat so close her presence was its own strength.

"That was some time ago," Coby said. "Dawn told me all of that just tonight, told me about the life and the death in these sheets and blankets. She had no idea what to do with them—with all of this--because she couldn't bring herself to toss them." She looked around at all the silent faces. "And that's why we're here. For something. For ceremony. For Dawn."

There had been tears from the beginning. Celine was a strong woman, but tears had come as soon as Coby told her what had happened. She simply didn't tend them. They dropped like jewels on her suede jacket.

She wanted him to speak

Maybe he shouldn't have. Later, much later, Trent wondered whether he should have said anything right then because nothing of this was his story. And yet it was, and he wanted everyone to know what the kid had done because saving one life means saving the world—isn't that the way it goes, he told himself, the old proverb?

"Marcus called it in," he told them. He smiled at Mrs. Pritchard. "Marcus is Mrs. Pritchard's grandson, and I want her and all of you to know that he's the one who called it in, called 911."

"He's the father?" Andrew asked, not angrily.

Trent shook his head.

Grandma Pritchard sat beside Celine. The smile he saw her give Coby early on was the one Mrs. Pritchard let grow just then because Marcus was hers.

Dawn and KayLee were still in the house. As long as they were, more had to be said.

"We found Mr. Faber out here," Coby said, pointing aimlessly with her arm. "It was me and Dawn, just the two of us." She reached for his hand once she got beside him again. "He'd been in an accident. He was out on one of the roads out here—his truck was. We found it on the way out." She looked at Scotty standing there helpless. "He'd hit a deer," she said.

Karin leaned away and held him suddenly at arm's length as if to check for injuries. Scotty must not have told her.

Coby told him that she and Dawn had followed his tracks in the snow, and then found him with that deer—it was a doe. "He —killed it," she said, "shot it because it was injured, you know, in the accident." She stopped to see if Scotty was up to talking himself.

There was enough wind outside to make the gaping siding sing, a mournful sound beneath the snapping fire. She wanted Scotty to say something, to draw an outline of what it was that all these people—even Karin—had to, know how Scotty came to be sitting out there in the middle of the field, as if he wanted to take his own life.

Scotty looked at Celine. No one spoke.

"There's more." Coby said, but she wanted him to talk.

"I wanted to talk to Dawn," Scotty said. "It was time. I got to thinking maybe it was time to talk to *your* daughter," he looked at Celine, "who's my daughter, too, even though I've never been her father." He looked at Karin "It was time," he said again.

The silence got prickly.

"When I left here," Scotty said. "I hit the deer on my way back to town, when I left." His eyes made it clear the story wasn't over.

"You didn't go in the house?" Trent asked him. "When you got here, you didn't go in?"

Scotty looked at Karin, her arm around his waist, and his face went somewhere beyond registering any emotion.

"Dawn wasn't here," Trent said. "She was with us, with Coby, all the time."

"It was our KayLee who was here," Scotty said. "I came out to find Dawn, but KayLee was the one who was here."

Her father had seen his daughter on that couch, Trent thought. It was a wonder someone wasn't dead. The man had seen his perfect daughter with that jerk, the other guy.

"KayLee was waiting for Dawn," Woody said. "The whole time she was with us, that's what she wanted—she wanted like nothing else to talk to Dawn."

"She was with LeRoy," Scotty said, his words distinct but in clusters. "Guy used to work for me. I know him, and they were, you know, together. They were on the couch." His eyes went down.

"LeRoy VanCamp?" Karin said.

"Dawn's guy?" Celine said.

"So we took Scotty here," Coby said. "Dawn and I—we took the man who is her father back here, and the two of them talked, didn't you?"

Scotty nodded.

"We'd all been out in the cold way too long, but the two of them talked a little, got introduced." She looked again at Scotty.

Karin stared into the fire.

The screen door back at the house slapped shut, hard enough to be heard over the wind's moans. They were coming, the two of them.

No one spoke

They weren't middle-schoolers, neither were they sweetheart little girls swinging hands. It was clear the two of them were no longer children. That's how Woody saw it. When Dawn and KayLee finally walked into that machine shed, their seriousness made them seem friends, maybe a little more than friends, even though, given what they'd both been through, the two of them could not have looked any different.

There they stood, alone, surprised at how many people were standing around that fire, all of them with a stake in their lives.

Coby let the two of them stand there. They were the ones who had to speak. None of the others had the right to say anything, he thought. What was to be said would begin and end with them.

Dawn put an arm around KayLee's waist. No one said anything. Old Mrs. Pritchard walked over, took both the girls' hands, and led them across the shed closer into the circle of the fire.

"Well," Dawn said, looking at her parents, her voice trembling a little, "some kind of party, is it?"

"Is already," Trent said, softly. "You two standing there together. Nice of you to show up."

Dawn hugged her new sister. Neither was dressed for the cold. KayLee still wore that vest she'd pulled on when she stood on the back step at the Dekkers a millennium ago. Dawn wore a wool pea coat, unbuttoned.

"This is Marcus's grandmother," Coby told KayLee, pointing at Priscilla with a nod. "Marcus lives here," she said, "Marcus Pritchard." And then, "He's been with Dawn quite a bit in the last couple of days."

KayLee stood there in a cold continuing stare. She had no idea who Marcus or his grandmother could have been.

So much that night was said and yet wasn't said. No matter, Woody thought, because so much was communicated wordlessly, They'd once attended a concert where the choir director never raised a baton or even a finger, simply stood before the choir and moved something in his face or shoulders, directed with motions so slight as to be indistinguishable.

That's what Woody thought of when he watched Grandma Pritchard, who said almost nothing for some time, didn't hypnotize those two kids or anyone else that night, didn't wave a magic wand or light a smudge and bathe them in smoke and spirit—didn't do any of that. Things just happened around her, as if others understood things they wouldn't have had any idea about if you would have asked them five minutes before. Woody had lived in a town bordering the reservation for a long time, even learned to love it some, as much as most people can; but he couldn't remember ever being that close to any man or woman with such extraordinary power. No *Twilight Zone*-thing either—that wasn't it. You just knew she was doing the right things. You just knew.

For months afterward, he tried to get hold of what it was that happened in those first few minutes the whole group was together in the shed, when old Mrs. Pritchard had been in charge. She seemed to know what medicine to supply and how much, how to manage the silence, what to say when something needed to be said.

He'd never claimed to have known Native ways all that well or understood them any better than he did the ranchers, their neighbors, or even himself.

But that night, from the moment it began, when those two kids came into the shed, that night, he knew what Grandma Pritchard was doing, just knew it. Not for a moment did any of it surprise Woody. Even so, it left him amazed.

The way of beauty

Two bales sat on the east end of the makeshift little circle, and that's where his grandma and the girls were standing when Marcus came back from the house all alone. No one saw him. No one was thinking about him, he figured. They were thinking about the girls, and that was fine with him.

His grandma was wearing his old man's high school jacket, the one she kept on a peg in the hall by the back door of the trailer. She wasn't saying anything, but neither were the girls, and neither were all those people—Dawn's parents and the guy Dawn had spotted in the café, who looked now as if his wheels were gone. They all looked beat. Had to be the guy's wife beside him, Marcus figured, because they looked like they were the ones who drove off the road and into the ditch.

His grandma twisted the top off one of the bottles of wine. She was standing right in front of the girls, all the others circled around that fire. If he'd had a drum, he would have used it, he thought, not because he knew much about singing or the songs a guy should sing, but because it just felt right in him at that moment to hear the beat of a person's heart, even his own. It would have been good.

Grandma poured wine into the top of Trent's thermos, not a little bit either, but plenty, all of that done out in front of them as if she were the priest or medicine man, which he'd always thought she was, sort of. Then she held up the cup, as if to make sure everyone saw it. She made all the people in that shed believe that what was in that thermos cap was nothing less than divine, he thought, bless her soul. There Grandma stood—a little woman really--holding on to what she'd poured in an old cup.

He hadn't made any noise when he'd come in. He didn't want anybody looking at him because what was going on here was all about those girls. All he could see of Dawn was from behind. Didn't matter-- it was as if her face was right in front of him now anyway.

Truth be known, he had no idea what his grandma was doing. He figured the girls would be sipping that wine somehow, but he wondered about all the others—there weren't enough cups. If she'd told him he needed a dozen, he'd have looked in the cupboard, because LeRoy always had a bunch of paper cups around somewhere just in case the party got big. It happened.

Instead, Grandma held that cup eye level, maybe higher, then brought it back down as if to let them all drink. Seemed right to him.

With the cup in both hands, she brought it right up before Dawn's eyes, a foot away maybe, holding it there with both hands, keeping it there until Dawn seemed to know what she had to do. Without being told Dawn brought her hands up and took that cup, keeping it up just as high as Grandma had carried it, as if celebrating something or other, something really good, which there hadn't been all that much of the whole night long.

Grandma made her hold that green cup up to the rest of them, as if it were something from the governor's house or whatever, as if what was in it wasn't just that Apple Farm or whatever he'd picked up from down in the basement, but some stuff that was way, way better. They stood there, all of them, and they said nothing, Dawn holding the blessing.

Then his grandma pointed, not with her fingers either, but with her eyes, pointed towards Celine, toward Dawn's mother. Everyone knew what had to happen.

Blew him away though, because he just caught on like everybody else did, as if they'd all been doing this whole thing forever. Dawn had to give away something to her mother, had to give up something precious. That's what Grandma was after, and he knew it—but he couldn't help thinking that everybody else understood it too, somehow, all those white people, all of them caught on, even though nothing was explained.

"Marcus," his grandma said.

She motioned him to come closer and into the circle of the others. He didn't stop watching Dawn. No one did. There was so much just plain beautiful about that girl, he thought. "I'm not going home," she had told him just last night. That's what he remembered as Dawn walked over to her mother. "I'm not going home—" it rang through his mind like barbed wire. It got him out of that bed they'd just shared to go look, because those words scared him, because they weren't just words.

What he didn't know was what there was or wasn't between her and her old lady, what kind of shit got left on the road they'd taken to get where they were. Dawn never said much to him about her mother, only that last night she wasn't going home. No way was she going home.

But right then in the shed, that girl went on a mission, that cup up in front of her eyes as she stepped around the bales and headed toward home. So much anger between them, he knew, and there was the whole miscarriage thing too, all that mess happening right downstairs when that baby just wasn't to be. And her mom hadn't known a thing. And then, that bullshit her little sister was telling her too, that Dawn was making the whole family live in hell. There was all of that inside her veins and running right up into her beating heart, Marcus thought.

But with that cup in her hands, he knew she knew exactly what she had to know, as if she'd been practicing for all of her life to give that sweet wine to her mother, to give it away. Grandma hadn't said a word to any of them, but everyone caught on that a giveaway was happening, what his grandma sort of made up.

When Dawn stood right there with her mother, his grandma told her what she seemed already to know. "Among our people, when what's inside is broken, we give away whatever it is we have. The way of beauty makes us strong."

Dawn waited for her mother to stand, all the while holding the cup between them in both her hands, letting it speak as if what it was belonged to neither of them. Her mother knew not to reach, not to take it. She had only to stand there as if she were herself a child when her daughter lifted it towards her. Something in him was singing, a voice and a song he'd heard before.

The two of them touched only each other's fingers, but something more passed between them, something healing. When Dawn stepped back, she looked again at his grandma, who nodded toward her stepdad to say that he too was to receive something in this giveaway in the machine shed. He was next. She had to be strong to keep giving. Wasn't just what his grandma wanted either. It was something bigger.

Dawn walked around the fire to face Andrew. Her step-dad knew not to touch the cup.

They all just knew.

Marcus was very proud. He moved out of the way, back into the shadows.

She was the only one who could give it all away

Each moment moved seamlessly. Dawn offered something Woody didn't know exactly how to explain, something to both her parents, to Celine and then her stepdad. He watched every precious moment.

No one explained that KayLee was next, but everyone knew it was time for Dawn's new sister to take this strange cup of blessing. No one said as much, but everyone understood. Dawn held that cup up until KayLee took it in both her hands. No words. The wind outside seemed a choir, sparks from the fire a kind of percussion.

Mrs. Pritchard started singing some reservation song, little more than a hum, not intended to change hearts, just accompaniment, something similar to what Woody's mother would have hummed years ago from a wholly different hymnbook.

Gently, Dawn took KayLee's shoulders in both hands, as if directing her, then pointed with her eyes where she needed to go, said something quietly, something no one else heard.

KayLee turned and took a step or two, but with her parents right in front of her eyes, she couldn't move, that stone they'd seen before returning to her face and her hands and her whole body. Still too much bad blood, Woody thought. It wasn't going to happen. Whether she wouldn't or couldn't do it made no difference. She didn't move.

Earlier that night, in their presence, even in their home, the girl screamed things her parents hadn't thought she'd even known, buried those words in their hearts, where they would never disappear. She'd never questioned them for a moment until a couple hours ago, when what she'd always felt beneath her simply fell away. It was something even this ritual couldn't heal. Too much hurt, Woody thought. Way too much anger.

No one moved. Scotty and Karin, supplicants, were powerless. Mrs. Pritchard, standing right there behind her, had done everything she could, and there was nothing he or Tieneke could do either, nothing. KayLee's face looked frozen, as if she were the one who'd run her car out in the cold alone.

There she stood, unmoving, heart of stone.

It was Dawn who took KayLee's hands away, wordlessly unwound KayLee's fingers, then held the cup out herself, as if to remind her sister of what was more pressing than what either of them held within.

Dawn took the cup, then stood there before Scotty and Karin and smiled an invitation. They knew that what she was offering was what they needed. When Woody replayed it all in his mind later, he was still astonished at how everything moved along as if they all knew the path that cup needed to take. To see it happen like it did that night was indescribable. They all were so beaten, so miserably beaten. All of them really, but all made strong.

Everything was said without words. If Dawn could give herself away, abandoned as she had been by this man, then KayLee could find the strength in her heart to give her dad—and her mom—the only gift either of them ever wanted, forgiveness.

KayLee took the cup when Dawn put it back into her fingers. Encouragement, admonition—whatever it was, it was clear that things had changed. KayLee looked at her mother, her face stiff as a mask. She lifted the cup to her mother's lips.

Karin reached for it hungrily. KayLee was her daughter, and if the only bit of her daughter she could touch that night was her hands, then she wouldn't be denied that much.

Then KayLee brought the cup to Scotty, who looked like some ragged beggar from the Bible. It was as easy to believe in his brokenness as it was in his daughter's strength. She gave it away, what both of them needed, all accomplished in silence, only the wind and the crackling fire.

Then Coby took what was in that Pendleton blanket and placed it in Dawn's arms as if to let her know she was only one who could give it away. It was obvious, painfully so, that

Dawn found it difficult to take that bundle. She stared at the blanket, pulled it closer. "I don't know what she would have been," she said. There were tears.

Mrs. Pritchard came over and stood there beside her. "I'm going to bring this home, where it belongs," she said, "with your people." Then she held out her arms. "It will never be mine and always be yours, but it is time for this 'something-of-you' to come home."

That's the way it went that night in the machine shed, mid-winter, Christmas coming, a night Woody would think of ever after as a firelit sacrament set in motion to bless the givers and the receivers, all of them penitents in all that cold.

They've been churchgoers all their lives. They've sat through a hundred baptisms, most of them white kids, some Indian, many others like Dawn and Marcus and Celine, something of one and something of the other. What happened that night was real and unreal, as blessed an event as any they'd ever practiced or witnessed—that's what they tell each. Something divine was there. He wouldn't have missed it.

They've been retired now for some time. Woody's finally out of school.

Coby and Trent got married, and there's a little one, adopted from just down the road.

Priscilla Pritchard is still around. The Dekkers stop by occasionally when they put flowers out on Teresa's grave.

KayLee is in college in Iowa, studying music; and Dawn is learning some computer skills in Mitchell.

There's a new, gorgeous Celine painting, a starry, starry night sky on the plains, hanging in the Dekkers' living room, a gift. Woody and Tieneke still live just up the road from Karin and Scotty.

Sometimes they wonder about LeRoy. He left that night. They think they would have done right by getting him in that machine shed, too, but his staying away just then was for the best. You can only go so far with a miracle.

Marcus Pritchard lives with them for some time most weeks—he'll be finishing high school this May. He mostly goes home to his grandma's place on weekends. He says he wants to go to Oregon when he graduates, "some place with trees," he says. Woody says that's nonsense. Fool kid grew up here. Nobody knows where he got that silly idea.

The day they got the news about Teresa is a day they'll never forget, but that cold night with a bottle of wine a Lakota woman pulled out of her grandson's basement—they often say nothing will come near to what it was that happened that night, so much pain and so much sadness, so much anger; and yet, out there in that windblown machine shed, such silent overpowering joy all around, something you just can't name.

The Brethower place is no more. Some rancher bought the land and burned down the buildings just last month. Cottonwood's fire department went out to keep tabs. The word on the street is that it took less than an hour. Woody wonders, he says, how many rats ran out—had to have been a score.

The whole place has returned to dust, to the land from whence it came.

When Woody saw the pictures of the fire in the paper last week, he told himself that before he woke up some morning on the other side of life, there were stories he had to tell--if he can, if anyone could.

That night's story is one of them. There were others, too, but what happened that night in the cold—that was something.

On a field of midnight snow

When Marcus Pritchard and his grandma got back in Trent's pickup that night, the three of them took off for her place. He offered to take that blanket and stuff in the skinny backseat with him, but his grandma would have nothing to do with giving it away.

"Someday down the line—maybe a year or so, who knows?" she said, "--somewhere down the line I'll give that girl that fine blanket the woman you're sweet on," she looked at Trent, "--what's her name again?"

"It's Coby," he told her.

"Sometime down the line I'll have that fine blanket cleaned and give it back to her, to Dawn Burnett, because sometime—you trust me on this, Marcus—someday she'll be more than happy to get it back."

"It's a good blanket," he said.

"You don't the half of it, boy," she told him. "But you know a whole lot more than you did a day and a night ago."

His grandma was right, he thought. Wasn't the first time either.

He'd just have to let somebody else be sure the fire was out back in the shed, he thought. When Dawn left, she was walking with her mother on her way to their car. She hadn't looked back.

Still, he had to giggle when he saw that Christmas tree on the bed behind him. What did Trent know anyway, thinking he was going to get his ass kicked for whacking down cedars? Not a bad guy anyway, he thought. And who wouldn't want to get it on with that Coby the Saint?

"After all this, Mr. Sterrett, you might think that tomorrow for sure Marcus is coming to school, but you'd be wrong," his grandma said. "He won't. Not tomorrow. He's got to be helping me with chili."

Marcus had forgotten about the riders. All she had to do was mention chili and he could smell it.

Trent looked over at her, surprised. "He's yours, you know. He's not mine. That kid back there's your responsibility. I expect you to get him there."

"I know—I know," she told him. "But tomorrow he's got to be coming with me. I got a heavy lugging to do, and I'm not up to getting done what I once could."

Why his grandma didn't just say where he was going to be, where they both would be, he didn't know. He'd heard the story a hundred times when she'd get in one of her "old days" routines. He didn't need to hear the whole Big Foot thing all over again.

Maybe it wasn't something she thought the principal should know—about the riders on their way south to Pine Ridge, about the chili she'd been brewing all day long to feed them. Maybe she didn't think her grandson needed an excuse for him not getting to school. Whatever the reason, his grandma didn't explain where he'd be, and Mr. Sterrett, the principal, didn't ask.

The three of them went back toward town for a couple miles to pick up his truck, because Marcus said he'd be needing it for all that lugging for his grandma. But once they got out there to where he'd left it, she told them both that she wasn't about to pull her stiff and creaky body from that warm truck, trade it for her grandson's frozen seats. "Besides," she said, "who knows if he's even got a heater that works?"

Marcus knew what was going on. It was a plot, his grandma's plot. The guy needed to get tipped off, he thought. So, he told him. "It's because of Wounded Knee," Marcus told Trent. "I'm not coming to school because the riders are coming through."

Trent was lost.

"The riders," Marcus said again. His grandma wasn't helping one little bit.

"What riders you talking about?" Sterrett said.

Marcus reached over the seat and grabbed his grandma's shoulder. "This grandma right here is going to tell you," he said to Sterrett. "All the way to her place, she's going ıd then you're going to know. You just be sure to .ear?"

rcus got out alone when Trent pulled up beside his truc. waited until Marcus found the keys and turned the old thing over. Once it started, off they went, the two of them leaving him back there, alone and freezing.

She wanted to talk to the boss alone anyway. The principal guy would have her gabbing all the way back to reservation, telling him the whole Wounded Knee story, every sad and awful bit. Probably she'd even pack some chili home with him since he didn't have a wife. Yet.

Right now, he thought, right at this moment, she was saying how people from right here on Cheyenne River were the ones down there at Wounded Knee. She'd tell him about the riders who'd be coming by, about why it was she wanted her grandson there, not just for the chili—that wasn't half of it. She wanted her grandson to see the riders out there in the cold, remembering. She'd tell Trent the principal that she wanted her grandson to get the riders some chili the way she'd given out the wine, because if those riders came all the way down from Standing Rock and would be going way down south to Pine Ridge, they deserved a whole lot more than the best chili his grandma could brew—that's what she'd be telling the school principal. That's what was going on, Marcus thought. The white guy had to know.

Then, she'd swear on a stack of Bibles that she'd get her grandson to school regular from then on, as long as he lived under her roof. That's the way it would go.

The wind had died, but the cold pressed down even harder all around. He pulled his hat down over his ears. The truck seemed hard as rock, stuck in an icebox. He thought of Dawn not looking at him when she got in the car, then remembered seeing her in her own room just last night, and finding her off in the ditch when he remembered how she'd told him she wasn't going home. He thought of standing out there in temperatures just as damned cold and seeing her inside that car, remembered waiting out there until he saw the red lights flashing all the way from town.

Something in him pulled him back outside just then, as if the truck might just heat up faster if he wasn't in it. He wanted to remember, too, wanted to feel what he did just last night. He stepped out of the truck as if she might still be there somewhere, looked up and around at a clear sky of a million stars, east to west, north to south, in the night sky.

He didn't smoke that much, just once in a while. He reached back in the cubby hole and took out a flat pack of dried cigarettes, flicked one out and lit up. It's what Indians do, he told himself, even him, half of one.

Way down the road, he could still pick up the flash of taillights from Trent's truck, and if he listened closely, he told himself—if he just stood here and listened hard, he figured he could hear his grandma tell the school man the story of her people, their people, dying out on some cold prairie just like this.

He could tell the story himself—how Big Foot and his people came from here or somewhere close, dead of winter, a whole band of Miniconjou and others frozen almost solid, sick and dying, all of them on their way south to Red Cloud's agency. It was late December, like this, maybe four hundred of them on a night that could have been just like this.

There he stood, the moon's shiny face lighting up the world around him so bright he could see them out there at the horizon in a broad swarm, dozens and dozens of them, robed in buffalo hides, some on horseback, some in wagons, all of them in the deep winter when no one should be out, scared and cold, moving south to what they thought might be safety.

He could hear his grandma's story just down the road somewhere, a bloody story she'd make sure to say the new guy needed to know, how so many of their people would die. He needed to know all of that to live here. She liked him, but she knew very well what he needed to understand.

So, Marcus stood there outside, smoking, his hat pulled down over his ears, hands in his pockets, honoring the story he could hear his grandmother telling, his own pickup rumbling clumsily behind him.

There he stood, alone in the night, up on a swell of land where he could see miles in all directions, looking far, far away, to a space in the dark sky where, just then, a dusky host of riders came down slowly and moved in silence across the midnight snow.

James Calvin Schaap is an emeritus professor of English at Dordt College, Sioux Center, Iowa, where he taught literature and writing for 37 years. He is the author of four novels, many short stories, essays, and meditations, and several other non-fiction books, including the *Things We Couldn't Say*, with Dutch resistance fighter Diet Eman.

He blogs at siouxlander.blogspot.com, and writes and reads *Small Wonder(s)*, historical vignettes broadcast weekly on KWIT, Siouxland Public Media, 90.3, in Sioux City, Iowa. Listen at https://plus.google.com/+JamesSchaap.

He and his wife Barbara live just outside of Alton, Iowa. They have two grown children, and a blue Russian cat named Smoke.

18616058R00216

Made in the USA
Lexington, KY
23 November 2018